Cannabis Indica

AF517520

Cannabis Indica

Perception vs Potential

2022

Dr Khagesh Gautam

Forewords by

Hon'ble Justice A K Jayasankaran Nambiar

Judge, High Court of Kerala

Sidharth Luthra

Senior Advocate

OakBridge

Published by
OakBridge Publishing Pvt. Ltd.
M 35, 1st Floor, Old DLF, Gurugram, 122001, Haryana, India
Tel.: +91 124 4305970, E-mail: info@oakbridge.in
www.oakbridge.in

Copyright © Khagesh Gautam, 2022

The views and opinions expressed in this book are the author's own and the facts are as reported by him which have been verified to the extent possible, and the publishers are not in any way liable for the same.

All rights reserved.

No part of this publication may be reproduced, transmitted, or stored in a retrieval system, in any form or by any means, electronic, mechanical, photocopying, recording or otherwise without the prior permission of the publishers.

Due care has been taken while preparing this book. Neither the author nor the publisher of the book holds any responsibility for any mistake that may have inadvertently crept in. The publishers shall not be liable for any direct, consequential or incidental damages arising out of the use of this book.

ISBN: 978-93-91032-84-5

This book is sold subject to the condition that it shall not, by way of trade or otherwise, be lent, resold, hired out, or otherwise circulated without the publisher's prior consent in any form of binding or cover other than that in which it is published.

For Parimal

Justice A.K. Jayasankaran Nambiar
B.Sc., LL.B., M.A. (Oxon.)

JUDGE HIGH COURT OF KERALA

High Court of Kerala
Ernakulam, Kochi - 682 031
Office : 0484 2562301

FOREWORD

I must admit to having been a tad hesitant when asked to write a foreword to this book that celebrates a substance whose cultivation, manufacture, possession, consumption et al is penalised under our laws. That, however, was before I read the manuscript.

On going through the pages of this scholarly work, I realised that there is much that has eluded the realm of our shared knowledge and understanding of Cannabis Indica, the plant that in India is variously known as 'marijuana, hemp, ganja, weed, pot etc'. Khagesh Gautam draws on history, religion, international trade and commerce as well as the provisions of our Constitution to put forth a compelling argument for the decriminalisation and legalisation of the substance in India. While one may disagree with the author at times, his views certainly cannot be ignored.

In a republic such as ours, where governance is by the rule of law, the laws cannot remain static and must evolve. Towards this end, the tribe of well-meaning academics in our country, to which the author undoubtedly belongs, constantly endeavours to persuade our legislators and policy makers to comprehend the entire spectrum of issues relating to an enactment and then decide whether or not the law requires to be amended. This erudite work must be seen as one such attempt that the author, Khagesh Gautam pursues with energetic elan.

Ernakulam
28.01.2022

Sidharth Luthra
M. Phil (Cambridge)
Doctor of Laws (Honoris Causa)
Visiting Professor, Northumbria University
Visiting Professor, National Law University, Delhi

SENIOR ADVOCATE

FOREWORD

When Prof. Khagesh Gautam reached out with a request to pen a foreword for his book, I was in the midst of reading a book called *'Opium Inc.' How a Global Drug Trade Funded the British Empire by Thomas Manuel.*[1] Thomas Manuel's book on the opium trade explains the intricacies of the trade and the British East India Company. Apart from the huge financial gains to Empire, it led to the Chinese getting opium, Britain getting tea (which it needed desperately) and India being completely colonized.

Yet the fact that *opium* is not *cannabis,* and that the plant that produces opium (*Papaver somniferum*) is distinct from the plant that produces *ganja* (i.e., *Cannabis sativa* L. (1753), *Cannabis indica* Lam. (1783), and *Cannabis ruderalis* Janish (1924), known to Indian law simply as 'hemp,' or 'cannabis') is a fact that is ignored by most people.

In common parlance the words *bhang* (a sweet drink that is made using cannabis seeds, milk, and nuts, etc.), *charas* (resin rubbed out of live cannabis plant) and *afeem (opium)* are indeed often used interchangeably or synonymously. But the author painstakingly explains the distinction between the two. In fact, this distinction between *opium* and *cannabis* was lost even when the debate on the Indian NDPS Act, 1985 took place in Parliament.

The book contains a comprehensive historical and legal analysis on the banning of cannabis. It questions the legitimacy of the ban of cannabis by the 1985 Act. Prof. Gautam's work is relevant for lawyers, law students and policy makers. He has delved deep into scientific and medical research and analyzed the Indian constitutional scheme to support his conclusion that there is a need for decriminalization of cannabis and its exclusion from the NDPS Act 1985. I was reminded of views expressed by the American writer *Robert M. Pirsig* who wrote the 1970's cult best seller *Zen and the Art of Motorcycle Maintenance*[2] on the use of *peyote.* In his subsequent book *Lila: An Enquiry into Morals*[3], he refers to the 1960's the debate in the USA on the acceptability and use of *peyote* (a plant hallucinogen) amongst Native Americans who consumed it to induce an altered mental state which they considered a form of religious communion. Pirsig endorsed the acceptability and use of *peyote* in native cultures.

Prof Gautam's work does not refer to *Pirsig's* work however as it is not proposing promotion of drug use. However, it sets out the historically prevalent use of cannabis and its byproducts in Indian culture, its historical & economic significance in India, in culture and in religion.

---

[1] Published in India 2021 HarperCollins Publishers, P-ISBN:978-93-5422-927-5
[2] Copyright © 1974 by Robert M. Pirsig, Corgi Books 0-552 10166 4.
[3] Copyright © 1991 Robert M. Pirsig, Bantam Books ISBN 978-0-553-29961-8

Off. : C-450, Defence Colony, New Delhi - 110024
Ph. : +91 11 41532816, 41532817, 41532818
Fax : +91 11 41500189
Res.: C-2, Defence Colony, New Delhi - 110024

He questions the constitutional validity of proscribing the use of cannabis, as defined under sections 2(iii) and (iv) of the NDPS Act, by its inclusion in the that Act. He argues that pre-1985 there was no restriction on cannabis and it was legitimately produced and sold, and also taxed under the Medicinal and Toilet Preparations (Excise Duties) Act, 1955. He contends *inter alia* that the basis of the legal ban on cannabis is misconceived. *Bhang* has been part of our civilization and culture.

I recall a visit in 2018 to the *Mahakaal* Temple at Ujjain where the *Jyotirlinga* is daily anointed with *bhang* paste during the early morning prayers *(Bhasma Arti)* and the excess paste distributed to a few lucky devotees. That the use of Cannabis was not restricted by religion or community is demonstrated in the *Babur Nama* which records of *Babur* that while *"his body couldn't tolerate opium, he was addicted to Ma'jun,"* – a concoction which was part drug, part sweets and made of *Ganja* leaves *(Marijuana)*, milk, sugar, poppy seeds and other ingredients. Even the subsequent three Mughal emperors *Humayun, Akbar and Jehangir* were consumers of opium as well as also of *Ganja*.[4]

Coincidentally my first brush with widespread growing of cannabis in the Garhwal Himalayas was in November 1985 on a college trek to Kuari Pass. While trekking we had an overnight halt in a village where we found an entire hillside covered with cannabis. To my chagrin the villagers informed that they used the cannabis seeds to spice their food, in the absence of availability salt and pepper. That cannabis was seen in common use was apparent as the hands of the porter traveling with were black as he was a daily consumer of *charas* and would begin the day with his daily dose. In that very year cannabis had been brought within the purview of the NDPS Act, 1985.

Prof. Gautam's book is a well-researched and documented academic work propounding the need for decriminalization of cannabis relying on historical materials, the religious, spiritual and cultural use of cannabis and its products, its use across different religious denominations including its medical use as far back as the 8th century AD *(referred to at page 39 of Chapter II and the Report of Indian Hemp Drugs Commission of 1894)*. He places for the reader's consideration, his understanding of the strong medical and beneficial qualities of cannabis, documented and recorded over more than a century.

The author considers different administrative and legal responses to *cannabis* specially from the 17th century till the present. The colonial period prior to the Government of India Act of 1935 was a time when trade in cannabis was permitted and often regulated and taxed. In the Government of India Act, 1935 (which later became our interim constitution), the author in depth discusses the separation of powers between the then federal and the provincial legislatures. He highlights the relevant legislative Entries, viz. Entry 45 in the Federal List and Entry 31 & 40 of the Provincial List to clarify that during that era, hemp (i.e. cannabis) was not only sold legitimately, it was taxed & the production, manufacture, possession, transport, purchase and sale of cannabis was then a legally recognized trading activity. Even Income tax was charged on

[4] Refer supra note 1

the income generated from cannabis trade with the exception that farmers were excluded from paying income tax on cultivating cannabis.

In the absence of any relevant entry in the Constitution 7th Schedule to justify the banning of cannabis, the book analyzes comprehensively the potential counter argument to justify the ban cannabis by examining *"criminal law" and "criminal procedure"* in the entries in the Concurrent Legislative List of the 7th Schedule. It argues that if legislative entries are to be interpreted, this must be done harmoniously. When the colonial government under the 1935 Act had no occasion to ban cannabis, is there any justification to ban it under the Indian Constitution, he argues.

The colonial approach, whether it was cannabis or opium cultivation and production and trade, cannot be assumed as a *grund norm* as the colonial government's decisions were focused on the commercial benefits this trade gave the British empire. Even opium trade ended when the British were pushed by the drug control policies driven by the USA to stop the trade in opium though in the past they had gone to war with China over the opium trade. [5]

Though opium was banned and *bhang* being used, Indian *cannabis* was produced and sold legitimately till 1985. However, the Single Convention on Narcotic Drugs, 1961 (18 USD 1407) in article 49(1) gave signatory nations, the right to have an exception for temporary permission for the use of cannabis, cannabis resin, extracts and tinctures of cannabis for non-medical use. Article 49(2)(f) of the treaty required restriction of use of *cannabis* and its production and manufacture for other than medical and scientific purposes within 25 years of signing of the treaty. It is this treaty that led to the enactment of the NDPS Act, 1985.

In India, Parliament sought to comply with the 1961 Single Convention to enact the NDPS Act, 1985 and even the statement of objects and reasons of NDPS Act referred to the international obligations. However, as pointed out in the book, the Indian Parliament legislates based on the power ascribed to it in List I and List III of Seventh Schedule of the Constitution.

The author rightly argues that the invocation of international treaty obligations cannot by itself justify the enactment of a law to criminalize any form of conduct if legislative competence is lacked & that the Constitution of India cannot be amended by the Single Convention which (according to him) is not consistent with the Constitutional text and interpretation. Challenging the very legitimacy of enactment of the NDPS Act, 1985 as specifically the prohibition on cannabis, Prof. Gautam seeks to carve out an exception for cannabis relying on historical text, scientific materials including medical data and then highlights the fallacies apparent in the debate that took place in August 1985.

The debates in Parliament prefacing the enactment of the NDPS Act, 1985 placed reliance on newspaper articles, which he rightly says cannot even past muster in a court of law. The constant mixing of the term *opium* with *hashish* or *charas* by different speakers during the debate is indicative of the only singular focus – prohibition of all drugs irrespective of their

[5] Refer supra note 1

medicinal or scientific use and the absence (as contended by the author) of adverse effects. He draws our attention to the hyperbolic claims and use words like abuse and addiction against cannabis use without an examination of the scientific data to determine whether use of Marijuana is either harmful, addictive or that there is no medically therapeutic use.

He deftly points out that the *gateway drug hypothesis* i.e., the use of cannabis in individuals graduates them to stronger and addictive drugs, has been debunked. The fact that the gateway hypothesis was in part relied upon or referred to, in 1985 to justify the banning of cannabis under the NDPS Act, 1985 is according to him a wholly illegitimate approach. The author relies on scientific material to contend that in moderation, *cannabis* use causes no harm. If so, why ban it? He relies upon data from around the world to justify his claims. His reference to data of the different states of the United States of America referred to in *Appendix A* (a consultation paper authored by him) is to contend that in the context of cannabis there is neither drug abuse nor dependency nor harm. Criminalization of cannabis use in India, he states has only added to the taxpayer's burden who have to also bear the enforcement costs of such prohibition which he believes is both legally and scientifically unwarranted.

The last portion of the book deals with the problem of arresting people for possession of small quantities of cannabis. As rightly stated by the author, possession of even a small quantity can be grounds for arrest under the NDPS Act. In a country like India where such offences are considered serious, other than post-trial incarceration, even pre-trial period in jail can run into months if not years. In entirety, the author has made a compelling argument for the decriminalization of cannabis highlighting its inherent positive qualities. While the author has clearly skirted away from seeking decriminalization of the prosecution of use of opium and opiates and contends that cannabis and opium stand on different footing, but on an academic plane his questions regarding the constitutional legitimacy of the NDPS Act, could have a bearing on some of the other substances proscribed by the NDPS Act.

In my view, the pace of criminalization of different kinds of conduct in India has led to a society which seeks to punish us from birth to death. In our nation, there are rare instances of decriminalization such as gold control in the 1980s and FERA in the year 2000. It is perhaps time for the Indian state to review its criminal law legislations keeping in view the culture and ethos of this nation and its people (irrespective of community, caste, religion or colour) and relook at the criminal law. Rampant criminalization of human conduct in the last four decades has led to a proliferation of prosecutable actions and the hapless citizens as also the hapless police officer seeks to keep pace with the myriad legislations, state and central, which contain criminal sanctions against the individual. Decriminalization of many forms of trivial harm is imperative, yet the Courts rarely apply the doctrine of *desuetude*. Decriminalization is not a job for the courts alone. Even section 377, IPC was never reviewed or repealed by the legislature but from start to finish the court verdict took almost a decade with the first decision of the Supreme Court quashing the High Court judgment legitimizing consensual homosexual sex and the Supreme Court striking it down in 2013 left citizens in a limbo. Only when a fresh batch of petitions came up before the Supreme Court and Section 377 IPC was struck down by a Constitution Bench, did the legal position change.

Foreword

The author's book is bold. It is challenging. It encourages us to think and provides a new look at the lack of justification for cannabis prohibition and propounds a historical basis for its legitimacy. I hope that it will be looked at by lawyers, judges and policy makers alike with the seriousness it deserves.

Sidharth Luthra
New Delhi
February 7, 2022

Preface

This book has an interesting journey. The work on this book actually started accidentally when I came across a book on legalization of cannabis in the United States in the library of Maurer School of Law, Indiana University, Bloomington, in August 2019. I had taken a sabbatical from Jindal Global Law School (JGLS), (where I have been on the faculty since July 2013) to begin work towards a doctoral degree. I reported to Bloomington a few days ahead of schedule and had a few spare days before the beginning of the course. I came across a few books on the subject and although I read only select chapters in them, I became interested in the subject. Later during my stay, I made friends with two undergraduate students who lived in the same building as mine: Ryan Zych (who was then doing a B.S. in neuroscience and chemistry), and Kayla-Norris Center (who has since graduated from Purdue with a degree in communication and media). One evening while chatting, I asked them their views on the legalization of cannabis in the United States, which lead to a very spirited discussion still fresh in my memory. As the coursework began there was not a lot of time to work on this side project, and I did what I could, but after the last week of September 2019, I had put all the materials and notes in a folder and forgot about it for some time. I continued to discuss this issue with whoever was willing to discuss and continued following legal developments in the US. I hardly encountered anyone who said it should not be de-criminalized. I took some time to study the legal industry in Canada and the United States (the states where it is legal) and was astonished by what I learned.

After finishing the coursework in late November 2019, and returning to Sonepat in December 2019, I got occupied with finishing the doctoral work. But in February 2020, as the new semester opened in Jindal, I made an effort to put together a group of students interested in working on the issue, and we did initially make a small group that did a lot of literature review. All that hard work and industry came in very useful at a later stage when the manuscript was being prepared. This first group of students comprised: Adv. Arindam Bharadwaj, now pursuing M.Sc. (Criminal Justice), London School of Economics; Adv. Yashowardhan Tiwari (Yash); Adv. Vidur Prabhakar, an Associate at J. Sagar Associates; and Adv. Anirban Chanda, now reading law in the chambers of Ms. Geeta Luthra, Senior Advocate, Supreme Court of India. As is the nature of all things human, the group did its work, and then disintegrated as slowly all the students went on to pursue their avenues in life. But this first group and our discussions gave birth to a lot of ideas in my mind.

After spending a considerable amount of time reviewing literature, and contemplating these ideas, a picture started emerging, which took about a year. Not much substantial work was done on the subject immediately following the Covid lockdown in late March 2020. After the semester ended, more time became available for this side-project. So I did all the required reading, and writing on the subject but at that point in time, as the first group of students above can also attest, none of us had any idea that a book will come out of this one day. I personally was in favor of writing law-review articles, a form of writing I am most familiar with. Chapters 3, and 4 of this work combinedly present the 'constitutional argument' that highlights some of the constitutional questions that do arise in respect of legalization of cannabis in India, were originally written as law-review articles, and do retain, I think, much of that original flavor. To this work, and much of Chapter 1, the Introduction, the first group contributed a lot by way of research assistance for which I am very thankful. The group was able to achieve its objective only partially. Yash and I were able to get one article published on the website of The Indian Express on November 3, 2020 ("Cannabis: The Other Prohibition"). I wanted to do much more writing but the doctoral dissertation had to be finished. The Covid lockdown added to our difficulties as everything had to be done online. It was around the time of publication of this newspaper article that I had decided to focus fully on the dissertation to the exclusion of everything else.

The first push to complete the manuscript started in March–April 2021, after submission of the doctoral dissertation in the last week of February, and real work started after I successfully defended the doctoral dissertation in an online defense on April 9, 2021. Some unfortunate circumstances visited us and it took all the resolve one could muster to continue this work in the first three months of 2021. My parents tested positive for Covid just a day before my father's birthday on March 18. My wife Shelja, the incredibly brave woman that she is, and I immediately decided to drop everything and go to Kurukshetra to help them and nurse them back to health. Luckily, they responded to treatment and whatever little care we could provide. They made sufficient recovery in about two weeks, and luckily because of the strict discipline that Shelja imposed, neither of us contracted Covid. It was during this time that the idea to write a full book on the subject took firm shape in my mind. The law-review route did not seem enough. But mostly my attention was on my upcoming defense, as I had submitted my dissertation to the committee by then.

The successful defense of the dissertation did provide a celebratory mood for a brief while, but things turned for worse very soon when my mother-in-law, and brother-in-law, also tested positive for Covid on April 13, 2021. Unfortunately, their respective cases worsened rapidly. They had to be hospitalized for a month and had to undergo intensive medical care. In the second week of April, Shelja had to report to battle duties one more time in her hometown Karnal where her family lives. Meanwhile, reports of tragic losses were coming routinely from everywhere, students, parents of students, in a few tragic cases both parents of students, fellow faculty members, old friends, new friends, there was death everywhere. This was right in the middle of the deadly second wave. It was at this point of time that I started writing the manuscript and had the assistance of a wonderful law student, Madhvi Wadhwan (B.A.LL.B. 2019–24), from Rajiv Gandhi National University of Law, Patiala, Punjab.

Earlier I was invited to write a blog post for the RGNUL Student Research Review (RSRR), and I requested the editors if they would be comfortable if I wrote a post on Cannabis Decriminalization in India, and they said they would welcome it. The editors then told me that a student can be assigned as a research assistant and that's how Madhvi got into the picture. She and I worked for a long period doing a lot of research on the drafting history of the Narcotic Drugs and Psychotropic Substances Act, 1985 (NDPS Act). This research was done to a certain extent earlier by the first group, but it had to be done again, and much more had to be added since the objective had changed a lot by now. Madhvi provided outstanding research assistance until the end, even offering to proofread the manuscript. Without her excellent research assistance, this work would have taken much longer. It was mostly in the months of April and May 2021 that Chapters 1, 2, and 5 were conceived and finished, and all throughout Madhvi provided reliable backup and research support. In fact, I got so focused on the manuscript at one point in time that Madhvi had to remind me that the editors are requesting for the requested blog post to be turned in. The post was published on July 27, 2021 ("Cannabis Decriminalization in India"), and is inspired by Chapter 5. An injury I encountered on May 25, 2021, that kept me in bed for a month, also contributed to these delays. Spending a month with my parents in Kurukshetra, and with my sister who had a baby boy on June 1, was a great source of joy except that pain from injuries disturbed the peace of mind on a few occasions. By June last week Shelly and I, both exhausted, returned to Sonepat. By then, her mother and brother were well enough for her to leave. After that started the second push to finish the manuscript and it fructified in a few days' space.

After completing writing the manuscript, Madhvi's proofreading, and one more final reading on my own part, the manuscript was finished sometime in the first week of July. On July 10, I went to Vice-Chancellor Prof (Dr.) C. Raj Kumar, Founding Vice-Chancellor, O.P. Jindal Global University, with a spiral-bound copy of the manuscript, and some chocolate cake. He congratulated me on finishing my doctoral dissertation, and after some coffee and cake, I showed him the spiral-bound copy and requested him to read the concluding part (Chapter

5) for me and share his thoughts. He proceeded to scan the pages, and then seemed to be getting deeper and deeper into the text, and I like to think he deliberately slowed down the fast pace at which he usually reads just for those pages. There was complete silence in his office, and after a while, it started to grow heavy as he kept on reading but did not say a word. I was anxious but kept on observing. I did not say a word either. After finishing the last page, he leaned over from his desk and started looking outside the window, very thoughtful and silent. I like to think that he liked what he read. He encouraged me to get the book published. I started making my efforts.

Sometime later that month, while I was busy submitting the manuscript to publishers, one of our talented graduate students from the Jindal School of Government and Public Policy (JSGP), Tejasi Panjiar, Master's in Public Policy, 2020-2022, who was interning with the Center of Policy Research, run by Dr. Ramanand Nand, reached out to me. She had been tasked with organizing a lecture and she reached out to me inquiring if I would be interested in doing such a lecture. I told her that about the recently finished manuscript, and that I would be interested to do a lecture on the issue if the organizers are okay with the topic. She called back in a few days, saying they would look forward to such a lecture, and a Zoom event was accordingly organized. The lecture was later published on YouTube by 'CPRJ India,' on August 3, 2021. I think we aptly titled it: "Legalization of Cannabis: The Next Big Question of Civil Liberties in India." It was around this time that the semester also commenced in Jindal, and we all had to report back to duties.

The next few months, as I tried to convince a publisher, my old-friend Deepu Krishna, now an associate professor at IFIM Law School Bangalore (then working with Jindal), suggested that I reach out to Vikesh Dhyani at Oakbridge Publishing, as they might be interested in publishing a book like this. I reached out to Vikesh, and we had long-spirited discussions over cannabis legalization in India, why such a thing would make sense, why now, etc. As a lawyer, I can say, it was probably one of the toughest cases to argue, but I think he saw the logic and the motivation behind the whole project, and slowly grew interested in it. Now I think I have been able to convince him completely and he has crossed over to 'our side,' as it were since his company is publishing this book. To this 'our side', belong all those minds who believe that cannabis is a healing herb and that its criminalization makes very little sense. They believe that cannabis should be decriminalized in India, and eventually, separate legislation should be brought to legally regulate it. They believe it should be available for personal, spiritual, and medicinal use like it was before August of 1985 when the NDPS Act was first enacted. In one sense, their case is essential to re-legalize cannabis in India.

The case is delicate. The case is not that the NDPS Act and the related state machinery should be dismantled. The NDPS Act and its enforcement machinery are important and should be retained. The NDPS Act and its machinery also require some reforms. The Supreme Court, in *Toofan Singh v. Tamil Nadu*, recently struck down section 67 of the NDPS Act, as it deserved to be struck down. I like to study this decision because it corresponds to my doctoral work, which is in the wider area of section 27 of the Indian Evidence Act, 1872, and the general law relating to the admissibility of custodial confessions during criminal trials. But the constitutional invalidation of section 67 of the NDPS Act is a significant step in NDPS Act reforms.

But in the case of cannabis re-legalization, the question is not really about reforming the NDPS Act and its machinery, it is about taking cannabis out of the NDPS Act and eventually making a new law for legally regulating it. There will be a period of time in between where it would unregulated, but that's a necessary part of the process. In addition, the moment cannabis is decriminalized, serious effort will be required to systematically identify all those NDPS Act convictions where the contraband seized was only cannabis as defined in the Act. I believe a ministry might be required to be set up at the state level, guided by the Union Law Ministry, or similar such union agency, to 'aid and advice' the Governor, or the President, as the case may be, to deal with the post-de-criminalization scenario where convicted prisoners might very fairly question, before a High Court, or the Supreme Court, the constitutional basis of their continued incarceration, if not a conviction. This I believe the state would have to do for all souls incarcerated for possessing solely cannabis. The way I see it, this is the penance that we as a nation, through our state, will need to do, for unjustly incarnating thousands of our own citizens, pre and post-conviction, for trading in a healing herb that has been a part of our culture, tradition, and even ancient medicine.

Insofar as the commercial or the economic angle is concerned, wider discussions among all stakeholders are required. Some of that is highlighted in this book but more work is required. A talented student of mine at JGLS, Aakash 'Josh' Joshua, who seems to have an incredible aptitude for Bitcoin and Crypto, introduced me to Zeus who is the owner of CannabisDoge, a US-based cannabis company working on using the blockchain to help further the industry. Zeus and I bonded over the shared belief that cannabis is essentially a 'healing herb', and that there is no case justifying its criminal prohibition either in the U.S., or in India, or for that matter anywhere on planet earth. CannabisDoge aims to act as a bridge for adopting cannabis as a means of healing and crypto as a financial and technological tool. Zeus and his team were interested in exploring the possibility of obtaining an export license from the Indian Government under the NDPS Act. They have already obtained such a license from the Brazilian government, and most of my initial discussions with Zeus took place when he was in Brazil. Zeus's help was instrumental in securing financial support for this project. We are currently working towards improving awareness about this issue in the Indian subcontinent, and South America. My long-time friend Anirban Bhattacharya, Partner, Shardul Amarchand Mangaldas, has agreed to take on the complicated legal challenge that CannabisDoge presented. All of us continue to work on spreading awareness about this issue in India, and we hope that the case for decriminalizing and eventually regulating cannabis in India as presented in this book will help in spreading awareness about this issue in India, and around the globe. Canada has already legalized cannabis across its territory, and the US seems very clearly to be on the same road. We hope that this book, and hopefully many others that would be written on the subject, would convince Indians to at least seriously consider, if not follow, the precedent of their 'long lost' Canadian 'siblings.'[1]

On November 9, 2021, Vikesh emailed me the agreement from Oakbridge. I remember I was driving to Rishikesh. On November 19, 2021, the contract was formally signed. Finally, the first version preface was written in Rishikesh on Christmas, 2021 as I working with the editors at Oakbridge, to whom I will always remain most thankful, especially to Priyanka Srivastava.

A second version was required because after detailed discussion with Vikesh, and later Priyanka, it was decided to examine the Uttarakhand Hemp Cultivation Policy of 2016 in light of the Medical and Scientific Use Amendment of 2014 (that inserted section 2(4)(da) into the NDPS Act). Parallel to these discussions, in early January, there was a separate development. An elective that I offered at JGLS (Cannabis Decriminalization in India: Law, History, and the Constitution) was approved by the academic board. 40 students enrolled, and I was working on preparing a detailed reading list for this course. To this end, I recruited the help of my former student, Saikeerthana Allamaraju. She was now charged additionally with assisting me in preparing an analysis of the Uttarakhand Policy. Without her help with legal research, and the long hours of dictations that she took it would have taken considerably longer to finish this additional work within time.

---

1. The expression "long lost siblings" is taken from Vivek Krishnamurthy in "Colonial Cousins: Explaining India and Canada's Unwritten Constitutional Principles", (2009) 34 Yale J Int'l L 207, at p. 207. *See also*, Khagesh Gautam & Sebastien Lafrance, 'A Comparative Survey of the law of Bail in India and Canada', in S. Khurshid et. al., *Taking Bail Seriously: The State of Bail Jurisprudence in India* 123 (LexisNexis, 2019) where we borrow this expression to present a comparative analysis of Indian and Canadian bail laws.

This is a very sensitive issue, and I do hope that this book will be able to achieve its purpose, which is to educate and not to create controversy. Decriminalization and re-legalization of cannabis in India will ultimately be beneficial to our nation, our people, our economy, and our health, further details of which are discussed in the book. But before 1985 there was no legal prohibition on cannabis in our land. These 37 years is the only period in our nation's history that has known this prohibition. It is time to end it. I hope this book will be the first of many, and one day the objective will be achieved. May this coming new year provide us with the wisdom to heal ourselves.

Khagesh Gautam
Sonepat
February 07, 2022

About the Author

Prof. (Dr.) Khagesh Gautam is currently an associate professor of law at the Jindal Global Law School, O P Jindal Global University, where he teaches constitutional law, criminal procedure, and evidence, and has taught indirect taxation, forensic evidence, and interpretation of statutes. He has also taught comparative evidence at China University of Political Science and Law, Changping, Beijing, PRC (June, 2016 & May-June, 2015); and Comparative Constitutional Law at William S. Richardson School of Law, University of Hawaii, USA (January, 2017). His research into cannabis decriminalization is a part of a larger project that seeks to comprehensive reform the Indian criminal justice system. This work is the result of concentrated research efforts that originally arose of this general theme. He continues to work on both independently now.

Dr. Gautam was awarded a S.J.D. from Maurer School of Law, Indiana University in May, 2021, where he finished his doctoral work in an 'extremely rare' 611 days. His doctoral thesis (unpublished) argues that constitutional validity of section 27 of the Indian Evidence Act, 1872 is suspect on the grounds that it violates Article 20(3) of the Indian Constitution. He graduated with distinction as a Stone Scholar from Columbia Law School in May 2013 were he obtained a LL.M, and received the LL.B. from Campus Law Centre, Delhi University in June, 2008. Before joining the academia, he practiced law before the Supreme Court of India, the Delhi High Court, and the Punjab & Haryana High Court from 2008 to 2012. He continues to be a part of the legal profession within constraints of academic life.

Dr. Gautam has published several law-review articles and book chapters in India and internationally. His work has appeared in several leading journals such as the Stanford Journal of International Law, Columbia Journal of Asian Law, Economic and Political Weekly, amongst others. He has also co-authored a book with Senior Advocate Dr. Abhishek Manu Singhvi titled *The Law of Emergency Powers: Common Law Perspectives* (2021).

Brief Contents

CHAPTERS

APPENDICES

Detailed Contents

APPENDICES

Table of Cases

1

Introduction

"[W]e need to think of the cannabis trade as a business and the challenge of regulating cannabis as a specific instance of business regulation."[*]

It has been observed that society sometimes may have a genuine concern in regulating, and even completely prohibiting such plants and substances the consumption whereof can be potentially hazardous to the human body.[1] In service of this societal goal, many societies often resort to its prohibition, at times going to the extreme of penalizing,[2] which is usually legislatively deployed, and rigorously enforced.[3] But to think that prohibiting the cultivation, manufacture, processing, distribution, sale, purchase, possession, and consumption of these substances can help achieve this objective is an idea fraught with considerable difficulties.[4] Unthoughtful and non-reflective prohibition of these plants and substances can also have potentially hazardous consequences for society as a whole.[5] A good example of this could be the case of *Uniao do Vegetal* (UDV), a

---

* Toby Seddon & William Floodgate, *Regulating Cannabis: A Global Review and Future Directions* 71 (2020, Palgrave Macmillan).

1. See David A.J. 'Richards, Drug Use and the Rights of the Person: A Moral Argument for Decriminalization of Certain Forms of Drug Use', 33 RUTGERS L. REV. 607, 607-608 (1981).
2. David Elkins, 'Drug Legalization: Cost Effective and Morally Permissible', 32 B.C. L. REV. 575, 588, 590 (1991).
3. *See e.g.,* Congressional findings and declarations: controlled substances, 21 U.S.C.A. § 801; Narcotic Drugs and Psychotropic Substances Act, 1985, No. 61, Acts of Parliament, 1985 (India); Dangerous Drugs Act, 1930, No. II, Acts of Parliament, 1930 (British India).
4. Margaret P. Spencer, 'Sentencing Drug Offenders: The Incarceration Addiction', 40 VILL. L. REV. 335, 365 – 372 (1995).
5. Randy E. Barnett, 'The Harmful Side Effects of Drug Prohibition', UTAH L. REV. 11, 17-23 (2009). (Hazardous consequences from criminal prohibition of drug consumption include punishing the users, making the users buy from criminals, inducing the invention of new intoxicating drugs, high amount of resources spent on drug law enforcement, increased crime rates, harms resulting from the "victimless" character of drug use, etc.).

small religious group from New Mexico who took the U.S. government to court challenging a ban on the group's use of a Brazilian imported hallucinogenic tea.[6] The use of 'hoasca,' a special tea prepared by blending two indigenous Brazilian plants 'banisteriopsiscaapi' and 'psychotria viridis,' contains dimethltryptamine (DMT) in the psychotria plant which is a federally prohibited substance under U.S. law, is 'essential' to UDV.[7] In fact, as recorded in the 2003 decision of the 10th Circuit, UDV's religious doctrine states that "members can perceive and understand God *only* by drinking hoasca."[8] The importance of hoasca for UDV is comparable to the importance of peyote to the Native American Church (NAC): "peyote, like hoasca, is cultivated primarily for its hallucinogenic properties and considered a vital religious sacrament, particularly by the NAC."[9] In situations such as these, on which this author has written elsewhere in detail,[10] members of religious groups desire to willingly consume entheogens and base their claim in the constitution, against which the government claims an interest in prohibiting the use of these substances.[11] I suppose we are lucky that in India, no *sadhu* ever had to go to a court to claim their spiritual right to consume cannabis, which they do and have been known to be doing for the last hundreds, probably thousands, of years.[12] This work is about one of such plants: the cannabis plant, law reform whereof has been a 'subject of public discourse for at least the last 50 years,' but has seen 'significant reform' in the last 10.[13]

---

6. *Gonzales* v. *O Centro Espirita Beneficente Uniao do Vegetal*, 126 S. Ct. 1211 (2006) (U.S. Supreme Court).
7. See David Garrett, 'Vine of the Dead: Reviving Equal Protection Rites for Religious Drug Use', 31 AM. INDIAN L. REV. 143, 144-45 (2006).
8. *O Centro Espirita Beneficente Uniao do Vegetal* v. *Ashcroft*, 342 F.3d 1170, 1174 (10th Cir. 2003).
9. Garrett, *supra* note 7 at 145.
10. Khagesh Gautam, 'Protecting Free Exercise of Religion under the Indian and the United States Constitutions: The Doctrine of Essential Practices and the Centrality Test', 8 VIENNA J. INT'L. CONST'L L. 305 (2014).
11. Garrett, *supra* note 7 at 145.
12. For more on the religious, spiritual, and cultural use of cannabis in India, *see infra* Chapter II, section (iii).
13. Toby Seddon & William Floodgate, *Regulating Cannabis: A Global Review and Future Directions* (2020, Palgrave Macmillan). (In the preface to their work, Seddon & Floodgate remark that even though cannabis law reform has been, "... a subject of public discourse for at least the last 50 years, but for much of that time actual change seemed a distant and unlikely prospect. ... [I]t has only been in the last decade that significant reform has started to develop in multiple places.").

i. Understanding 'Cannabis'

Cannabis has a complicated history. Some say it is a plant, others say it is a pleasure-giving intoxicant,[14] yet others say it is a medicine, some say it is a dangerous illegal drug, and yet some others say it can lead to deeply spiritual and mystical experiences.[15]

'Cannabis,' a plant that has been used 'therapeutically for millennia,'[16] is also known as 'marijuana, hemp, ganja, weed, pot, Mary Jane,'[17] and by several other names, it means the same thing: a cannabis plant of the 'genus cannabis.'[18] Whereas the psychoactive properties (i.e. they get you 'high') of this plant's leaves, flowers, seed, and resin were discovered 2500 years ago,[19] it was being used medicinally 4000 years ago in China, Egypt, and Mesopotamia.[20] The harmful effects of cannabis continue to be debated but no 'definitive conclusions about causation' have been drawn yet and many people 'view it as a relatively benign and low-harm substance'.[21]

---

14. Cannabis remains the most widely consumed prohibited intoxicant in the world, *see* Seddon & Floodgate, *supra* note 13 at 5. The United Nations Office of Drug Control estimates that nearly 200 million adults (4% of global adult population) used cannabis in 2017. *See* United Nations Office on Drugs and Crime, *World Drug Report 2019*, United Nations (2019), available at: https://wdr.unodc.org/wdr2019/. Government of India, Ministry of Social Justice & Empowerment estimates that a total of 31 million individuals (2.8% of the total population) had consumed cannabis within the past year. *See* Government of India, Ministry of Social Justice and Empowerment, Magnitude of Substance Use in India 2019, p.17 (2019).
15. Seddon & Floodgate, *supra* note 13 at 1-2.
16. Lewis A. Grossman, 'Life, Liberty, [and the Pursuit of Happiness]: Medical Marijuana Regulation in Historical Context', 74 FOOD & DRUG. L.J. 280, 287 (2019); Seddon & Floodgate, supra note 13 at 3.
17. *See e.g.* Report of the Indian Hemp Drugs Commission 1893-94 ('IHDC REPORT'), *See infra* Chapter 2; Nitin B., 'Legalizing Cannabis in India: Is it time the Parliament starts talking about it?', The News Minute, August 24, 2015, available at: https://www.thenewsminute.com/article/legalizing-cannabis-india-it-time-parliament-starts-talking-about-it-33635 (last accessed April 1, 2021).
18. Narcotic Drugs and Psychotropic Substances Act, 1985 ('NDPS Act'), § 2(iv) (defining 'cannabis plant' to mean 'any plant of the genus cannabis'.).
19. Seddon & Floodgate, *supra* note 13 at 3 (observing that, "[t]he psychoactive properties of the plant's resin, leaves and flowers may have been found a little later but can be identified at least as far back as 2500 BCE in Xinjiang and parts of Siberia, and quite probably were discovered earlier than that …").
20. *Id.*
21. Seddon & Floodgate, *supra* note 13 at 6. Seddon & Floodgate highlight that, "the association between cannabis and schizophrenia has been particularly controversial."

Tracing the 'historical geography' of cannabis it has been noted that by the medieval period, "it was well established across the Muslim world and had come to form *an important part of religious and cultural tradition in India*."[22] Of course, some of the historical material discussed in this work would tend to suggest that cannabis already was a part of religious and cultural tradition in ancient India.

Sometimes the words 'cannabis,' 'marijuana,' and 'charas' are also used synonymously,[23] and going strictly by the law 'charas' and 'cannabis' may fairly be used in such a manner since the most important definition of the word 'cannabis' is provided in section 2(iii) of the Narcotic Drugs and Psychotropic Substances Act, 1985 ('NDPS Act'):

> *"2(iii) "cannabis (hemp)" means—*
>
> *(a) charas, that is, the separated resin, in whatever form, whether crude or purified, obtained from the cannabis plant and also includes concentrated preparation and resin known as hashish oil or liquid hashish;*
>
> *(b) ganja, that is, the flowering or fruiting tops of the cannabis plant (excluding the seeds and leaves when not accompanied by the tops), by whatever name they may be known or designated; and*
>
> *(c) any mixture, with or without any neutral material, of any of the above forms of cannabis or any drink prepared therefrom;"*

Two things are clear from this definition. First: that even though technically *charas* and *ganja* might be two distinct things, they are both *legally* defined to *mean* cannabis because ultimately, they are either a part of, or extracted from the *cannabis plant*, which itself is defined in section 2(iv) of the NDPS Act to mean, "any plant of the genus cannabis." The law doesn't work in mysterious ways, it just works in complicated ones. And second: that the *seeds* and *leaves* of the *cannabis plant* are exempted from this definition if they are not accompanied by *ganja*.

A clear understanding of the legal meaning of the word 'cannabis' was necessary before introducing the key thesis of this work, which is: (a) from a legal standpoint, the case that possession of cannabis[24] in India should be 'decriminalized,' is very strong; (b) from a policy standpoint, trade in cannabis in India should be 'legalized,' but it is beyond the brief of this work to contemplate as to what type of model would be most suited for Indian market; and (c) from a

22. *Id.* at 4. (Emphasis Added).
23. *See e.g.* Namrata Reddy Sirupa, 'Why Cannabis Should Be Legalized in India', *Business World*, January 13, 2019, available at: http://www.businessworld.in/article/Why-Cannabis-Should-Be-Legalised-In-India/13-01-2019-166025/ (last accessed April 1, 2021).
24. As defined in the NDPS Act, *supra* note 18, § 2(iii).

constitutional standpoint, it is highly doubtful whether Parliament has the power to criminalize it.

For the sake of fullness and clarity, we would use the following non-legal definition of cannabis, but it is easy to see how the definition of cannabis as provided in sections 2(iii), and (iv) of the NDPS Act is subsumed in the following one (note here that the word 'hemp' is used as synonymously with 'cannabis' in the NDPS Act):

> *""Marijuana" is the Mexican colloquial name for a plant known to botanists as Cannabis Sativa. It is a hemp plant that contains cannabinoids, chemicals that initiate psychological effects when they bind to cannabinoid receptors in the brain. It has approximately 525 known components, and at least eighty-five different known cannabinoids can be derived from it. However, the most common plant-derived cannabinoids, ... are Phtocannabinoid tetrahydrocannabinol ("THC"), and Cannabidiol ("CBD"). THC ingestion is most often associated with psychological effects such as euphoria, analgesia, sedation, cognitive impairment, and appetite stimulation. CBD is the cannabinoid most often associated with healing. Among other potential health benefits, CBD has been shown to relieve convulsion, inflammation, anxiety, and nausea; prevent short-term memory loss; and inhibit cancer cell growth in breast cancer."*[25]

ii. The Medicinal and Toilet Preparations (Excise Duties) Act, 1955

In India, the use of cannabis for personal, recreational, religious, spiritual, or medicinal, use is currently criminally prohibited under the Narcotics Drugs and Psychotropic Substances Act, 1985 ("NDPS Act").[26] In fact, it would not be incorrect to say that the use of cannabis for such use was criminalized in India, for the first time, by the NDPS Act.[27] Before 1985, the use of cannabis for medicinal purposes seems to have been expressly regulated by the Medicinal and

25. Elena M. Quattrone, 'The Catch 22 of Marijuana [Il]Legalization', 22 B.U. J. SCI. & TECH. L. 299, 303-04 (2016).
26. *See* Narcotic Drugs and Psychotropic Substances Act, 1985, No. 61, Acts of Parliament, 1985 (India).
27. Khagesh Gautam & Yashowardhan Tiwari, 'Cannabis: The other prohibition', *The Indian Express*, November 3, 2020, https://indianexpress.com/article/opinion/cannabis-the-other-prohibition-6927254/; Shashi Tharoor & Avinash Tharoor, Opinion, 'High time India, the land of bhang, legalises marijuana', *The Print*, October 18, 2018, https://theprint.in/opinion/when-india-legalises-weed/66245/; Adrija Roychowdhury, Research, 'Cannabis in India: A rather long story, with its highs and lows', *The Indian Express*, September 12, 2020), https://indianexpress.com/article/research/cannabis-in-india-a-rather-long-story-with-its-highs-and-lows-6592020/.

Toilet Preparations (Excise Duties) Act, 1955 ("MTP Excise Act").[28] The MTP Excise Act was enacted by our Parliament to 'provide for the levy and collection of duties on medicinal and toilet preparations,' that contained either alcohol or any narcotic drugs.[29] Even though enacted in 1955, this Act came into force on April 1, 1957.[30] As per the MTP Excise Act, duties of excise could be levied on 'dutiable goods' that were defined as 'medicinal and toilet preparations' specified in the Schedule appended to the Act.[31] Medicinal preparations in 'Ayurvedic, Unani or other indigenous systems of medicine' that involved the use of any narcotic drugs attracted a 20% *ad valorem* excise duty.[32] 'Indian hemp' has been defined in section 2(e) of this Act the following way:

> *"(i) the leaves, small stalks and flowering or fruiting tops of the Indian hemp plant (Cannabis sativa L.), including all forms known as bhang, siddhi or ganja;*
>
> *(ii) charas, that is, the resin obtained from the Indian hemp plant, which has not been submitted to any manipulations other than those necessary for packing and transport;*
>
> *(iii) any mixture, with or without neutral materials, of any of the above forms of Indian hemp or any drink prepared therefrom; and*
>
> *(iv) any extract or tincture of any of the above forms of Indian hemp;"*[33]

However, the NDPS Act, also enacted by our Parliament, criminalizes trade in cannabis (including its cultivation, cross-breeding, agricultural and other scientific research, manufacture, etc.) throughout the length and breadth of the Republic of India.[34] Whereas the constitutional authority to regulate and tax trade in cannabis for medicinal purposes is quite clearly made out from the text of the Indian Constitution itself,[35] it is not possible to say the same with equal

---

28. Medicinal and Toilet Preparations (Excise Duty) Act, 1955, No. 16, Acts of Parliament, 1955 (India).
29. *Id.* Preamble.
30. *Id.* § 1(3).
31. *Id.*§ 2(c) read with Schedule, Entries 1(iii), 2(iv), 4.
32. *See e.g.,* Medicinal and Toilet Preparations (Excise Duty) Act, 1955, Schedule, Entry 2(iv).
33. Medicinal and Toilet Preparations (Excise Duty) Act, 1955, § 2(e).
34. *See* Narcotic Drugs and Psychotropic Substances Act, 1985, § 8, § 20.
35. India Constitution, 7th Schedule, List I: Union List, Entry 84 (as it stood before the enactment of the Constitution (One Hundred and First Amendment) Act, 2016, §17(a)(i). Entry 84, before 101st Amendment read as follows:
    "84. Duties of excise on tobacco and other goods manufactured or produced in India except —
    (a) alcoholic liquors for human consumption;
    (b) opium, Indian hemp and other narcotic drugs and narcotics, *but including medicinal and toilet preparations* containing alcohol or any substance included in sub-paragraph (b) of this entry."

    (Emphasis Added).

certainty when it comes to its criminalization. At the first go, it might seem quite implausible, even unthinkable, to suggest that the Parliament does not have the authority to criminalize cannabis under the Constitution. However, one of the claims made in this book is that upon a fair and reasonable interpretation of the Constitution, consistent with the relevant principles of constitutional interpretation that are a part of our jurisprudence as well as the law laid down by the Supreme Court, some questions on the Parliament's competence do arise and need to be addressed. Parliament is our highest law-making body, and we reserve our highest respect for it. But questions of constitutional competence are a factor in the interpretation of the Constitution. If we respect our Parliament, it is only because we respect our Constitution even more since the Constitution has established our Parliament. Therefore, we must be careful and methodical when we examine the foundational document of our republic. For instance, if the State Legislatures are specifically competent to impose duties of excise on cannabis, it would require considerable strain to be placed on the clear text of the Constitution, and perhaps some innovation in the doctrine of federalism and settled principles of interpretation to say that Parliament can criminalize cannabis across the Union of India. When we realise that this federal arrangement was continued in our Constitution from the Government of India Act, 1935, it does push us to pause and to take a closer look. These questions do arise, and simply invoking the famous 'entry 97' of List 1 of Schedule 7 would not answer these questions, or at most offer a very unsatisfactory solution to the extent that we might have to base them on contradictory basic principles. Besides, text and history are not the only relevant considerations in constitutional interpretation. We must take the economic dimension into account, and this can be done in a much more efficient way by our Parliament, and Cabinets, at the State and Union levels. We should keep on reminding ourselves from time to time that the Parliament and the Cabinet are both constitutionally established institutions as well.

Speaking of Cabinets, a 2019 study conducted by the Union Ministry of Social Justice and Empowerment, Government of India, shows that a total of 31 million individuals (2.8% of the total population) had consumed cannabis within the past year.[36] I suspect that if such a study is conducted again today and respondents are honest then this number might be much higher, but could

36. Government of India, Ministry of Social Justice and Empowerment, Magnitude of Substance Use in India 2019, p. 2 (2019) (available at: http://socialjustice.nic.in/writereaddata/UploadFile/Magnitude_Substance_Use_India_REPORT.pdf.).

anyone really blame the people in the light of the incredible stress, anxiety, death, depression, hopelessness, and misery that have been visited upon us since this study was published. This study found that only 0.25% of cannabis users are dependent on the substance, compared to 19% of alcohol users.[37] Another recent study conducted by a Delhi-based think-tank 'Vidhi Centre for Legal Policy'[38] shows that those worst hit by enforcement of the prohibition of cannabis are economically and socially the weakest.[39] These include mostly daily wage workers and slum or street dwellers.[40] In Mumbai alone, where 10,669 pending cases before a Magistrate's court were analyzed, the study found that 99.9% of these cases included charges that involved 'consumption of a narcotic substance' but the details of the substance were not always available.[41] However, whenever details of the substance were available, 87% of those cases were cases of cannabis consumption.[42] Even though the public debate has now definitively shifted in the direction of decriminalization of cannabis for medicinal and personal use in what Prof. Huntington has described as the 'west,'[43] predominantly in the United States of America, and Canada; in India even though unfortunately it has not been possible to have an informed public debate on this issue yet, I believe the time has come to address this issue with the seriousness that it deserves. There is truly much at stake here. With the cost-cutting alone that can be easily achieved by simply 'decriminalizing' possession of small quantities, say 30 grams (roughly the equivalent of 1 ounce, but since we don't use ounces in India), and by refusing to call such possession an offence so serious that it deserves 5 years in jail or similar disproportionate penalty, we can substantially reduce the load on our criminal justice system. For every investigation officer, prosecutor, and judge that we free up from investigating, prosecuting, and deciding mere possession offences, we make one more officer, prosecutor, and judge available to focus on more serious crimes like rape, murder, and several national security offences. We need our police to be engaged in actual policing, and while reserving my greatest respect for our police forces (both at the state and the union level), it is my belief

37. *Id*, at 4.
38. Neha Singhal & Naveed Ahmad, 'A Case For De-Criminalization of Cannabis Use in India', *Vidhi Centre For Legal Policy*, August 20, 2020, https://vidhilegalpolicy.in/wp-content/uploads/2020/08/Cannabis_Final.pdf.
39. *Id*, at 7.
40. *Id*.
41. *Id*, at 5.
42. *Id*.
43. Samuel P. Huntington, *The Clash of Civilizations and The Remaking of World Order*, Simon & Schuster (1996).

that we are wasting national resources when we allow our laws to say that possessing a few ounces of cannabis is such a serious offence that we should put people in jail for half a decade, with probably another decade spent fighting the case through the already overburdened judicial system. It is my view that the case to decriminalize possession of small quantities (more discussion to follow) in India, on the grounds of the reduction of burden on the already overburdened judicial system (especially the trial judiciary, and the High Courts, acting as the last court of criminal appeal), is quite strong, and will be presented as such in this book. In any case, this is an argument that needs to be made, and this book is a modest attempt to fill what seems to be a substantial gap in Indian cannabis legalization scholarship by presenting legal, policy, and constitutional arguments as to why the prohibition of cannabis in India could safely be ended.

iii. Contemporary Debate: Around Half a Decade Old

The debate around the legalization of trade in cannabis may be said to have been going on in India for about half a decade now. On August 25, 2015, leading Indian newspaper *The Hindu* reported that a four-time Member of Parliament, of Lok Sabha from Dhenkanal, Odisha, who was also the chief whip of the political party Biju Janata Dal, Shri Tathagata Satpathy, "shook awake a rather somnolent Lok Sabha in the recent monsoon session by advocating the legalization of cannabis. This startling advocacy was certainly not the official position of his party."[44] Shri Satpathy gave the following statement to the newspaper: "Cannabis is a drug that has been given a bad name the alcohol lobby, peddling something far more dangerous, has managed to club cannabis with more dangerous narcotics ... Not only legalisation of cannabis, I'm in favour of decriminalising Section 377 of the Indian Penal Code, and against the ban on pornography."[45] The MP seems to be sensitive to the fact that politicians 'as representatives of a very young population' will have to make 'common cause with young people.'[46]

Satpathy is not the only lawmaker at the Union level who has taken a public stand against the prohibition of cannabis. On December 15, 2017, it was reported that Shri Dharamvir Gandhi, MP from Patiala, Punjab, and a

44. Nistula Hebbar, 'When some MPs choose to go by their heart', *The Hindu*, August 24, 2015, available at: https://www.thehindu.com/news/national/when-some-mps-choose-to-go-by-their-heart/article7572827.ece (last accessed April 1, 2021).
45. *Id.*
46. *Id.*

'cardiologist by profession' sought 'to legalize marijuana possession and consumption in India' by moving a private member's bill.[47] As can be guessed he earned the support not just of Satpathy, but also of the famous film star turned politician late Shri Vinod Khanna, who was an MP and member of the currently-in-office Bharatiya Janata Party (BJP).[48] On October 18, 2018, The Print carried an opinion piece co-authored by Dr. Shashi Tharoor, MP (Lok Sabha), Thiruvananthapuram, Kerala, and a leading member of the Congress party, and a noted public figure in India and abroad,[49] and his nephew Avinash Tharoor, who is a Policy and Communications Officer at the UK Drugs Charity Release.[50] Unlike his parliamentary colleague Satpathy, who is open about his personal cannabis use,[51] and has spoken about it on occasion,[52] Tharoor begins his co-authored piece by a qualification: "I have never tried a recreational drug in my life."[53] Perhaps there is an important lesson here: one's personal use of cannabis is, and ought to remain private, and is ultimately irrelevant in such discussions. Later in this piece, the Tharoors develop an argument and present their case as to why trade in cannabis should be legalized in India. But Sathpathy's work here is at a different level. When asked the following question: "Why do you think cannabis consumption was criminalized? Was it wrong to do so and attach such stigma to its use?", this is what the MP had to say:

> *"Intoxication, in various forms, has been part of societies across the world. Shiva had some kind of 'ras' and Christ's blood was wine. Since biblical times and even prior to that, including Romans and South Americans, people have been using*

---

47. HT Correspondent, 'Bill for legalised supply of opium, marijuana cleared for Parliament', *Hindustan Times*, November 02, 2016, available at: https://www.hindustantimes.com/punjab/aap-mp-gandhi-s-bill-seeking-opium-legalisation-cleared-for-tabling-in-parliament/story-itanKX3vRrhuXJPdgnJD6N.html (last accessed April 1, 2021); TNM Staff, 'You want ganja to be legal in India? These MPs want it too', *The News Minute*, December 15, 2017, available at: https://www.thenewsminute.com/article/you-want-ganja-be-legal-india-these-mps-want-it-too-73218 (last accessed April 1, 2021).
48. *Id.*
49. For more information *see* https://www.shashitharoor.in/ (last accessed April 1, 2021).
50. Shashi Tharoor & Avinash Tharoor, 'High time India, the land of bhang, legalises marijuana', *The Print*, October 18, 2018, available at: https://theprint.in/opinion/when-india-legalises-weed/66245/ (last accessed April 1, 2021).
51. Tathagata Satpathy, 'Should Marijuana be legalised?', *The Hindu*, August 20, 2017, available at: https://www.thehindu.com/opinion/op-ed/should-marijuana-be-legalised/article19466725.ece (last accessed April 1, 2021).
52. Deeptiman Tiwary, 'Cannabis ban is elitist. It should go: Tathagata Satpathy', *Times of India*, March 29, 2015, available at: https://timesofindia.indiatimes.com/india/cannabis-ban-is-elitist-it-should-go-tathagata-satpathy/articleshow/46732106.cms (last accessed April 2, 2021).
53. Tharoor & Tharoor, *supra* note 50.

intoxicants. Whether it's part of Indian culture, I don't know. But it's definitely a way of life in India. In Odisha (where cannabis consumption is not illegal), people smoking chillum is a common sight. It is not something you make note of just as you don't notice someone drinking water or having tea. The only difference that I have experienced in life is whether you let an intoxicant overpower your life or you take it as a learning process, do something and then get out of it."[54]

iv. The Case of Himachal Pradesh: High Times Ahead?

It was recently reported that the Chief Minister of Himachal Pradesh, Shri Jai Ram Thakur, is considering legalizing the trade in cannabis.[55] According to some news reports, there seems to be a growing bipartisan consensus on legalizing trade in cannabis at least in the state of Himachal Pradesh.[56] This has been acknowledged by CM Thakur himself when he reportedly told some media people: "Considering the growing demand for legalizing the cannabis cultivation, we are willing to consider it but a decision will be taken only after looking at the existing laws and its implications."[57] This is a significant development for two reasons.

One, according to the third argument that this work makes (i.e., it is highly doubtful whether Parliament has the power to criminalize it), the competence to levy taxes on trade in cannabis is vested in the state legislatures only. From this argument's perspective, the statement of the Chief Minister is particularly important. If the position presented in this work is accepted, and if the Chief

54. Tiwary, *supra* note 52 (emphasis added).
55. 'Plan to legalise cannabis cultivation, says Thakur', *The Tribune*, November 13, 2018, available at: https://www.tribuneindia.com/news/archive/himachal/plan-to-legalise-cannabis-cultivation-says-thakur-682159 (last accessed April 1, 2012).
56. *Id.*; Gagandeep Singh Dhillon, 'Explained: Why is Himachal Pradesh planning to legalise cannabis cultivation?', *The Indian Express*, March 16, 2021, available at: https://indianexpress.com/article/explained/explained-why-himachal-is-now-planning-to-legalise-cannabis-cultivation-7219802/ (last accessed April 4, 2021);
Gaurab Dasgupta & Amrita Das, Map by Urvashi Makwana, 'Himachal Pradesh Is Legalizing Cannabis Cultivation For Medicinal, Industrial Use', *The Tennessee Tribune*, March 29, 2021, available at: https://tntribune.com/himachal-pradesh-is-legalizing-cannabis-cultivation-for-medicinal-industrial-use/ (last accessed April 4, 2021);
Gaurav Bisht, 'Himachal to legalise cannabis cultivation to boost economy', *Hindustan Times*, March 22, 2021, available at: https://www.hindustantimes.com/cities/chandigarh-news/himachal-to-legalise-cannabis-cultivation-to-boost-economy-101616413074575.html (last accessed April 4, 2021).
57. *The Tribune*, *supra* note 55.

Minister's party commands the confidence of the state legislature, constitutionally there is nothing preventing the State of Himachal Pradesh from enacting legislation to this effect notwithstanding the prohibition in the NDPS Act. In fact, as discussed later in this work, there is evidence from the pre-1985 era, or more correctly the pre-NDPS Act era, where cannabis, as defined in section 2(iii) of the NDPS Act, was actually an item on which duties of excise were routinely levied by the state legislatures. Also, in this context, there might be some constitutional concerns arising from the trade and commerce clauses[58] of the Constitution that could be raised having a significant bearing on this issue. Such issues are not articulated in this work, but the possibility of these issues cannot be denied.

And two, according to the first two arguments made in this work, and as is the publicly stated position of several other members of Parliament as noted above, (a) there is no cause for the prohibition of cannabis in the Republic of India; (b) there is a strong case for legalization of trade in cannabis; and (c) decriminalization and eventual legalization will ultimately be beneficial for our country, our society, and our future. More specifically, legalization in Himachal Pradesh will be particularly beneficial for not just the people of Himachal but for 'we, the people of Union of India.' The state of Himachal Pradesh, also called 'Dev Bhoomi'[59] (quite literally: 'the land of gods' (depending on how you translate 'dev' that is translated here as god, but could also mean 'lords,' which could be a reference to a god-like yet mortal being), is *inter alia*, famous for areas like 'Mallana Valley'[60] (Mallana is sometimes spelled as Malana) and 'Parvati Valley,'[61] both in Kullu District of Himachal and both famous for its cannabis. There are many other such places in India that are famous for the cannabis that grows in that region. I am not an expert in intellectual property rights, and perhaps a person more learned should look into this, but to my mind, such type

58. India Constitution, Arts 301-304 (collectively referred to here as 'trade and commerce clauses').
59. *See e.g.,* Arvind Sehgal, 'Himachal Pradesh as "Dev Bhumi": Sociological Paradoxes', 49, ECONOMIC & POLITICAL WEEKLY, 59, (Jan. 18, 2014), https://www.jstor.org/stable/24478987.
60. Gagandeep Singh Dhillon, 'Explained: What is Mallana Cream, Himachal's unique cannabis product?', *The Indian Express*, December 15, 2020, available at: https://indianexpress.com/article/explained/what-is-mallana-cream-himachal-pradesh-cannabis-7098907/ (last accessed April 1, 2021).
61. *See e.g.* Pierre-Arnaud Chouvy, 'Cannabis cultivation and hashish production in the Parvati Valley, Himachal Pradesh, India (2015)', GEOPIUM, 2015, available at: https://www.geopium.org/cannabis-cultivation-and-hashish-production-in-india-2015/#:~:text=Cannabis%20cultivation%20and%20hashish%20production%20in%20the%20Parvati,Himachal%20Pradesh%2C%20India%20(2015)&text=Hashish%20produced%20in%20the%20Parvati,as%20the%20world's%20very%20best. (last accessed April 1, 2021).

of geographical referencing is usually reserved for locally grown plants, and crops, and seems to correspond very closely to the legal definition of a 'geographical indicator' as provided in section 2(1)(e) of the Geographical Indications Act, 1999:

> *""geographical indication", in relation to goods, means an indication which identifies such goods as agricultural goods, natural goods or manufactured goods as originating, or manufactured in the territory of a country, or a region or locality in that territory, where a given quality, reputation or other characteristic of such goods is essentially attributable to its geographical origin and in case where such goods are manufactured goods one of the activities of either the production or of processing or preparation of the goods concerned takes place in such territory, region or locality, as the case may be.*
>
> *Explanation. For the purposes of this clause, any name which is not the name of a country, region or locality of that country shall also be considered as the geographical indication if it relates to a specific geographical area and is used upon or in relation to particular goods originating from that country, region or locality, as the case may be;'*[62]

In fact, according to a report published by *Cannabis Now Magazine*, hashish (covered by the definition of 'charas' under section 2(iii)(a) of the NDPS Act) produced in Parvati Valley 'is of extremely high quality' and, "... Malana Cream that has long been produced in the isolated village of Malana has often been rated as the world's very best."[63] Though there are some reports which suggest that Indian *charas* is smuggled to foreign countries and 'is one of the costliest forms of hash sold in cafes of Amsterdam,'[64] Pierre-Arnaud Chouvy reports that:

> *"Indian charas is very rarely found outside of India as most of the Indian production is consumed locally or nationally (immediate neighbours to India - such as Nepal, Pakistan, and Afghanistan - also produce hashish) and as trafficking outside of India mostly involves small quantities. Of course, one can find Indian charas on the menus of most coffee shops in the Netherlands but one would be hard-pressed to determine if the Manali, Malana or Tosh charas sold in Amsterdam is real high-quality charas or if it even is Indian charas. In any case, the vast majority of the*

62. Geographical Indications of Goods (Registration and Protection) Act, 1999 (Act No. 48 of 1999, enacted December 30, 1999) available at: https://legislative.gov.in/sites/default/files/A1999-48.pdf (last accessed July 2, 2021).
63. Pierre-Arnaud Chouvy, 'Himalayan Highs', *Cannabis Now Magazine*, Issue 19, March 2016, available at: http://www.geopium.org/himalayan-highs/ (last accessed April 1, 2021).
64. Dhillon, *supra* note 60.

hashish consumed in Europe clearly comes from Morocco, reportedly the world's first producer of hashish."[65]

v. Substantial Potential for State Revenue

"What is the goal of the current federal policy prohibiting all use of marijuana? Is it to make criminals of those individuals? Or is the goal to educate the public about potential risks associated with using marijuana and to direct efforts toward deterring use, especially among the young? ... [T]he goals of education and deterrence could be more effectively pursued through a policy of full legalization, regulation, and taxation of marijuana than through the current policy of marijuana prohibition."[*]

In India, cannabis has been around for centuries and going by Indian as well as western experience, it is not going anywhere notwithstanding its legal status.[66] The most inspiring reforms in this area are taking place in Canada, and some States of the United States. These efforts began from decriminalizing and later legalizing cannabis for medicinal and recreational use.[67] As at the time of this writing, 13 States in the U.S., following widespread public support,[68] have enacted legislation to legalize recreational use, and 11 of these States have further established commercial supply chains from 'seed to sale' (with other 2 using non-commercial models).[69] The use of the model is important in determining the most efficient way of bringing this trade within the indirect tax umbrella.[70]

---

65. Chouvy, *supra* note 63.

* Cynthia S. Duncan, *The Need for Change: An Economic Analysis of Marijuana Policy*, 41 CONN. L. REV. 1701, 1705-06 (2009).

66. For the western experience, *see* Nachshon Goltz & Ekaterina Bogdanov, 'Lessons from Washington and Colorado: The Potential Financial Gains of Recreational Marijuana to Canada', 40 CAN.-U.S. L.J. 126 (2016). After comparing the Canadian and limited US experience of legalizing cannabis, the authors note: "Marijuana use is here to stay, whether or not it is criminalized." *Id.* at 137.

67. Seddon & Floodgate, *supra* note 13 at 17.

68. *Id.* Seddon & Floodgate note that in Vermont and Illinois cannabis was legalized through the state legislatures. In other 11, it was the result of "ballot initiatives, demonstrating the growing public support for reforming cannabis laws." In December, 2013 Uruguay became the first country in the world to legally regulate the cannabis market. In Uruguay, the drive was also voter driven and was ultimately approved by politicians. *See id.* at 26. Same thing happened in Canada in October, 2018. *See id.* at 31.

69. *Id.* at 18.

70. *See e.g.*, Seddon & Floodgate, *supra* note 13 at 20-21.

It can't be denied that trade in cannabis represents a significant addition to the indirect tax base, not to mention the income tax base. Significant public revenue could be generated by income tax that would in its ordinary course be collected by employers in cannabis and its related sister industries. It will be noted here that without any amendment to the Income Tax Act, 1961, we could significantly expand our tax base, and after a few amendments in the Goods and Services Tax regime, we could significantly expand our indirect tax base. Experts have also noted that legalization of medical cannabis often 'smoothed the transition' to recreational cannabis, "along with revealing how the federal government would allow the generation of tax revenues from the sale of cannabis."[71]

According to a widely reported[72] study conducted by an independent Berlin-based data-driven campaign outlet *ABCD*, along with an Israel-based firm *Seedo*, New Delhi and Mumbai ranked globally amongst the top-ten cannabis consuming cities in the world, with New Delhi placed at third and Mumbai at the sixth position respectively.[73] The total cannabis consumption per year for New Delhi was reported to be 38.26 metric tons, while for Mumbai the figure was placed at 32.38 metric tons. New Delhi was also ranked 10th amongst the least expensive cities for cannabis, with the price estimated to be US$ 4.38 per gram[74], though the correctness of this price needs to be independently confirmed. That's 38,260 kilograms of cannabis consumed per year in the nation's political capital, and 32,380 kilograms consumed in the nation's financial capital. Going by the price of US$ 4.38 per gram, in monetary terms,

---

71. *Id.*
72. FE Online, 'Delhi, Mumbai ranked among top 10 cities in cannabis consumption globally, capital bags third spot', *Financial Express*, September 10, 2019, available at https://www.financialexpress.com/india-news/delhi-mumbai-ranked-among-top-10-cities-in-cannabis-consumption-globally-capital-bags-third-spot/1701538/; India Today Web Desk, 'Delhi 3rd largest cannabis consumer in the world, Mumbai 6th: Study', *India Today*, September 13, 2019), *available at* https://www.indiatoday.in/education-today/latest-studies/story/delhi-3rd-largest-cannabis-consumer-in-the-world-mumbai-6th-study-1598845-2019-09-13; TNN, 'Delhi ranks high 3rd on global weed list', *Times of India*, September 10, 2019, available at https://timesofindia.indiatimes.com/city/delhi/delhi-ranks-high-3rd-on-global-weed-list/articleshow/71057555.cms.
73. *ABCD 2018 Cannabis Price Index*, ABCD, (Apr. 20, 2018), available at: http://weedindex.io.
74. *ABCD 2018 Cannabis Price Index*, ABCD, (Apr. 20, 2018), available at: http://weedindex.io. Placing reliance on this study, it was reported, "A study estimated that around 725 crore could be raised in Delhi alone if cannabis is taxed. This number was pegged at 641 crore for Mumbai;" Neha Singhal & Naveed Ahmad, 'A Case For De-Criminalization of Cannabis Use in India', Vidhi Centre For Legal Policy, 5 (Aug. 20, 2020), https://vidhilegalpolicy.in/wp-content/uploads/2020/08/Cannabis_Final.pdf.

that's US$ 167,578,800/-[75] worth of cannabis sold in New Delhi alone per year. Taking the conversion rate of US$ 1 = INR 70, it amounts to INR 11,73,05,16,000/-. That's INR 1173 crores worth of cannabis is sold just in New Delhi every year. If taxed at a modest rate of 5%, a total of INR 58,65,25,800/- worth of net revenue could be collected by the State Government of Delhi. This phenomenon seems to have been noted by some commentators. For instance, this recent detailed analysis in India Today calculates that annual revenue equivalent to US$ 101.2 million (INR 725 crore) could be earned if cannabis is taxed at the same level as cigarettes.[76] This analysis, however, presumes that cannabis should be taxed at the same unreasonable level as cigarettes, and it is not clear on what basis such a presumption could be made. If anything, according to the weight of the opinion of public commentators on the subject, as well as the arguments presented in this work, there is no reason for cannabis to be taxed at the same exorbitant level as tobacco. Whereas tobacco has zero redeeming medical qualities, the medicinal benefits of cannabis for physiological as well as psychological issues are well documented, well tested, and strongly recommended. The fact remains, cannabis use is here to stay, and a study of the Canadian and limited US experience shows that 'legal, but tightly regulated, sales of marijuana could bring millions of dollars into municipal, provincial, and federal treasuries.'[77]

It will be noted here that any government infrastructure that might be required to be erected for regulating trade in cannabis can be easily built by this money, and as such, it is highly unlikely that any such need might arise since all state governments as such have well-staffed revenue departments headed by a minister answerable to the cabinet that is collectively answerable to the state legislature. Additional revenue officers, specially trained to deal with cannabis cultivators and dealers, can be recruited into these departments and their salaries, etc. can be easily paid from this money. And therein lies the opportunity for the State of Himachal Pradesh. If the trade in cannabis (cannabis as defined in section 2(iii) read with section 2(iv) of the NDPS Act) is fully legalized (i.e. decriminalization of cultivation,[78] production, manufacture, possession, sale,

75. 38,260 kilograms = 38260000 grams. 38260000 grams at the rate of US $ 4.38 per grams amounts to US $ 167,578,800.
76. Sonali Acharjee, 'Should India make Cannabis legal?', *India Today*, September 19, 2020, available at: https://www.indiatoday.in/magazine/cover-story/story/20200928-should-india-make-cannabis-legal-1723088-2020-09-19 (last accessed April 1, 2021).
77. Goltz & Bogdanov, *supra* note 66 at 136.
78. NDPS Act, § 8(b) criminally prohibits cultivation *inter alia* of 'cannabis plant'.

purchase, transport, warehousing use, consumption, import inter-State, export inter-State,) in the State of Himachal Pradesh, something that according to this work the legislature of Himachal Pradesh has the full constitutional authority to do, the revenue windfall that will be incurred by the Consolidated Fund of the State of Himachal Pradesh[79] might alone more than justify such a legislative decision.

vi. Criminal Justice Reforms

In a consultation paper submitted to the National Level Committee for Reforms in Criminal Law (the 'Committee'), constituted by the Ministry of Home Affairs, Government of India in 2019 at the National Law University, Delhi, the 'fiscal case for cannabis decriminalization in India' was presented to the Committee.[80] This paper reports that after its legalization, following popular support, in the State of California, USA, in November 2016, California's revenue records have noted a massive inflow of revenue, and a total of US$ 1.4472 billion were collected in form of cultivation tax, excise tax, and sales tax from the beginning of 2018 till June 2020.[81] Data from the States of Washington (legalized: November, 2012), Oregon (legalized: November, 2014), Colorado (legalized: November, 2012), Alaska (legalized: November, 2014), Nevada (legalized: November, 2016), Massachusetts (legalized: November, 2016), Michigan (legalized: November, 2018), and Illinois (legalized: June 2019) shows similar trends. These trends have been noted briefly.[82] Many other foreign (mostly European) countries have already legalized cannabis as noted here in this report.[83]

---

79. India Constitution, Art. 266, § 1 (establishing a Consolidated Fund of India and that of the States).
80. Khagesh Gautam & Yashowardhan Tiwari, 'Consultation Paper No. 1: The Fiscal Case for Cannabis Decriminalization in India', October 28, 2020 (reproduced here as Appendix A).
81. *Id.* at 11.
82. *See e.g.* Khagesh Gautam & Yashowardhan Tiwari, 'Cannabis: The Other Prohibition', *The Indian Express*, November 03, 2020, available at: https://indianexpress.com/article/opinion/cannabis-the-other-prohibition-6927254/ (last accessed April 1, 2020); Neha Singhal & Naveed Ahmad, 'Could Indian Economy Get a New High by Removing Ban on Cannabis?', *The Quint*, September 05, 2020, available at: https://www.thequint.com/voices/opinion/weed-marijuana-cannabis-prohibition-indian-govt-united-states-war-on-drugs-racist-origins (last accessed April 1, 2021).
83. Syed Wajid, 'Is decriminalization of marijuana in India a better move?', *National Herald*, October 09, 2019, available at: https://www.nationalheraldindia.com/opinion/is-decriminalisation-of-marijuana-in-india-a-better-move (last accessed April 1, 2021). The list includes: Poland, Moldova, Macedonia, Luxembourg, Italy, Greece, Germany, Georgia, The Czech Republic, Croatia, Chile, Austria, and Antigua & Barbuda.

In addition to this, certain other incidental benefits to our already overburdened judicial system, starting from the judicial magistracy all the way up to Hon'ble the Supreme Court of India, have been noted. First, the decriminalization of cannabis wipes out the illegal drug market[84] and opens it up as a potential tax base.[85] Second, decriminalization quite literally removes 'a substantial amount of currently pending cases in trial courts.'[86] As this author has elsewhere explained: "If the very law under which a person was going to be charged, or tried and convicted, ceases to exist, there is no reason for that case to go on in court, or for the police to keep on investigating such cases. Those who are currently serving prison sentences for cannabis-related offences can be pardoned, or paroled by the Governor, or the President, as the case may be."[87] This is one potential benefit that needs to be investigated at the highest levels of decision making with an urgency that cannot be stressed enough, and it is the considered view of this author that in addition to the certain revenue windfall noted above, this ought to be one of the most pressing reasons why we, the people of India, should take the question of decriminalization of cannabis very seriously. In the U.S., post decriminalization, "cannabis-related arrests have declined in [the] States that have legalized cannabis."[88]

It would be noted here that even though the NDPS Act is a parliamentary legislation, it is the Consolidated Fund of the State of Himachal Pradesh that pays for *most* of the prosecutions under that Act. For the *most* part, enforcement of the NDPS Act is left to the state police, state prosecutors, and the magistracy and trial courts, all of which are being paid for by the Consolidated Fund of the State of Himachal Pradesh. This argument applies *mutatis mutandis* to all State governments and legislatures as established by our Constitution. The criminal justice machinery of the State governments is constitutionally enjoined to enforce the laws enacted by the Union Parliament as well as the State Legislature and to that extent, it would be fair to say that this argument might appear to be heavily one-sided, i.e., on the side of the State government. It is correct to say that the criminal justice machinery of the State governments cannot refuse to enforce the laws enacted by the Union Parliament, for to claim otherwise would

84. *See e.g.,* Seddon & Floodgate, *supra* note 13 at 69, noting that, "[w]ithin both legalisation and decriminalisation models, income can be generated (or clawed back) through criminal justice cost savings.". *See also* Tharoor & Tharoor, *supra* note 50; Sirupa, *supra* note 23; Gautam & Tiwari, *supra* note 82.
85. Consultation Paper No. 1, *supra* note 80.
86. Gautam & Tiwari, *supra* note 27.
87. *Id.*
88. Seddon & Floodgate, *supra* note 13 at 69.

be inconsistent with the Constitution. Furthermore, the manner in which the Union and State governments share the revenues and financial resources is also a particularly tricky issue, and in the scheme of things, it is generally wise to leave enough elbow-space to account for changing conditions. However, the important point to note here is that the State Legislatures are expressly authorised under the Constitution to impose duties of excise, *inter alia*, on cannabis. This express authority vested exclusively in the State Legislatures has a deeper history that is traced to the Government of India Act, 1935, and that is further traced back to the Indian Drugs and Hemp Commission Report of 1894. It is not just the text of the Constitution, but also the peculiar history of this particular arrangement that must be considered. If we keep our attention on this peculiar history and then examine the picture presented in Appendix A, we will see that the criminal prohibition of cannabis in 1985 (by the enactment of the NDPS Act) appears rather to be an aberration from the normal. The normal has actually been quite the reverse in our country. It would be noted that it is not being suggested that the criminal justice machinery of the State government should simply refuse to enforce the law, and such a claim could never be made. For this reason, the suggestion is that in the first stage we may consider 'decriminalizing' cannabis by removing it from the purview of the NDPS Act (*see* Appendix B that provides a list of 98 provisions of the NDPS Act that have been identified for this purpose; the list of course if not exhaustive). In the second stage, we may set up a ministry at the Union, or at the State level whose work whereof will include, but not limited to, systematically cataloguing all prisoners convicted under the NDPS Act where the contraband seized was only cannabis. These prisoners will have to be released from the prisons and the government should take the lead instead of waiting for *habeas corpus* petitions to be filed questioning the continued incarceration, if not convictions, of these prisoners. This ministry will also have to work with all the stakeholders as the groundwork for the third stage is prepared: drafting of model legislation legally regulating the cannabis industry at the State level. The revenues generated from decriminalization, and eventual legalization, should be sufficient to offset the expenses required to run such a ministry, and if we are wise and careful, we might just end up providing a reliable line of perpetual revenue that ultimately will be used for the benefit of the people.

Laws exist for us; we do not exist for the laws. In our country, we have the freedom to openly and freely discuss whether a particular law should be retained in the statute book or not. This is what distinguishes us from most of our neighbours in the region, and this is indeed our heritage that we cherish. The question here is not about repealing the NDPS Act wholesale and doing away with the drug-law enforcement machinery at the Union and State levels. The question is only whether there is a case for cannabis to be kept within the purview of the NDPS Act? This book claims that there is no case and on more grounds than one. Once the constitutional text is examined in the light of the peculiar history of that text a very different picture emerges. To the extent it might seem odd to us, it is only because we have not seen that picture before. The more we look at it, contemplate on it, examine the basis on which it stands, we realise this picture makes more sense: looking backward and going forward. At some point in time orthodoxy has to be abandoned and even seemingly settled interpretations must give way to the necessities of the times.

vii. Cannabis decriminalization, or full legalization?

> *The prohibition of drugs is a public policy matter, and the decision to legalize marijuana would require a radical change in that policy. … The extent to which the current system of marijuana prohibition has been successful in preventing abuse of the substances must be weighed against any benefits derived from removing the criminal sanctions associated with recreational and medical use.*[*]

Full decriminalization of cannabis therefore benefits the people of Himachal Pradesh in the following ways: (a) decriminalization frees up considerable financial resources of the State government that are now available to be deployed for other purposes ; (b) it can potentially pave the way for eventual legalization, and open up a potential tax base that cannot be tapped right now only because of a parliamentary legislation the constitutionality whereof itself is suspect; (c) it can potentially bring in crores of rupees to the Consolidated Fund of the State; (d) it potentially opens up cannabis tourism opportunities in Himachal Pradesh, another industry that exists peacefully and operates efficiently right below the radar of legality, and yet is beyond the reach of our tax laws; and (e) provide gainful employment and entrepreneurial opportunities to the people, especially the enterprising youth, of Himachal Pradesh, who would have to be involved in cultivation, production, manufacture, possession, sale, purchase, transport, warehousing, use, consumption, import inter-State, export inter-State, of cannabis and other cannabis related products. These activities would require a team of cultivators, manufacturers, packers, movers, and sellers of cannabis and

---

* Cynthia S. Duncan, *The Need for Change: An Economic Analysis of Marijuana Policy*, 41 CONN. L. REV. 1701, 1709 (2009).

cannabis-related products. This in turn provides more work for accountants, lawyers, sales-people, logistics professionals, and a whole host of professionals. Perhaps Satpathy, the MP from Dhenkanal, Odisha had seen the writing on the wall much earlier than CM Thakur, or maybe he just spoke about it earlier. The fact remains that similar benefits have been demonstrably experienced by other economies, and there is no reason to presume that such benefits would not accrue to our economy.

viii. A Larger Issue at Stake

In addition, there is a larger issue at stake here. A lot of public commentary on the subject notes that cannabis use for personal, religious, spiritual, and medicinal purposes has a very long history in India.[89] In fact, 'the cannabis plant is one of the oldest herbal products currently in use.'[90] In the popular commentary, it has been noted that cannabis has been used in India since 2000 BCE, and finds mentions in several ancient Indian scriptures, with the oldest reference being to the *Atharva Veda* as 'one of the most sacred plants on Earth.'[91] Another claim is the use of cannabis in the worship of one of the gods in the Hindu trinity - Lord Shiva.[92] This author, being born and brought up in the holy city of Kurukshetra, Haryana, is personally aware of the ritualistic use of cannabis in Shiva worship where cannabis is not only consumed by the worshipper but on the prescribed day(s) as per the Hindu calendar, a paste made out of cannabis is applied on the Shiva *linga* in ritual worship (known to this author as *ganja shringar*). Such claims are important and should be investigated more carefully. Unfortunately for this author, two things prevented further study: (a) access to authentic copies of such scriptures; and (b) knowledge of the language(s) in which they are written. One hopes that this investigation is undertaken soon and taken to its logical conclusion.

---

89. *See e.g.* Sirupa, *supra* note 23; Gautam & Tiwari, *supra* note 27; Priya Mishra, 'High time India legalised cannabis', *Firstpost*, May 03, 2019, available at: https://www.firstpost.com/india/taking-pot-shots-its-high-time-we-legalised-cannabis-6564001.html (last accessed April 1, 2021).
90. Amanda Reiman, 'The Fallacy of a One Size Fits All Cannabis Policy', 35 HUMBOLDT J. OF SOC. RELATIONS, 104 (2013).
91. *See e.g.* Sameeruddin Shaik, 'Legalization of Cannabis in India', *Times of India*, August 29, 2020, available at: https://timesofindia.indiatimes.com/readersblog/sameer/legalization-of-cannabis-in-india-25286/ (last accessed April 2, 2021).
92. *Id.*

Furthermore, a widely noted recent study by the All-India Institute of Medical Sciences ('AIIMS') reported that about 7.2 million Indians had consumed cannabis within the past year,[93] another widely quoted 2019 study published by the Ministry of Social Justice and Empowerment found that cannabis is the second most commonly used substance in India after alcohol[94]. The fact remains that cannabis cultivation, production, manufacture, possession, sale, purchase, transporting, warehousing, use, consumption, in India is nothing new and has a very old history. It may not be unfair to state that cannabis consumption in India might perhaps be as old as India itself, and certainly much older than the birth of the modern Indian republic in 1947. If the cultivation and consumption of cannabis would have been harmful, it is doubtful that it would have survived and continued to be preserved by tradition for so long. In fact, as is demonstrated in this work later, cannabis cultivation, production, manufacture, possession, sale, purchase, transporting, warehousing, use, consumption, in India was totally legal in 1947, in 1950, and continued to be so until 1985 when the NDPS Act was enacted by our Parliament. It was legal when the first war of independence was fought in 1857. One might be speculating a bit, but given the consumption patterns of the substance during that time, it might be fair to presume that the odd tola[95] of hash might have brought much comfort to the brave soldiers of that war on the battlefront, and one prays, later too as memories of war do continue to oppress the minds of warriors for long, even if their forgotten histories might not. As this story from Forbes magazine reports, sufferers of Post-Traumatic Stress Disorder ('PTSD') who used cannabis were 2.5 times more likely to recover.[96] One scientific study found "indications that cannabis or some of its components, primarily THC and CBD, diminish particular symptoms of PTSD."[97] Priya Mishra also reports medicinal benefits from personal experience as well as independent study.[98]

---

93. *Id.*
94. Gautam & Tiwari, *supra* note 27; Shaik, *supra* note 91.
95. A 'tola' (measuring around 10 grams) is the traditional weight by which cannabis continues to be traded in India, never mind the legal prohibitions of the NDPS Act.
96. *See* Emily Earlenbaugh, 'PTSD Sufferers Who Used Cannabis Were 2.5 Times More Likely To Recover In A Recent Study', *Forbes*, December 22, 2020, available at: https://www.forbes.com/sites/emilyearlenbaugh/2020/12/22/ptsd-sufferers-who-used-cannabis-were-25-times-more-likely-to-recover-in-a-recent-study/?sh=1d75261d4321 (last accessed April 1, 2021).
97. Abizaid, A., Merali, Z., & Anisman, H. (2019), 'Cannabis: A potential efficacious intervention for PTSD or simply snake oil?', *Journal of psychiatry & neuroscience: JPN*, *44*(2), 75–78. https://doi.org/10.1503/jpn.190021 (available at: https://www.ncbi.nlm.nih.gov/pmc/articles/PMC6397040/).
98. Mishra, *supra* note 89.

Dr. Deepak Raheja, a senior psychiatrist, and psychotherapist, reportedly told the National Herald that cannabis 'can be used for medical purposes' but highlighted the difference between medical use and dependence.[99] Dr. Raheja said: "Medically, cannabis use is recommended by doctors to treat various symptoms such as nausea /vomiting during chemotherapy, improving the appetite of HIV/AIDS patients, and reducing chronic pain. Marijuana helps in altering mood and its functioning resembles that of a "stress buster"."[100] In addition, experts have noted that cannabis 'consumption in moderation is not deemed to pose significant public health issues'.[101] In this light, why did our Parliament ever criminalize/ prohibit cannabis?

This question is addressed later in this work, but for now, it may be noted that in August, 1985, when our Parliament debated the NDPS Act, an important fact seems not to have been brought to the attention of the MPs who spoke that day: the infamous legacy of Mr. Harry J. Anslinger. Luckily, much of the popular commentary also seems to have missed this crucial connection. Writing for the Huff Post, Johann Hari notes the contribution of Anslinger, who in 1929 was in charge of the Department of Prohibition in Washington, DC, and after alcohol prohibition ended suddenly, 'found himself in charge of a huge government department, with nothing for it to do'.[102] Thus he invented 'reefer madness'[103] (reefer is a synonym for cannabis) and turned his focus on enforcing cannabis prohibition.[104] It was Anslinger's aggressive campaign,

99. Wajid, *supra* note 83.
100. *Id.*
101. Seddon & Floodgate, *supra* note 13 at 62, noting that, "While cannabis consumed in moderation is not deemed to pose significant public health issues, issues arise over excessive or problematic consumption.".
102. Johann Hari, 'Why Is Marijuana Banned? The Real Reasons Are Worse Than You Think', *HuffPost*, February 11, 2016, available at: https://www.huffpost.com/entry/real-reasons-marijuana-is-banned_b_9210248 (last accessed April 1, 2021).
103. Steve Bloom, 'The Legalization Equation: It's for Everyone', March 31, 2021, available at https://www.celebstoner.com/blogs/steve-bloom/2021/03/31/legalization-equation-it-is-for-everyone/ (last accessed April 1, 2021).
104. Reiman, *supra* note 90 at 110 ("The media helped develop this societal fear surrounding cannabis. In 1937 a movie entitled "Reefer Madness" ... was released with the purpose of instilling Anslinger's anti-cannabis message into mainstream society. The movie begins during a PTA meeting where a High School Principal is warning parents of the dangers of cannabis. The movie then tells the tale of a young man who is lured into an apartment where cannabis is being smoked. After he himself is intoxicated, he's framed for the murder of his girlfriend. The movie ends with the real killer (and regular cannabis smoker) being committed to an institution due to insanity brought on by smoking cannabis ... ").

affected also by racist tendencies that resulted in the demonization of cannabis.[105] Racial undertones in the regulation of illicit substances in the US have been known to exist and have been well documented.[106] It is well known that during Ansligner's days, cannabis consumption was largely restricted to members of the African-American and Latin-American communities, and with jazz musicians. American scholars have painstakingly documented the disproportionate effects of cannabis criminalization that have largely affected members of these two communities, and some have gone to the extent of arguing that cannabis prohibition was an indirect way to oppress the members of these communities. It is the considered view of this author that we, the people of India, through our Parliament, should never have become a part of such a sinister operation, and this is the larger issue at stake here.

Unfortunately, the MPs who debated the NDPS Act were unaware of the racist history of cannabis prohibition in the United States, the primary driving force being the 1961 Single Convention on Narcotic Drugs ('Single Convention') that was signed by the Indian representative Shri B. N. Banerji on July 31, 1961. Article 49(2)(f) of the Single Convention provided that, "The use of cannabis for other than medical and scientific purposes must be discontinued as soon as possible but in any case, within twenty-five years from the coming into force of this Convention as provided in paragraph 1 of article 41." According to Tharoor & Tharoor, there is a way out of the Single Convention for India, which is to interpret the phrase 'medical and scientific research' in Article 49(2)(f) in an expansive manner.[107] Even though the approach is not without its critics,[108] legally speaking this seems to be an attractive proposition but requires careful legal research and analysis in order for it to be developed into a workable legal argument. A big challenge in this 'all marijuana is medical

---

105. Grossman, *supra* note 16 at 289-90 ("Harry Anslinger, the first commissioner of the Federal Bureau of Narcotics in the Treasury Department, conducted an aggressive campaign to persuade states to embrace the law and to include cannabis. His explicitly racist crusade-bolstered by the Hearst newspaper chain-demonized marijuana as a promoter of violence, crime, sexual depravity, and insanity, particularly in minority communities. By 1937, 35 states had enacted the Uniform Act with its optional marijuana provisions, and every other state had passed alternative anti-cannabis legislation. This early wave of anti-marijuana laws culminated with the 1937 passage of the federal Marihuana Tax Act. This statute, modeled on the Harrison Act, was another product of Anslinger's anti-drug zealotry. It sought to tax and regulate marijuana out of existence.").

106. Reiman, *supra* note 90 at 108.

107. Tharoor & Tharoor, *supra* note 50.

108. *See e.g.,* Grossman, *supra* note 16 at 283 (speaking in the context of legalization of medical marijuana in California, USA, noting that, "[M]any proponents of legal recreational use were also irritated by Peron's "all marijuana use is medical" declaration.").

marijuana' approach is that medical marijuana is 'administered only in doses sufficient to produce the desired clinical effect and only for as long as is medically necessary.'[109] The distinction between recreational use and medical use of cannabis has been captured perfectly by Prof. Peter J. Cohen of Georgetown University Law Center: "[I]t may be misleading to assume that marijuana's properties as manifested in individuals who have used it frequently, often in large quantities, and over a long period of time, can predict the effects of marijuana in patients who use it only as often as necessary under the advice of a medical professional and who carefully titrate the drug to achieve a desired clinical effect."[110]

However, independent of this approach, this work presents an alternative approach. According to the arguments developed here, our Parliament is not, and cannot be, enabled by the Single Convention to enact the prohibition on cannabis as it has done by enacting the NDPS Act. The Single Convention is not binding on our Parliament and therefore is not the law of our land. Since it is not binding on us, there is no question of expansively interpreting a particular phrase in Article 49(2)(f) thereof in order to decriminalize cannabis in India. These arguments are developed fully in Chapter 4, part (iii).

ix. Conclusion

Decriminalization, full legalization, eventual regulation, and fair taxation of cannabis in India is a very pressing issue that we, the people of India, must address. The core reason why criminal prohibition of cannabis has failed in every single nation remains the same: "very large amounts of money have been spent enforcing prohibitive cannabis laws that have not only failed to reduce or eliminate consumption but have in fact coincided with increasing use."[111] This is also an issue that is right at the cutting edge of law and policy and requires careful attention and study. This issue is being publicly debated and lawmakers at the Union, as well as State level, have started taking this issue seriously. Experts have noted the need to, "think of cannabis trade as a business and the challenge of regulating cannabis as a specific instance of business regulation."[112]

---

109. Peter J. Cohen, 'Medical Marijuana: the conflict between scientific evidence and political ideology', 2009 UTAH L. REV. 35, 53 (2009).
110. *Id.*
111. Seddon & Floodgate, *supra* note 13 at 8.
112. *Id.* at 71.

There are several potential benefits to be drawn from it and very little downside. There is a very large tax base that even if taxed at very moderate levels is capable of generating much-needed revenue for the State. This tax base involves not just cannabis cultivators, but a much larger workforce that will be involved in the cultivation and subsequent manufacturing and processing operations that are involved with trading in almost everything else. It will give legitimate status to the hard work of the cannabis cultivators, and generate legitimate work for a whole host of professionals. A very large number of pending legal cases can be simply removed from the legal pipeline that is already fully choked. The police and law enforcement agencies can then be deployed to fight serious crimes, and not chase charges of small possession. The ridiculousness of our cannabis prohibition is clear from the following statement made by a former Chief of Mumbai's Anti-Narcotics Cell, given two days after a celebrity's arrest on cannabis possession charges: "A sadhu's chillum holds more marijuana than what she is being convicted of."[113]

This author hopes that this modest contribution will fill some of the gaps in cannabis legalization scholarship in India, provide some answers, hopefully, raise more questions, and entice some bright young legal minds to take up further legal research in this area and come up with workable solutions to this very urgent problem.

---

113. Acharjee, *supra* note 76.

2

The Early to Late Early Years (1600 to 1930)

i. No Legal Prohibition: 1600-1857 (Company Rule)

In another context, this author has referred to this period as 'Company Rule' and the period before the year 1600 as 'Pre-British India,'[1] and would use these expressions again here. To examine the legal status of cannabis cultivation and consumption in this time period, we can examine the issue from three angles: (i) personal use; (ii) medicinal use; and (iii) religious or spiritual use. In this period, cannabis was consumed for these three purposes predominantly by three methods: (a) smoking,[2] and (b) eating[3] (by way of sweetmeats; today in many jurisdictions where cannabis consumption is legal brownies, chocolates, and other such sweetmeats are widely available for your enjoyment); and (c) drinking. Understood in terms of section 2(iii) of the NDPS Act, discussed in the earlier chapter, *ganja* and *charas* are usually smoked (and also 'vaped'), and *bhang* usually made into a sweetened drink, *charas* is also quite capable of being consumed by way of eating.

In Pre-British India, and as well as during Company Rule, there was no legal prohibition on the cultivation, trade, and consumption of cannabis for any of the said three purposes, though smoking remained the most popular mode of consumption, followed closely by drinking, and eating. There was no legal

---

1. Abhishek Singhvi & Khagesh Gautam, *The Law of Emergency Powers: Comparative Common Law Perspectives* 175, 182 (Springer, 2020).
2. *See e.g.,* Report of the Indian Hemp Drugs Commission 1893-94 154, 55 ('IHDC REPORT') ("Ganja is used principally for smoking. ... [Charas] is almost wholly used for smoking."). *See also* Lewis A. Grossman, 'Life, Liberty, [and the Pursuit of Happiness]: Medical Marijuana Regulation in Historical Context', 74 FOOD & DRUG. L.J. 280, 287 (2019) (noting that, "Cultures around the world have used marijuana therapeutically for millennia. They have taken it orally, smoked it, and applied it topically.").
3. IHDC REPORT, *supra* note 2 at 158. ("There is, however, a very considerable consumption of sweetmeats made with ganja or bhang, or even sometimes charas. They are all prepared in very much the same way, ...".).

prohibition or regulation on the use of cannabis for (i) recreational, (ii) medicinal, and (iii) religious or spiritual purposes during these two periods. Any regulations on cannabis cultivation, trade, possession, and consumption, would either have been self-imposed or societally imposed by those engaged with its cultivation and trade and the most reliable piece of evidence remains the 1893-94 Report of the [British] Indian Hemp Drugs Commission.

For personal consumption, it would appear that cannabis leaves and derivatives were most probably smoked, *inter alia* by adding them to tobacco. These methods of consuming cannabis for recreational purposes continue to remain the preferred method in India, and worldwide, even today.[4] However, due to the widespread use of cannabis among Hindu ascetics and *sadhus* in India by way of religious practices, customs, or ceremonies, many of whom also consume cannabis and its derivatives by way of smoking it via a *chillum*, it might not be accurate to state that smoking cannabis is restricted only to personal use.[5]

The first British source that gives an account of the use of cannabis in India is Whitelaw Ainslie's account of Indian medicines published in 1826 which records the recreational use of cannabis in India.[6] This work also records the widespread medicinal use of cannabis in India. In this book it is noted that cannabis leaves, "... in India, are frequently added to tobacco to increase its intoxicating power; they are also sometimes prescribed in cases of diarrhoea; and in conjunction with turmeric onions, and warm ginglie oil, are made into an unction for painful, protruded piles."[7] A second source that confirms not just the fact of widespread medicinal use of cannabis in India, but also confirms medicinal properties thereof, is the work of British physician W.B. O'Shaughnessy, who in the 1830s, after conducting experiments with 'hemp derivatives' in Kolkata found that, "Rheumatism, Hydrophobia, Cholera, Tetanus and 'infantile convulsions' were all treated successfully with various hemp concoctions ..."[8] On this basis, O'Shaughnessy concluded that "... in Hemp the profession has gained an anti-convulsive remedy of the greatest value."[9]

4. India Today Web Desk, 'Delhi 3rd largest cannabis consumer in the world, Mumbai 6th: Study', *India Today* (New Delhi), September 13, 2019. Editor, 'The joint campaign: Should we not legalize recreational use of Cannabis?', *The Times of India* (New Delhi), November 10, 2012.
5. R. N. Chopra, 'Use of Hemp Drugs in India', IND. MED. GAZ. 356, 360 – 361 (1940).
6. James H. Mill, 'Madness, Cannabis and Colonialism: The 'Native-Only' Lunatic Asylums of British India, 1857-1900', 45 (2000).
7. *Id.*
8. *Id.* at 45. *See also* Grossman, *supra* note 2 at 288.
9. *Id.*

ii. No Legal Prohibition: 1857 to 1930 (Early British Colonial Government)

Company Rule was abolished and direct rule of the British Government was imposed in 1858 through the Government of India Act, 1858, despite the protestations of the British East India Company.[10] This period is called 'Early British Colonial Government' here, and during this period too there was no legal prohibition on cannabis. However, consumption of cannabis was systematically and falsely connected with the propensity to engage in violent and criminal acts, as well as insanity, by colonial administrators of the British Government in India. These systematic efforts were overwhelmingly the result of incomplete and incorrect data gathering that was ultimately found totally unreliable by the colonial Government's own officers.[11] The raw information and data that ultimately became the basis on which the colonial Government demonized not just cannabis but also those who consumed it[12] (i.e. Indian subjects of the colonial Government) have now been shown to be collected from 'small and unrepresentative' samples, and without any expert supervision.[13] But despite all this, the British colonial Government's mission to ultimately develop a negative and perhaps even dangerous image of Indian hemp users as 'dangerous, lunatic and potentially violent' ultimately proved successful.[14]

An important reason behind the unreliability of the British colonial government's data (as noted in 1874 by another British Government official Dr. Simpson) was the need to fill official forms prescribed by the Government.[15] These forms compelled the police to 'come up with a cause of insanity to complete the forms correctly'.[16] When faced with the prospect of submitting an incompletely filled form versus an incorrectly filled one, colonial Government's police officials preferred to submit patently incorrectly filled ones.[17] This resulted

10. Singhvi & Gautam, *supra* note 1 at 186, Chapter 2.
11. *See e.g.,* James H. Mill, *supra* note 6 at 58 (2000), quoting a British colonial officer Surgeon-Major Cayley from 1873 where he questions the reliability of official data.
12. *See id.* at 178-79.
13. *Id.* at 55, noting that medical officers of the British colonial government in India "based their opinions of all in India who consumed cannabis substances on that small and unrepresentative sample.".
14. *Id,* at 63.
15. *Id.* at 50.
16. *Id.*
17. *Id.* at 51, noting that violent and criminal acts were falsely ascribed to the use of cannabis by "... Indian policemen who had very little evidence that this was indeed the case."

in a situation where the police, when filling a form where the cause of insanity had to be prescribed, overwhelmingly stated artificially created reasons. James Mill notes that in situations like these, "... 'ganjah-smoking' was a convenient and accepted way of filling the form up and one that was likely to be believed".[18] In this manner, "... 'ganjah-smoking' as cause of insanity on the form was likely to be accepted by the medical officers at the asylums despite the dubious ways in which the police arrived at that judgment".[19] He ascribes this to the nineteenth-century struggle in Europe between the medical profession and the clergy to 'assert their authority over the psyche'.[20] In this struggle, blame was cast on cannabis, a substance totally unfamiliar to the British colonial Government's officials at that point.[21] In addition, the influence of the now-discredited science of phrenology (used to validate theories of racial superiority) in the British perspective on cannabis use in India in this period has also been documented.[22] The general misgivings of colonial Government officials in equating cannabis with opium and alcohol casts further doubts on the reliability of the British Government's data.[23]

During the 1860-70s, this biased approach of the British colonial Government in India not only unfairly demonized cannabis and its users,[24] it also became a powerful weapon in the hands of a colonial Government to humiliate colonized people by casting their age-old customs in a negative light in order to project their own superiority as a ruling race. The non-representativeness and therefore total unreliability of the British Government's data has been noted by James Mill in the following words:

> "*The ordinary Indian who while going about his business enjoys a smoke or a drink of some hemp preparation will never come to the attention of the British and be examined or recorded by them. Rather it is the disordered individual available to the*

18. *Id.*
19. *Id.*
20. *Id.* at 51.
21. *See* James H. Mill, *supra* note 6 at 51 (2000), noting that, "Blaming hemp was a simple and plausible was of ascribing the aetiology of mental disease in India which thereby reinforced the medical officer's claim that he knew what he was talking about.".
22. James H. Mill, *supra* note 6 at 53-55 (2000). The British officer Surgeon Hutchinson came up with an 'easy means of identifying' a 'confirmed ganjah-smoker'. The 'ganjah-corn' on the fingers of a person was identified as an 'irrefutable sign', one of the 'fool proof ways to uncovering' a cannabis user.
23. *Id.* at 55.
24. *Id.* at 57, 178-79 (noting that the demonization and criminalization of 'customs or habits' in India, such as cannabis use, was the result of the 'power-relations of the period'.).

medical gaze in the institutional setting of the asylum and produced on the case note as a hemp user that represents the sole access that the British have to Indians thought to use hemp. Thus their violence, weakness or disruption comes to be regarded as typical of people who use hemp."[25]

In 1871, though, British officials started voicing concerns and questioning the Government's methods. Surgeon Wise, in 1872, noted that an attempt made that year to distinguish cases where the use of cannabis 'clearly' caused insanity and those where the use of cannabis was merely 'occasional' was unsuccessful.[26] The negligent (at best), and deliberately false (at worst) form-filling exercise by the Indian policemen, the raw data on the basis of which statistics were compiled for governmental decision-making in this phase[27], was judged to be its cause.[28] James Mill notes, "... the statistics of the asylums were directly responsible for governmental decisions about cannabis use and cannabis users. It did not matter that medical officers responsible for those statistics actually reported that there were problems with understanding exactly what they signified. ... [N]umerical data, however dubious, their accuracy and relevance, were the meta-language of colonial government."[29] The dubiousness of the data, as it appeared from these official forms was that for the colonial police, "... if the man be a ganjah-smoker the drug is invariably put down by them as the cause of insanity".[30] It was noted again in 1873 by Surgeon-Major Caley that, "... 'not much reliance can be placed on alleged causes of insanity ... it is difficult to ascertain if ganja was the actual cause in so many cases'."[31]

Consequent upon a question raised in the British House of Commons by William Caine in March 1893, the colonial Government, in April 1893, established a Parliamentary Commission known as the Indian Hemp Drugs Commission[32] (IHDC).[33] The IHDC was given the responsibility of going to India to, "... inquire into the cultivation of hemp plant in Bengal, the preparation of drugs from it, the trade in these drugs, the effect of their

25. *Id.* at 53.
26. *Id.* at 57.
27. *See e.g.,* James H. Mill, *supra* note 6 at 64, noting that heavy propensity during this time of the colonial government to heavily rely on 'information about the governed' as a 'tool of effective administration'.
28. James H. Mill, *supra* note 6 at 58.
29. *Id.*
30. *Id.*
31. *Id.*
32. *See* IHDC REPORT, *supra* note 2.
33. IHDC REPORT, *supra* note 2 at 1. *See also* James H. Mill, *supra* note 6 at 44.

consumption upon the social and moral conditions of the people, and the desirability of prohibiting the growth and the sale of ganja and allied drugs".[34] But then it was thought that these inquiries should be extended to the whole of India as a result whereof this commission ended up conducting a pan-India survey.[35] One of the most important questions inquired into by the IHDC was, "... whether there is ground for the statement that bhang is less injurious than ganja to consumers."[36]

To make these inquiries, the IHDC examined three types of witnesses: (i) 'official witnesses' (who gave information based on their 'official and local experience'; (ii) 'non-official witnesses' (these were witnesses of 'all ranks' who were 'able to give information regarding the drugs generally or in connection with certain classes of the people'); and (iii) 'other persons or associations' (who gave whatever information by way of facts or opinions that they desired to give to the Commission).[37]

The IHDC made a comprehensive survey and submitted its final report in April 1894.[38] The IHDC in its final report concluded that, "... there was no trustworthy basis for a satisfactory and reasonably accurate opinion on the connection between hemp drugs and insanity in the asylum statistics appended to the annual reports", and rubbished the connection between cannabis consumption and crime when it concluded that, "... as a rule these drugs do not tend to crime and violence."[39] But the prejudiced mindset of the British colonial Government manifested in the IHDC's final report when despite all these findings the report still concluded that, "... admitting (as we must admit) that hemp drugs as intoxicants cause more or less cerebral stimulation, it may be accepted as reasonably proved in the absence of other causes that hemp drugs do cause insanity."[40]

---

34. IHDC REPORT, *supra* note 2 at 1; James H. Mill, *supra* note 6 at 44.
35. *See* IHDC REPORT, *supra* note 2 at 1 ("Lord Kimberley was of the opinion that the inquiry could hardly be confined to Bengal, but should extend to the whole of India, and that the Commission should ascertain to what extent the existence of the hemp plant all over India affects the practical difficulty of checking or stopping the consumption of ganja as distinguished from other narcotic drugs prepared from the hemp plant, ...".).
36. *Id.*
37. *Id.* at 13.
38. James H. Mill, *supra* note 6 at 44.
39. *Id.* at 63.
40. *Id.*

The IHDC Report found that cannabis in India was considered a 'poor man's narcotic,' and its criminalization could 'deprive the very poorest of the population of the use of a narcotic to which they have always been accustomed'.[41] It was found that the cannabis plant is widely cultivated and consumed across the length and breadth of India.[42] Especially in the Himalayas, it was found that the 'climate and mode' of its cultivation resembled those of Europe.[43] With respect to Amritsar, a prominent Indian city in the state of Punjab, the IHDC found:

> *"Amritsar is not only a great market for bhang as well as charas, but it is the head-quarter of the Sikh region, and the former drug is largely consumed by the followers of that faith. It seems to be a regular drink or refreshment with the visitors to the Golden Temple. When members of the Commission visited the city, a dense growth of bhang flourished over a large area in the outlying parts of the public gardens and countless plants in the hedgerows surrounding the city. The seeds discarded from the large quantity of bhang that is daily consumed in the city sufficiently account for this growth, and it is probable that the ways leading to Amritsar from the country round are sown with hemp in the same way. The plant is probably propagated in the same manner, but to a less degree, around Lahore, the capital town of the province, and the head-quarters of the Administration. East of Umballa and Karnal the bhang-bearing belt appears to widen out, and its southern boundary would probably pass across the Karnal district."*[44]

The survey conducted by the IHDC found that in the entire North-Western provinces, cannabis was 'very largely consumed' in all its three forms, *viz.* ganja, charas, and bhang.[45] It was grown throughout the 'Himalayas from Kashmir to the extreme east of Assam,' from the 'southern slope of the mountains' into the 'Punjab and Gangetic plains,' in the 'hill tracts of Assam,' along the 'frontiers of East Bengal, Assam, and Upper Burma from Independent Tippera, through Lushailand, Manipur, and the country of Kanchins, to the frontiers of China,' and several other geographical regions spread across the length and breadth of India.[46] There was no prohibition in Garhwal (a prominent region in the lower

41. IHDC REPORT, *supra* note 2 at 3.
42. In Bengal, it was found in 'nearly every district' and that 'it grows abundantly in several places'. IHDC REPORT, *supra* note 2 at 19. (Throughout the Himalayas, it grows 'spontaneously' and 'in a broad belt along the foot of the mountains. *Id.* at 24. The female plant cultivated in Kumaon region, grown primarily for its fibre, yielded a 'very considerable amount of charas.') *Id.* at 17.
43. IHDC REPORT, *supra* note 2 at 18.
44. *Id.* at 25.
45. *Id.* at 135.
46. *Id.* at 33-34.

Himalayas),[47] and it was widely cultivated and consumed in Bombay,[48] Gujarat,[49] and the Rajputana[50] (today known as Rajasthan).[51] As it moved from northern India to the south, the IHDC found that in the Madras presidency, the preferred form of consumption of cannabis was in drink form,[52] compared to the north where those who consumed it preferred to smoke it.[53] In Hyderabad also, charas was 'almost unknown' and bhang was widely consumed.[54] Even otherwise as well 'the occasional use of bhang in the form of drink' was found 'almost universal with Hindus'.[55]

In 1878, the cultivation of cannabis was found prohibited in the small princely state of Cooch Behar[56] but regulated by law in Bengal whereby a license was required from the Collector in order to cultivate plants from which intoxicating drugs can be produced.[57] This law seems to have been complied with as there was no 'clandestine cultivation' found in the region.[58] This could also be because the total surface area of land used for cultivation was very small, and was further 'greatly curtailed' between 1875 and 1886.[59] In the year 1892-93, there were 86 arrests and 71 convictions, but these were all for 'growing a few plants (very often a single plant) in the courtyards of houses'.[60] This is

47. *Id.* at 43.
48. *Id.* at 98-99. ("The preparation of ganja in Bombay is described by several witnesses.") In Bombay, it seems cannabis was being consumed in form of 'ganja,' 'charas,' and 'bhang'. Whereas 'ganja' and 'charas' are smoked, 'bhang' is the drink made from cannabis seeds, etc.
49. *Id.* at 99. ("The bhang crop in Gujarat is turned into drug by drying the plants and shaking or beating them so as to detach the leaves, flower, and fruit.").
50. *Id.* at 123. ("The Rajputana States appear to grow most of the bhang they require, and to import ganja and charas.").
51. The Editors of Encyclopaedia, 'Rajputana', ENCYCLOPEDIA BRITANNICA, 5 Mar. 2009, https://www.britannica.com/place/Rajputana, (last accessed 6 April 2021).
52. IHDC REPORT, *supra* note 2 at 93. ("In the Madras Presidency, especially towards the south, the name bhang is applied almost exclusively to the prepared drink, which may be made from the pure leaves, but is generally made from the material which is known and sold as ganja.").
53. *See e.g.,* IHDC REPORT, *supra* note 2 at 93-94. ("After the charas has been extracted from the female flower, the powdered or broken flowers are mixed with hemp seed and smoked in a *chillum.*").
54. IHDC REPORT, *supra* note 2 at 122-23.
55. *Id.* at 132.
56. *Id.* at 37.
57. *Id.* at 35.
58. *Id.*
59. *Id.*
60. *Id.* at 36.

probably why 'ganja smokers' started growing them 'in places hidden from the public view'.[61]

iii. Religious, Spiritual, and Cultural Use

"Siddhis are born of practices performed in previous births, or by herbs, mantra repetition, asceticism or by Samadhi."[*]

—Maharishi Patanjali, Yoga Sutras, *Kaivalya Pada,* Verse 1

In 2004, a story reported in *The Tribune* quoted the Vice-President of Malana village Panchayat in Himachal Pradesh as saying: "Cannabis has been grown here since time immemorial," and further reported that "*villagers consider cannabis*

61. *Id.* at 37, 38.

* *See* Sri Swami Satchidananda, The Yoga Sutras of Patanjali 197 (Internal Yoga Publications, Virginia 1979, ninth reprint 2020). The Yoga Sutras of Maharishi Patanjali were 'like a Bible' to Swami Satchidananda (*id.* at vii). He considered them to be, "... a living scripture to illuminate our spiritual path." (*id.*) The Yoga Sutras are divided into four books (or *padas*): (i) Samadhi Pada (book on Contemplation); (ii) Sadhana Pada (book on Practice); (iii) Vibhuti Pada (book on Accomplishments); and (iv) Kaivalya Pada (book on Absoluteness). Translating the first verse of the fourth book, and focusing on the word 'herbs' (Sanskrit: *aushadhi*), Swami Satchidananda notes: "Patanjali begins this book by reviewing the methods by which the *siddhis* can be obtained by the Yoga practitioner. Some people attain the *siddhis* without even doing any practice in this life. ... He also gives us cues about the people who get some experiences through their LSD and marijuana. The so-called "grass" is an herb, is it not? Mushrooms could also be considered herbs also." (*id.* at 197). The use of herbs, and chemicals to induce spiritual and mystical experiences is nothing new. For a powerful modern day account *see* Sam Harris, Waking Up: Searching for Spirituality Without Religion (Penguin, Great Britain 2014). Harris talks about use of the drug MDMA (3,4-methylenedioxy-N-methylamphetamine) commonly known as *ecstacy*, and how his experiments lead to a state of deep spiritual awakening. Harris's work seems to indicate a similarity between the altered states of mind, or consciousness, caused by use of herbs such as cannabis, or some synthetic drugs, and the altered states of mind, or consciousness experienced through meditative practices, and long periods of contemplative silence. Deep spiritual realizations are possible in either case. This would tend to support Maharishi Patanjali's observations in the fourth book of Yoga Sutras, i.e. a deeply meditate state, through which *siddhis* (i.e. spiritual perfections) are caused by attaining states of deep concentration that may be caused variously by: (i) consumptions of herbs (including but not limited to cannabis); (ii) meditative practices (including but not limited to *mantra* repetition); (iii) asceticism and silent contemplation (on this *see e.g.* Radhanath Swami, The Journey Home: Autobiography of an American Swami *infra* note 65); and (iv) through attaining state of *Samadhi*. The author can confidently report that the first three methods of have been known to, and indeed are, very effective in attaining spiritual realizations, though the same can't be reported about the fourth one.

cultivation to have been approved by their village deities."[62] In fact, "a number of villagers claimed that 'unless Jamlu God tells us to grow other crops, we will grow only cannabis."[63] Jamlu God, or Jamlu Rishi is considered by some to be one of the seven mythical sages of Hindu mythology (the *sapta rishis*): Rishi Jamdagni. This is not the first time these facts have been reported or documented. The use of cannabis, referred also to as 'Shankar Mahaprasad,' for instance by the highly revered sect of Naga sadhus (who worship the divine in the form of Lord Shiva), continues to be a part of Indian spiritual tradition even today.[64]

'Charas', a substance obtained from the resin in the cannabis plant,[65] and considered an 'expensive luxury' in Bengal,[66] was cultivated, it seems, primarily in the Himalayan region (where there was no prohibition), but much of it was not sold rather it was given away to from 'fakirs' visiting Badrinath and Kedarnath.[67] This would seem to indicate that act of extraction of 'charas' from cannabis resin itself was not necessarily indicative of any intent to possess, or sell, or even consume. A villager might genuinely believe that extraction of 'charas' from the cannabis plant for it to be offered to 'fakirs' and *sadhus* etc. (essentially religious or spiritual men, and sometimes women, who have renounced the

62. Daniela Berti, 'Binding Fictions. Contradicting Facts and Judicial Constraints in a Narcotics Case in Himachal Pradesh', 94, 97 in Daniela Berti & Devika Bordia, *Regimes of Legality: Ethnography of Criminal Cases in South Asia* (Oxford University Press, 2015).

63. *Id.*

64. *See e.g.,* Radhanath Swami, The Journey Home: Autobiography of an American Swami 138-140 (Jaico, 2013, tenth impression 2019). Shri Radhanath Swami, formerly Richard Slavin, narrates an incident from his spiritual travels where he came across a 'fearsome tribe' of Naga sadhus in the Himalayas. Swamiji describes the Naga ceremony as follows (*id.* at 139): In the center of the sacrificial fire, they planted an upright trident representing Shiva. Then, chanting mantras, they offered oblations of clarified butter and at a certain point in the ceremony, presented a clay pipe called a *chillum* before their altar. Still chanting mantras, they ceremoniously filled the chillum with a type of marijuana called ganja and gave the first honors to a senior Naga. He reverentially held the chillum to his forehead and changed incantations before putting it. Then they passed the pipe around the fire, each Naga chanting mantras before smoking." The Nagas offered the chillum to Swamiji but when he respectfully told them of his vow of never taking intoxicants, they honored his vow and continued with their ceremony.

65. The procedure to make 'charas' from cannabis is described by the IHDC Report in detail. *See* IHDC REPORT, *supra* note 2 at 93. (The procedure described is: "The *sujango* or female plants, having been cut in November, are spread out to dry for twenty-four hours. The people then sit around in the heat of the day, and pluck off the flower heads, which are now full of seed, discarding the coarser leaves. Each handful is rubbed between the palms for about ten minutes and thrown aside. In the course of time a quantity of juice accumulates on the palms which is scraped off and rolled into balls. These are charas.").

66. IHDC REPORT, *supra* note 2 at 133.

67. IHDC REPORT, *supra* note 2 at 41.

world and just wander about without any possessions, etc.) itself is a part of their religious practices much of which are customary in such regions. Furthermore, this gives rise to an interesting jurisprudential question. We know that: (i) Maharishi Patanjali in the Yoga Sutras lays down four methods through which spiritual realizations may be obtained. These methods include deep meditation, asceticism, and silent contemplation, and may be supplemented or aided by use of certain herbs; and (ii) the state of mind, or consciousness caused upon the consumption of cannabis (presumably THC that has now been identified as the psychoactive compound) is conducive to spiritual practice. In light of this knowledge, have we not criminalized a method to obtain spiritual insights that itself is sanctioned by the Yoga Sutras? This ought to force our collective consciousness to seriously reconsider the question of decriminalization of cannabis by removing it from the scope of the NDPS Act.

Assume the following scenario: a citizen is arrested for being in possession of a small quantity of cannabis, presumably, for personal consumption? The citizen claims that this small quantity is for consumption for spiritual practices. In light of the Yoga Sutras, and the above discussion, how do we decide such a case?

Clearly the Yoga Sutras cannot be said to be a source of law within the scope of Article 13 of our Constitution (that lays down all sources of law). But the existence of this document cannot be ignored while deciding this case. The famed 'doctrine of essential practices', developed by the Supreme Court, cannot really help us resolve this question either. We would have to be supremely unfair to our highest judicial body, in particular, and our entire judiciary, in general, to put on this institution's already overburdened shoulders with the additional and rather onerous responsibility of being an authority on spiritual matters. Here again, as responsible citizens, we must be responsible for our choices. Whether a person chooses to consumer cannabis for spiritual purposes is a personal decision, and is seemingly supported by scriptural authority, and generally reliable experiences of our fellow human beings. In such circumstances, to reduce such a person down to the legal status of a criminal seems to be a very cruel thing to do, and in the language of Maharishi Patanjali, is bound to bring bad karma! To protect against this bad karma, we may begin first with decriminalizing possession of small quantities, and eventually removing cannabis altogether from of the NDPS Act.

Speaking of *sadhus* and *charas*, the IHDC Report noted that nearly the whole of 'charas supply of India comes through the Punjab'.[68] At this point of time in

68. *Id.* at 113.

history, a large part of the Himalayan region came under Punjab as it was made a part of his large empire by the Sikh Emperor Raja Ranjit Singh.[69] These two places are considered holy by the Hindus, and the giving away of 'charas' to Hindu *sadhus* clearly supports the religious background and purposes for which cannabis was used in this period. The then King of Oudh himself promoted the cultivation of ganja, and a particular strain called the '*Mahadev* ganja' was cultivated in large numbers in this area.[70] Surprisingly, the holy places of Badrinath and Kedarnath, are dedicated respectively to Lord Vishnu, and Lord Shiva (who is also called *Mahadev*), and the Commission noted that the use of cannabis plant in Shiva worship seems to be an essential practice[71] thereof.[72] The Commission also found that 'charas', grown from the 'wild hemp is of superior quality,' grown near a Shiva temple, and is often 'given to fakirs and pilgrims.'[73] The religious mendicants of Puri (also a holy city of Hindus famous for its Konark Sun Temple in current day Orissa) were found to be 'the most determined consumers of ganja'.[74] In Bengal, there was a custom where guests and family members were offered 'an infusion of the leaves of the hemp plant' on Durga Puja, an important Hindu festival.[75] The use of cannabis in 'Tantric religious works' was a custom that originated from 'immemorial usage' and

69. J. S. Grewal, *The Sikhs of the Punjab*, 101 (Cambridge University Press, 1991).
70. IHDC REPORT, *supra* note 2 at 42.
71. On the doctrine of essential practices developed by the Supreme Court of India, see Khagesh Gautam, Protecting Free Exercise of Religion under the Indian and the United States Constitutions: The Doctrine of Essential Practices and the Centrality Test, 8 VIENNA J. INT'L CONST'L. L. 305 (2014). See also IHDC REPORT, supra note 2 at 161. ("The special form of worship by the followers of Siva, called the Trinath or Tinnath Mela, in which the use of ganja is considered to be essential, is mentioned by many witnesses, and deserves more than a passing notice.").
72. IHDC REPORT, *supra* note 2 at 160-61. ("It is chiefly in connection with the worship of Siva, the Mahadeo or great god of the Hindu trinity, that the hemp plant, and more especially perhaps ganja, is associated. The hemp plant is popularly believed to have been a great favourite of Shiva, and there is great deal of evidence before the Commission to show that the drug in some form or other is now extensively used in the exercise of the religious practices connected with this form of worship. ... The religious ascetics, who are regarded with great veneration by the people at large, believe that the hemp plant is a special attribute of the god Siva, and this belief is largely shared by the people. ... At the Shivaratri festival, and on almost all occasions on which this worship is practiced, there is abundant evidence before the Commission which shows not only that ganja is offered to the god and consumed by these classes of the worshippers, but that these customs are so intimately connected with their worship that may be considered to form in some sense and integral part of it.").
73. *Id.* at 93.
74. *Id.* at 128.
75. *Id.* at 159.

'regarded by many people as part of their religious observances'.[76] The legend of the tenth *guru* of Sikhs, and the founder of the Sikh faith, Guru Gobind Singh was also noted whereby in the battle between the Guru and his armies with forces of the 'Hill Rajas of the Simla, Kangra, and the Hoshiarpur districts' for the 'attack and capture of Lohgarh fort,'[77] the following transpired:

> *"[T]he Rajas sent an elephant, who was trained in attacking and slaying the forces of the enemy with a sword in his trunk and in breaking open the gates of forts, to attack and capture the Lohgarh fort near Anandpur. The guru gave one of his followers, Bachittar Singh, some bhang and a little opium to eat, and directed him to face the elephant. This brave man obeyed the word of command of his leader and attacked the elephant, who was intoxicated and had achieved victories in several battles before, with the result that the animal was overpowered and the Hill Rajas defeated."*[78]

All this provides considerable support to the proposition that cannabis was widely cultivated and used in various forms, such as 'ganja' and 'charas', for religious-spiritual purposes in India in this period, and was in fact used for said purposes since time immemorial. The Commission was certainly convinced by all this evidence and accordingly recommended that these social and religious practices be not interfered with, as such interference would be taken by consumers as an 'encroachment upon their religious liberty'.[79] It should be noted that the use of cannabis for spiritual, or sacramental purposes is not unique to India. The Rastafarians of Jamaica have been fighting for their spiritual rights[80] and finally in 2015 possession of up to 2 ounces was decriminalized and home cultivation for medicinal or sacramental use was legalized.[81]

76. *Id.*
77. *Id.* at 162.
78. *Id.*
79. *Id.* at 166.
80. For a detailed survey of the people of Rastafari faith and their fight to practice their faith (which involves use of cannabis for spiritual and sacramental purposes) *see* Melissa Bone, 'From the Sacrilegious to the Sacramental: A Global Review of Rastafari Cannabis Case Law' in Beatriz Caiuby Labate & Clancy Cavnar (Ed.), *Prohibition, Religious Freedom, and Human Rights: Regulating Traditional Drug Use*, 89-109 (Springer, 2014).
81. *See* Toby Seddon & William Floodgate, *Regulating Cannabis: A Global Review and Future Directions* 37 (Palgrave Macmillan, 2020).

iv. Medicinal Use

Currently, cannabis is criminally prohibited in India by the NDPS Act, 1985. Taking the U.S. Controlled Substances Act, 1971[82] ('CSA,' enacted on May 1, 1971) as a comparative reference point, it will be seen that cannabis is listed in Schedule I of the CSA, meaning that it has 'no currently accepted medical use in treatment' in the U.S.[83] But cannabis has been 'recognized as a therapeutic agent across many cultures for over 5,000 years.'[84] It was used in ancient 'Indian Ayurvedic medicine,' and neighbouring China's 'medical use of marijuana' is recorded from 'about 2700 BC'.[85] In fact, a leading American expert has noted that from the "millions of persons who started smoking marijuana as college students in the late 1960s, some of whom have been taking the drug more or less regularly ever since, have suffered neither obvious immediate damage nor dramatic aftereffects ... [I]f occasional marijuana smoking over [decades] carried substantial health risks, the evidence should have started to come in by now."[86] On this authority, legal scholarship in the U.S. has highlighted that the so-called 'harmful and addictive' properties of cannabis 'have been greatly exaggerated.'[87] In fact, the United Nations 2006 World Drug Report also highlights that 'much of the early material on cannabis is now considered inaccurate'.[88] This U.N. report also notes that "a series of studies in a range of countries have exonerated cannabis of many of the charges levelled against it."[89] And most importantly it

82. Controlled Substances Act, 1971 (U.S. Congress), 21 U.S.C. ch. 13.

83. Cynthia S. Duncan, 'The Need for Change: An Economic Analysis of Marijuana Policy', 41 CONN. L. REV. 1701, 1704 (2009).

84. Elena M. Quattrone, 'The Catch 22 of Marijuana [Il]Legalization', 22 B.U. J. SCI. & TECH. L. 299, 301 (2016).

85. Grossman, *supra* note 2 at 287 (noting that, "In Central Asia, cannabis's native region, people apparently used the plant for medicinal purposes (and other reasons) for many thousands of years before the dawn of recorded history. The first written mention of the medical use of marijuana appears in Chinese sources from about 2700 BCE. As cannabis cultivation propagated around the Old World, culture after culture absorbed the plant into their armamentariums. Marijuana was used in ancient Indian Ayurvedic medicine, in African shamanistic healing, and as a peasant folk remedy in Europe.").

86. Mark A.R. Kleiman, *Against Excess: Drug Policy for Results*, 256 (Basic Books, 1992).

87. Duncan, *supra* note 83 at 1706 (n. 18).

88. Office on Drugs & Crime, *2006 World Drug Report: Analysis*, United Nations, 156 (2006), available at: http://www.unodc.org/pdf/WDR_2006/wdr2006_volumel.pdf ('U.N. World Drug Report').

89. *Id. See also* Drug Policy Research Center, RAND, 'Research Brief: Using Marijuana May Not Raise the Risk of Using Harder Drugs' (2002) stating that, "[T]he harms of marijuana can no longer be viewed as necessarily including an expansion of hard-drug use and its associated harms.").

should be remembered that, unlike recreational use, "when used as medical therapy, marijuana is administered only in doses sufficient to produce the desired clinical effect and only for as long as is medically necessary."[90]

The use of cannabis for medical purposes in India was also noted by the Commission. It is interesting to note that the IHDC Report was given in 1893-94. Around that time, another authoritative source, the *Dispensatory of the United States*, an 'unofficial companion to the *U.S. Pharmacopoeia*, and published in 1885, noted that, "extract of hemp was known "to cause sleep, to ally spasm, to compose nervous disquietude, and to relieve pain," and was also prescribed for "neuralgia, gout, rheumatism, tetanus, hydrophobia, epidemic cholera, convulsions, chorea, hysteria, mental depression, delirium tremens, insanity, and uterine hemorrhage."[91] It may therefore be said that the medicinal use of cannabis was then known in the United States, and was known in India and China much earlier.

Very few witnesses denied medicinal benefits being obtained from moderate use of the drug and a 'vast majority' gave evidence to the contrary.[92] One official witness gave evidence that, "... having searched through all the Sanskrit and Hindi books accessible, he found the first mention of *bhanga* as a medicine in the works of Sucruta, written before the eighth century A.D."[93] The Commission found that the use of cannabis for medicinal purposes goes back to 'fifth and twelfth century'.[94] Among its medicinal uses, recorded as early as 1300 A.D., the following are mentioned: "[I]t destroys phlegm, expels flatulence, induces costiveness, sharpens the memory, and excites appetite.".[95] Going back to 1500 A.D., the following medicinal uses are recorded: "Ganja, which is soporific and corrects derangements of the humours, which produces a healthy appetite, sharpens the wits, and acts as an aphrodisiac."[96] And going back to 1600 A.D., the following medicinal uses are mentioned: "antiphlegmatic, pungent, astringent, digestive, easy of digestion, and bile-affecting, and increases infatuation, intoxication, the power of the voice, and the digestive faculty. ... [c]reates energy, mental powers, and

---

90. Peter J. Cohen, 'Medical Marijuana: The Conflict between Scientific Evidence and Political Ideology', 2009 UTAH L. REV. 35, 53 (2009).
91. 2006 World Drug Report: Analysis, *supra* note 87 at 288.
92. IHDC REPORT, *supra* note 2 at 180-81.
93. *Id.* at 174. The witness was one Mr. George A. Grierson, an Indian Civil Service officer.
94. *Id.*
95. *Id.*
96. *Id.*

internal heat, corrects irregularities of the phlegmatic humour, and is an elixir vitae."[97]

Apart from this historical evidence, witnesses before the Commission gave contemporary evidence of medicinal use, to which even 'European practitioners' had warmed up,[98] a fact that is independently corroborated.[99] Cannabis was found useful in treatment of 'cholera during epidemics,' was occasionally used as a prophylactic, and was recommended in 'malarial area to counteract the effects of "bad air and water"'.[100] It was found useful in diseases of the 'urinary organs' and used to treat "diabetes, impotency, stricture, spermatorrhoea, hydrocele, incontinence of urine, and swellings of the testicles".[101] Its use to treat impotency was found supposedly to be based on its aphrodisiac effects,[102] though the direct aphrodisiac effects of cannabis were contested, and the Commission observed that these effects might be more indirect than direct.[103] Evidence suggested that cannabis was regularly used to 'prevent insomnia' and 'relieve anxiety,' and to that extent, its use in India, from a socio-cultural perspective, was nothing more than a 'glass of wine when [one] is of heavy heart'.[104] Based on this, and other evidence, the IHDC concluded that "*Cannabis indica* must be looked upon as one of the most important drugs of Indian Materia Medica."[105]

Cannabis has medicinal and pain-relieving qualities and people who have used it for this purpose have reportedly felt that cannabis as a pain reliever works better

97. *Id.* at 174-75.
98. *Id.* at 176. ("Witnesses refer to the use of the drugs in the treatment of "brain fever," cramps, convulsions of children, headache, hysteria, neuralgia, sciatica, and tetanus. In certain of these diseases, *e.g.*, convulsions of children, neuralgia, and tetanus, the use of hemp preparations has also been advocated by European practitioners.").
99. *See also* Quattrone, *supra* note 84 at 301 ("In Western culture, marijuana was prescribed in 1830s Ireland to treat muscle spasms and pain. Even in the U.S. in 1860, physicians "reported success in using marijuana to treat chronic cough, gonorrhea, pain," and other ailments. By the turn of the 20th century pharmaceutical companies such as Parke-Davis (now known as Pfizer), and Eli Lilly researched the development of painkillers and sedatives featuring marijuana extracts to treat epilepsy and migraines.").
100. IHDC REPORT, *supra* note 2 at 176.
101. *Id.*
102. *Id.* at 179.
103. *See* IHDC REPORT, *supra* note 2 at 179, relying on works of medical text-book writers and their opinions. The Commission noted that, "Meanwhile it is enough to say that the alleged aphrodisiac action seems to be merely the indirect effect of the drug as a stimulant. The effect explains the use of these drugs in the houses of prostitutes, regarding which there is a good deal of evidence, just as alcohol in one form or another is used in similar houses in Europe.").
104. IHDC REPORT, *supra* note 2 at 182.
105. *Id.* at 175.

compared to opium-based pain relievers. For instance, according to this report in Australian Quarterly, the use of opium-based pain killers was reduced once they were substituted with medical cannabis.[106] The use of cannabis is a much safer alternative, compared to opium-based pain relievers (also called 'opioids') since the number of people worldwide who have ever died of a cannabis overdose is zero.[107] A leading U.S. authority on the subject of addiction notes that in 'healthy young users' cannabis's 'cardiovascular effects are unlikely to be of clinical significance,' and that, "[d]ocumented evidence of death resulting from recreational use, even in large doses, is lacking."[108] The possibility of death by cannabis overdose is also not mentioned in what is considered to be a standard textbook on pharmacology, calling attention only to the 'most consistent effect' of cannabis on the cardiovascular system (i.e. an increase in heart rate, and systolic blood pressure) with no 'consistent changes in respiratory rate.'[109] Cannabis could, however, be dangerous if consumed with other potent drugs (like heroin, or cocaine) or when consumed during activities that require full human attention and alertness, e.g. operating heavy machinery, sharp instruments, and driving, etc.[110] On the other hand, cannabis may make the operation of certain types of non-dangerous heavy machinery (such as a washing machine!) a pleasant experience! Pun aside, the fact remains that no one has ever died of a cannabis overdose, and it seems that it is highly unlikely that someone could overdose on it. If it is mixed with tobacco for smoking, the traditional risks associated with tobacco continue to be present. If it is mixed with other more potent drugs, it might cause physical injury, or worse even death. But on its own, cannabis is not a dangerous or a poisonous plant, and its occasional consumption for whatever purpose causes no discernable harm to the human body, or the society at large. It has clearly proved medicinal uses, and apart from that people have been using it to celebrate innocent personal events like a new job, a birthday, graduation, etc., and it has provided physical and psychological comfort to many suffering from not just cancer, but also clinical depression, post-traumatic stress, anxiety, etc. In another time, and in another age, this plant would perhaps have been worshipped like a deity. In another age, in our

106. Suvi Mahonen, 'A nation in pain: Can medicinal cannabis help?', 89 AUSTRALIAN QUARTERLY: AUSTRALIAN INSTITUTE OF POLICY AND SCIENCE, 3-7 (2018).

107. *Id.* at 5. *See also* Cohen, *supra* note 89.

108. Sandra P. Welch & Billy R. Martin, 'The Pharmacology of Marijuana', *Principles of Addiction Medicine* 249, 261-63 (Allan W. Graham et al., eds., 3d. ed. 2003).

109. See, e.g., Jerome H. Jaffe, 'Drug Addiction and Drug Abuse', in Goodman and Gilman's: *The Pharmacological Basis of Therapeutics* 535, 561-62 (Alfred Goodman Gilman et al., eds., 6th ed. 1980).

110. Cohen, *supra* note 90 at 55.

country, it indeed was. Perhaps those days will return in our promising republic when we would redeem the spiritual legacy of our forefathers.

Despite all this, the medical establishment, at least in India, has not yet been able to effectively engage with the potential beneficial effects of 'medical marijuana.'[111] This, in large measure, could be explained by the lack of research on the potentially beneficial effects of marijuana.[112] An interesting case is the 1976 trial of Robert Randall.[113] He (suffering from a severe case of 'glaucoma'[114]) initially obtained medical marijuana illegally, but later decided to grow it himself, and when arrested and charged with its possession was successfully able to use the 'necessity defence' in criminal law whereby 'a crime may be excused if the defendant committed the criminal act in an emergency situation to prevent a greater harm from occurring'.[115] The 'necessity defence' almost never works in practice, but after Randall's ophthalmologist testified in his defence, and other medical evidence was presented, the judge ruled that Randall had no other acceptable alternative except to smoke cannabis since 'treatment with other drugs has become ineffective, and surgery offers only a slim possibility of favourable results with significant risk of immediate blindness.'[116] Randall, after that, famously became 'America's only legal pot smoker'.[117] The pun aside, this case, and the Australian case, both show that cannabis has legitimate medical applications for diverse purposes; that itself is a very strong ground to decriminalize cannabis for medicinal use. In the least, it calls for further careful scrutiny and informed public debate. It must be noted that in the United States, where calls to legalize cannabis federally are getting stronger, and several States have fully legalized it, the law currently does not recognize that cannabis has any

111. The word 'marijuana' is used here in the same manner as defined *supra* Chapter 1, section (i). The word 'medical' here means the use of marijuana for curative as well as palliative purposes. *See* Amanda Reiman, 'The Fallacy of a One Size Fits All Cannabis Policy', 35 HUMBOLDT J. OF SOC. RELATIONS, 104 (2013).

112. David C. Peters II, 'Patients and Caregivers Report Using Medical Marijuana to Decrease Prescription Narcotics Use', 35 HUMBOLDT J. SOC. RELATIONS, 24-40, 25 (2013).

113. He was tried before the Superior Court, Washington D.C., by Judge James Washington, who was formerly the dean of Howard University Law School. *See* Grossman, *supra* note 2 at 292.

114. Glaucoma is a disease that destroys vision by increasing pressure within the eyeball. *See* Grossman, *supra* note 2 at 292.

115. Grossman, *supra* note 2 at 292.

116. *United States* v. *Randall,* 104 Dly. Wash. Law Report. 2249, 2252 (1976).

117. Grossman, *supra* note 2 at 293.

medicinal purpose,[118] the need to reschedule cannabis from schedule 1 of the Controlled Substances Act, 1970 has been strongly highlighted.[119]

Another problem with much of the cannabis research in the west is that most of it have been conducted to prove the 'gateway hypothesis,' according to which cannabis was hypothesized as a gateway drug that leads to consumption of more dangerous drugs.[120] It is interesting to note that S. Jaipal Reddy, M.P. (Mahbubnagar) actually opened his speech supporting the NDPS Bill in the debate in Parliament on August 28, 1985, by relying on the now-debunked[121] gateway hypothesis.[122] The gateway hypothesis has now been thoroughly debunked. Prof. Kleiman, a leading U.S. authority on the subject, in 1992 found that "The gateway hypothesis is not the only plausible relationship between marijuana use and the use of other drugs."[123] Other experts have found that cannabis, "does not appear to be a gateway drug to the extent that it is the *cause* or even that it is the *most significant predictor* of serious drug abuse," and therefore, "care must be [taken] not to attribute cause to association."[124] Rather the 'reverse gateway hypothesis,' according to which cannabis decreases the use of other drugs seems to be gaining traction in the scientific community, and there seems to be enough reliable evidence to warrant further investigation.[125] There is reliable evidence to show that medical marijuana clearly reduces the consumption of opiates. Researchers have found that those who were using opiates for pain management were quite open to substituting cannabis for opiates for managing their pain.[126] However, those who were already using cannabis expressed no desire

118. 21 U.S.C. § 812(b)(1). Cannabis (known here as 'marijuana,' is classified as a schedule I drug that include drugs that have 'no currently accepted medical use in treatment in the United States'.).

119. *See also* Quattrone, *supra* note 84 at 300-301 (2016).

120. David C. Peters II, *supra* note 112 at 24-25 (2013).

121. *Id.* at 25; Quattrone, *supra* note 84 at 308 (noting that the gateway hypothesis applies to marijuana only in the 'broadest sense' to the extent that 'many of the factors associated with a willingness to use marijuana are the same as those associated with a willingness to use other illicit drugs.).

122. Lok Sabha Debates (August 28, 1985), Third Session (Eighth Lok Sabha), Vol. IX, No. 25 (Lok Sabha Secretariat), column 50 ("Studies conducted by Indian Council of Medical Research in several Universities of the country have confirmed that the drug addiction amongst students has assumed alarming proportion. They start off with hashish, charas and then go on to heavier stuff like LSD, cocaine and barbiturate etc"). For a detailed discussion, *see infra* Chapter V.

123. Kleiman, *supra* note 86 at 259-61 (1992).

124. Division of Neuroscience & Behavioral Health, Inst. of Medicine, Marijuana and Medicine: Assessing the Science Base 99-101 (Janel E. Joy et al. eds., 1999).

125. David C. Peters II, *supra* note 112 at 25; Mahonen, *supra* note 105.

126. David C. Peters II, *supra* note 112 at 30.

to substitute cannabis for opiates.[127] Thus, those who were using opiates preferred to use cannabis, but those who used cannabis do not, in fact almost never go back to opiates, even though they legally can. This further debunks the gateway hypothesis and rather supports the reverse gateway hypothesis.

v. Personal and Recreational Use

"The [U.S.] Office of the National Drug Control Policy ... estimates that [100 million] Americans (over [40%] of the population) have tried marijuana in their lifetime and that nearly [15 million] (almost [6%] of the population) used marijuana in the past month."[*]

People with tendencies to impose their moral judgments on others tend to make a mountain out of a molehill over the issue of personal and recreational use. For the ones who continue to support the ill-conceived, and now proven to be a totally failed, idea of criminalisation and prohibition of cannabis, it would appear that the word 'recreational' itself is an anathema, as if 'recreation' was something so sinister that no human being should ever engage in it. Tendencies like these are to be easily found in the U.S., as well as in India, where some people would gladly pay for a pack of their favourite cigarettes and a glass of their favourite liquor while enjoying a game of Russian roulette in a Goa casino, pointing out the many imaginative harms of cannabis consumption.[128] Meanwhile, cigarette and alcohol sales keep on rising, and many people continue to peacefully consume cannabis without causing any harm to either themselves or others, tobacco and alcohol remain legal but cannabis remains criminally prohibited. A 2008 report from the U.S. Center for Disease Control and Prevention shows that at least 60.8% of adults in the U.S. were currently using

127. *Id.*

* Cynthia S. Duncan, *The Need for Change: An Economic Analysis of Marijuana Policy*, 41 CONN. L. REV. 1701, 1705 (2009).

128. *See e.g.* Nat'l Inst. on Drug Abuse, U.S. Dep't of Health & Human Services, Research Report Series: Marijuana Abuse (2005) (pointing out the potential health risks associated with cannabis use, such as increased risk of lung disease and even some types of cancers); Letter written by Keith B. Nelson, Principal Deputy Assistant Attorney General, U.S. Dep't of Justice to Rep. John Conyers, Chairman, House Commission on the Judiciary (July 25, 2008) available at http://judiciary.house.gov/hearings/pdf/Nelson080725.pdf (making the astonishing claim that data from adequate and well-controlled clinical trials do not support any of the claimed therapeutic uses for smoked cannabis.).

alcohol and 20.8% were using cigarettes.[129] A 2019 survey conducted by the Government of India, Ministry of Social Justice and Empowerment, in collaboration with the National Drug Dependence Treatment Centre, AIIMS, New Delhi, found that out of the 2.8% of Indians aged 10-75 years (3.1 crore individuals) who were current users of any cannabis product(s), [o]verall, just about 0.25% Indians use cannabis in a dependent pattern."[130] Studies conducted in the U.S. have now shown that "[l]ong-term and even daily marijuana use doesn't appear to cause permanent brain damage."[131] These studies also found that cannabis typically caused much less impairment as compared to alcohol or any other drugs, and even when it does cause impairment it was only a 'very small' impairment.[132] Quite consistent with the results of the 2019 survey quoted above, studies in the U.S. have found that only a few cannabis users develop a dependence on the plant.[133] Even in the few cases where users develop dependence, cannabis dependence 'appears to be less severe' than alcohol and other drugs.[134] It is perhaps for this reason that Prof. Mark Kleiman, a highly respected U.S. authority on the subject, in an interview with CBS in 1998 said: "Marijuana is the most widely-used illicit drug, and the illicit drug most likely to be used by respectable folks. ... It is the mostly widely used illicit drug, precisely because its negative impact on most users tends to be much smaller than the impact of cocaine or methamphetamine."[135]

On its personal and recreational use, the following passage from the IHDC Report should be enough to put the matter to rest:

> *"Among the beneficial effects attributed to the drugs is their effect as a food accessory or digestive. This effect is more generally attributed to bhang ... [b]ut there are a large*

---

129. Center for Disease Control & Prevention, U.S. Dep't of Health & Human Services, Health, United States, 2008, at 305 (2009).
130. Government of India, Ministry of Social Justice and Empowerment, Magnitude of Substance Use in India 2019, p. 17 (2019).
131. *See e.g.,* Sid Kirchheimer, Heavy Marijuana Use Doesn't Damage Brain: Analysis of Studies Finds Little Effect from Long-Term Use, WebMD, July 1, 2003, http://www.webmd.com/mental-health/news/ 20030701/heavy-marijuana-use-doesnt-damage-brain. (15 different studies, conducted over 3 months to 13 years, are cited here. These studies involved 700 regular cannabis users, and 484 non-users. These studies showed that "long-term and even daily marijuana use doesn't appear to cause permanent brain damage.").
132. *Id.*
133. Division of Neuroscience & Behavioral Health, *supra* note 124 at 98.
134. *Id.*
135. Quoted at Cynthia S. Duncan, 'The Need for Change: An Economic Analysis of Marijuana Policy', 41 CONN. L. REV. 1701, 1706, 1707 (n.15, 19, respectively) (2009).

number of witnesses who attribute it also to the smoking of ganja. ... [T]here seems quite equally good ground for believing that the chillum of ganja taken by the laboring man after his food with the object of allying weariness and assisting digestion is no more harmful; and there are many witnesses whose evidence is in this sense. The use of bhang in the one case is sometimes compared to the glass of wine taken at meals by a moderate consumer of alcohol, and the use of ganja in the other case to be laboring man's glass of beer or even to his pipe of tobacco. It is possible also that the effects of hemp drugs in this respect may be to a certain extent comparable with those of tea."[136]

The Commission found that people engaged in physically taxing vocations (such as gymnasts, wrestlers, porters, divers, postal runners, blacksmiths, miners, and even musicians) 'use the hemp drugs on occasion of especially severe exertion'.[137] It was used by 'religious persons, such as fakirs'[138] and by tradesmen such as jewelers to 'produce concentration of attention.'[139] The Commission's recommendations in this context were very similar to its recommendation against criminalisation and prohibition in the context of religious-spiritual use.[140] It was believed that moderate users will 'feel a sense of deprivation,' [141] and it might not be wise to prohibit the use of cannabis. It will be noted that it is now known that cannabis consumed in moderate quantities does not present any significant public health issues.[142] A 2019 study conducted in Colorado that has legalized recreational cannabis found, "no significant effect on cannabis consumption among high school students related to the introduction of commercial sale."[143] However, it should be noted that studies in Oregon show that while legalization of recreational cannabis, "does not appear to have increased use among youth who did not already use cannabis, use among existing users has increased."[144] While it is encouraging to learn that legalization of recreational cannabis did not entice the youth to it; existing users may fairly be expected to increase their use immediately following legalization. In other words, there is nothing unpredictable and dangerous here.

136. IHDC Report, *supra* note 2 at 181.
137. *Id.* at 181-82, 194.
138. *Id.* at 182, 194.
139. *Id.* at 182.
140. *Id.* at 183.
141. *Id.*
142. Seddon & Floodgate, *supra* note 80 at 62.
143. *Id.*
144. *Id.* at 62.

Compared with consumption of opium and alcohol, cannabis consumption was found far less dangerous or injurious, even when consumed excessively.[145] Excess consumption was found to be an exception in any case.[146] President Nixon appointed bipartisan National Commission on Marijuana and Drug Abuse, known popularly as the 'Schafer Commission,' which in its 1972 Report titled *Marihuana, A Signal of Misunderstanding*, found that 'looking only at the effects on the individual there is little proven danger of physical or psychological harm from the experimental or intermittent use of cannabis.'[147] We should once again take note of the 2019 'Magnitude of Substance Use' survey conducted by the Ministry of Social Welfare & Empowerment that found that out of the 3.1 crore Indians who reported being current users of any cannabis products, overall only 0.25% of Indians were reported to be using cannabis in a dependent pattern.[148]

vi. Cannabis Consumption and Crime

In so far as the use of cannabis and its correlation with crime was concerned, the Commission did not find any. Colonel Hutchinson, Commissioner of Lahore, gave the following evidence: "I remember no case from which I can deduce the theory that the use of the drugs is in any way connected with crime; that is to say, from my own personal experience. I cannot say the same regarding alcohol even among the natives of this country."[149] Mr. Toynbee, Commissioner of Bhagalpur, gave the following evidence: "I have never had persons pointed out to me as social wrecks from the effects of ganja. As far as I have seen, many more cases of evil effects from alcohol than from hemp have come before me".[150] And lastly we may consider the evidence of Colonel Bowie, Commissioner in the Central Provinces: "I can call to mind a great many cases which I had to deal with as a Magistrate and as a Sessions Judge, in which serious hurt and homicide have been caused by persons under the influence of alcohol, but not a single case

145. *Id.* at 185. ("But even in cases of excessive consumption, the difficulty appears to be less with ganja than with alcohol or opium."). *See also Id.* at 195. ("[I]t is a striking fact that of these witnesses a majority of about three to one declare alcohol to be more injurious than hemp drugs.").
146. *Id.* at 194.
147. Raymond P. Shafer, Report of the National Commission on Marihiuana and Drug Abuse (1972), http://www.druglibrary.org/schaffer/library/studies/nc/ncmenu.htm.
148. Magnitude of Substance Use in India 2019, *supra* note 130 at 17.
149. IHDC Report, *supra* note 2 at 195.
150. *Id.* at 195-96.

of crime of any kind which had been committed under the influence of bhang or ganja."[151] Other witnesses reported that indigenously use of cannabis was preferred to 'ardent spirits and wine'.[152] Surgeon-Lieutenant-Colonel Crombie said: "I believe that the habit of using ganja moderately is absolutely harmless; but I think moderate use of alcohol is liable to produce tissue changes in the long run."[153] Another witness said: "Prohibition, [of cannabis] I fear, would lead many to take to the use of ardent liquors, and this, in my humble opinion, would be replacing one evil by another of still greater magnitude."[154] This sentiment was shared by other 'much experienced' witnesses.[155] The connection between cannabis consumption and commission of crimes including the connection between international drug smuggling and cross-border terrorism was pointed out by a few Lok Sabha M.P.s during the debates concerning the NDPS Act.[156] Unfortunately, the nature of this connection was misunderstood in August 1985 when the NDPS Act was debated in Lok Sabha. The nature of this connection and the error into which the 8th Lok Sabha was betrayed is highlighted later in the last chapter of this work.

vii. Early Medical Experiments on Cannabis Use in India

Medical experiments were conducted regarding the use of cannabis and their results were shared with the Commission. Sir William O'Shaughnessy reported the results of tests conducted on pupils at the Medical College, Calcutta: "The result of several trials was that in as small doses as ¼ of a grain the pulse was increased in fullness and frequency; the surface of the body glowed; the appetite became extraordinary; and, with scarcely any exception, great aphrodisiac was experienced."[157] Lauder Brunton reported: "Its chief effect is on the brain, and is of a twofold nature; it excites a form of delirium and hallucinations generally of a

151. *Id.* at 196.
152. *Id.*
153. *Id.*
154. *Id.*
155. *See e.g.*, IHDC Report, *supra* note 2 at 197. ("One witness of much experience (Khan Bahadur Kadir Dad Khan, C.I.E., Sind Witness No. 4) says: "All classes of the people, from the most influential spiritual leader to the lowest beggar, will say that the British Government, while not interfering or prohibiting the use of alcohol in their own country, are stopping them here from the use of less intoxicating drugs, which they have been using from time immemorial, and which is also religiously respected.").
156. Lok Sabha Debates (August 28, 1985), Third Session (Eighth Lok Sabha), Vol. IX, No. 25 (Lok Sabha Secretariat), columns 47-48.
157. IHDC Report, *supra* note 2 at 186.

gay character causing much merriment, accompanied by a great inclination to muscular movements. ... The drug produces in some persons a curious loss of sense of space and time. This stage is generally followed by deep sleep. ... The process of digestion (sic) is less altered by *Cannabis indica* than by opium, and the after effects of opium (nausea, headache, etc.) are not produced."[158] The most interesting results were reported by Dr. Russell, through a note furnished to Dr. Prain:

> *"Mental effects appear in from three to five minutes; exhilaration and excitement of a pleasing nature: the subject talkative and merry; laughs and gesticulates; plays on imaginary music instruments and sings; converses with imaginary persons; illusions and delusions, usually of a pleasing nature; objective of these very responsive to external impressions and suggestions; rarely quarrelsome or combative. Then ensues a condition of repose and quiet contemplation with fixed stare and immobile pupil."*[159]

Results of other experiments reported to the Commission showed the, "... absence of morbid changes in the brain and of tissue changes generally under the action of hemp drugs even when used in excess."[160] Experiments conducted on animals showed that there was no, "... appreciable indication of the development of any cerebral excitement either during the administration of the drug or after intoxication had been fully established. ... The general health of the animal remained excellent during the entire course of the experiment."[161] The post-mortem examinations of monkeys on whom experiments of use of cannabis were conducted showed that the body of the animal was 'fairly well nourished' with a 'considerable amount of subcutaneous fat'.[162] The lungs were found 'exceptionally healthy,' and the liver, spleen, and pancreas 'appeared to be perfectly normal'.[163] The Commission also found that there was no evidence worth 'any weight' regarding any 'mental or moral injury' that might result from moderate use of cannabis.[164] Judging from all this evidence, the Commission observed:

> *"[T]he immediate effect of the moderate use of any of the hemp drugs on the habitual consumer is refreshing and stimulating, and alleviates fatigue, giving rise to*

---

158. *Id.* at 186-87.
159. *Id.* at 187.
160. *Id.* at 188.
161. *Id.* at 189.
162. *Id.* at 190.
163. *Id.*
164. *Id.* at 202.

pleasurable sensations all over the nervous system, so that the consumer is "at peace with everybody" – in a grand waking dream. He is able to concentrate his thoughts on one subject: it affords him pleasure, vigour, ready wit, capacity for hard work, and sharpness for business; it has a quieting effect on the nervous system, and removed restlessness and induced forgetfulness of mental troubles; all sorts of grotesque ideas rapidly pass through the mind, with a tendency to talk; it brightens the eyes, and, like a good cigar, given content; the man feels jolly, sings songs, and tells good stories; it causes bravery in the brave and cowardice in the timid, and, like alcohol, brings out the real character of the man. In young men it may give rise to sensual thoughts, and aphrodisiac effects are mentioned."[165]

viii. Average Selling Price and State Revenue

Trade in cannabis was permitted, and in some cases regulated and taxed in this period. 'Ganja' was found to be the most important of all three (i.e. ganja, charas, and bhang), and it was further found that it contributed 'nearly the whole of hemp drug revenue' in India.[166] While, cannabis was found to be a 'poor man's narcotic,'[167] the IHDC also found that its use among the 'well-to-do classes' was, "... by no means rare, and the probability is that with people who have acquired the taste and can afford to gratify it freely the indulgence is not stinted either to themselves or their friends."[168] The highest consumption was found in Calcutta, with shops in Darjeeling, Jalpaiguri, Shahabad, Bhagalpur, Purnea, and other areas in the Bengal region.[169] Even the price at which cannabis was being brought and sold was recorded by the IHDC Report.[170] The price of Rs. 20/- for 1 kilogram of ganja was reported by several reliable 'official

---

165. *Id.* at 191-92.
166. *Id.* at 127.
167. *Id.* at 63.
168. *Id.* at 128.
169. *Id.*
170. *See e.g.,* IHDC REPORT, *supra* note 2 at 129. ("The Excise Commissioner reports that the average retail price of ganja is Rs. 20 per sèr. It ranges from Rs. 12 in Calcutta, in Mymensingh, or 2½ annas to more than 6 annas per tola, the average being 4 annas. It appears from the evidence that 1/10th of a tola is the smallest quantity that will suffice for one *chillum*, and that more is required if more than two or three smokers have to partake of it. That quantity apparently affords one smoke to two persons, and the refreshment seems to be generally taken twice a day. For the most moderate habitual smokers, therefore 1/16th of a tola may be taken as the daily allowance. This represents an expenditure of ¼ anna a day and a yearly allowance of 23 tolas.").

witnesses',[171] and no excessive consumption was reported by any of them. In fact, their reports, which appeared to be sound to the Commission,[172] seem to indicate that whatever was being consumed could not be 'considered as excessive.'[173] The Commission found that not more than 5% of all cannabis consumers could be considered 'excessive consumers'[174] According to the calculations in the IHDC Report, in total only 0.5% of the general population could be said to be regular consumers of cannabis.[175] Despite its low cost,[176] bhang was also consumed only by 0.6% of people.[177] This is consistent with the Commission's finding that cannabis consumption in India, especially if being smoked, was largely a private affair, and that, "... it would be only rarely that a man would smoke in the presence of a neighbour who had not specially come to join him."[178] This was a 'negligible percentage' of the total population, and a witness (Rev. Laflamme) was actually, "... surprised to hear that the Government is concerned about a practice which is confined to so small a portion of the people as is ganja and bhang, and is not concerned about the widespread, rapidly increasing, and much more injurious habit of alcoholic drink, from which greater harm results."[179]

---

171. IHDC REPORT, *supra* note 2 at 129-30. (One Excise Commissioner and another Deputy Magistrate and Collector reported the price of Rs. 20/- for One Sèèr. One Sèèr, contains 80 Toläs. One Tolä is approximately 11 grams. This makes One Sèèr approximately 1 kilogram. The Deputy Magistrate and Collector of Malda gave the following evidence: "I have taken some statistics on this point. The ganja shop at this town of English-bazar sells ganja at the rate of Rs. 20 a sèr. I enquired of a large number of persons who come to purchase ganja at this shop as to their daily consumption of their drug. Altogether 378 persons were examined. Of these, 247 persons stated that they spent a pice (¼ anna) a day on this drug, 106 persons gave 2 pice (½ anna) as their daily expenditure on ganja, whilst only 13, 7, 1, 3, and 1 stated their daily consumption to be 3 (¾ anna), 4 (1 anna), 5 (1¼ annas), 8 (2 annas), and 10 (2½ annas).").
172. *Id.* at 130.
173. *Id.* (The Deputy Magistrate and Collector of Malda reported: "The retail price of ganja in this district is about Rs. 20, so that two pice (½ anna) can fetch a man only 1/8th tola of ganja. This is not sufficient for more than three *chillums*. I think it cannot be considered as excessive. As regards occasional consumers, all that can be said is that their number is extremely small. In fact, it is impossible for a man to consume a pretty large quantity unless he is a habitual consumer and has kept up the habit by daily use.").
174. *Id.*
175. *Id.* at 131-32. (The district wise calculation of ganja consumption shows that out of a total population of 71,271,080 souls only 376,880 could be said to be regular consumers, which brings it to 0.5% of the total population. The highest, at 1%, was found in Bhagalpur.).
176. *Id.* at 140. ("Bhang is so cheap, 3 or 4 annas a sèr, as to give very wide latitude for individual indulgence. ... Occasional use, either regulated by the season, or prompted by the weather, or connected with social and religious observances, is also very common.").
177. *Id.* at 143.
178. *Id.* at 167.
179. *Id.* at 197.

Nevertheless, the average price of Rs. 20 per kilogram was likely the cause of this negligible percentage of 0.6% of people.[180] Charas, however, was doubly expensive compared to ganja and was sold at Rs. 40 per kilogram, and was naturally used by 'people with better means.' [181] Between the years 1873 and 1892, the IHDC Report notes, the total yearly 'hemp drug revenue' from the North-Western provinces (where it was 'very largely consumed'[182]) grew from Rs. 400,000/- to Rs. 700,000/-.[183] An increase of 193% was noted in Oudh[184] (where the King himself was interested in its cultivation,[185]) and 50% in the North-Western provinces.[186] The changing habits among higher classes and their growing preference for liquor were also noted as the 'principal cause' of the decrease in consumption.[187]

ix. Conclusion: IHDC Recommendations (Regulation and Taxation Without Unnecessary State Intervention)

The IHDC Report ended with a list of eight primary recommendations. Chief among them was that prohibition of cannabis would be, "neither necessary nor expedient in consideration of their ascertained effects,"[188] and advocated for a policy of systematic and uniform.189 regulation and taxation.[190] However, it recommended that cannabis cultivation be licensed and centralized.[191] Trade in cannabis was not to be monopolized by the Government, "for practical reasons, though there [was] no theoretical objection to it."[192] The Commission stressed that: "When sufficient provision has been made for restricting consumption of the drugs by the means above detailed, there should be as little interference as possible on the part of the Government with their distribution."[193]

180. *Id.* at 132. ("At the average price of ganga, Rs 20 per sèr, the Commission's estimate of half a sèr is equivalent to a yearly expenditure of Rs. 10, and it is not likely that the poor people, who form the great bulk of the consumers, could afford more than this amount.").
181. *Id.* at 133.
182. *Id.* at 135.
183. *Id.* at 136.
184. *Id.*
185. *Id.* at 42.
186. *Id.* at 136.
187. *Id.* at 134, 138.
188. *Id.* at 359, Conclusion I.
189. *Id.* Conclusion IV.
190. *Id.* Conclusions II, III, VI.
191. *Id.* Conclusion III(b).
192. *Id.* Conclusion V.
193. *Id.* Conclusion VII.

3

The Later British Colonial Government Leading upto Indian Independence (1930 to 1947)

So far we have seen that there was no legal prohibition on cultivation, processing, sale, purchase, possession, and consumption, etc. of cannabis during the years 1600 to 1930. This period was divided into three parts: (i) the Pre-British India (the year 1600 and earlier), and (ii) the Company Rule (the year 1600 to 1857), and (iii) Early British Colonial Government (1857 to 1930). Throughout this period there was no prohibition on cannabis, and in fact, the British Colonial Government was advised by its own advisors not to criminalize it. This situation remained largely unchanged in so far as cannabis was concerned throughout the period 1930 to 1947. Besides demonstrating the fact that cannabis was not prohibited in this period, this chapter will also lay the foundation of the third claim made by this work: from a constitutional standpoint, it is highly doubtful whether Parliament has the power to criminalize it.

The Government of India Act of 1935,[1] (the '1935 Act') one of the longest legislation ever enacted by the Parliament of the United Kingdom that may fairly be said to be the first properly written constitutional document[2] was put in place to govern British India.[3] The 1935 Act lasted for 12 years when the current day Republic of India won its independence from British rule.[4] Thereafter, the 1935 Act was proclaimed to be the interim constitution for independent India by the Governor-General of India.[5] The Constituent Assembly that was also to serve as an

1. Government of India Act 1935, 26 Geo. 5 c. 2 (U.K.).
2. Sarath Pillai, 'Fragmenting the Nation: Divisible Sovereignty and Travancore's Quest for Federal Independence', 34 LAW & HIST. REV. 743, 762 (2016). ("Also, the GOI Act (1935), one of the longest constitutions ever enacted by the British Parliament, was shaped by imperial constitutionalism.").
3. H.M. Seervai, *Constitutional Law of India* 287, 288 (4th ed. 1996).
4. Indian Independence Act 1947, 10 & 11 Geo. 6 c.48 (U.K.).
5. The India (Provisional Constitution) Order 1947, 10 & 11 Geo., c. 30 (U.K.); *K.M. Rajagopalan* v. *The State of Madras and another* (1954) 2 MLJ 254 (India).

interim Parliament,[6] was tasked with drafting a new constitution for independent India.[7] After about three years of intense labour and long deliberations, and under the leadership of Babasaheb Dr. Bhim Rao Ambedkar,[8] the Constitution of India was adopted by the Constituent Assembly on November 26, 1949,[9] with some provisions coming into force the same day while some other provisions came into effect the following year on January 26,[10] which we celebrate every year as our Republic Day.[11] This means that between August 15, 1947, and November 26, 1949, the 1935 Act served as the interim constitution of independent India,[12] and will be henceforth referred to as such in this chapter.

i. Distribution of Legislative Powers

Having established a federal legislature,[13] and a provincial one,[14] the interim constitution had further distributed the legislative powers between these two.[15]

---

6. India Constitution Art 379, *repealed by* The Constitutional (Seventh Amendment) Act, 1956 ("Until both Houses of Parliament have been duly constituted...the body functioning as the Constituent Assembly of the Dominion of India immediately before the commencement of this Constitution shall be the provisional Parliament"). *See also* 1 B. Shiva Rao, *Framing of India's Constitution: Select Documents* 581 ("Nehru's Note to the President of the Constituent Assembly, August 23, 1947"). In this note Pandit Nehru noted that, "Recent changes and developments have put an end to the old Legislative Assembly and the Constituent Assembly will now function as the Legislative Assembly of India. The Legislative Assembly Department is for the present rather headless till such time as the Constituent Assembly functions as a Legislative Assembly. Probably, the correct view is that the President of Constituent Assembly becomes automatically the head of the Legislative Assembly Department."
7. Indian Independence Act 1947, 10 & 11 Geo. 6 c. 30, §§ 8(2), 8(3) (U.K.).
8. Dr. Ambedkar was a man of extraordinary learning having obtained doctorates from both the London School of Economics and the Columbia Law School. *See* J. Krishnamurty, 'Ambedkar's Educational Odyssey', *1913–1927*, 5(2) JOURNAL OF SOCIAL INCLUSION STUDIES 147 (2019).
9. India Constitution, Preamble ("We, the people of India, having solemnly resolved to constitute India into a sovereign, socialist, secular, democratic republic … [i]n our Constituent Assembly this twenty-sixth day of November, 1949, do hereby adopt, enact and give to ourselves this Constitution.")
10. Madhav Khosla, India's Founding Moment 14 (2020).
11. Know India, Republic of India, https://knowindia.gov.in/republic-day-celebration/republic-of-india.php.
12. B.N. Rau, India's *Constitution in the Making* 2 (1960); Uday S. Mehta, 'Indian Constitutionalism: Crisis, Unity, and History', in *The Oxford Handbook on The Indian Constitution* (S. Choudhry, M. Khosla & P.B. Mehta eds. 2016).
13. Government of India Act 1935, 26 Geo. 5 Ch. 2, § 18 (U.K.).
14. *Id.* § 60.
15. *Id.* §§ 99-107.

Under the interim constitution, these powers were distributed on the twin basis of territoriality, and subject matter.[16] Territorially, the federal legislature was allowed to 'make laws for the whole or any part of British India or for any Federated State',[17] whereas the provincial legislature was allowed to 'make laws' only for the 'Province or for any part thereof'.[18] Subject-matter wise, the interim constitution divided all the subjects of legislation into three lists that were all put in Schedule 7,[19] and the legislative power was divided in the following broad manner:

a. First, it was laid down that in all the 'matters enumerated' in the Federal Legislative List,[20] only the Federal legislature[21] could exercise legislative power,[22] but it could also exercise these powers in the Provincial Legislative List[23] in the following four situations: (i) in respect of a territory that was not a 'Province';[24] (ii) if the Governor-General had declared an emergency;[25] (iii) if two or more Provincial Legislatures passed resolutions to the effect that it appeared to them that 'any of the matters enumerated in the Provincial Legislative List should be regulated in those Provinces by Act of the Federal legislature';[26] and (iv) if the subject-matter pertained to implementation of 'treaties and agreements with other countries', but here the power could only be exercised with the 'previous consent of the Governor'.[27]

---

16. *Prafulla Kumar Mukherjee & Others* v. *Bank of Commerce Ltd.*, AIR 1947 PC 60 (Privy Council) (Ind. App.).
17. Government of India Act 1935, 26 Geo. 5 Ch. 2, § 99 (U.K.).
18. *Id.*
19. *Id.* sch. 7, List I: Federal Legislative List (containing a total of 59 entries); List II: Provincial Legislative List (containing a total of 54 entries); List III: Concurrent Legislative List (containing a total of 36 entries).
20. *Id.*
21. *Id.* § 100(1). Section 100, sub-section (1) begins with a non-obstante clause and provides: "Notwithstanding anything in the two next succeeding subsections, the Federal Legislature has, and the Provincial Legislature has not, ...".
22. *Id.*
23. *Id.* sch. 7, List II: Provincial Legislative List.
24. *Id.* § 100(4) ("The Federal Legislature has power to make laws with respect to matters enumerated in the Provincial Legislative List except for a Province or any part thereof.").
25. *Id.* § 102(1).
26. *Id.* § 103.
27. *Id.* § 106(1) ("The Federal Legislature shall not by reason only of the entry in the Federal Legislative List relating to the implementation of treaties and agreements with other countries have power to make any law for any Province except with the previous consent of the Governor; or for a Federated State except with the previous consent of the Ruler thereof.").

b. Second, it was laid down that in the 'matters enumerated' in the Provincial Legislative List,[28] only the provincial legislature could exercise legislative power.[29]

c. Third, it was laid down that in the 'matters enumerated' in the Concurrent Legislative List,[30] both the federal and provincial legislatures could concurrently exercise legislative power.[31]

d. Fourth, if any particular matter was found 'not enumerated in any of the Lists in the Seventh Schedule' the Governor-General could, by public notification, empower either the Federal or the Provincial legislature to 'enact a law' on such matter.[32] This authority was discretionary,[33] and extended to making any law 'imposing a tax not mentioned in any such list'.[34] It was necessary for an express provision pertaining to tax legislations to be mentioned in the interim Constitution because in *The Matter of Central Provinces and Berar Act No. XIV of 1938*[35] it was held by the Federal Court of India that in order for either the Federal or the Provincial legislature to have subject-matter competence to levy and collect a tax, it has to be expressly mentioned in one of the taxing-entries in one of the three lists in Schedule 7.[36]

e. Fifth, and specifically applicable to the Concurrent List where both the Federal and Provincial legislatures had concurrent authority, in case of repugnancy between Federal law and Provincial law, the federal one would prevail, and the Provincial law to the extent of its repugnancy to

---

28. *Id.* sch. 7, List II: Provincial Legislative List.
29. *Id.* § 100(3) ("Subject to the two preceding subsections, the Provincial Legislature has, and the Federal Legislature has not, power to make laws for a Province or any part thereof with respect to any of the matters enumerated in List II in the said Schedule …".)
30. *Id.* sch. 7, List III: Concurrent Legislative List.
31. *Id.* § 100 (2) ("Notwithstanding anything in the next succeeding subsection, the Federal Legislature, and, subject to the preceding subsection, a Provincial Legislature also, have power to make laws with respect to any of the matters enumerated in List III in the said Schedule …".)
32. *Id.* § 104(1).
33. *Id.* § 104(2) ("In the discharge of his function under this section the Governor-General shall act in his discretion.").
34. *Id.*
35. *In Re. The Central Provinces and Berar Act No. XIV of 1938*, (1939) FCR 18 (India).
36. *Id.* at 74. ("There is no general power given to the Federation to impose indirect taxes, nor any general power given to the Provinces to impose direct taxes. The heads have been separately specified in great detail"); *See* H.M. Seervai, *Constitutional Law of India* 166 (4th ed. 1996).

the Federal law would be 'void'.[37] But a Provincial law could prevail over a Federal one if it received the assent of the Governor-General of India.[38]

ii. Constitutional Competence to Criminalize Trade in Cannabis

Having thus understood the broad framework of the manner in which legislative competence was distributed under the interim Constitution, let us now try to locate this power in the text of the interim Constitution. If this power cannot be located in the interim Constitution then it must follow that there was no power under the interim Constitution to criminalize trade in cannabis.[39] This conclusion is consistent with the fact that there was no legal prohibition on trade in cannabis at the time India gained back its independence from the British in 1947.[40] This could be because neither the Federal nor the Provincial legislature was constitutionally authorized to criminalize trade in cannabis.[41]

The Federal legislature could not criminalize trade in cannabis because it was authorized to legislate only on the matters enumerated in List I of the Seventh Schedule ("Federal Legislative List"). In the case of cannabis, none of the four exceptions mentioned above was satisfied. In addition, there is reliable evidence to the effect that during these years cannabis was widely consumed in India for religious/spiritual, medicinal, and recreational purposes.[42] However, Entry 45 of the Federal Legislative List provided:

"45. Duties of excise on tobacco and other goods manufactured or produced in India ***except--***

37. Government of India Act, 1935, § 107(1), 26 Geo. 5 Ch. 2, (U.K.).
38. *Id.* at § 107(2).
39. *Union of India* v. *H. S. Dhillon,* AIR 1972 SC 1061 (India) ("Under the Govt. of India Act, the residuary powers were not given either to the Central Legislature or to the Provincial Legislatures."); H.M. Seervai, *Constitutional Law of India* 2484 (4th ed. 1996). *See Melbourne Corporation* v. *Commonwealth,* (1974) 74 CLR 31 (Austl.) ("The Commonwealth Parliament is a Parliament which possesses only "enumerated or selected legislative powers" - a proposition as to which this Court has never faltered"); *Citizens' and The Queen Insurance Cos.* v. *Parsons,* 1880 Can LII 6 (SCC), 4 SCR 215 (Canada).
40. Under the Dangerous Drugs Act of 1930 (India) enacted by the Federal Legislature of India, "...in order to centralize and vest in the Governor-General in Council the control over certain operations relating to dangerous drugs" the use of cannabis was not controlled or regulated even after defining cannabis in the Act.
41. Government of India Act, 1935, §§ 100, 104, read with, sch. 7, List I: Federal Legislative List, Entry 45, read with List I: Provincial Legislative List, Entries 31, 40, 26 Geo. 5 Ch. 2 (U.K.)
42. *See e.g.,* Government of India, Report of the Indian Hemp Drugs Commission 159 (1894).

(a) alcoholic liquors for human consumption;

(b) opium, Indian hemp and other narcotic drugs and narcotics; non-narcotic drugs;

(c) medicinal and toilet preparations containing alcohol, or any substance included in sub-paragraph (b) of this entry."[43]

Entry 45 is the only entry in the Federal Legislative List that uses the word 'hemp', which was at that point in time was, and even today is used as synonymous with 'cannabis'.[44] The only entry in the Federal Legislative List in the interim Constitution that even mentions the word 'hemp' mentions it in the negative. The use of the word 'except' above is clearly intended to tell the Federal legislature that it may impose duties of excise on tobacco and all goods manufactured in India *except* the ones stated in (a), (b), and (c).

This use of the word 'except' in Entry 45 of the Federal Legislative List is further clarified by Entries 31 and 40 of the Provincial Legislative List that provided:

"31. Intoxicating liquors and narcotic drugs, that is to say, the production, manufacture, possession, transport, purchase and sale of intoxicating liquors, opium and other narcotic drugs, but subject, as respects opium, to the provisions of List I and, as respects poisons and dangerous drugs, to the provisions of List III."[45]

"40. Duties of excise on the following goods manufactured or produced in the Province and countervailing duties at the same or lower rates on similar goods manufactured or produced elsewhere in India—

(a) alcoholic liquors for human consumption;

(b) opium, Indian hemp and other narcotic drugs and narcotics; non-narcotic drug;

---

43. Government of India Act, 1935, sch. 7, List I: Federal Legislative List, Entry 45, 26 Geo. 5 Ch. 2 (U.K.) (Emphasis Added).

44. Dangerous Drugs Act 1930 (India) § 2I (" hemp means – (i) the leaves, small stalks and flowering or fruiting tops of the Indian hemp plant (Cannabis Sativa L.), including all forms known as bhang, siddhi, or ganja; *(ii) charas,* that is, the resin obtained from the Indian hemp plant, which has not been submitted to any manipulations other than those necessary for packing and transport; and *(iii)* any mixture, with or without neutral materials, of any of the above forms of hemp or any drink prepared therefrom; *See* Government of India, Report of the Indian Hemp Drugs Commission (1894).

45. Government of India Act, 1935, 26 Geo. 5 Ch. 2, sch. 7, List II: Provincial Legislative List, Entry 31.

> *(c) medicinal and toilet preparations containing alcohol or any substance included in sub-paragraph (b) of this entry.*"[46]

iii. Lack of Constitutional Competence to Criminalize Trade in Cannabis under the Government of India Act, 1935

On a conjoint reading of Entry 45 of the Federal Legislative List and Entries 31 and 40 of the Provincial Legislative List, it is abundantly clear that the production, manufacture, possession, transport, purchase, and sale, etc. of cannabis was a legally recognized trading activity that was subject to duties of excise (which is a tax on manufacturing), and in addition to this routine sales tax.[47] It further stands to reason that people who engaged in this trading activity further paid income tax as the Federal legislature was competent to levy an income tax, except on the farmers that cultivated cannabis.[48]

One may perhaps be tempted to argue that 'criminal law'[49] and 'criminal procedure'[50] are both entries in the Concurrent Legislative List of the Seventh Schedule and therefore even though the Federal legislature is not competent to impose any taxes on the trade in cannabis, it can certainly invoke its subject-matter powers under the Concurrent Legislative List to federally criminalize trade in cannabis across the length and breadth of British India. Similarly, the Provincial legislature may take recourse to the same entries and subject to the rules of repugnancy, criminalize within that Province's trade in cannabis. These arguments, however, do not survive scrutiny.

First, it would amount to a manifestly absurd interpretation of the interim Constitution. It cannot be the case that legislation that authorizes a legislature it has created to impose taxes on commercial trading activity will simultaneously also authorize the same legislature, or another legislature, to criminalize the very same

---

46. *Id.* Entry 40. (Emphasis Added).
47. *Id.* Entry 48. ("Taxes on sale of goods and on advertisements.").
48. *Id.* sch. 7, List I: Federal Legislative List, Entry 54 ("Taxes on income other than agricultural income.").
49. *Id.* sch. 7, List III: Concurrent Legislative List, Entry 1 ("Criminal law, including all matters included in the Indian Penal Code at the date of passing of this Act, but excluding offences against laws with respect to any of the matters specified in List I or List II and excluding the use of His Majesty's naval, military and air forces in aid of the civil power.").
50. *Id.* Entry 2 ("Criminal Procedure, including all matters included in the Code of Criminal Procedure at the date of the passing of this Act.").

activity. The entries must be interpreted harmoniously.[51] And the only way the above-stated argument could be true would be when these entries in the Concurrent Legislative List are read in a totally disharmonious manner. Furthermore, the manner in which Entry 1 of the Concurrent Legislative List is worded leaves very little room to argue that this entry can be used by either legislature to claim the subject-matter competence that is constitutionally necessary to criminalize trade in cannabis. Second, criminalizing this trade would have been quite counter-productive since trade in cannabis was bringing a handsome sum of money annually to the British colonial Government.[52]

iv. Conclusion

It is therefore clear that not only was trade in cannabis legal, taxed, and actually rather widespread given the amounts in which it was consumed annually across the length and breadth of British India in diverse forms, it is also clear that under the interim Constitution neither the Federal nor the Provincial legislature was constitutionally competent to criminalize this trade. The taxation of this trade by way of imposition of duties of excise and a sales tax was left to the Provincial legislature. This arrangement seems consistent with the patterns of cultivation and consumption of cannabis that the British colonial Government had surveyed and identified.[53]

51. *Calcutta Gas Company* v. *State of West Bengal* AIR 1962 SC 1044 (India).
52. Government of India, Report of the Indian Hemp Drugs Commission (1894) ("It has been recorded from 1873 to 1892 that the hemp drug revenue of the North-Western Provinces and Oudh has grown from INR 4 to 7 lakhs. The Increase in Oudh has been 193 per cent., and in the North-Western Provinces 50 per cent.").
53. *See e.g.*, Government of India, Report of the Indian Hemp Drugs Commission (1894).

4

Independent Indian Government: Pre and Post Adoption of The Constitution of India (1947 to 1985)

It is a peculiar feature of written constitutions of geographically large nations in the modern-day world that almost all of them resort to some sort of constitutional formulation to divide legislative powers between a federal, or a union, and a provincial, or a state legislature.[1] The manner in which these formulations are laid down in any given constitution might differ, but the fact of these formulations and the desire to distribute legislative powers between a state and a federal legislature cannot be denied.[2]

The Constitution of India follows this principle and has distributed legislative powers between the Union Parliament and State Legislatures.[3] This distribution is based on and largely follows the original formulation laid down in the Government of India Act of 1935, which was British legislation enacted by the U.K. Parliament to govern British India.[4] The Commonwealth of Australia Act of 1901, another British legislation that went on to become the Australian Constitution, also distributes legislative powers between a federal legislature (the

---

1. F. J. Stimson, 'Intention and Wisdom of the Division of Legislative Power between Congress and the States', 56 U. PA. L. REV. 361 (1908); Antun Marinac, Mirela Mezak Matijevic & Jasmina Mladenovic, *Division of Competences between the European Union and the Member State*, 3 ECLIC 79 (2019).
2. N. Selvakkumaran, 'The Legislative Relations between the Union Parliament and the State Legislatures under the Indian Constitution', 11 SRI LANKA J. INT'L L. 207 (1999); Nicholas P. Zalany, 'The European Union Constitution and Its Effects on Federalism in the EU', 66 OHIO ST. L. J. 615 (2005).
3. Khagesh Gautam, 'Sales Tax and Cloud Computing in India', 68 TAX. LAW. 671 (2015); Khagesh Gautam, 'Taxing Offshore Transactions in India and the Territoriality Clause - A Case for Substantial Constitutional Limitations on Indian Parliament's Power to Retrospectively Amend the Income Tax Act', 40 INT'L TAX J. 17 (2014).
4. H.M. Seervai, *Constitutional Law of India* 285 (4th ed. 1996).

Australian Parliament) and provincial legislatures of Australia.[5] The British North America Act of 1894, again British legislation that went on to become the Canadian Constitution, also distributed legislative powers between a federal legislature (the Canadian Parliament) and the provincial legislatures of Canada.[6] The U.S. Constitution, the oldest of all these documents, uses a version of a similar device to divide legislative powers between a federal legislature (the U.S. Congress) and state legislatures.[7]

This chapter, building on the argument made in the previous chapter, argues that the manner in which legislative powers were distributed in the Government of India Act of 1935, and later under the Constitution of India, makes the constitutionality of those parts of the Narcotic Drugs and Psychotropic Substances Act of 1985 ('NDPS Act') highly suspect on the grounds that Union Parliament lacks the legislative competence to enact such a law.

The Constitution of India is one of the longest written constitutions in the world.[8] It took a long time to draft[9] and was finally adopted on November 26, 1949.[10] The manner in which legislative powers were distributed between the federal and provincial legislatures in the interim constitution was by and large retained in the Indian Constitution.[11] Having established the Union Parliament[12] (comprising of two houses: the House of the People, and the Council of States), and State Legislatures,[13] the Constitution distributed legislative powers between these two on largely the same lines as in the interim constitution.

---

5. Alan Fenna, 'Commonwealth Fiscal Power and Australian Federalism', 31 U. N.S.W. L. J. 509 (2008).
6. *Manitoba (Attorney General)* v. *Canada (Attorney General)*; *Canada (Attorney General)* v. *Newfoundland (Attorney General)*; *Quebec (Attorney General)* v. *Canada (Attorney General)* (1981) 1 SCR 753 (Privy Council) (Appeal taken from Can.); Brian Bird, 'The Unbroken Supremacy of The Canadian Constitution', 55 ALBERTA L. REV. 755 (2018).
7. *Sturges* v. *Crowninshield*, 17 U.S. 122 (1819); *U.S. Term Limits, Inc. v. Thornton*, 514 U.S. 779 (1995).
8. Ravi P. Bhatia, 'Evolution of Judicial Activism in India', 45 JILI 262 (2003).
9. The Constituent Assembly of India took almost three years (two years, eleven months and seventeen days to be precise) to draft the Constitution. *See* Lok Sabha, First Day in The Constituent Assembly (India), http://164.100.47.194/loksabha/constituent/facts.html.
10. India Constitution Preamble.
11. H.M. Seervai, *Constitutional Law of India* 2305 (4th ed. 1996).
12. Indian Constitution Art. 79 (There shall be a Parliament for the Union which shall consist of the President and two Houses to be known respectively as the Council of States and the House of the People.)
13. *Id.* Art. 168, § 1 ("For every State there shall be a Legislature which shall consist of the Governor, and (a) in the State of Andhra Pradesh, Bihar, Madhya Pradesh, Maharashtra, Karnataka, Tamil Nadu, Telangana and Uttar Pradesh, two Houses; (b) in other States, on House.)"

i. Distribution of Legislative Powers

As noted above, under the interim Constitution, legislative powers were distributed on the twin basis of territoriality, and subject matter.[14] The same formula was adopted by the Constitution.[15] Territorially, the Union Parliament was authorized to 'make laws for the whole or any part of the territory of India'[16] and the State Legislatures could 'make laws for the whole or any part of the State'.[17] Subject-matter wise too, the Constitution, following the formula used in the interim Constitution, expanded and divided all the subjects of legislation into three lists that were all put in Schedule 7,[18] and the legislative power was divided in the following broad manner:

a. First, in all the 'matters enumerated' in the Union List the Union Parliament alone could exercise legislative power,[19] but it could also exercise powers in the State List in the following five situations: (i) in respect of a territory that was 'not included in a State';[20] (ii) if the President of the republic declared an emergency;[21] (iii) if the Council of States in the Union Parliament declares, "... by resolution supported by not less than two-thirds of the members present and voting that it is necessary or expedient in national interest that Parliament should make laws with respect to ... any matter enumerated in the State List specified in the resolution ...";[22] (iv) if two or more State Legislatures passed resolutions to the effect that it appeared to them, "... desirable that any of the matters with respect to which Parliament has no power to make

14. *Prafulla Kumar Mukherjee & Others* v. *Bank of Commerce Ltd.* AIR 1947 PC 60 (Privy Council) (Ind. App.).
15. H.M. Seervai *supra* note 4.
16. India Constitution Art. 245, § 1.
17. *Id.*
18. *Id.* Sch. 7 (Art. 246), List I: Union List (containing a total of 97 entries); List II: State List (containing a total of 66 entries); List III: Concurrent List (containing a total of 47 entries).
19. *Id.* Art. 246, § 1 (Notwithstanding anything in clauses (2) and (3), Parliament has exclusive power to make laws with respect to any of the matters enumerated in List I in the Seventh Schedule (in this Constitution referred to as the "Union List".)
20. *Id.* Art. 246, § 4 ("Parliament has power to make laws with respect to any matter for any part of the territory of India not included in a State notwithstanding that such matter is a matter enumerated in the State List".)
21. *Id.* Art. 250, § 1 read with Art. 356, § 1, cl. (b). *See generally* Abhishek Singhvi & Khagesh Gautam, *The Law of Emergency Powers: Comparative Common Law Perspectives*, Springer 259-296 (2020) for a detailed treatment of this specific issue.
22. *Id.* Art. 249, § 1. Such a resolution can remain in force only for one year, but could be extended by following the same procedure for another year. *See Id.* Art. 249, § 2.

laws for the States ... should be regulated in such States by Parliament by law ...";[23] and (v) if the subject-matter pertained to implementation of, "... any treaty, agreement or convention with any other country or countries or any decision made at any international conference, association or body."[24]

b. Second, in the 'matters enumerated' in the State List, only the State Legislature could exercise legislative power.[25]

c. Third, in the 'matters enumerated' in the Concurrent List, both the Union Parliament and the State Legislatures could concurrently exercise legislative power.[26]

d. Fourth, with respect to 'matters not enumerated in the Concurrent List or the State List' only the Union Parliament is authorized to 'make any law'.[27] This authority extended to make any law 'imposing a tax not mentioned in either of those Lists'.[28] It was necessary for this express provision pertaining to tax legislations to be mentioned in the Constitution for the same reason as it was necessary to make it express in the interim Constitution.[29]

e. Fifth, and specifically applicable to the Concurrent List alone where both the Union Parliament and State Legislatures have concurrent authority, in case of repugnancy between a Parliamentary law and State law, the Parliamentary one would prevail, and the State law, to the extent of its repugnancy to the Parliamentary law, would be 'void'.[30] But a State Law could prevail over a Parliamentary one if it received the assent of the President of the republic.[31]

---

23. *Id.* art. 252, § 1
24. *Id.* § 253.
25. *Id.* art. 246, § 3.
26. *Id.* art. 246, § 2.
27. *Id.* art. 248, § 1.
28. *Id.* art. 248, § 2.
29. *Sundararamier* v. *State of AP*, AIR 1958 SC 468 (India). ("Entries in the Lists-leads to the inference that taxation is not intended to be comprised in the main subject in which it might on an extended construction be regarded as included, but is treated as a distinct matter for purposes of legislative competence. And this distinction is also manifest in the language of Art. 248, Cls. (1) and (2), and of Entry 97 in List I of the Constitution."); *All India Federation of Tax Practitioners* v. *UOI*, AIR 2007 SC 2990 (India); *See also supra* notes 42 and 43.
30. India Constitution Art. 254, § 1.
31. *Id.* Art. 254, § 2.

ii. Constitutional Competence to Criminalize Trade in Cannabis

Having thus understood the broad framework of the manner in which legislative powers were distributed under the Constitution of India, this part of the book will try to locate this power in the text of the Constitution. If this power cannot be located within the Constitution then it must follow that there is no power under it to criminalize trade in cannabis.[32] This conclusion would be consistent with the fact that there was no legal prohibition on trade in cannabis at the time India gained its independence from the British in 1947,[33] and in fact trade in cannabis in India was criminalized only in 1985 when the NDPS Act was enacted by the Indian Parliament.[34] This could also be because neither the Union Parliament nor the State Legislatures (just like the federal and provincial legislatures under the interim Constitution) were constitutionally authorized to criminalize trade in cannabis. Constitutional competence to criminally prohibit any activity at the pain of arrest, trial, and incarceration (first during the investigation, then during the trial, and finally upon conviction) is a very serious matter. Any attempt to interpret the Constitution with a predetermined mindset to find something in the text to fit the interpretation, it will be seen, will ultimately have to be based on contradictory doctrines. Substantial liberties with the text will have to be taken, and established rules of interpretation will have to be ignored. In our attempt to somehow find something in the text of the Constitution in favour of Parliament's power to criminalize trade in cannabis we will have to ignore in the text that vests express powers with the State Legislatures to levy duties of excise on such trade. Such a federal bias, in the case of cannabis, is neither warranted nor desirable, unless, of course, we are willing to admit that the Supreme Court has been correct every single time it has interpreted the Constitution. We should be grateful that our Supreme Court, on the other hand, has on more occasions than one realized that an earlier

32. *Subrahmanyan Chettiar* v. *Muttusami Goundan*, AIR 1941 FC 47 (India). If the subject-matter cannot be located in any of the three lists in Schedule 7 of the 1935 Act, then the legislature cannot enact a law on it, and if it does the law would be null and void; *A.G. for Alberta* v *A.G. for Canada*, AIR 1943 PC 76 (80) (Privy Council) (Appeal taken from Can.); *See* Dr. C.D. Jha, *Judicial Review of Legislative Acts* 519 (2nd Ed 2009).

33. *See supra* Chapter 2.

34. Jonathan P. Caulkins, Beau Kilmer, & Mark A. R. Kleiman, 'Marijuana Legalization: What Everyone Needs to Know' 191 (2016); Manavi Kapur, W'hy are weed and hash illegal in India, but not bhang? The association of cannabis with crimes is an import from the United States', SCROLL.IN (September 12, 2020), https://scroll.in/article/972852/why-are-weed-and-hash-illegal-in-india-but-not-bhang; *See infra* Chapter 5.

interpretation of the Constitution was erroneous, and thus has never hesitated from reversing it or removing the error from an earlier position. It will be appreciated that the case of cannabis has never been examined from the federalism perspective in our country. It will be pertinent to note that even the 8th Lok Sabha did not fully appreciate the federalism issues that do arise in this case, as will be clear from a reading of the following chapter.

The Union Parliament could not criminalize trade in cannabis because it was authorized to legislate only on the matters enumerated in the Union List and none of the entries in the Union List authorized the Parliament to criminalize trade in cannabis. Entry 84 of the Union List, as it stood before the 101st Amendment in 2016,[35] provided:

> *"84. Duties of excise on tobacco and other goods manufactured or produced in India except—*
>
> *(a) alcoholic liquors for human consumption;*
>
> *(b) opium, Indian hemp and other narcotic drugs and narcotics, but including medicinal and toilet preparations containing alcohol or any substance included in sub-paragraph (b) of this entry."*

As was the case with entry 45 of the Federal List of the interim Constitution,[36] entry 84 of the Union List was the only entry in this list that used the word 'hemp', which (as has been shown above) was at that point of time, used as synonymous with 'cannabis'.[37] Furthermore, and again similar to entry 45 of the Federal List, entry 84, the only entry in the Union List that even mentions the

---

35. Entry 84 of the Union List, after the enactment of the Constitution (One Hundred and First Amendment) Act, 2016, now reads as follows:
    "84. Duties of excise on the following goods manufactured or produced in India, namely:
    (a) petroleum crude;
    (b) high speed diesel;
    (c) motor spirit (commonly known as petrol);
    (d) natural gas;
    (e) aviation turbine fuel; and
    (f) tobacco and tobacco products."
    See India Constitution Sch. 7, List I: Union List, Entry 84, as amended by the Constitution (One Hundred and First Amendment) Act 2016, § 17(a)(i) (with effect from September 16, 2016).
36. Government of India Act 1935, 26 Geo. 5 Ch. 2, sch. 7, list I: Federal Legislative List, Entry 45 (U.K.).
37. Dangerous Drugs Act 1930 (India) § 2(c) ("hemp mean - (i) the leaves, small stalks and flowering or fruiting tops of the Indian hemp plant (Cannabis Sativa L.)); *See also* Punjab Excise Act 1914, § 3(13)(i)(ii)(iii) (India); *See* Government of India, Report of the Indian Hemp Drugs Commission 15-18 (1894).

word 'hemp', mentions it in the negative. The use of the word 'except' above is clearly intended to tell the Union Parliament that it may impose duties of excise on tobacco and all goods manufactured in India *except* the ones stated in (a), and (b). The use of the word 'except' in Entry 84 of the Union List is further clarified by Entry 51 of the State Legislative List that provided:

> *"51. Duties of excise on the following goods manufactured or produced in the State and countervailing duties at the same or lower rates on similar goods manufactured or produced elsewhere in India—*
>
> *(a) alcoholic liquors for human consumption;*
>
> *(b) opium, Indian hemp and other narcotic drugs and narcotics;*
>
> *but not including medicinal and toilet preparations containing alcohol or any substance included in sub-paragraph (b) of this entry."*[38]

On a conjoint reading of Entry 84 of the Union List as it stood before the 101st Amendment in 2016, and Entry 51 of the State List, it becomes clear that the production, manufacture, possession, transport, purchase, and sale of cannabis was a legally recognized trading activity that was subject to duties of excise (which is a tax on manufacturing), and in addition to this routine sales tax.[39] It further stands to reason that people who engaged in this trading activity paid income tax as the Union Parliament is competent to levy an income tax, except for the farmers that cultivated cannabis.[40] It is therefore clear that the constitutional arrangement as provided in the interim Constitution under which not only was trade in cannabis legal, taxed, and actually rather widespread given the amounts in which it was consumed annually across the length and breadth of British India in diverse forms was largely carried over to the Indian Constitution. As per this arrangement trade in cannabis was liable to duties of excise and other forms of indirect taxation, but neither the Union nor the State legislatures were authorized to criminalize this trade.

This was to continue until 1985 when the time limit of 25 years imposed by Article 49(2)(f) of the Single Convention on Narcotic Drugs, 1961 became

---

38. India Constitution Sch. 7, List II: State List, Entry 51. (Emphasis Added)
39. State Legislatures were exclusively authorized to levy 'Taxes on the sale or purchase of goods other than newspapers' before the 101st Amendment in 2016 that ushered in the modern Goods and Service Tax regime. *See* India Constitution Sch. 7, List II: State List, Entry 54, omitted by Constitution (One Hundred and First Amendment) Act, 2016, § 17(b)(ii) (with effect from September 16, 2016).
40. India Constitution, Sch. 7, List I: Union List, Entry 84 ("Taxes on income other than agricultural income.")

applicable and in order to fulfil an international obligation, the Union Parliament enacted the NDPS Act, 1985. The Single Convention on Narcotic Drugs[41] was signed by India's representative on July 31, 1961, but, "... [s]ubject to ... the reservation provided for in Art. 49, paragraph 1 (a), (b), (d) and (e) with a reservation."[42] On a bare analysis it will be clear that as a result of this the Union Parliament could now take recourse to the fifth exception to the first rule of legislative power distribution as deduced above in order to claim the requisite legislative competence to criminalize trade in cannabis, which it did by enacting the NDPS Act.[43] There is nothing in the three lists in the Seventh Schedule that expressly or even impliedly authorizes the Union Parliament to criminalize trade in cannabis. The only entry in the Seventh Schedule that authorizes any legislative activity pertaining to trade in cannabis is Entry 51 of the State List and that too only authorizes imposition of duties of excise on this trade and not its criminalization. Furthermore, and as also argued above in the context of the interim Constitution, it cannot be the case that a Constitution that authorizes a legislature it created to impose taxes on a commercial trading activity can be read in a manner whereby it simultaneously also authorizes the same legislature, or another it might have created, to criminalize the very same activity. It is therefore clear that the Indian Parliament draws the requisite constitutional competence to criminalize trade in cannabis by recourse to the Single Convention[44] as the subject-matter thereof pertains to the implementation of, "... any treaty, agreement or convention with any other country or countries or any decision made at any international conference, association or body."[45] The material part of Article 49 of the Single Convention provides:

> *1. A Party may at the time of signature, ratification or accession reserve the right to permit temporarily in any one of its territories:*
>
> *(a) The quasi-medical use of opium;*

---

41. Single Convention on Narcotic Drugs 1961, 18 U.S.T 1407 (U.S. Treaty) ("Single Convention")
42. *Id.* Mr. B. N. Banerji, India's representative, signed the Single Convention with the following reservation: "Subject to ratification and to the reservation provided for in Art. 49, paragraph 1 (a), (b), (d) and (e). The Government of India will, in accordance with the second sub-alinea of Article 42, endeavour to secure, within the shortest time possible, the consent of Sikkim to the application of the Convention to that territory."
43. *See infra* Appendix. A detailed list of the all the provisions of the NDPS Act, 1985 the combined effect whereof is criminalization of trade in cannabis is provided in this Appendix appended at the end of this paper.
44. Single Convention, *supra* note 41, Art. 49.
45. India Constitution Art. 253.

(b) Opium smoking;

(c) Coca leaf chewing;

(d) The use of cannabis, cannabis resin, extracts and tinctures of cannabis for non-medical purposes; and

(e) The production and manufacture of and trade in the drugs referred to under (a) to (d) for the purposes mentioned therein.

2. The reservations under paragraph 1 shall be subject to the following restrictions:

(a) The activities mentioned in paragraph 1 may be authorized only to the extent that they were traditional in the territories in respect of which the reservation is made, and were there permitted on 1 January 1961.

(b) No export of the drugs referred to in paragraph 1 for the purposes mentioned therein may be permitted to a non-party or to a territory to which this Convention does not apply under article 42.

(c) Only such persons may be permitted to smoke opium as were registered by the competent authorities to this effect on 1 January 1964.

(d) The quasi-medical use of opium must be abolished within 15 years from the coming into force of this Convention as provided in paragraph 1 of article 41.

(e) Coca leaf chewing must be abolished within twenty-five years from the coming into force of this Convention as provided in paragraph 1 of article 41.

(f) The use of cannabis for other than medical and scientific purposes must be discontinued as soon as possible but in any case within twenty-five years from the coming into force of this Convention as provided in paragraph 1 of article 41.

(g) The production and manufacture of and trade in the drugs referred to in paragraph 1 for any of the uses mentioned therein must be reduced and finally abolished simultaneously with the reduction and abolition of such uses.[46]

iii. International Law and Indian Parliament's Constitutional Competence to Criminalize Trade in Cannabis

It is a long-standing principle of constitutional interpretation that treaty-making power must be exercised in accordance with the constitution and the limitations

46. Single Convention, *supra* note 41, Art. 49. (Emphasis Added).

if any, that it might have imposed.[47] That international obligations mandate acts or omissions that are inconsistent with its own constitution cannot be an acceptable defence when the government is sued for violation of constitutional rights, or for transgressing constitutional limitations.[48] This position is well supported by judicial authority from the supreme courts of the United States,[49] India,[50] and elsewhere.[51] Even though the rule of interpretation whereby the judges are required to harmonize international law and domestic law can be found in principles of constitutional interpretation in comparable jurisdictions such as the United States,[52] India,[53] and others,[54] 'two important caveats' attached to this rule have been noted:

> "... *(i) the international treaty or convention must be ratified by the government, and if required it must have been made a part of domestic law; and (ii) the rule does not require the domestic courts to bend over backwards to accommodate international law, and if the conflict cannot be resolved in a harmonious manner, domestic law or the constitutional provisions must override international law.*"[55]

The underlying rationale behind these caveats has been explained thus:

---

47. Khagesh Gautam, 'The Use of International Law in Constitutional Interpretation in the Supreme Court of India', 55 STAN. J. INT'L. L. 27, 35 (2019). *See also* Roger P. Alford, 'Misusing International Sources to Interpret the Constitution', 98 AM. J. INT'L L. 57, 61 (2004); Henry Wade Rogers, *The Treaty-Making Power,* 16 ANNU. REP. A.B.A. 243, 249 (1893); Note, 'Matters of Domestic Concern: A Potential Judicial Limitation on the Treaty-Making Power', 34 IND. L.J. 57, 61 (1958).
48. Gautam, *supra* note 47 at 35; *See also* Peter J. Spiro, Treaties, 'International Law, and Constitutional Rights', 55 STAN. L. REV. 1999, 2018 (2003) (noting that, "A consensus continues to hold that treaties cannot result in the diminishment of constitutional rights"); Jack Goldsmith and Daryl Levinson, 'Law for States: International Law, Constitutional Law, Public Law', 122 HARV. L. REV. 1791, 1794 (2009).
49. *See Reid* v. *Covert,* 354 U.S. 1 (1957) ("This Court has regularly and uniformly recognized the supremacy of the Constitution over a treaty.")
50. *See In re Berubari Union and Exchange of Enclaves,* AIR 1960 SC 845 (India).
51. *See generally* Gautam, *supra* note 47.
52. *See Societe Nationale Industrielle Aerospatiale* v. *United States Dist. Court for S. Dist. of Iowa,* 482 U.S. 522, 567 (1987) ("The final component of a comity analysis is to consider if there is a course that furthers, rather than impedes, the development of an ordered international system").
53. India Constitution Art. 51, cl. (c). *See also Comm'r of Customs, Bangalore* v. *G.M. Exp. and Others,* (2016) 1 SCC 91, 115 (India), *GVK Indus.* v. *ITO,* (2011) 4 SCC 36, 64-65 (India), *Githa Hariharan* v. *Reserve Bank of India,* (1999) 2 SCC 228, 229 (India), *Giani Bakshish Singh* v. *Govt of India,* (1973) 2 SCC 688, 694 (India).
54. *See generally* Gautam, *supra* note 47.
55. Gautam, *supra* note 47 at 37.

> *"At the heart of either of these is the essential nature of a sovereign democratic constitution. Ultimate sovereignty vests in people, and it is the people who get to decide what laws will bind them, how they will be enacted, and what restrictions are to be put on the powers whereby these decisions are taken. This ultimate sovereignty finds an expression, first and foremost, in the constitution. The constitution establishes certain sources wherefrom binding legal norms flow, and if international law is not one of those norms then it falls upon the constitutional authorities and constitutional rules that [bind] them to decide whether a rule of international law should be made a part of binding domestic law."*[56]

The Supreme Court of India has held that "National courts cannot say yes if Parliament has said no to a principle of international law. ... National courts being organs of national State and not organs of international law must perforce apply national law if international law conflicts with it."[57] On the basis of this judicial statement a principle of statutory interpretation has been deduced whereby, "If a constitutional provision appears to be in conflict with a provision of international law, the courts will try to avoid the conflict and observe the principle of comity of nations so far as practicably possible, but ultimately, the conflict has to be resolved in favour of the constitutional provision. Anything less than that and the practical result will be declaring a constitutional provision in effect unconstitutional because it violates a principle of international law."[58] From this, it follows that the Indian Parliament being created by the Indian Constitution cannot transgress the limitations that the Constitution itself imposes on it, and certainly cannot indirectly amend the Constitution by signing an international treaty such as the Single Convention.

Even though the Single Convention recognized *inter alia* that medical use of cannabis, "... continues to be indispensable for the relief of pain and suffering and that adequate provision must be made to ensure the availability of narcotic drugs for such purposes,"[59] it also recognized that, "... addiction to narcotic drugs constitutes a serious evil for the individual and is fraught with social and economic danger to mankind."[60] One of the 'general obligations' in the Single Convention on the parties thereof is: "To give effect to and carry out the provisions of this Convention within their own territories."[61] In the specific

56. *Id.* at 40 (Internal Footnotes Omitted).
57. *Gramophone Co. of India* v. *Birendra Bahadur Pandey*, (1984) 2 SCC 534, 540 (India).
58. Gautam, *supra* note 47 at 41.
59. Single Convention, *supra* note 41, Preamble.
60. *Id.*
61. *Id.* Article 1(a).

context of cannabis, this is supposed to be done by limiting the "production, manufacture, export, import, distribution of, trade in, use and possession of" [cannabis] "exclusively to medical and scientific purposes".[62] However, as seen above, both under the interim constitution and later under the Constitution of India, the production, manufacture, possession, transport, purchase, and sale of cannabis was a legally recognized trading activity that was subject to duties of excise (which is a tax on manufacturing), and in addition to this routine sales tax, and consequently therefrom income tax.

iv. Conclusion

Since the federal and provincial legislatures under the interim Constitution, and later the Union Parliament and State Legislatures under the Constitution of India were only allowed to regulate the production, manufacture, possession, transport, purchase, and sale of cannabis by the imposition of excise and other indirect taxes, and there is no express, or necessarily implied, authority to be inferred from the subject-matter jurisdiction as laid down in the three lists in Schedule 7, and other connected arguments presented above, it follows that none of these legislatures had any authority to criminalize trade in cannabis. To that extent the constitutionality of several provisions of the NDPS Act becomes highly suspect.[63] Furthermore, it is not possible for the Indian Parliament to obtain the necessary constitutional competence to criminalize trade in cannabis merely by signing the Single Convention for to say otherwise is to admit that the Constitution of India can in effect be amended by the Single Convention and such an argument is not admissible since it is inconsistent with the Constitution's text[64] and interpretation.[65]

62. *Id.* Article 1(c).
63. *See infra* Appendix B.
64. India Constitution Art. 368.
65. Gautam, *supra* note 47.

5

The Prohibition Era: Enactment of the Narcotic Drugs and Psychotropic Substances Act, 1985 (1985 to 2021)

"Marijuana is the most widely-used illicit drug, and the illicit drug most likely to be used by respectable folks. ... It is the most widely used illicit drug, precisely because its negative impact on most users tends to be much smaller than the impact of cocaine or methamphetamine."[*]

In this concluding chapter of this work, we continue our narrative from the previous two chapters, and here we will take a critical look at the manner in which Lok Sabha handled this issue. We must be sensitive to the fact that cannabis is not a dangerous plant, that even its regular consumption causes very little harm and only a very few people actually end up being dependent on it. It is used by people across the socio-economic, cultural, religious, educational, and educational spectrums. The rich and the poor have used it; the urban and the rural have used it; the lettered and the unlettered have used it; atheists, spiritualists, and religious people have all used it (perhaps with best results); those with recurring physical pain and serious psychological problems have used it; those who just wanted to relax their mind and body and have some harmless fun have used it; the young have used it and the old have used it; Hindus have used it[1] (in fact seems to have been using it even before the 'west' as we know it even existed on the globe), the Muslims have used it, the Christians have used it, the Sikhs have used it,[2] and I am quite sure if a survey is conducted no religion

* Prof. Mark Kleiman, author of Against Excess: Drug Policy for Results (1992); quoted at Cynthia S. Duncan, *The Need for Change: An Economic Analysis of Marijuana Policy*, 41 CONN. L. REV. 1701, 1706, 1707 (2009).

1. *See supra* Chapter 2, section (iii).
2. *Id.*

found and practiced in India would be left unrepresented in this list. Perhaps we might, in a 'light-hearted' moment, note the incredibly secular potential of this plant that seems to promote world peace by simply existing for human consumption! In a more serious context though, note that not one human being in the recorded history of cannabis has ever died of cannabis overdose.[3] And yet in India, criminal prohibition of cannabis (designated here as the 'Prohibition Era'[4]) was started in 1985 with the enactment of the Narcotic Drugs and Psychotropic Substances Act, 1985 ('NDPS Act'), the principal Indian legislation on the point that continues to be on statute book till the writing of this chapter. Parliament followed up the NDPS Act with the 'Prevention of Illicit Traffic in Narcotic Drugs and Psychotropic Substances Act' (Act 46 of 1988) that was given Presidential Assent on July 4, 1988. The statement of object and reasons of the 1988 Act says: "In recent years, India has been facing a problem of transit traffic in illicit drugs. The spillover from such traffic has caused problems of abuse and addition."[5] It is a short legislation with just 16 sections. The key provision is section 3 that allows any officer of either the Union, or State government above the rank of Joint Secretary to 'make an order directing that such person be detained.'[6] The preventive detention order so made can be 'executed at any place in India' and police powers for executing a warrant under the Code of Criminal Procedure, 1973 are available to execute such an order.[7] Surprisingly, the detention orders cannot be declared invalid or inoperative on the grounds that the detained person is outside the limits of territorial jurisdiction of the Government, or that the place of detention is

---

3. *See supra* Chapter 2, section (iv); see also Nick Wing, 'The Exhaustive List Of Everyone Who's Died Of A Marijuana Overdose', *Huffington Post*, August 30, 2018, available at: https://www.huffingtonpost.com.au/entry/marijuana-lethal-dose_n_58f4ec07e4b0b9e9848d6297 (last accessed July 3, 2021).
4. The title 'Prohibition Era' is drawn from a news-paper article this author earlier co-wrote. *See* Khagesh Gautam & Yashowardhan Tiwari, 'Cannabis: The Other Prohibition', *The Indian Express* (November 3, 2020), https://indianexpress.com/article/opinion/cannabis-the-other-prohibition-6927254/.
5. Prevention of Illicit Traffic in Narcotic Drugs and Psychotropic Substances Act, 1988, Statement of Object and Reasons, para 1.
6. *Id.* § 3(1). The full provision says: "Power to make orders detaining certain persons. (1) The Central Government or a State Government, or any officer of the Central Government, not below the rank of Joint Secretary to that Government, specially empowered for the purposes of this section by that Government, or any other officer a State Government, not below the rank of a Secretary to that Government, may, if satisfied, *with respect to any person (including a foreigner)* that, with a view to preventing him from engaging in illicit traffic in narcotic drugs and psychotropic substances, it is necessary so to do, make an order directing that such person be detained."
7. *Id.* § 4.

outside these limits.[8] The maximum period of detention is 'one year from the date of detention order,' but in some circumstances could be even 'two years from the date of detention.'[9] This summary legislation may raise additional constitutional concerns but concerns against the existence, and use of the emergency-like powers of preventive detention have been expressed in our country since even before the drafting of the Constitution. The power of preventive detention is the power of the government to detain any person in their custody without the benefit of any constitutional or procedural right (i.e. right to bail, right to be informed of the charges on which one is arrested, right to be tried by an independent criminal court, right to confront adverse evidence in open court, and several such rights mentioned in the Code of Criminal Procedure, 1973, as well as enunciated by the Supreme Court from time to time). This is a highly discretionary power that according to many constitutional experts is of an emergency character. Perhaps for this reason it has been kept largely immune from judicial review, but courts do intervene from time to time on established constitutional grounds.

In this chapter, we will critically examine the manner in which the 8th Lok Sabha debated the Narcotic Drugs and Psychotropic Substances Bill, 1985 ('NDPS Bill'). A brief history of the drafting of the NDPS Act is provided in part (i), a critical analysis is provided in part (ii), and ends with some concluding remarks in part (iii). Since every chapter has a concluding portion, and since you have made it to the last chapter, I trust you to draw your own conclusions, and therefore no separate concluding chapter is being provided. I rest this case, started in chapter 1, in part (iii) of this chapter.

i. Proceedings in Lok Sabha leading up to the enactment of NDPS Act

The Narcotic Drugs and Psychotropic Substances Bill, 1985 ('NDPS Bill') that later became the NDPS Act was introduced in the 8th Lok Sabha on August 23, 1985, by former Prime Minister Shri. Vishwanath Pratap Singh, who was the then Minister of Finance and Commerce in the cabinet led by the then Prime Minister Shri Rajiv Gandhi.[10] The NDPS Bill seems to have been introduced in response to

8. *Id.* § 7.
9. *Id.* § 11.
10. Lok Sabha Debates (August 23, 1985), Third Session (Eighth Lok Sabha), Vol. IX, No. 23 (Lok Sabha Secretariat), columns 331-332.

a 'calling attention' motion moved on August 7, 1985, by Shri Mool Chand Daga, MP (Pali).[11] This motion, titled 'Calling Attention to a matter of Urgent Public Importance,' was moved in response to a 'reported increase in the *smuggling* of heroin and other narcotic drugs in the country and its evil effects on our society, particularly the younger generation'.[12] Responding to this motion the Minister of State for Finance Shri Janardhana Poojary ('MoS Finance') noted:

> *"There has been an increase in drug trafficking particularly in heroin and cannabis resin in recent past. This is mainly due to the fact that the Near and Middle East Region, and more particularly Pakistan, in recent years, has emerged as a major producer and supplier of opiates and cannabis resin. ... This is also evident from the recent reports of International Narcotics Control Board. In its report from the year 1984 the Board has, inter alia, observed that, "India is increasingly used as a transit country for opiates and cannabis destined for other regions of the world and New Delhi and Bombay are reportedly the most important exit points for these drugs."*[13]

After assuring the House that 'field formations remain vigilant to *check smuggling* including that of narcotics,' and that 'appropriate *anti-smuggling* measures' to '*curb smuggling of drugs*' were being taken by Union and State authorities, MoS Finance further assured the House that, "A draft comprehensive legislation on Narcotic Drugs and Psychotropic Substances inter-alia providing deterrent punishment to check smuggling of such drugs is at an advanced stage of finalisation for introduction in Parliament."[14] Thereafter, the NDPS Bill was introduced in the Lok Sabha on August 23, 1985, by the then Minister of Finance and Commerce,[15] which was debated on August 26[16] and August 28, 1985,[17] before being enacted into law. On August 29, 1985, the Secretary-General, as per 'rule 127 of the Rules of Procedure and Conduct of Business in Rajya Sabha' informed the Lok Sabha that the Rajya Sabha had, "... at its sitting held on 29th August, 1985, agreed without any amendment to the Narcotic Drugs and Psychotropic Substances Bill, 1985, which was passed by

11. Lok Sabha Debates (August 7, 1985), Third Session (Eighth Lok Sabha), Vol. VIII, No.12 (Lok Sabha Secretariat), column 272.
12. *Id.*
13. *See* Lok Sabha Debates (August 7, 1985), *supra* note 11, columns 273-276. (Emphasis Added)
14. *Id.* at columns 274-75.
15. Lok Sabha Debates (August 23, 1985), *supra* note 10.
16. Lok Sabha Debates (August 26, 1985), Third Session (Eighth Lok Sabha), Vol. IX, No. 24 (Lok Sabha Secretariat), columns 193-202.
17. Lok Sabha Debates (August 28, 1985), Third Session (Eighth Lok Sabha), Vol. IX, No. 25 (Lok Sabha Secretariat), columns 15-79.

the Lok Sabha at its sitting held on the 28th August, 1985."[18] A copy of the NDPS Bill, now passed by both Houses of Parliament and assented to by the President became the NDPS Act. It was laid on the table of the Lok Sabha on November 18, 1985.[19]

ii. Critical Analysis of Lok Sabha Debates on the NDPS Act

A critical analysis of the Lok Sabha debates on the NDPS Bill leading up to the enactment of the NDPS Act shows that these debates left much to be desired. This work deals specifically with cannabis, but cannabis was not the plant that captured the imagination of the 16 MPs[20] who contributed to this debate. The Lok Sabha debates leading up to the enactment of the NDPS Act are liable to be criticized on the following eight grounds. It should be stated at the outset that these eight critiques are by no means intended to be exhaustive, and only illustrative. For the sake of brevity, note in advance that these eight critiques are variously, as well as independently, capable of supporting any of the three key points made in this work, *viz.* (a) from a legal standpoint, the case that possession of cannabis[21] in India should be 'decriminalized,'; (b) from a policy standpoint, trade in cannabis in India should be 'legalized,' but it is beyond the brief of this work to contemplate as to what type of model would be most suited for the Indian market; and (c) from a constitutional standpoint, it is highly doubtful whether Parliament has the power to criminalize it.

(a) The Debate was mostly about opium

First, the plant that captured the imagination of the MPs who participated in this debate was opium. There was hardly any discussion on any other plant except opium, and a large part of the debate was dominated by a discussion to

18. Lok Sabha Debates (August 29, 1985), Third Session (Eighth Lok Sabha), Vol. IX, No. 26 (Lok Sabha Secretariat), column 154.
19. Lok Sabha Debates (November 18, 1985), Fourth Session (Eighth Lok Sabha), Vol. X, No. 1 (Lok Sabha Secretariat), column 348, 349 (entry 12).
20. A total of 16 MPs participated in the debate. MoS Finance Janardan Poojari noted their contribution in his closing speech when he rose to answer the questions posed by many of these members, who all spoke in favour of the NDPS Bill but not without pointing out several limitations therein. *See* Lok Sabha Debates (August 28, 1985), *supra* note 17 at column 56. Addressing the Deputy Speaker (who was in Chair) MoS Finance noted, "Sir, about 16 hon. Members participated in this debate."
21. As defined in the NDPS Act, 1985, § 2(iii).

protect the interests of the opium farmers cultivating opium on license. Cannabis was not spoken about in any intelligent detail by any member on these two days. Even though the NDPS Bill was introduced to 'consolidate and amend' the law relating to all sorts of 'narcotic drugs,'[22] on August 26 and 28 almost all MPs focused their attention on opium cultivation.[23] Cannabis cultivation was mentioned only once and the claim, consistent with the general tone of the debate, was overstated[24] and clearly did not inspire as much emotion as the plight of the opium farmers.

(b) Cannabis plant equated with opium plant

Second, the MPs that spoke on these two days, especially the one who had moved the calling attention motion on August 7, 1985, himself equated the cannabis plant with the opium plant. Shri Mool Chand Daga, MP (Pali), who had moved the calling attention motion just a few days earlier,[25] on August 26 and 28, 1985 made the following statements in Lok Sabha while speaking in support of the NDPS Bill:

> *"Recently, we came across a news item that the students and the research scholars in the laboratory of Lucknow University were selling opium in the form of heroin and hasish.*[26] *... Heroin and Hasish is also the same thing. They are all derived from opium."*[27]

22. *See e.g.,* Lok Sabha Debates (August 26, 1985), *supra* note 16 at column 193 (MoS Finance introducing the NDPS Bill on behalf of Minister of Finance and Commerce); Narcotic Drugs and Psychotropic Substances Act, 1985, Preamble.
23. Lok Sabha Debates (August 7, 1985), *supra* note 11, column 279 (Mool Chand Daga (Pali)), columns 287-88 (Amitabh Bachchan (Allahabad)); Lok Sabha Debates (August 28, 1985), *supra* note 17 at column 16 (Manoj Pandey (Bettiah) equating cannabis consumption with opium consumption), at columns 22-25 Balkavi Bairagi (Mandsaur) highlighting the plight of opium farmers general and specifically in his constituency and surrounding areas); at column 32-37 (Jujhar Singh (Jhalawar), supporting Balkavi Bairagi and also highlighting the plight of opium farmers in his constituency); at column 41 Ramashray Prasad Singh (Jahanabad) highlighting the fact that, "Opium is cultivated in many States of our country ...,"at column 52 (Mool Chand Daga (Pali)), at columns 41-42 (Ramashray Prasad Singh, MP (Jahanabad), highlighting that, "Opium is cultivated in many States in our country.").
24. Lok Sabha Debates (August 28, 1985), *supra* note 17 at column 43-44 (Somnath Rath (Aska) stating that, "In Jammu and Kashmir, charas and ganja are being cultivated in the fields and the fields meant for vegetables, cereals etc. are converted for this cultivation.")
25. Lok Sabha Debates (August 7, 1985), *supra* note 11 at columns 272-73.
26. Lok Sabha Debates (August 26, 1985), *supra* note 16 at column 52.
27. Lok Sabha Debates (August 28, 1985), *supra* note 17 at column 54.

This was a very unfortunate remark to be made in Lok Sabha, and Daga was not the only one who made it.[28] What makes it even more unfortunate is that it was made by the very same MP whose calling attention motion led to the introduction of the NDPS Bill. The propriety of making a grave allegation against 'students and research scholars of Lucknow University' such as this on the basis only of a news item itself is questionable but is perhaps explained by the Daga's personal views on heroin addiction.[29] It will be seen Daga cites nothing (not even the name of the newspaper, or the date of the 'news item') in support of this serious allegation. But Daga had made a similar unsubstantiated remark on August 7, 1985, when he rose to speak in support of his calling attention motion.[30] On top of that, adding to the misfortune of the above-quoted remark is the fact that it was made *after* the introduction of the NDPS Bill. 'Cannabis' as defined in section 2(iii) the NDPS Act (and also so defined in the NDPS Bill) includes three things: the "flowering or fruiting tops of the cannabis plant (*except* the seeds and leaves when not accompanied by the tops),"[31] the "separated resin, in whatever form, whether crude or purified, obtained from the cannabis plant and also includes concentrated preparation and resin known as hashish oil or liquid hashish,"[32] and any 'mixture' or 'drink' prepared 'therefrom.'[33] A 'cannabis plant' means 'any plant of the genus cannabis.'[34] If Daga would have taken care to consult just the definition of cannabis as provided in the NDPS Bill, it would have become clear to him that what he called 'hasish,' and what the NDPS Bill defined as *charas*, is just another name for the substance obtained from 'cannabis resin,' and has nothing to do with opium. This would also have been clear to

---

28. Lok Sabha Debates (August 28, 1985), *supra* note 17 at column 16 (Manoj Pandey (Bettiah) equating cannabis consumption with opium consumption).
29. Lok Sabha Debates (August 7, 1985), *supra* note 11, column 276 (Mool Chand Daga (Pali), speaking in support of the calling attention motion, "Heroin has ruined the lives of many people.").
30. *Id.* ("One lack young men of India have become addicts of these narcotics and as a result thereof they are leading a miserable life.") Daga offers no support for this, cites no source to support this number, and at no point of time he explains what he means by an 'addict'.
31. NDPS Act, 1985, § 2(iii)(b) ("*ganja*, that is, the the flowering or fruiting tops of the cannabis plant (excluding the seeds and leaves when not accompanied by the tops), by whatever name they may be known or designated;").
32. *Id.* at § 2 (iii)(a) ("*charas*, that is, the separated resin, in whatever form, whether crude or purified, obtained from the cannabis plant and also includes concentrated preparation and resin known as hashish oil or liquid hashish;").
33. *Id.* at § 2(iii)(c), ("any mixture, with or without any neutral material, of any of the above forms of cannabis or any drink prepared therefrom;").
34. *Id.* at § 2(iv) ("cannabis plant means any plant of the genus cannabis").

Daga if he would have taken care to consult the Dangerous Drugs Act, 1930.[35] This lack of information about these plants (perhaps for want of study,) and the narcotics that are derived from them led to a misunderstanding or a lack of proper understanding that then, unfortunately, plagued the views of almost all 16 MPs who participated in this debate. Made in another place, and at another time, some might agree that this alone might provide sufficient legislative grounds for this issue to be re-debated. There is, of course, an urgent need for this to be publicly discussed, and academically examined. And this brings us to the third critique.

(c) Debate filled with contradictory, unsubstantiated, and outlandish claims

Third, MPs who spoke on August 7, 1985, *before* the NDPS Bill was introduced, and those who spoke in its favour on August 26 and 28, 1985 *after* it was introduced made contradictory remarks filled with insensitive, unsubstantiated, and outlandish claims. For instance, take the following remark of Shri Daga, made on August 7, 1985:

> *"Narcotic consumption is not confined to universities and their campuses alone. Religious places have also come under its grip. In religious places like Puri in India, priests consume charas and ganja in front of the deity. The people of Orissa know it very well. Even in Varanasi, in temples sadhus consume ganja, charas, etc. in front of the deity chanting "Bum-Bum Bhole Nath". This is a common scene everywhere in Varanasi. No religious place is free from the use of narcotics."*[36]

The practice of using cannabis to induce or facilitate spiritual experience(s) is nothing new in India and has been discussed earlier in this work.[37] For Daga to claim that 'no religious place is free from the use of narcotics' is a totally baseless, unsubstantiated, hyperbolic, and insensitive claim. The use of narcotics, specifically cannabis, e.g., Shiva and Shakti worship has a long tradition in Indian civilization and is either permissible or even considered necessary in some forms of worship. To the extent it is used in some forms of worship, the fact is nothing new and was recorded after a detailed survey by the Indian Hemp Drugs Commission as far back as 1894.[38] As if adding insult to injury, Daga then links the spirituo-religious use of cannabis with 'terrorists and extremists' but then

35. *See* Dangerous Drugs Act, 1930, § 2(c) (defining 'hemp' in similar way as 'cannabis' is defined in the NDPS Act); § 2(e) (defining 'opium').

36. Lok Sabha Debates (August 7, 1985), *supra* note 11, column 276.

37. *See supra* Chapter 2, section (iii), section (vi), section (viii), and read accompanying text of notes 71, 154 and 175.

38. *See supra* Chapter 3, section (ii), note 42.

immediately contradicts his own remarks by now saying that it is not cannabis but 'heroin and smack' (that are derived from opium, not cannabis) that is reaching temples.[39]

As noted above, it was smuggling of opium-based narcotics from neighbouring states,[40] most notably Pakistan, that was the key concern in the minds of MPs who spoke on August 26 and 28, 1985. With respect to opium cultivation in neighbouring Nepal, the concern of the MP who stated this fact seems more to do with highlighting the 'big scale' of international opium trade and unfairness of prices fetched for the substance.[41] We will return to this point later. Shri Anoopchand Shah, MP (Bombay North) on August 28, 1985, said:

> *"Narcotic drugs are being used in abundance in our Metropolitan cities like Bombay, Madras, Calcutta, etc. ... I do not want to name any country, but a country which has never been able to defeat nor can it defeat India in any of the wars may, by demoralising the people by making them addicts of these drugs defeat this country."*[42]

Shri Daga, speaking on August 7, 1985, in support of his calling attention motion had also alluded to similar facts in the larger context of illegal drug smuggling from Pakistan.[43] This fact was also alluded to by one of our greatest and internationally acclaimed film-actors Shri Amitabh Bachchan, MP (Allahabad),[44] acknowledged by the MoS Finance,[45] and re-stated by other MPs who contributed to the debate.[46] Almost all of these claims were also, consistent with the general tone of the debate, either baseless or highly exaggerated.[47]

---

39. Lok Sabha Debates (August 7, 1985), *supra* note 11, column 279 ("Now, terrorists and extremists are also engaged in these activities. May I know how and why this heroin and smack have reached temples, sacred places and big institutions?").
40. Opium cultivation in Nepal and its smuggling into India was noted by Dr. G. S. Rajhans, MP (Jhanjharpur). *See* Lok Sabha Debates (August 7, 1985), *supra* note 11, at column 298.
41. Lok Sabha Debates (August 7, 1985), *supra* note 11, at column 298 (Dr. G. S. Rajhans, MP (Jhanjharpur) said: "Opium is cultivated in Nepal without any restriction. Its cultivation is legal there. I have seen it with own eyes. One Kg. of opium costs Rs. 2,000 in Nepal. After coming into India, it sells at Rs. 30,000 and in U.S.A. it sells at Rs. 3 lacks. You are not aware that this trade is going on a big scale.").
42. Lok Sabha Debates (August 28, 1985), *supra* note 17, at columns 35, 36.
43. Lok Sabha Debates (August 7, 1985), *supra* note 11, at column 281.
44. *Id.* at column 287-88.
45. *Id.* at column 282.
46. *See e.g.,* Lok Sabha Debates (August 28, 1985), *supra* note 17, at columns 46-47 (Shantaram Naik, MP (Panaji)).
47. *Id.*

On the other hand, Dr. Krupasindhu Bhoi, MP (Sambalpur) was of the view that it was Central Intelligence Agency (CIA) that was involved in hooking Indian youth to opium.[48] Dr. Bhoi, raised the question: "What are the CIA people in the name of 'box item' doing about the use of narcotics by the students?"[49] and moments later answered it himself: "Some CIA and other people educate the students in the anti-India culture. They give smack in the cigarette, tobacco etc."[50] In so far as the claim of drug smuggling from Pakistan, and the larger geographical area known as the Golden Crescent, the fact of opium cultivation and international smuggling thereof has been painstakingly documented by highly respected journalist Gretchen Peters in her 2010 book 'Seeds of Terror.'[51] Even though written more than a decade ago, the work is still relevant to understanding the narco-smuggling trade routes. Very few journalists have been able to document international opium smuggling originating in Afghanistan as Peters has done in her book. Flying in the face of these documented facts pertaining to opium cultivation was the following remark of Dr. G. S. Rajhans, MP (Jhanjharpur): "With the occupation of Afghanistan by the Soviet Union, U.S.S.R. laws are strictly enforced there due to which drug abuse is not possible in Afghanistan. All these activities have now been shifted to Pakistan. Drug abuse in Iran is also not possible due to Islamic Laws."[52] No such thing ever happened or is even happening now.[53] To say that Pakistan is actively involved in using opium smuggling into India as a way to destabilize the country (notwithstanding the factual merit of such a claim, an investigation whereof is outside the stated scope of this work,) and the fact that India happens to be in a geographical location that makes several seaports and land-locations in India to be attractive transit points in a much larger international drug shipping routes are two very different things. As noted by Shri Amitabh Bachchan, MP (Allahabad) on August 7, 1985: "Geographically, India happens to be sandwiched between the two regions which are known for narcotics and its growth. In the international terminology, they are generally called "the golden crescent" and "the golden triangle."[54]

---

48. Lok Sabha Debates (August 28, 1985), *supra* note 17, at columns 55, 64.
49. *Id.* at column 55.
50. *Id.* at column 64.
51. Gretchen Peters, *Seeds of Terror: How Drugs, Thugs, and Crime Are Reshaping the Afghan War* (2010, Macmillan).
52. Lok Sabha Debates (August 7, 1985), *supra* note 11, at column 298.
53. *See generally* Peters, *supra* note 51.
54. Lok Sabha Debates (August 7, 1985), *supra* note 11, at column 287.

On August 7, 1985, speaking in support of Daga's calling attention motion, the MoS Finance noted that there was indeed "an increase in drug trafficking *particularly in heroin and cannabis resin* in recent past. *This is mainly due to the fact that the Near and Middle East Region, and more particularly Pakistan, in recent years, has emerged as a major producer and supplier of opiates and cannabis resin.*"[55] Quoting a report from the International Narcotics Control Board the MoS Finance noted that India "*is increasingly used as a transit country for opiates and cannabis resin destined for others regions of the world and New Delhi and Bombay are reportedly the most important exit points for these drugs.*"[56] But from this, the Minister jumps to the following: "In India the abuse of opium and cannabis (Ganja), the traditional drugs of abuse continues in a limited way. ... [T]he magnitude of the problem will be known only on completion of the comprehensive survey which has been undertaken by the Ministry of Social and Women's welfare."[57] Several other members referred to this pending survey and on the basis thereof made hyperbolic claims.[58] It is not clear from the speech of MoS Finance what he meant by 'abuse.' This brings us to the fourth critique.

(d) Lack of proper understanding of 'addiction', 'abuse,' 'gateway drug theory,' etc.

*"Millions ... have used marijuana on a regular, almost daily basis for decades. Despite these massive numbers of long-term users, no reliable evidence has appeared that such use has any adverse effects on their physical health ... [I]n no less than nine official investigations of the problem, in both the United States and elsewhere, none have found any significant adverse effects on humans."**

Fourth, several key concepts like 'abuse,' and 'addiction' were never explained by any MP who spoke on these three crucial days: August 7, 1985 (*before* the NDPS Bill was introduced) and August 26, and 28, 1985 (*after* the introduction

55. *Id.* at column 273. (Emphasis Added).
56. *Id.* at column 274. (Emphasis Added).
57. *Id.*
58. *See e.g.*, Lok Sabha Debates (August 28, 1985), *supra* note 17, at columns 46-47.

* Steven B. Duke & Albert C. Gross, America's Longest War: Rethinking Our Tragic Crusade Against Drugs 51 (1993).

of the NDPS Bill, and leading up to its enactment).[59] What exactly did the MoS Finance, and several other MPs who used these terms, mean by them was never explained or debated? To begin with, it is not clear on what basis the MoS Finance claimed that drug 'abuse' is going on in metropolitan cities when the very survey to find out whether there is any 'abuse' going on was pending.[60] Shri Daga's speech on August 7, 1985, suffers from the same defect when he claims, without citing any source to support his claim that 100,000 'young men of India have become addicts.'[61] It will be seen that even in the U.S. there are those who, despite mounting evidence,[62] continue to 'maintain that marijuana is extremely harmful and addictive, with no medically therapeutic use.'[63] Legal scholars have been at pains to point out that cannabis is 'far less addictive' than opioids, and that 'there is no documented evidence of death resulting from its use, even in large doses.'[64] Pharmacology professionals have now demonstrated that an overdose of delta-9 THC (the psychoactive compound in cannabis) is not lethal.[65] At most, it increases the heart rate and systolic blood pressure but that is 'dose related' and its 'onset and duration correlate well with the concentration of [THC] in blood.'[66] No consistent changes in respiratory rate were found as well.[67] As Dr. Maté, a highly respected Canadian medical

59. *See e.g.* Lok Sabha Debates (August 7, 1985), *supra* note 11, at columns 292, 296 (Dharam Pal Singh Malik, MP (Sonepat) staing that, "The addiction to heroin and other narcotic drugs has badly affected the social and economic fabric of the country," Dr. G. S. Rajhans, MP (Jhanjharpur); Lok Sabha Debates (August 28, 1985), *supra* note 17, at columns 18 (R. P. Das, MP (Krishnagar)), at column 26 (Ajay Mushran, MP (Jabalpur)), at column 37 (V. S. Krishna Iyer, MP (Bangalore South)); Lok Sabha Debates (August 28, 1985), *supra* note 17 at column 43-44 (Somnath Rath (Aska)).
60. Lok Sabha Debates (August 7, 1985), *supra* note 11, at column 274.
61. *Id.* at column 276.
62. *See e.g.,* Mark A.R. Kleiman, 'Against Excess: Drug Policy for Result' 256 (1992) stating that, "[M]illions of persons who started smoking marijuana as college students in the late 1960s, some of whom have been taking the drug more or less regularly ever since, have suffered neither obvious immediate damage nor dramatic aftereffects ... [I]f occasional marijuana smoking over [decades] carried substantial health risks, the evidence should have started to come in by now."
63. Cynthia S. Duncan, 'The Need for Change: An Economic Analysis of Marijuana Policy', 41 CONN. L. REV. 1701, 1706 (2009).
64. Peter J. Cohen, 'Medical Marijuana: The Conflict between Scientific Evidence and Political Ideology', 2009 UTAH L. REV. 35, 37 (2009).
65. Michael Walker & Susan M. Huang, 'Cannabinoid Analgesia', 95 PHARMACOLOGY & THERAPEUTICS, 127, 133 (2002).
66. Jerome H. Jaffe & William R. Martin, 'Opioid Analgesics and Antagonists', in *Goodman & Gilman's The Pharmacological Basis of Therapeutics* 561 (Alfred Goodman Gilman et al., eds., 6th ed. 1980).
67. *Id.*

authority on addiction observes: "There is nothing more intrinsically criminal in the average drug user than in the average cigarette smoker or alcohol addict. The drugs they inject or inhale do not themselves induce criminal activity by their pharmacological effect, *except* perhaps in the way that alcohol can fuel a person's pent up aggression and remove mental inhibitions that thwart violence. ... *The criminality associated with addiction follows directly from the need to raise money to purchase drugs at prices that are artificially inflated owing to their illegality.*"[68]

Daga then goes on to make another outlandish claim that politicians at the highest level are involved in drug smuggling, and that it cannot be stopped unless these politicians are disqualified from holding office.[69] And pray how exactly are they to be disqualified, and upon what evidence, is something that Daga perhaps left to the judicial branch. Luckily, when an MP asked the MoS Finance to respond to Daga's patently outlandish claim that '50 per cent of the students in Delhi' are somehow addicted to an assortment of narcotic drugs,[70] the Minister skilfully sidestepped this landmine.[71]

One MP made his remarks based on the now-debunked 'gateway drug theory,'[72] but to be fair this theory was debunked only recently[73] and these remarks can be explained away on the ground that we did not know better in 1985. However, medicinal uses of cannabis were well known in India in 1985 and it is fair to say that members were familiar with Title 21 of the United States Code, section 812(1), which lists the following three criteria of schedule I drugs or substances: (a) it should have a high potential for abuse; (b) has no currently accepted medical use in treatment in the U.S.; and (c) lack of accepted safety for

---

68. Gabor Maté, *In the Realm of Hungry Ghosts: Close Encounters with Addiction* 306 (2018, Vermilion London).
69. Lok Sabha Debates (August 7, 1985), *supra* note 11, at column. 279. ("Unless politicians found involved in smuggling irrespective of their being members of Lok Sabha, Rajya Sabha or Vidhan Sabha are disqualified from membership of these bodies and are disgraced it is not possible to check smuggling.").
70. *Id.* at column 282 (E. Ayyapu Reddy, MP asking a question to MoS Finance: "Shri Daga has said that 50 per cent of the students in Delhi are affected by it. Do you agree with that?").
71. *Id.* (MoS Finance Janardan Poojari responding to question asked as stated in note 53).
72. *See e.g.,* Lok Sabha Debates (August 28, 1985), *supra* note 17 at column 50 (S. Jaipal Reddy, MP (Mahbubnagar) said: "They start off with hashish, charas and then go on to heavier stuff like LSD, cocaine and barbiturates etc.").
73. David C. Peters II, 'Patients and Caregivers Report Using Medical Marijuana to Decrease Prescription Narcotics Use', 35 HUMBOLDT JOURNAL OF SOCIAL RELATIONS, 24-40, 25 (2013). *See* Chapter 2, section (iv).

use of the drug or other substances under medical supervision.[74] None of these three grounds, if they are superimposed on Indian conditions, would be satisfied. Like any other substance that is capable of being abused, cannabis is not special and not exempt from such a charge. But it is not correct to say that cannabis is inherently addictive. Just like many people who consume a glass of beer in college (in many cases more than just a glass!) and do not go on to become alcoholics, and are able to live responsible adult lives, many people who consume cannabis live their lives the same way. Just like many of these responsible adults who still might enjoy a glass of beer now and then, many still might enjoy a bit of cannabis now and then. In absence of anything inherently dangerous in the plant itself, and it being subject to the same type of abuse that tobacco, or alcohol, or gambling,[75] or any number of other substance and behavioural addictions; and in light of all the arguments made in this book, it would appear that there are good grounds for cannabis prohibition in India to be reconsidered. We now know better. We therefore must change our laws. Note here again that not only no one has ever died of a cannabis overdose, it seems to be highly unlikely that death could be caused by it anyway; and it is safe to consume under medical supervision, or otherwise. It is a sad tragedy that not one member of the 8th Lok Sabha pointed this out in Lok Sabha. It is not correct to suggest that relevant authorities and materials were not available in 1985, so somehow the 8th Lok Sabha should not be responsible for this grievous oversight. Much research has been published thereafter, but in 1985 itself plenty of authoritative materials were available for these points to be raised. Perhaps if the Bill was sent to some sort of bipartisan parliamentary committee for further study, as was pointed out during the debates,[76] some of these issues would have become clearer to the law-makers. If this suggestion seems impertinent, it would be only because of my own ignorance of how parliament actually works. But still, much of this would have been clear if the issue would have been treated with the care that it deserved by the 8th Lok Sabha. But there is nothing stopping future Lok Sabhas to correct such errors of the past.

74. *See* 21 U.S.C. § 812(1), Schedule I.

75. *See e.g.*, Maté, *supra* note 68 at 215, for a discussion on gambling, and other behavioral addictions, e.g., shopping, sex, eating, etc., and it is submitted that an addiction to excessive use of social-media can safely be added to this illustrative list. This highlights the fact that addictions could be substantive or behavioral, and this indeed is a grave limitation in the 8th Lok Sabha's approach, as is highlighted throughout this section.

76. Lok Sabha Debates (August 28, 1985), *supra* note 17, at column 37-38.

Similarly, Shri Shantaram Naik, MP (Panaji) made the claim that "In Pakistan, almost 61 per cent of the drug addicts are in rural areas and only 39 per cent of them are rural areas. Even in Madras Medical College, about 70 per cent of male interns are resorting to drug addiction and 20 per cent female interns. These are factual figures that we are well aware of."[77] But Naik offers no support for these figures, cites no source to support them, and everyone else in the House seems to have taken these figures on their face. But Naik goes further and makes a further outlandish claim that "terrorism and drug addiction are very much related to each other *because those who are not taking to these drugs are being administered and they are asked to commit this heinous crime. It is only by taking these drugs, this heinous crime can be committed and we have also to see this in the light of this terrorism which is increasing.*"[78] At this point, the third critique and the fourth critique merge. It is not clear whether the word 'addiction' is being used as synonymous with 'use'. Furthermore, it is unfortunate that Naik makes this connection between drug 'addiction' and 'terrorism' for it is based on a fundamental misunderstanding of both.

While it is correct to say that the illegal drug trade is a source of revenue for terrorist outfits operating out of Afghanistan and Pakistan,[79] such outfits routinely resort to all sorts of the criminal enterprise (e.g. kidnapping, extortion, contract-killing, illegal drug-smuggling, etc.) in order to finance their nefarious activities, but the day cannabis prohibition ends and it is converted into a legitimate business activity and legitimate capital is infused with talented and enterprising young minds, from that day illegal drug-smuggling would cease to be an area from where such groups could finance their activities. There is a more detailed national security perspective that perhaps needs to be articulated rather than just asserted, but it falls outside the scope of this work.

It is important to understand the core of the argument about illegal drug smuggling. The point here is not that if you cannot beat them, you join them. The point is that what you are trying to beat is actually your friend and there is no need to engage in conflict with it. In that sense what you are trying to beat is joining you, waiting, as it were, like a long-lost friend, for you to open the door! Maybe it wonders why you are so mad at it! All it wants to do, it seems, is to make you smile. If tomorrow, suddenly alcohol and tobacco were to be prohibited across the territory of our republic, in my considered opinion, it

77. *Id.* at column 46.
78. *Id.* at 46-47.
79. *See generally* Peters, *supra* note 51.

would be quite unreasonable, and even irrational to believe that such a prohibition would have the desired effect. Such prohibitions have never worked in the past, and are unlikely to work in the present since they are not consistent with human nature. Life is full of pain, and it is human, all too human, to desire relief from that suffering. For some humans, it can take the form of physical pain, and for others psychological. The argument that cannabis should be legalized cannot be invalidated on the ground that it sets a precedent, for e.g., to legalize kidnapping! Since we cannot stop these criminal groups from kidnapping, why don't we legalize kidnapping itself and license this activity? That is absurd. Being kidnapped cannot provide relief from human suffering. It would probably traumatize the victim who might actually require medicinal cannabis to heal.

Growing and selling ganja, and charas (as any other illegal substance) are profitable activities with a relatively stable demand, respectable margins, and a well-organized distribution network.[80] This activity is criminal only because our laws have declared it to be so, and it should be clear by now that before 1985 the very same activities were subject to duties of excise under our own laws. There is no reason why the situation can't be the same again.

I hope it would be clear by now that terror outfits will resort to any criminal activities that provide a sufficiently high rate of return. Hypothetically speaking, if trade in cannabis is legalized and regulated, cannabis farmers in Afghanistan, Pakistan, Nepal, or India can carry on their trade legally, pay taxes to their respective governments and to those where their products are exported, provide employment to thousands, create sister industries like cannabis tourism, and secure a life of relative peace and prosperity for themselves and their families. This pie (in terms of market size) seems to be pretty big and there seems to be plenty for everyone! To say that cannabis farmers, unlicensed opium cultivators in India, and opium cultivators in Afghanistan and Pakistan are the same as terrorists and should be legally and politically treated as such is to make a very fundamental error of attribution. Terror outfits resort to the illegal drug trade to raise finances for their nefarious operations. The farmers who cultivate these plants are not necessarily terrorists. The distinction is crucial to identify the true

80. *See e.g.*, Maté, *supra* note 68 at 277. ("A major study conducted on behalf of British government in 2005 illustrated both the rich benefits that current drug legislation confers on major traffickers of heroin and the ludicrous impotence of law enforcement efforts against the drug trade. "The profit margins for major traffickers of heroin into Britain are so high they outstrip luxury goods companies such as Louis Vuitton and Gucci," reported the *Guardian*. ... In North American the situation is no different.").

troublemakers and distinguish them from those whose who freely decide to cultivate cannabis or opium. In this context it would be important to note the findings of Daniela Berti who studied NDPS Act prosecutions at ground level in Himachal Pradesh, and in the course of the study found that:

> *"[V]illagers involved in the cultivation of cannabis strongly emphasize the cultural value attributed to cannabis, the cultivation of which, they say, is a traditional practice that has been maintained exclusively for domestic and religious purposes. Local newspapers give a great deal of visibility to this discourse, often reporting that villagers consider cannabis cultivation to have been approved by their village deities. For example, an article appeared in The Tribue in 2004, entitled 'Where devta tells them [villagers] to grow cannabis' includes statements from a number of villagers, who claimed that 'unless Jamlu god tells us to grow other crops, we will grow only cannabis'. Furthermore, the vice-president of Malana village, a place in the region famous for growing cannabis, is quoted as saying, 'Cannabis has been grown here since time immemorial'."*[81]

A closer examination of the debates also shows that the misunderstanding with respect to the question of substance abuse was central to the introduction of the NDPS Bill. Shri Dal Chander Jain, M.P. (Damoh) noted in his speech supporting the NDPS Bill, 'as the use of narcotics has increased in our young generation, the need to bring this Bill has arisen."[82] Speaking before him, the MoS Finance, who defended the Bill in the Lok Sabha, had also highlighted that 'abuse of opium and cannabis' continued in India in a limited way.[83] The MoS expressed concern about 'heroin emerging as a drug of choice,' and also said that the abuse of these substances has mostly been reported from 'metropolitan cities.'[84] Here, it will be interesting to note that a recent survey conducted in 2019 by the Ministry of Social Justice and Empowerment, in collaboration with the National Drug Dependence Treatment Centre, AIIMS, New Delhi, showed that, "[a]bout 2.8% of Indians aged 10-75 years (3.1 crore individuals) are current users of any cannabis product. More number of people use bhang (2%) as compared charas/ganja (1.2%). There is a preponderance of men among

81. Daniela Berti, 'Binding Fictions: Contradicting Facts and Judicial Constraints in a Narcotics Case in Himachal Pradesh', 94, 97 in Daniela Berti & Devika Bordia, *Regimes of Legality: Ethnography of Criminal Cases in South Asia* (2015, Oxford University Press). (Internal Citations Omitted).
82. Lok Sabha Debates (August 28, 1985), *supra* note 17, at column 59-40.
83. Lok Sabha Debates (August 7, 1985), *supra* note 11, column 274.
84. *Id.*

consumers of cannabis. ... *Overall, just about 0.25% Indians use cannabis in a dependent pattern.*"[85]

Daga, who had moved the 'calling attention' motion on August 7, 1985, also said that, "[h]eroin has ruined the lives of many people. ... One lakh young men of India have become addicts of these narcotics and *as a result thereof* they are leading a miserable life."[86] Even though it is unfortunate that neither of these two speakers provided any definitive or even helpful description or definition of addiction, Daga did call upon the Minister who explained to the House, "what the Department of Social Welfare had done to save the young men from becoming drug-addicts ?"[87] Shri Dharam Pal Singh Malik, M.P. (Sonepat) also stated that addiction to heroin and other narcotic drugs had 'badly affected the social and economic fabric of the country.'[88] Some members made the astonishing claim that substance addiction is an inherently western phenomenon and that corrective measures are urgently required to be taken to arrest its import into India.[89] Even though awareness campaigns were recommended by some members as a preventive measure designed to arrest the problem of addiction,[90] it is submitted that such campaigns would have been hopelessly ineffective because of a complete misunderstanding of what is it that people are required to be made aware of. For instance, Shri V.S. Krishna Iyer, MP (Bangalore South), narrated the following instance in his speech supporting the NDPS Bill: "One

---

85. Government of India, Ministry of Social Justice and Empowerment, Magnitude of Substance Use in India 2019, p. 17 (2019) (available at: http://socialjustice.nic.in/writereaddata/UploadFile/Magnitude_Substance_Use_India_REPORT.pdf.)
86. Lok Sabha Debates (August 7, 1985), *supra* note 11, column 276.
87. *Id.* at column 277.
88. *Id.* at column 292. Malik also highlighted that cannabis was being cultivated in 'our country alone.' He however seems to be completely unaware of the long history of religious, spiritual and cultural use of cannabis in India that has been highlighted earlier in this work. *See* Chapter 2, section (iii). Malik also overemphasized the extent of the problem. In his own words, "If we do not fight this evil the country will be like a deadbody in no time." *Id.* The problem with this suggestion is that the evil that the country has to fight is not clearly defined anywhere. On the other hand, going by the 2019 Ministry of Social Justice and Empowerment Magnitude of Substance Use in India survey only 2.8% of Indians were found to be current cannabis users. *See* Magnitude of Substance Use in India 2019, *supra* note 85 at 17. It is not very clear how the consumption of a plant by 2.8% of the people could possibly be an evil that would leave the country like a dead body. Furthermore, it is not possible to call such an activity an 'evil' in the first place.
89. *See e.g.,* Lok Sabha Debates (August 28, 1985), *supra* note 17, at column 38 (V. S. Krishna Iyer); column 45 (Somnath Rath).
90. Lok Sabha Debates (August 28, 1985), *supra* note 17, at column 38-39.

instance I would like to mention that one of the rickshaw pullers who was engaged in this drug peddling became suddenly rich because of his drug peddling since there is huge profit in this trade. It so happened that he had become very familiar with the drug addicts, particularly with those Hippies. He married one of the French women to whom he supplied that drug. He went with her to France. Ultimately, she deserted him and he remained a drug addict. Now he is completely ruined. This is authentic information which has been reported in Karnataka papers."[91] It is unclear from this instance exactly what this is supposed to prove! To begin with, the narration of the story betrays a lack of proper understanding of the physiological as well as psychological nature of addiction. In addition to that, it is not clear if it was an addiction to drugs that caused the ruin of the drug addict in this case or his marriage to the French woman! It is highly possible that it was the wife's desertion that caused the drug addiction and that in turn caused his ruin!

It is also very unfortunate that at times fantastical claims, almost all of the times unsubstantiated, such as that, (i) 50% of students in Delhi, and 72% students in Government Medical College, Patiala were harmfully exposed to potentially addictive substances;[92] (ii) 35% students in Delhi alone are regularly consuming these substances; (iii) certain plants and substances are so inherently addictive so as to cause addiction upon administration of second or third dose itself;[93] (iv) consuming these substances three times can damage a child 'beyond repair;'[94] and (v) consumption of, and addiction to, narcotic drugs was somehow restricted to 'rich people' and now has started 'affecting the common man,'[95]

91. *Id.* at column 38.

92. Lok Sabha Debates (August 7, 1985), *supra* note 11, at column 282 (E. Ayyapu Reddy); Lok Sabha Debates (August 28, 1985), *supra* note 17, at column 19 (R.P. Das, M.P. (Krishnagar)). *See also* Lok Sabha Debates (August 28, 1985), *supra* note 17, at column 18 (R.P. Das, M.P. (Krishnagar), relying on a survey conducted by the Indian Council of Medical Research, claimed that "1,52,000 students were surveyed and it was seen that the increase of drug abuse among the Delhi students grew from 3.6 per cent in 1975 to 12 per cent in 1983. The Delhi University itself was the biggest victim in this matter; the menace is as high as 33 per cent among the students of the Delhi University." It will be immediately seen that the figure of 50% as claimed by Reddy stands clearly contradicted by the figure of 33% as claimed by Das.

93. Lok Sabha Debates (August 28, 1985), *supra* note 17, at column 57 (MoS Finance Janardhana Poojary stating that, "When they go out for second dose or a subsequent does, they will become addicts."); Lok Sabha Debates (August 7, 1985), *supra* note 11, at column 288 (Amitabh Bachchan stating that, "it only takes three helpings for a child to get permanently hooked on to [narcotic drugs such as 'smack,' 'brown sugar,' 'angel dust'], and it damages the child beyond repair.").

94. Lok Sabha Debates (August 7, 1985), *supra* note 11, at column 288 (Amitabh Bachchan).

95. *Id.* at column 292 (Dharam Pal Singh Malik).

were made by several members. These views seem to indicate that the members had accepted the position that people, including children, get addicted to these substances because the substances are inherently addictive.[96] These views also seem to indicate that the members adopted a 'blame the addict' approach whereby the addict is seen, in the words of Dr. G. S. Rajhans, M.P. (Jhanjharpur) as 'gradually advancing towards *their* death,' and are themselves responsible for destroying their lives, their health, as well as the lives of their families.[97] In fact, the manner in which some of the members presented their views, it seems to be the case that they were using the phrases 'drug addiction' and 'drug consumption' synonymously. For instance, when Shri Shantaram Naik, M.P. (Panaji) says that drug addiction 'is *going on to a large extent* so much so that tourism in a sense has become a menace in the territory of Goa,' the reference seems to be to a social menace that is sometimes created on account of excessive recreational consumption of narcotic drugs.[98]

Medical authorities on the subject, however, point out the limitations that this debate suffered from. To begin with, it must be noted that cannabis, just like any other drug could be abused. But 'cannabis dependence syndrome' (as it is called these days) is caused in 'heavy chronic users,' and is, "exhibited by a lack

---

96. *See e.g.,* Lok Sabha Debates (August 28, 1985), *supra* note 17, at column 26 (Ajay Mushran). According to Mushran, M.P. (Jabalpur), children are 'inadvertently getting inducted into the habit of taking drugs.' The view expressed by Mushran could be taken to be correct if it were the case that either the 'drugs,' or the substances from which these drugs are extracted, or the substances were inherently addictive. From an exhaustive reading of the debates it is clear that this view was either impliedly or expressly accepted by an overwhelming majority of the members, and that the maintainability of this view was never actually questioned in the House.
97. Lok Sabha Debates (August 7, 1985), *supra* note 11, at column 296 (Dr G. S. Rajhans). Dr. Rajhans described his experience in the following words: "I have seen how they are gradually advancing towards death, how they are destroying their health and how their health and how their wives and other members of their family are suffering. I would like to say that this is a very serious problem and it should be dealt with seriously." Whereas the experience of Dr. Rajhans is valuable, it should be pointed out that this view has now been demonstrated to be inconsistent with the best-known medical practices most suited to heal the addict. It is submitted that the view represented by the before quoted words of Dr. Rajhans is liable to be misconstrued in such a way that the society, and therefore by continuation the legal system, ends up blaming the addict. *See also* Lok Sabha Debates (August 28, 1985), *supra* note 17, at column 48 (Dr. Phulrenu Guha). Dr. Guha, M.P. (Contai) said that, "[D]rug Addiction ruins families and women are the worst sufferers ... The use of drugs ruins not only the person concerned, but also his family. ... When the son is addicted, the mother suffers psychologically. In many cases, they are helpless. ... The husband may say that he will not do it anymore, but the next day, he again comes as the addicted person."
98. Lok Sabha Debates (August 28, 1985), *supra* note 17, at column 46.

of control over use and continued use of the drug *despite adverse personal consequences*."[99] This knowledge is not limited to the medical establishment. The Washington Post, in an article in May 2002 noted: "Fewer than one in 10 marijuana smokers become regular users of the drug, and most voluntarily cease their use after 34 years of age. By comparison, 15 percent of alcohol consumers and 32 percent of tobacco smokers exhibit symptoms of drug dependence."[100]

An international authority on *inter alia* the psychology of addiction, Canadian physician and researcher Dr. Gabor Maté, points out the Roman roots of the word 'addiction.' An "*addictus*, was a person who having defaulted on a debt, was assigned to his creditor as a slave – hence, addiction's modern sense as enslavement to a habit."[101] The Latin *addicere*, however, has a more 'innocuous' meaning, "a habitual activity or interest, often with a positive purpose."[102] Rejecting the 'disease model' to view addiction, Dr. Maté says, "Viewing addiction as an illness, either acquired or inherited, narrows it down to a medical issue. It does have some of the features of the illness, and these are more pronounced in hardcore drug addicts I work within the Downtown Eastside. But not for a moment do I wish to promote the belief that the disease model by itself explains addiction or even that it's the key to understanding what addiction is all about."[103] Almost all members of the 8th Lok Sabha who spoke in favour of the NDPS Bill, as is shown above, consciously or unconsciously subscribed to the 'disease model.' The patent incorrectness of this view, on which the entire NDPS Act is based, is dismissed by the following words of Dr. Maté:

> *Although tolerance is a common effect of many addictions, a person does not need to have developed a tolerance to be addicted. And then there's physical dependence. As defined in medical terms, physical dependence is manifested when a person stops taking a substance and, due to changes in the brain and body, she experiences withdrawal symptoms. Those temporary, drug-induced changes form the basis of*

---

99. Sandra P. Welch & Billy R. Martin, 'The Pharmacology of Marijuana', *Principles of Addiction Medicine* 249, 260 (Allan W. Graham et al., eds., 3d. ed. 2003) (emphasis added). Welch & Martin also point out that the risk of, "becoming dependent on cannabis probably is more like the risk for alcohol than for nicotine or the opioids, with around 10% of those who ever use cannabis eventually meeting the criteria for dependence."
100. Keith Stroup & Paul Armentano, 'The Problem is Pot Prohibition', *Wash. Post*, May 4, 2002.
101. Maté, *supra* note 68 at 128.
102. *Id.* at 127.
103. *Id.* at 130.

physical dependence. Although a feature of drug addiction, a person's physical dependence does not necessarily imply that he is addicted to it.[104]

Most MPs probably were not aware that withdrawal symptoms could be experienced even by a non-addict, "you just have to have been taking a medication for an extended period of time."[105] It is a medical fact that the 'addictive' (or the 'feel good') effect of narcotics acts in a different part of the part than the one that leads to addiction.[106] Even laboratory animals can be 'induced into addiction' if they are forced to live under 'unnatural circumstances of captivity and stress.'[107] There is also good reason to believe that some human beings might be more prone to drug-dependence than others, on account of no fault of their own, rather on account of a reduced number of dopamine receptors.[108] The law must therefore distinguish between 'physical dependence' (that can be caused by long exposure to any drugs (legal or illegal) including cannabis) on the one hand, and 'addiction' on the other. As Dr. Maté points out that, "[t]here is no addiction centre in the brain, no circuits designated strictly for addictive purposes. The brain systems involved in addiction are among the key organizers and motivators of human emotional life and behaviour; hence, addiction's powerful hold on human beings."[109]

The 8th Lok Sabha's understanding of addiction suffers from an additional grave limitation: this approach can be successfully adopted only at the cost of ignoring the existence of behavioural addictions.[110] But accepting the existence of behavioural addictions as real would mean acknowledging that the true cause of every addiction (substance, or behavioural) essentially lies deep inside our own childhood, our past and present experiences, and our own self, and such an acknowledgement, it would be seen by the perceptive reader, will be immediately destructive of the 8th Lok Sabha's approach. This is the good type of destruction, the kind that is eventually required in every democratic republic, and one that is consistent with our traditions. It seems almost ironic that this book is about a plant that is used in Shiva worship in the Hindu tradition, and considered by

104. *Id.*
105. *Id.* at 131.
106 *See* Maté, *supra* note 68 at 131. Quoting a study done on rats using morphine, it is stated that, "When morphine is infused only into the "reward" circuits of a rat's brain, addiction-like behaviour results, but there's no physical dependence and no withdrawal."
107. Maté, *supra* note 68 at 137. Quoting Bruce Alexander, a psychologist at Simon Fraser University in British Columbia, Canada.
108. *Id.* at 143.
109. *Id.* at 150.
110. *Id.* at 229-47 (Chapter 22, Poor Substitutes for Love: Behavioural Addictions and Their Origins).

some to be his favourite: Lord Shiva is also the lord of destruction, but he is also the lord of stability, self-control, and patience.

The following words of Dr. Maté, in my opinion, call for a more humane approach to the issue of addiction, something that upon much reflection and study I found lacking in the 8th Lok Sabha's approach to the issue thus causing a grave error in their conclusions. In addition, they provide much support to the idea that possession of small quantities should be immediately decriminalized in India. These words deserve extensive quotation:

> *Addicts are locked into addiction not only by their painful past and distressing present, but equally by their bleak view of the future. ... They are unable to develop compassion towards themselves and their bodies while they are regarded as outcasts, hunted as enemies and treated like human refuse. ...* ***If we want to support people's potential for healthy transformation, we must cease to impose debilitating stresses on their already burdened existence. Recall that uncertainty, isolation, loss of control and conflict are the major triggers for stress and that stress is the most predictable factor in maintaining addiction and triggering relapse.*** *The addict is re-traumatized over and over again by ostracism, harassment, dire poverty, the spread of disease, the frantic hunt for a source of the substance of dependence, the violence of the underground drug world and harsh chastisement at the hands of the law – all inevitable consequences of the War on Drugs.*[111] ...
>
> *In relegating the addict to the bottom of the social and moral scales and in our contemptuous rejection of her as a person, we have created the exact circumstances that are most likely to keep her trapped in pathological dependence on drugs. There is no island of relief, only oceanic despair. ...* ***[W]e want to eradicate or limit addiction, yet our social policies are best suited to promote it, and we condemn the addict for qualities we dare not acknowledge in ourselves. ... If we want to help people seek the possibility of transformation within themselves, we first have to transform our own view of our relationship to them.***[112]

Many members, however, ultimately advocated for a strong policy of awarding heavy deterrent punishment to not just the drug smugglers.[113] The response of the Minister to these exhortations was expected to take a strong stand, and accordingly, he declared that it was 'the basic responsibility of the Government' to prevent and punish addiction.[114]

---

111. *Id.* at 300 (emphasis added).
112. *Id.* at 301 (emphasis in *italics* provided).
113. *See e.g.*, Lok Sabha Debates (August 28, 1985), *supra* note 17, at column 20 (R.P. Das).
114. Lok Sabha Debates (August 7, 1985), *supra* note 11, at column 296.

As noted above, now we know better, and therefore must change our laws. According to a landmark 2003 study conducted on over 17,000 'middle-class Americans: "The basic cause of addiction is pre-dominantly experience-dependent during childhood, and not substance-dependent, ... The current concept of addiction is ill-founded."[115] Addiction, it seems, is neither genetic nor substance-dependent (i.e., the view that some substances are inherently addictive; in fact, more and more it seems that substances are not inherently addictive, though could cause dependence, which is a different thing from addiction,) and therefore views of addiction based on these assumptions need to be discarded. An addict is not born, but made; her addiction is the 'result of a situation that [she] had no influence in creating.'[116]

(e) Warned against likely abuse of Criminal Justice System, but warning ignored

Fifth, governmental corruption in the implementation of the proposed NDPS Bill was pointed out by a lot of MPs.[117] Shri Dal Chander Jain, MP (Damoh) used the fable of the crocodile to make this point:

> *"In a pond, there were many crocodiles. A special force was set up to kill them. The special force killed half of the crocodiles in the first month and in the second month, they killed one fourth of the crocodiles. In the third month also they worked efficiently. The people felt relieved and they were patted for their good work. Later on it was seen that they have become almost inactive. People asked them that previously they worked hard, but what had happened further. They replied that they could kill all the crocodiles if they so desired, but what would they do after that. So, they wanted that crocodiles might also remain in the pond and they might also be there to kill them."*[118]

---

115. *See* Maté, *supra* note 68 at 180-81.
116. Maté, *supra* note 68 at 259. ("The addict, in other words, is not born but made. His addiction is the result of a situation that he had no influence in creating.")
117. *See e.g.,* Lok Sabha Debates (August 28, 1985), *supra* note 17, at column 55 (Mool Chand Daga, "I am submitting that opium is being smuggled into our country through the Nepal border and our Border Security personnel are also involved in it. I have mentioned the names of 44 police posts and how the BSF personnel are working hand in glove with the smugglers. How do you expect that your Bill would be implemented successfully when the public servants themselves are not honest and patriotic? Through this Bill, you have opened the floodgates of corruption and this Bill will further encourage corruption.")
118. Lok Sabha Debates (August 28, 1985), *supra* note 17, at column 40.

In this context, the only reference to cannabis cultivation was made by Shri Ramashray Prasad Singh, MP (Jahanabad). He narrated the following incident:

> *"I would like to narrate one incident. I went to a Police Station. A 'Ganja' tree was there. I saw a tree in the compound of Jahanabad Police Station. People told me that it was a 'Ganja' tree. Now, you tell us if there would be 30 kgs. 'Ganja' on the tree located in the Police Station, how the police personnel there, who have to implement the law, will implement it. If the police personnel, who have to apprehend the culprits, indulge in such acts, what to say of others."*[119]

Shri Jujhar Singh, MP (Jhalawar) highlighted this specifically in the context of 'unlicensed cultivation of opium,'[120] and we should pay careful attention to his speech:

> *"I had asked a question in this very session regarding unlicensed cultivation of opium that was got done in Jhalawar district during the last year. Sir, the Narcotics department itself is responsible for it and the then Deputy Commissioner is also involved in it. Many officers themselves were involved in unlicensed cultivation in Jhalawar constituency. ... It is my firm belief that the Narcotics department is itself involved in the racket and is forcing the farmer to resort to illegal cultivation of opium. ...*
>
> *Monitoring the process of collecting opium from the fields is the most crucial stage in the opium cultivation. When opium is taken out from the fields, the inspectors undertake door-to door visit. During this period, constables of Narcotics Department are vested with powers of inspectors and sub-inspectors for those 45 days and they carry out their duty in their new capacity. ... You can yourself imagine the harassment caused to the people when these persons, who have no openings in service, are vested with powers of the inspectors and sub-inspectors during weighing and purchasing period."*

It would therefore appear to be the case that domestic illegal opium trade is not the same as the illegal drug trade. When opium cultivation is licensed, the obvious way to game the system is to grow more than what one is licensed to grow and siphon off the excess harvest to the illegal market. Another way would be to have some harvest destroyed and siphon this off into the illegal market. All this cannot be done without the collusion of government officials, and that is the point being made by Shri Jujhar Singh. The motivation, on the part of government officials, is as stated above, *viz.* the excessive powers granted to these officials and a lack of promotional avenues in government service itself. It would

119. *Id.* at column 43.
120. *Id.* at column 32.

immediately be noticed that this phenomenon is not unique to opium cultivation, rather it is unique to *licensed* cultivation (whether it be of opium or any other crop). The motivation, on part of the farmers, was also stated by Singh, and again deserves extensive quotation:

"My other submission is that the rate of heroin and refined opium is very high, but rate given to the farmers by the Government is Rs. 150 per kg. upto 7½ kg. If they produce upto 11 and a quarter kg., then after 7 and a half kg, they are paid Rs. 240 per kg. If the farmer produces more than 11¼ kgs., then he gets Rs. 280 per kg. upto 15 kgs. If the farmer gives upto 15 kgs of opium to the Government, he gets Rs. 3,075 by merging various slabs whereas if he sells that much quantity in market he can get Rs. 15,000 to Rs. 25,000. You pay only Rs. 3,000 for a thing which can fetch Rs. 25,000 in the market. Because of this difference people are tempted to pilfer a small quantity."[121]

Making an impassioned plea for opium farmers, and highlighting that cultivating opium poppy involved a lot of hard work on the part of the farmers, Shri Balkavi Bairagi, MP (Mandsaur), who spoke before Singh, was the first MP to raise this in Lok Sabha. His words also deserve extensive quotation:

"I am talking about those farmers for whom Shri Vishwanath Pratap Singh is the Finance Minister, Shri Janardhana Poojary is the Minister of State for Finance and Shri Rajiv Gandhi is the Prime Minister. ... Is any Member of this House aware of this fact that a farmer has to care a lot for the opium plant and he has to nurse it with his own hands at least 40 times before it gets ripe? Is there any other crop in which a plant has to be touched by farmers 40 times? ... What is the price you pay for opium? A compulsory levy has been imposed. The yield per hectare should not be below 28 kgs and the maximum price that is paid is Rs. 130 per kg if it is below 30 kgs. Rs. 150 per kg if it is between 30 to 45 kgs., and Rs. 180 per kg if it is between 45 to 60 kgs and Rs. 220 per kg if the yield exceeds 60 kgs. This is your slave system. I would like to point out that it is the Government which forces the farmer to become a thief and later it frames laws to apprehend him. ... It is very unfortunate that the Government which cannot make its farmers brave, self reliant and prosperous, is ready to sign such a Bill which is prepared by those very bureaucrats. I am serious when I say that the Government is playing with the livelihood of farmers. ...

I would suggest that if opium is confiscated from a farmer's possession, he [should] be treated as a smuggler, but what will happen if opium is concealed by somebody in the farmers' house because of political enmity. The village headman fraudulently gets

---

121. *Id.* at column 34.

50 grams, 100 grams or 200 grams of opium concealed in the farmer's house and implicates him in a case. What will happen with Girdawar, the Patwari or the Inspector himself gets the opium concealed in the farmer's house and gets him arrested? ... About 75 lakhs people are engaged in opium cultivation and about 50 lakhs of them depend directly on opium cultivation for their livelihood. We have never said that a lenient view should be taken of the smugglers, but if you do not adopt a liberal attitude towards the farmer, then I am of the opinion that it is basically against the very policies of Shri Rajiv Gandhi and the Congress Party. ... It is unfortunate because the Government first forces them to become thief and when they become helpless to survive, and when we speak the truth we are told to speak in low tone, because then it becomes a question that concerns the entire nation. This does not concern the entire nation, but it concerns a few bureaucrats who get a share in it. ...

[Y]ou have created new kings, who are leading luxurious life and the farmers are continuously paying a heavy price for it. I would like to submit very humbly to you that the farmers have not been taken into confidence while fixing the price of opium."[122]

These two speeches (by Singh, and Bairagi) are the only occasions when any sensible discussion took place about the modalities of regulating opium cultivation and trade, and the issues of governmental corruption and inefficiency were pointedly highlighted.[123] Since the stated scope of this work is restricted to cannabis, there is no occasion to engage with opium here, but it certainly gives food for thought. However, one interesting question does arise. If Singh and Bairagi were so dissatisfied with the law on the issue of opium cultivation, a dissatisfaction shared by some other MPs, then why did they vote to support the NDPS Bill? That question is answered by Daga's speech on August 28, 1985, where he stated: "Our whip Shri Gulam Nabi Azad is insisting on passing it at the earliest. We will vote as our party directs us, but then it will be the sole responsibility of Government and not ours if any injustice is done."[124] The NDPS Bill, it would appear, was passed in haste, and this brings us to our next critique.

---

122. *Id.* at columns 22-25.

123. But *see also* Lok Sabha Debates (August 28, 1985), *supra* note 17, at column 52 (Mool Chand Daga, "The farmers in Rajasthan are being played with. Opium is produced in Chittor district of Rajasthan. They merely get Rs. 250 for 5 kgs of opium while the same quantity is sold off for Rs. 1 lakh abroad.").

124. *Id.* at column 54.

(f) NDPS Bill was being drafted in undue haste

Sixth, many MPs said that the NDPS Bill was drafted in a hurry, being pushed through Parliament in haste, and this should be avoided. Ajay Mushran, MP (Jabalpur) said that the NDPS Bill was 'drafted in a hurry' and cautioned that the House should extensively debate the issue of 'small quantity' and related offences proposed in the Bill before it is enacted.[125] Chinta Mohan, MP (Tirupati) 'at the outset' cautioned that the Narcotic Drugs and Substances Committee should have included experts and not politicians.[126] V. S. Krishna Iyer, MP (Bangalore South) said that even though the NDPS Bill was a 'comprehensive bill', "... unfortunately there is no time to think over it and the Bill is rushed through the House and there are a number of defects in the Bill."[127] Madhu Dandavate, MP (Rajapur), who was the Minister of Railways (in Prime Minister Morarji Desai's cabinet), and subsequently became the Minister of Finance (in Prime Minister Vishwanath Pratap Singh's cabinet), also said that the NDPS Bill should be 'referred to Select Committee.'[128] Mood Chand Daga, MP (Pali), the mover of August 7, 1985, calling attention motion himself proposed that the NDPS Bill be, "... referred to the Joint Select Committee. The Bill which has such a wide scope and which affects the interests of so many people should be referred to a Select Committee so that people can get justice. Heavens will not fall if it is delayed for a month or two. ... I would once again strongly request you to get it examined by the Select Committee and discuss it clause by clause and make no haste in this regard."[129] The NDPS Bill, however, despite all this, was never sent to any parliamentary committee, and was later enacted into the NDPS Act and continues to be the principal legislation in India prohibiting trade in cannabis in the territory of the Indian republic.

(g) Questions of Constitutional competence

Seventh, there was no discussion in Lok Sabha about the constitutional competence of Parliament to criminalize trade in cannabis. This point is made explained in detail above[130] and there is no need to restate it here.

125. *Id.* at columns 29-30.
126. *Id.* at column 31.
127. *Id.* at columns 37-38.
128. *Id.* at column 57.
129. *Id.* at column 54.
130. See *supra* Chapter 4, section (ii) and (iii).

(h) The 'Small Quantities Loophole'

Eighth, the NDPS Act criminalizes possession of small quantities of narcotic drugs and psychotropic substances.[131] As per the NDPS Act not only the 'cultivation,'[132] but the 'production, manufacturing, possession, sale, purchase, transport, domestic and international trade in cannabis,'[133] prohibited, the possession of a small quantity of cannabis or any cannabis extracts[134] is also punishable with rigorous imprisonment for one year, or a fine of INR 10,000 (approximately USD 133).[135] As per a notification issued by the Ministry of Finance, Department of Revenue exercising the powers conferred by section 2 of the NDPS Act (dated October 19, 2001) 100 grams of cannabis is considered to be a 'small quantity,' and 1 kilogram is considered to be 'commercial quantity.'[136] However, this 'small quantity notification' is not of much avail because the police arrest people for possession of 'minimum quantity,' which is not the same as 'small quantity,' and unfortunately is not prescribed anywhere thus providing the opportunity for police discretion in these matters to be abused. The problem is identical to the one faced in the U.S., where, "[t]he definition of *small amount* can vary from jurisdiction to jurisdiction but most often refers to an amount of marijuana with a total weight of less than one ounce."[137] To be fair, however, it should be noted that 13 States in the U.S. have done away with criminal prohibition for medical use, and 31 States and the District of Columbia have recognized the value of medical use.[138] Earlier in this work, we have discussed the medicinal uses of this plant and know that it has

---

131. NDPS Act, § 2(xxiia) defining 'small quantity' as 'any quantity lesser than the quantity specified by the Central Government by notification in the Official Gazette.' A list of these quantities is provided in a notification issued by the Ministry of Finance, Department of Revenue dated October 19, 2001. *See* Gazette of India, Part II, Section 3, October 19, 2001, available at https://egazette.nic.in/WriteReadData/2001/E-2510-2001-0773-113878.pdf (last accessed May 20, 2021) (hereinafter 'Small Quantities Notification').
132. NDPS Act, § 20(a).
133. *Id.* § 20(b).
134. *See e.g.*, NDPS Act, § 2(iii) defining cannabis (hemp) to include *charas* (crude or purified separated resin extracted from the cannabis plant including *hashish oil* or liquid hashish), *ganja* (the flowering or fruiting tops excluding the leaves), or any mixture or drink prepared from the cannabis plant. *See also id.* § 2(iv) defining 'cannabis plant' to mean 'any plant of the genus cannabis.'
135. NDPS Act, § 20(ii).
136. Small Quantities Notification, *supra* note 131, Entry 23.
137. Cynthia S. Duncan, 'The Need for Change: An Economic Analysis of Marijuana Policy', 41 CONN. L. REV. 1701, 1704 (n.4) (2009).
138. *Id.*

been used for such purposes for a very long time in India, much earlier than the modern-day conception of a nation-state even emerged.[139]

Compared to this, the 'coffee-shop' system of the Netherlands is the most well-known around the globe. This system came about in the 1980s when prompted by the 'concerns over growing heroin use by young people in early 1970s' the Dutch Government decided to decriminalize possession of small quantities in 1980 as a result of which the coffee-shop system came to be established and tolerated.[140] Today it is one of its most famous tourist attractions thus establishing, and limited only by one's imagination, the amazing potential of cannabis tourism. Possession of small quantities for personal use was never criminal in Spain and was 'typically subjected to 'administrative sanctions,'[141] and is tolerated in Belgium.[142] Australia has been slowly decriminalizing cannabis since 1987 and medical cannabis has been legal in Australia since 2016.[143] Closer to home, medical cannabis is legal in Israel since 1995, in Sri Lanka since 2018, Thailand since 2019, and Lebanon since 2020.[144] In addition, in 2019 Israel also decriminalized possession of up to 15 grams of cannabis attracting only a fine.[145]

Across the Atlantic in the United States, and very recently, the District of Columbia and Vermont have permitted personal possession of cannabis for recreational purposes in small quantities limited at 57 grams and 28.5 grams, respectively.[146] Driving under influence of cannabis is an offence in the States of Colorado and Washington with a legal THC limit of 'five nanograms per millilitre as measured in whole blood (as opposed to blood serum)'.[147] On the other hand, the laws of those States in the U.S. that have stopped short of full legalization and had only decriminalized cannabis also no longer criminally prohibit it. In some States, possession of 1 ounce (28.5 grams) of cannabis is considered a civil violation with a fine of USD 25 or 50.[148] Draft legislation has already been introduced in the U.S. Congress whereby federal penalties for

139. *See supra* Chapter 2, section (iv).

140. Toby Seddon & William Floodgate, *Regulating Cannabis: A Global Review and Future Directions* 43 (2020, Palgrave Macmillan).

141. *Id.* at 46.

142. *Id.* at 50.

143. *Id.* at 59.

144. *Id.* at 61.

145. *Id.*

146. *See* Seddon & Floodgate, *supra* note 140 at 26.

147. *Id.* at 26.

148. *Id.*

possession (up to 100 grams or less) for personal use are to be removed, 'not-for-profit transfer between adults of marijuana for personal use' (up to 1 ounce i.e. 28.3 grams) is to be permitted,[149] and cannabis is to be reclassified as a Schedule II substance.[150] At the time of writing this book 13 States in the U.S. have decriminalized small quantity possession for personal use and treated first-time possession of small amounts 'like a minor traffic violation.'[151] In Jamaica, where there is a 'long-standing cultural association'[152] with cannabis (or *ganja*, as it is popularly called in India as well) possession of up to 2 ounces was decriminalized in 2015 and home cultivation for medicinal or sacramental use was legalized.[153]

This issue of criminalization of the possession of small quantities of cannabis in the context of the NDPS Bill was raised by Shri Ajay Mushran, M.P. (Jabalpur).[154] Mushran pointed out that criminalization of the possession of large or commercial quantities of controlled substances is a 'noble idea' but cautioned that criminalization of small quantities might be 'misused by the officials.'[155] He gave the following illustration: "They can catch a person having 100 gms. and say that only 10 gms. was found in his possession. ... What is the guarantee that even this one year's punishment will be given? They will impose a fine of Rs. 50 or Rs. 100 and the officers also, by declaring a lesser quantity, they will take a share of the booty."[156] However, Mushran felt that 'too little punishment' had been prescribed for possession of small quantities in the NDPS

---

149. *See e.g.*, H.R. 5843, 110th Congress (2008) (U.S. Congress), Act to Remove Federal Penalties for the Personal Use of Marijuana by Responsible Adults, removing federal penalties for: (i) possession of up to 100 grams or less of cannabis; and (ii) not-for-profit transfer between adults.
150. *See e.g.*, H.R. 5842, 110th Congress (2008) (U.S. Congress), Medical Marijuana Patient Protection Act, calling for rescheduling cannabis from Schedule I to Schedule II of the Controlled Substances Act, and providing "for the medical use of marijuana in accordance with the laws of the various States"). *See also* 21 U.S.C. § 812(a)-(c) (2006), providing a comprehensive list of all controlled substances. Schedule I lists the most dangerous substances and Schedule V lists the least dangerous.
151. Cynthia S. Duncan, 'The Need for Change: An Economic Analysis of Marijuana Policy', 41 CONN. L. REV. 1701, 1703 (2009).
152. For details of this 'long-standing cultural association,' *see* Melissa Bone, 'From the Sacrilegious to the Sacramental: A Global Review of Rastafari Cannabis Case Law' in Beatriz Caiuby Labate & Clancy Cavnar (Ed.), *Prohibition, Religious Freedom, and Human Rights: Regulating Traditional Drug* Use 89-109 (2014, Springer).
153. Seddon & Floodgate, *supra* note 140 at 37.
154. Lok Sabha Debates (August 28, 1985), *supra* note 17 at column 29 stating that he wanted 'this point to be debated in this House, and that this 'small quantity' should be defined.'
155. *Id.*
156. *Id.*

Bill.[157] Dal Chandar Jain, M.P. (Damoh), speaking in the context of opium cultivation, also pointed out that the *small quantities loophole* (as pointed out by Mushran) 'will result in many malpractices.'[158] He suggested that some sort of certification or permit mechanism be put in place to possess small quantities of certain controlled substances. [159] It will be seen that the suggestion to regulate, via licensing or certification, the possession of small quantities of cannabis was a suggestion that seems to have been inspired by an earlier similar legal arrangement whereunder ownership and possession of small quantities of gold was heavily regulated. This arrangement, as experience has shown, has turned out to be economically undesirable, and was anyway rejected. Even though in the proper context, the use of licenses or permits might not be the most conducive way forward, it is submitted that the suggestion to regulate, via licensing or certification, the cultivation, and possession of small quantities of cannabis either procured or self-grown, is a superior alternative to its criminalisation and prohibition.[160] The manner in which our criminal justice system as a whole (starting from the police constable all the way up to the Supreme Court) will benefit from this approach has already been noted earlier.[161] In addition to this, because of the known psychoactive qualities found in THC (tetrahydrocannabinol) which is the primary psychoactive component found in the cannabis plant, it might be desirable to prescribe by law the maximum quantity that may be possessed [162] by one person. A review of the relevant legislation from some of the several States in the U.S., and Canada shows that: (a) their domestic experience with criminalization of possession of small quantities of cannabis directly contributed to the problem of an inflated prison population; and (b) legalization of cannabis for medical as well as personal use has very often resulted in a legal arrangement that resembles the one suggested above.

157. *Id.*

158. *Id.* at column 41.

159. *See* Lok Sabha Debates (August 28, 1985), *supra* note 17 at column 41 ("Under the Gold Control Act, one cannot keep primary gold. Permit is required to keep it. Some sort of certificate must be obtained to possess even a small quantity of such drugs also. Only after obtaining the permit, one would be allowed to possess small quantity.").

160. *See e.g.,* Seddon & Floodgate, *supra* note 140 at 10 (2020, Palgrave Macmillan) pointing out that a, "central theoretical insight that we draw on in this book is that regulation is not simply a matter of applying external controls to markets; rather, regulation is constitutive of those markets."

161. *See* Chapter 1, section (vi).

162. By the word 'possessed' here is meant the total quantity retained on the body and in the immediate personal belongings of the person who is in possession.

iii. Uttarakhand Hemp Policy *vis-à-vis* NDPS (Amendment) Act, 2014

The 'Uttarakhand Hemp Cultivation Policy' of 2016[163] is a welcome development in the direction of creating a hemp economy in India. However, a closer examination of the Policy reveals that there is much scope for improvement. As of December 5, 2016, the state of Uttarakhand acting under section 14 of the Narcotic Drugs and Psychotropic Substances Act, 1985 ('NDPS Act') has approved the cultivation, stocking, warehousing, sale and purchase, and transportation[164] of 'industrial hemp'. It is important here to note that 'Industrial hemp' is only one type of cannabis plant, whereas the NDPS Act defines cannabis plant to mean 'any plant of the genus cannabis.' As would be noted later in this chapter, generally speaking the plant cannabis includes *Cannabis sativa* L. (1753), *Cannabis indica* Lam. (1783), and *Cannabis ruderalis* Janisch (1924). The NDPS Act makes no discrimination when defining the plant for the purposes of the Act. And it defines cannabis plant to include *any plant* of the genus cannabis, and does not restrict itself to industrial hemp only. In understanding this key botanical point, perhaps, lies the key to unlocking the doors to a prosperous and peaceful future.

(a) Understanding the Uttarakhand Hemp Cultivation Policy (2016)

According to the Policy, any individual, research institution, commercial or industrial institution may approach the District Collector to obtain a license either for cultivating, stocking, warehousing, sale and purchase, and transportation of industrial hemp if the following general conditions are fulfilled: (i) the applicant must either be the owner or leaseholder of the land where cultivation of industrial hemp will be permitted;[165] and (ii) the applicant must submit the relevant details of: (a) the tract of land where industrial hemp will be cultivated;[166] (b) the relevant application duly filled and supported with

163. *See* Letter No. 639/XXIII/2016/04(02)2016, dated December 05, 2016, by the Chief Secretary, Uttarakhand Government addressed to the Excise Commissioner, Dehradun, Uttarakhand (hereinafter 'Uttarakhand Hemp Cultivation Policy') (on file with author) (available at, Uttarakhand Excise Department's Website, http://uttrakhandexcise.org.in/Docs/bhang.pdf, accessed on February 02, 2022).

164. Uttarakhand Hemp Cultivation Policy, *supra* note 163, at page 5 (letter dated August 17, 2017 by the Excise Commissioner Uttarakhand, addressed to all district authorities across Uttarakhand).

165. Uttarakhand Hemp Cultivation Policy, *supra* note 163, cl. (2).

166. *Id.* at cl. (2)

prescribed documentation;[167] and (c) the license fee for the application.[168] However, it must be noted that industrial hemp is prohibited to be cultivated in any tract of land except for the notified tract(s).[169] This system of notifying tracts of land for cannabis cultivation is borrowed from the legal regime whereby the cultivation of opium is regulated.[170] Before the District Collector decides as to whether or not the license application is approved, the Policy authorises the Collector to conduct such inspection as the same may deem necessary.[171] In this context, it is evident from the manner in which the Policy is worded, that the decision-making authority of the Collector is subject to the requirements of natural justice. For instance, in the event that the application is declined, the Collector is required to provide reasons for the decision. Furthermore, the Collector's decision is subject to appeal before the Excise Commissioner within 30 days of the decision being communicated. All this would seem to indicate the quasi-judicial nature of the Collector's authority under the Policy.

(b) Anomalies and Resolutions in the Uttarakhand Hemp Cultivation Policy

(i) Policy inconsistent with the Medical and Scientific Use Amendment of 2014

The Uttarakhand Hemp Cultivation Policy leaves much to be desired. An anomaly is visible in clause (2) of the policy Policy itself. According to clause (2), an individual is allowed to make a joint application with a commercial or industrial institution, but the same individual is not allowed to make a joint application with a research institution. This anomaly is not easily explained, and it is suggested that the Policy may be suitably amended. Furthermore, there is no reason for the Uttarakhand government to restrict individuals from

---

167. *Id.* at cl. (1) read with Letter dated August 17, 2017, *supra* note 164, cl. (1) to (6), e.g., an application for a 'cultivation and warehousing' license can be made using Form IHA-A1, but if one desires only cultivation only license on must use Form IHC-1.

168. *Id.* at cl. (3).

169. *Id.* at cl. (1).

170. *See* Ministry of Finance, Department of Revenue Notification No, 01/2021-Narcotics Control-1, dated October 11 2021.This notification, issued in pursuance of Rule 8 of the Narcotic Drugs and Psychotropic Substances Rules, 1985 notifies the general conditions for grant of license for cultivation of opium poppy during the opium crop year commencing on October 1, 2021 and ending on September 30, 2022. Clause (1) of this notification says: "Opium poppy cultivation may be licensed in any tract as may be notified in this behalf by the Central Government."

171. Uttarakhand Hemp Cultivation Policy, *supra* note 163, cl. (1).

making joint applications with research institutions, especially in light of the newly inserted words '*medical and scientific use*' in Section 4(2)(da) of the NDPS Act.[172] While research institutions are better equipped to give effect to 'scientific use', however situations where individual citizens may need cannabis for genuine medical conditions cannot be ruled out. Since the Policy is restricted to industrial hemp, it excludes the use of the plant in genuine medical need as industrial hemp is known mostly for its industrial applications. In the event the Policy is amended, and a decision is taken to extend it to all plants of the genus cannabis, as the NDPS Act defines it, individual cultivation license might require suitable reinterpretation in order to accommodate the needs of genuine medical users.

Section 4 of the NDPS Act allows the Union Government, "to take such measures for preventing and combating abuse of and illicit trade in narcotic drugs."[173] Section 4(1) of the NDPS Act, most recently amended by the Parliament in 2014, now enjoins the Union Government to take all such measures as it deems necessary or expedient for the purpose of: (i) preventing and combating abuse of *inter alia* cannabis, and also (ii) to *ensure* its 'medical and scientific use'.[174] The insertion of the phrase "ensuring their medical and scientific use" by the Parliament in 2014 (the 'Medical and Scientific Use Amendment') may fairly be said to be indicative of a liberal and forward-thinking approach of the Parliament. It has to be carefully noted that the medical and scientific use of all narcotic drugs and psychotropic substances as defined in the NDPS Act has now been sanctioned by Parliament. But this work is limited to *cannabis*, i.e., hemp that is defined variously in section 2(iii) read with section 2(iv) of the NDPS Act. The Union Government's authority under section 4 however extends to all types of narcotic drugs and psychotropic substances as defined under the Act and later added to its ambit by relevant notifications, one of which is *cannabis*. By this analysis, it should be clear that the medical and scientific use of cannabis is certainly one of the purposes for which the Union Government has now been legally enjoined. However, care must be taken to realise that the argument being made in this book is restricted to cannabis.[175] Whether or not these arguments apply to other narcotic drugs

---

172. Narcotic Drugs and Psychotropic Substances Act, 1985, § 4(2)(da), inserted by Act 16 of 2014, § 3(b), *with effect from* May 1, 2014.
173. NDPS Act, *supra* note 172, § 4 (section heading).
174. NDPS Act, *supra* note 172, § 4(1) (emphasis added).
175. *See* Chapter 2, part (iii): Religions, Spiritual, and Cultural Use.

and psychotropic substances as mentioned in the NDPS Act is an open question.[176]

(ii) Policy not conducive to fully realise potential Medical and Scientific Use

A rather curious part of the Uttarakhand Hemp Cultivation Policy is that it restricts itself to 'industrial hemp.' The Policy very specifically states that the cultivation license can and will only be granted to cultivate crops of industrial hemp with a maximum of 0.3% THC[177] content.[178]

Furthermore, the Policy restricts itself to allowing the use of industrial hemp only to obtain the seed and the fiber of said plant.[179] These are two very peculiar anomalies here that are not very easy to explain.

First, since the State is now directed through legislation to take measures to see that cannabis is made available for medical and scientific use, as may fairly be inferred from the newly inserted 2014 Medical and Scientific Use Amendment to the NDPS Act, it is not very clear why the Uttarakhand Hemp Cultivation Policy should restrict itself only to industrial hemp. The Uttarakhand government would be well advised to follow the liberal and forward-thinking approach of the Parliament, as evidenced by the insertion of the phrase "ensuring their medical and scientific use" in section 4(1) of the NDPS Act. If the matter is examined, it would be seen that there is no reason for the Uttarakhand Hemp Cultivation Policy to restrict itself to industrial hemp or to impose the maximum 0.3% THC barrier.

Second (and this is where we may foreshadow a potential civil liberties issue as well), arises out of the following scenario. Assuming that a patient has a doctor's

---

176. *See e.g.,* Sri Swami Satchidananda, The Yoga Sutras of Patanjali 197 (Internal Yoga Publications, Virginia 1979, ninth reprint 2020) on the use of cannabis in spiritual practices; Sam Harris, *Waking Up: Searching for Spirituality Without Religion* (Penguin, Great Britain 2014) also on the use of cannabis and some other synthetic drugs conductive to cause spiritual experiences.
177. THC, or delta 9 tetrahydrocannabinol, is the psychoactive compound found in all plants of the genus cannabis, with varying concentration levels in each type of the plant. Ingestion of THC is 'most often associated with psychological effects such as euphoria, analgesia, sedation, cognitive impairment, and appetite stimulation.' See, Elena M. Quattrone, 'The Catch 22 of Marijuana [Il]Legalization', 22 B.U. J. SCI. & TECH. L. 299, 303-04 (2016).
178. Uttarakhand Hemp Cultivation Policy, *supra* note 163, cl. (5) read with cl. (6).
179. *Id.* at cl. (1).

prescription, or recommendation[180] for medical cannabis, and the prescribed strain in question is one that requires more than 0.3% THC, what is such a patient to do? On the one hand, in light of the 2014 Amendment to the NDPS Act, it clearly seems to be the case that once the doctor's prescription, or recommendation is available, all possible measures should be taken to either provide or to enable such a patient to procure or cultivate such a strain themselves. However, on the other hand, from the manner in which the rest of the NDPS Act is structured and its attendant rules and notifications are drafted, it is clear that if such a patient were either to cultivate such a strain himself/herself or were to cause such a strain to be cultivated, they would be acting in a manner contrary to the law. Now, looking at this scenario from the perspective of the Uttarakhand Hemp Cultivation Policy, we again find ourselves in an anomalous situation. On the one hand, the NDPS Act requires that all plants of the genus cannabis be made available for medical and scientific use, per the Medical and Scientific Use Amendment. The Policy could have very easily accommodated the needs of all people who have a genuine medical need (i.e., a medically diagnosed condition where cannabis has been known, or shown to be helpful), and who might be sourcing medical cannabis from unauthorised sources, by allowing them to cultivate, or cause to be cultivated, or simply procure medical cannabis from a licensed cultivator. But the Policy restricted itself to industrial hemp, which is a very useful plant with many industrial and commercial applications. But industrial hemp is just one of the several plants of the genus cannabis. When examined closely, it would be seen that there is actually no reasonable case for the Policy to restrict itself either to industrial hemp, or to regulate cannabis cultivation using the maximum 0.3% THC requirement.

(iii) Excessive powers and The Flowering Top Conundrum

However, the Policy takes the maximum 0.3% THC content requirement very seriously. Clause (6) of the Policy authorises the District Collector to conduct such inspections as they may deem necessary in order to enforce the 0.3% THC requirement. In the event the cultivated crop is found to be in violation of this

180. Dave Bewley-Taylor, Tom Blickman, & Martin Jelsma, *The Rise and Decline of Cannabis Prohibition: The History of Cannabis in the UN Drug Control System and Options for Reform* p. 29 (Transnational Institute, Global Drug Policy Observatory, 2014). This report cites the 1996 Compassionate Use Act (Proposition 215) that was enacted by the voters in California that exempted medical use of cannabis from criminal penalties. California's law allows individuals to possess, cultivate, and transport cannabis so long as it is used for medical purposes with a doctor's written 'recommendation' as opposed to a prescription.

rule, the District Collector is authorised to destroy the cultivated crop without the cultivator having any resort to any claim or compensation. These requirements, in conjunction with the rest of the Policy, do present to us a very anomalous situation that, for the sake of convenience, we may call the 'Flowering Top Conundrum.'

The Flowering Top Conundrum unfolds as follows. The 'flowering or fruiting tops' of the cannabis plant (excluding the seeds and leaves when not accompanied by the tops)'[181] as well as 'the separated resin in whatever form'[182], are currently prohibited by the NDPS Act. This 'flowering or fruiting top' is called *ganja* that contains THC. The 'separated resin,' usually hand-rubbed out of a live plant, is called *charas*, or *hashish*. It is arguable though that the phrase *hashish* may only be used for the resin coming from Morocco, and the phrase *charas* may only be used for the resin coming out of India. (Note here in passing that issues such as these may foreshadow several legal disputes that may involve intellectual property law.) The 2014 Medical and Scientific Use Amendment to the NDPS Act directs the Union Government to take all such measures as may be deemed necessary or expedient in order to ensure medical and scientific use of cannabis. It may fairly be said that any criminality associated with the use of flowering or fruiting top, as well as the separated resin has now been removed after the enactment of the Medical and Scientific Use Amendment. But since the Uttarakhand Hemp Cultivation Policy seems to have been drafted in ignorance of this legal position, re-consider the scenario of the hypothetical medical user as mentioned above.

Let us assume that a medical user of the flowering or fruiting top of a particular strain of cannabis with a higher concentration of THC as is currently permitted by the Policy wants to apply for a cultivation license. Let us further assume that alternatively, this medical user has found a cultivator with the requisite knowledge and skills who has agreed to cultivate, process, and transport this strain to the concerned medical user. It will be seen that in either of these two scenarios, the license application of such a user or a cultivator will have to be denied on the ground that the strain for which cultivation license is sought is not covered by the Policy. This denial seems to be rather arbitrary on its own, and also seems to be inconsistent with the general tone of the Medical and Scientific Use Amendment giving rise to the Flowering Top Conundrum: Parliament says yes, but state government says no! However, the way I read the Policy, the state

181. NDPS Act, *supra* note 172, § 2(iii)(b), sub-definition of 'ganja.'
182. *Id.* at § 2(iii)(a), sub-definition of 'charas.'

government has not said no, it is only yet to say yes. Furthermore, medical and scientific use amendments in foreign jurisdictions have been sensitive to the natural diversity inherent in all types and varieties of the cannabis plant itself.[183] According to many botanical experts, there is no genuine botanical basis to distinguish between the three types of cannabis varieties that are supposedly found across the globe.[184] These three types of cannabis varieties are commonly known as: *Cannabis sativa* L. (1753), *Cannabis indica* Lam. (1783), and *Cannabis ruderalis* Janisch (1924).[185]

(iv) Tract Notification System: A Legal Relic of Colonial Times

Finally, we may note the tract notification system mentioned earlier that is borrowed from the legal regime applicable to the cultivation of opium. The Uttarakhand Hemp Cultivation Policy follows this tract notification system, whereunder cultivation of industrial hemp is permitted only on tracts of land pre-approved by the state by issuing a notification under the relevant provisions of the NDPS Act.[186] The use of tract notification system was envisaged under the opium licensing regime, and has not undergone any substantial or even unsubstantial review since the time the British originally put it in place. The tract notification system, whereby not only the cultivation of a plant, but also the land on which such cultivation is possible is restricted might or might not be the most suitable method to regulate opium cultivation. However, this extremely and sometimes even prohibitively restrictive legal regime is not conducive for full medical, scientific, commercial, and industrial exploitation of the cannabis plant in all its natural and biological varieties.

Upon sober reflection, and careful analysis, it would be seen that it might perhaps be better to follow a path more conducive to the potential medicinal users, and those scientifically curious. If licensed cultivation is the preferred way forward, then it might be more suitable to have an independent state-wide licensing authority. In order to protect the Collectors from unnecessary litigation, this quasi-judicial authority to grant licenses for cannabis cultivation that is currently being exercised by the Collectors of all districts should be exercised by such a consultative body. The Collectors of districts must be on the

183. *See generally* Jocelyn Bosse, 'Before the High Court: The Legal Systematics of Cannabis', 29 Griffith L. Rev. 302 (2020). Bosse exposes the botanical defense to criminal charges of cannabis cultivation and possession, etc, which is based on the rules of botanical nomenclature.

184. *Id.* at p. 311.

185. *Id.*

186. Uttarakhand Hemp Cultivation Policy, *supra* note 163, cl. (1).

concerned license-granting panel though, so that their valuable inputs are given their due consideration. It would be seen that having a wider panel comprising of professionals trained in the process of taking quasi-judicial decisions would be more suitable to, and consistent with the general objectives of the Medical and Scientific Use Amendment. In addition, such a panel might be more effective in achieving these general objectives given the fact that the decisions of such a panel will be subject to appeal, and if the need arises to judicial review as well.

(c) Conclusion

As can be seen from the above analysis, the 2016 Uttarakhand Hemp Cultivation Policy on the one hand, and the 2014 Medical and Scientific Use Amendment on the other hand seem to be pointing in opposite directions. Both of them represent significant developments in Indian Cannabis Law. The Medical and Scientific Use Amendment, for the first time in the history of independent India, positively enjoins the Union Government to take such measures as may be deemed to be necessary in order to ensure that cannabis as defined in the NDPS Act is available for medical and scientific research. The Uttarakhand Hemp Cultivation Policy could have been drafted in a manner more consistent with the Medical and Scientific Use Amendment.

The areas of improvement as mentioned in the analysis above are not mere policy recommendations. Article 21 of our Constitution protects the fundamental right of a dignified human existence. The right to health has more than one facet to it. It may be argued that the right to health includes within itself the right of a citizen to cultivate, or to have cultivated, that particular strain of cannabis that their doctor has prescribed or recommended. As per the constitutional position outlined in chapters 3 and 4 of this book, the regulatory authority in this regard to trade in cannabis vests with the state legislature. In fact, if we examine the pre-independence position, we find out that in those years as well, this authority was always vested with the provincial legislature. In either case this authority was limited to imposition of excise duties, and this limited vesting of authority was consistent with the recommendations of the Indian Hemp and Drugs Commission Report of 1893-94 ('IHDC Report'). The IHDC Report, whose recommendations have been hailed as pragmatic more than 100 years after they were originally made,[187] did categorically recommended that cannabis should never be criminalized in India in any

187. Bewley-Taylor, Blickman, & Jelsma, The Rise and Decline of Cannabis Prohibition, *supra* note 180 at 9.

form.[188] Later, the structure of the Dangerous Drugs Act of 1930 was consistent with these recommendations. It is also a fair assumption that this Report was still fresh in institutional memory the time the Dangerous Drugs Act was enacted. In 1926, the New York Times had referred to the IHDC Report to dispute the connection between cannabis use and insanity and criminality.[189]

The key point to note is that at no point of time in our history, it seems, was the power to criminally prohibit cannabis vested with the federal legislature, or later parliament at all. Even though the Uttarakhand Hemp Cultivation Policy has opened up one way to potentially access the cannabis plant, the limitations of the Policy as pointed out above do leave much to be desired. For the sake of our collective physiological and psychological well-being, for the sake of our national economy, for the sake of our criminal justice system, and in the name of our cultural, religious, and spiritual history, one hopes that calmer and sober heads prevail when the time comes to draft detailed policies with respect to decriminalization, and eventual legalization of cannabis in the Republic of India.

iv. Conclusions

This work attempted to make the following three points: (a) from a legal standpoint, the case that possession of cannabis[190] in India should be 'decriminalized,'; (b) from a policy standpoint, trade in cannabis in India should be 'legalized,' but it is beyond the scope of this work to contemplate as to what type of model would be most suited for the Indian market; and (c) from a constitutional standpoint, it is highly doubtful whether Parliament has the power to criminalize it. The third position is laid down in detail in chapters 3 and 4, and the first two are highlighted in chapters 1, 2, and the above discussion. In addition, the chapters are organized in a manner so as to present a historical narrative of the legal status of cannabis in India, before and after gaining independence in 1947, and after the proclamation of the modern-day republic in 1949. There isn't much point in restating the key points once again since every chapter has its own concluding part. Suffice it to mention here that

188. *See* Chapter 2, section (ix): Conclusion: IHDC Recommendations (Regulation and Taxation without unnecessary State intervention).

189. Bewley-Taylor, Blickman, & Jelsma, 'The Rise and Decline of Cannabis Prohibition', *supra* note 180 at 17.

190. As defined in the NDPS Act, § 2(iii).

the case for decriminalizing possession of small quantities, and for eventual full legalization of cannabis for personal, spiritual, religious, recreational, and medicinal purposes is rationally very strong on its own, and now there are growing precedents all over the globe. This work has also attempted to make such arguments in the Indian context and hopefully has served its purpose. But I would seek your indulgence to allow me to finish this work on a more philosophical note.

That human existence is full of pain, suffering, misery, and despair is a state of being confirmed by deliberations of philosophers, meditations of warriors, discourses of spiritualists, and most importantly from the lived experience of humanity. One of the oldest surviving schools of Indian philosophy, the *Sankhya* school,[191] in its primary scripture *Sankhya Sutras*, Book I, Verse 1, says that the 'absolute cessation of the threefold pain is the absolute aim of the soul.'[192] Richard Garbe translates 'threefold pain' to comprises of: (i) '*adhyatmika*' (i.e., due to one's own self); (ii) '*adhibhautika*' (i.e., due to beings of the outer world, such as beasts and birds, etc.); and (iii) '*adhidaivika*' (i.e., due to planets, demons, and the like).[193] Henry Thomas Colebrooke, Esq., also translates 'threefold pain' to include: (i) *adhyatmika* (natural and inseparable); (ii) *adhibhautika* (natural and extrinsic); and (iii) *adhidaivika* (non-natural or superhuman).[194] Detailed spiritual inquiry into the diverse ways in which cessation of pain can be brought about notwithstanding, question of human suffering and misery seem to have occupied the philosophical minds of India's sages since time immemorial. The authorship of *Sankhya Sutras*, attributed to Kapil Muni, is dated back to Buddha.[195]

The causes of pain are diverse, and not easily apprehended by the human mind. The incredible tragedies and traumas that we all, as human beings, have experienced after the COVID-19 global pandemic will surely extract a huge toll

191. *See* S. Radhakrishnan, Indian Philosophy, Vol. II 248-335 (George Allen & Unwin, London 1966, eight impression)

192. Richard Garbe (tr.), Aniruddh's Commentary and the Original Parts of Vedantin Mahadeva's Commentary on The Samkhya Sutras 2 (Baptist Mission Press, Calcutta 1892). *See also* Henry Thomas Colebrooke (tr.), The Sankya Karika 1 (Oxford, London 1837), who translates the same verse as: "The inquiry is into the means of precluding the three sorts of pain; for pain is embarrassment: nor is the inquiry superfluous because obvious means of alleviation exist, for absolute and final relief is not thereby accomplished."

193. *Id.* at 2-3.

194. Colebrooke, The Sankhya Karika, *supra* note 192 at 1-2.

195. *See e.g.* Radhakrishnan, Indian Philosophy, *supra* note 191 at 251.

on our public as well as private healthcare infrastructure. This toll will be paid, one way or the other, by future generations to come; and this burden will fall most immediately on the younger generation (i.e., between 23-45 years of age), and the generations that will follow. Apart from the physical pain that many have experienced on account of being infected by the COVID-19 virus, and the long and arduous road to recovery that is filled with incredible physical pain for most, it is my belief that it will be psychological trauma that this generation has suffered that will be left unattended. This trauma, I suspect, will be unsuspectingly transferred to the next generation, and this intergenerational trauma will extract a heavy toll in terms of the general levels of stress (including post-traumatic stress), anxiety, clinical depression, panic attacks, and other such psychological issues. I am not being a doomsday predictor here: people are suffering psychologically, and we do not know how to deal with it. This is not a very good state to be in for any economically developing society; we can't have a psychologically traumatized, and stressed workforce. On a deeper human level, it would be a tragedy. The perceptive reader would immediately sense that psychological issues that some of our fellow human beings have to deal with today, and some unfortunate others would have to deal with in the future, do not necessarily have any correlation with their economic status. Rich or poor, educated or uneducated, urban or rural, young or old, we are all equally subject to the same afflictions of the mind, as well as of the body. I suspect these traumas are highly likely to manifest themselves in forms of increased violent crime, social unrest, and increased dissatisfaction with social, cultural, legal, and constitutional institutions. Here is a plant growing in the state of nature, consumption whereof: (i) is so safe that no one has ever died of an overdose; (ii) is known to provide reliable relief from the physical pain of diverse varieties; (iii) is known to provide reliable relief from psychological suffering of diverse varieties; (iv) has been consumed, not just in India, but wherever it was found, and its known use goes back thousands of years; (v) is not associated with any type of rise in violent crimes; (vi) can actually help in reducing dependency on much more dangerous and potentially lethal substances (e.g. alcohol, and opioids, etc.); and (vii) the criminal prohibition whereof is so bad an idea that in 1894 a British commission studying the issue reported to its Parliament that it should never be criminally prohibited; (viii) can provide reliable and steady sources of the public revenue; and lastly (ix) is being consumed, was being consumed, and highly likely will continue to be consumed by human beings. It is also beyond dispute that all plants of the genus cannabis have been used in India since time immemorial for spiritual, recreational, pain-relief, and other medicinal purposes. They continue to be used today as well, and not just in India but world over. Cannabis consumers and non-consumers have been living in harmony with each other since the history of either cannabis or its consumers has been recorded. Entire economies have been, and continue to be, built around this plant and there is undisputed evidence of that as well.

The Medical and Scientific Use Amendment of 2014 in the NDPS Act is a welcome development that has potentially opened up the door for legally accessing all plants of the genus cannabis. This gives hope to the current day medicinal user. The Uttarakhand Hemp Cultivation Policy of 2016, drafted under the NDPS Act, is a good first step in this direction. As demonstrated above, there is neither a case nor cause for Uttarakhand, or for that matter any other State government: (i) to restrict their respective hemp policies to industrial hemp only, (ii) to impose restrictions on THC concentration in the cultivated plant, or (iii) import the tract notification system into cannabis law from the opium regulatory regime. State governments would perhaps be convinced from this analysis to consider going for more liberal and enabling licensing regimes as compared to the Uttarakhand Model. Contemplating a model state hemp cultivation policy could perhaps be left as 'homework' after reading this book, and one hopes that a wider discussion will follow.

In the times that we are living in, in light of the known pain-relieving properties of cannabis to the human body, and the human psyche, in light of all the stresses and anxieties that we all have to live and deal with on a daily basis, and in light of all that is highlighted and argued in this work, it is my view and hope that the average middle-class consumer of cannabis in India, perhaps with a historical bent of mind, might be compelled to contemplate on the following: symbolically speaking, consuming cannabis might just be one of the biggest acts of peaceful civil disobedience in our country right now!

I hope and trust that these arguments will educate the reader, whether a cannabis consumer or not, about this substance, its place in our culture, the history of its legal status, and constitutional arrangement pertaining to it that has been in place since the Government of India Act, 1935 was enacted, and was carried forward into our Constitution in 1949. I also hope and trust that these arguments will encourage you to form an opinion on the subject, should you feel the need to have one (but since you are reading this sentence, this is covered!), and at least to reconsider your position if you are a cannabis-prohibitionist (someone who supports the criminal prohibition of cannabis). If you support cannabis-decriminalization, then chances are that you further support cannabis-legalization, and in either case, I hope and trust that this work might provide you with a systematic manner with which to approach this subject, and encourage you to take up a further study on your own. If you are a cannabis-grower, I hope and trust that the day is not too far away in the future when you can cultivate this plant, and earn your livelihood with the same dignity of a vegetable, or dairy, or crop farmer. If you are a cannabis-seller or distributor, I hope and trust that you will one day be a registered dealer under the indirect tax laws, with your own respectable operation, and you and your employees will proudly submit your income tax returns at the end of the financial year. If you are a cannabis entrepreneur, well, the road ahead would be bumpy, but it's the journey that matters right!

And lastly, if you are a cannabis consumer, I hope and trust that the day is not too far away in the future when you can safely order online some cannabis from the privacy of your home and are able to partake in it based on your judgment without being judged by the law. As for society, I hope that follows too. I hope and trust that one day you will be able to go to Connaught Place, enter a dispensary, buy a pre-roll, get a cup of coffee, walk to the Central Park and enjoy all this with your friends, or a good book, or some good music, without being bothered by anyone! Pray tell, why should an honest taxpayer not be able to enjoy his evening cup of tea with a pre-roll while enjoying the view at Gateway of India, or while waiting for his 15-hour flight to take-off (when the same taxpayer can easily conceal his whiskey in a flask at the same spot; and don't we already have smoking rooms in airports!)?!

I end this work in the hope that whatever is causing your suffering, it makes itself comprehensible to you so that you can find a way to heal it; for there seems to be no end to human suffering; it seems to be a permanent condition that all humans must constantly struggle against. If consuming cannabis helps you heal, or manage your pain better, if it provides an island of relief amidst an ocean of suffering and despair, if it helps you be a better human being more sensitised to the suffering of your fellow humans, if it adds to your joys and reduces your miseries, and if it helps you to find the path to a more stable, peaceful, and less painful human existence, then know that it is alright to consume cannabis. It is the law, in this case, that seems to be wrong; not your desire to be human. We are all after all human, all too human!

APPENDICES

Appendix A

Consultation Paper No. 1: The Fiscal Case for Cannabis Decriminalization in India

Submitted By:

Prof. Khagesh Gautam,
S.J.D. Candidate (Indiana University, Maurer School of Law); LL.M. (Columbia); LL.B. (Delhi),
Associate Professor of Law,
Assistant Director, Centre on Public Law and Jurisprudence,
Jindal Global Law School,
email: kgautam@jgu.edu.in

Assisted By:

Yashowardhan Tiwari,
B.A.LL.B. (Hons) (JGLS),
GRIP Scholar,
Jindal Global Law School,
email: 15jgls-ytiwari@jgu.edu.in

October 28, 2020

Professor (Dr.) G. S. Bajpai,
Convenor and Member,
National Level Committee for Reforms in Criminal Laws,
(constituted by the Ministry of Home Affairs, Government of India, vide its notification '1-2-19 Judicial Cell (Part I)' dated 02-03-2020, 04-05-2020, and 29-05-2020)
Centre for Criminology and Victimology,
National Law University Delhi
New Delhi -- 110078

Subject:	Consultation Paper No. 1 titled '**The Fiscal Case for Cannabis Decriminalization in India**', submitted *in response to* the general notification issued by National Law University Delhi dated 26-06-2020, and *further in response to* the public notice on 'Open Consultation on the Narcotic Drugs and Psychotropic Substances Act, 1985' bearing the serial no. CRCL/PN/10/2020 dated 07-10-2020.

Dear Sir,

We are pleased to submit the attached **Consultation Paper No. 1: The Fiscal Case for Cannabis Decriminalization in India** in response to the general notification issued by National Law University Delhi dated 26-06-2020, and further in response to the public notice on 'Open Consultation on the Narcotic Drugs and Psychotropic Substances Act, 1985' bearing the serial no. CRCL/PN/10/2020 dated 07-10-2020.

The present paper attempts to study the fiscal gains that directly emerge from decriminalization and legal regulation of trade in cannabis. The paper makes an economic case for the decriminalization of cannabis consumption in India by analysing the state revenue earned by those states in the United States where its trade has been decriminalized and is now legally regulated. Various studies by federal and independent organizations corroborate the fact that the annual tax revenue of the USA estimates around $ 9 billion (approx.) only from the legalized sale of cannabis. Similar effects could also be observed in Canada and European countries but have not been studied in this paper. The massive spike in revenue collection is also supported by the reduction in state costs to enforce the criminal prohibition of trade in cannabis. The fiscal case for cannabis has been made in the west since the mid-twentieth century. The present article adds to the same debate to make a case for India. Studies conducted by the Indian government, as well as those by the independent group, show that cannabis is the most commonly consumed substance after alcohol. The economic case for legalization of trade in cannabis is strongly supported by the growing trends of cannabis consumption across the adult populations in the civilized world (e.g., the U.S.A., Canada, Spain, etc.) and has immense potential to boost economic growth by adding a permanent and steady source of tax-revenue to general state revenues that can be utilized for a diverse variety of public spending. In addition, legalizing trade in cannabis has immense potential to create jobs in a diverse variety of areas, cultivation of specific strains of cannabis for medicinal as well as recreational purposes. Furthermore, if legalized the cost of enforcing this criminal prohibition will disappear thus saving the public exchequer a substantial amount. In addition, all relevant pending cases currently in the investigation, inquiry, or trial stage would lapse thus reducing pendency in the judicial system (starting from Sessions Court all the way up to the Supreme Court). The rising cases of arrests under the NDPS Act due to cannabis consumption anyway reflects poorly on the success of law and policy regarding the same. The paper finally concludes on the predicament that the state by pushing a substantial number of people into the criminal justice system is not only creating a social problem rather is also forfeiting a substantial amount of revenue that can help in all kinds of public benefits that the people desire.

We would like to congratulate the Committee on undertaking this arduous yet necessary task, and we are indeed very honoured to assist the Committee in this historic work in any small way. Decriminalization of trade in cannabis is a necessary and long-pending discussion in our country and there could not have been a better place to begin this discussion than the National Law University Delhi and under the leadership of leading lights of Indian legal academia.

We hope that the Committee will find the attached consultation paper useful for its purposes. However, we would like to clarify that we are submitting this consultation paper in our personal capacity and these views do not necessarily reflect the views of the Jindal Global Law School, or the O.P. Jindal Global University on these issues in any way, shape, or form.

We look forward to assisting the Committee in this task and do undertake to answer any questions connected with the attached consultation paper.

Regards,

Khagesh Gautam,
LL.M. (Columbia); LL.B. (Delhi),
Associate Professor of Law,
Jindal Global Law School,
O.P. Jindal Global University,
Sonipat, Haryana
email: kgautam@jgu.edu.in

Copy to:	Professor (Dr.) Ranbir Singh, Chairperson, National Level Committee for Reforms in Criminal Laws, *(constituted by the Ministry of Home Affairs, Government of India, vide its notification '1-2-19 Judicial Cell (Part I)' dated 02-03-2020, 04-05-2020, and 29-05-2020)*

Consultation Paper No. 1:

The Fiscal Case for Cannabis Decriminalization in India

Khagesh Gautam and Yashowardhan Tiwari#*

Introduction

Decriminalization of cannabis for medical, and recreational purposes is an important and well-known legal-reforms debate in the west, most notably in the US.[1] The manner in which criminalization of cannabis has most severely impacted the economically weaker sections of society is also well documented.[2] In India, the cannabis legalization debate had been lurking around for quite some time.[3]

Regulation of the cannabis trade has been found to be economically beneficial for the state as it opens up a steady stream of revenue that can be utilized for diverse purposes.[4] In addition, the criminal law enforcement costs also go down

* Associate Professor of Law, Jindal Global Law School. The author may be contacted at kgautam@jgu.edu.in.

\# Graduate Research Immersion Program (GRIP) Scholar, Jindal Global Law School. The author may be contacted at 15jgls-ytiwari@jgu.edu.in.

1. Matthew B. Hodroff, *The Controlled Substances Act: Time to Reevaluate Marijuana*, 36 WHITTIER L. REV. 117 (2014).
2. David R. Katner, *Up in Smoke: Removing Marijuana from Schedule I*, 27 B.U. PUB. INT. L.J. 167 (2018).
3. Shashi Tharoor & Avinash Tharoor, Opinion, *High time India, the land of bhang, legalises marijuana*, The Print (Oct. 18, 2018), https://theprint.in/opinion/when-india-legalises-weed/66245/; *Bill for legalised supply of opium, marijuana cleared for Parliament*, HINDUSTAN TIMES (Nov. 02, 2016), https://www.hindustantimes.com/punjab/aap-mp-gandhi-s-bill-seeking-opium-legalisation-cleared-for-tabling-in-parliament/story-itanKX3vRrhuXJPdgnJD6N.html; Soibam Rocky Singh, *HC issues notice on plea against cannabis use*, THE HINDU (Nov. 06, 2019), https://www.thehindu.com/news/national/hc-issues-notice-on-plea-against-cannabis-use/article29902666.ece; Aditi Singh, *Delhi HC issues notice in plea challenging prohibition and criminalization of Cannabis use in India*, BAR & BENCH (Nov. 06, 2019), https://www.barandbench.com/news/delhi-hc-issues-notice-in-plea-challenging-prohibition-and-criminalization-of-cannabis-use-in-india; *Vision & Mission*, THE GREAT LEGALISATION MOVEMENT-INDIA, https://www.glm.org/vision-and-mission.
4. Carl Davis, Misha E. Hill & Richard Phillips, *Taxing Cannabis*, INST. ON TAX'N & ECON. POL'Y 19-25 (Jan. 2019), https://itep.sfo2.digitaloceanspaces.com/012319-TaxingCannabis_ITEP_DavisHillPhillips.pdf.

as the burden on the police, judicial, and penal systems are considerably relaxed.[5] The fiscal[6] case for decriminalization and legal regulation of the trade in cannabis is a considerably crucial one given the fact that revenue streams for the Indian state are currently severely constrained and are predicted to remain in such a state for the foreseeable future.[7] In addition, if a steady stream of tax revenue could be added to, for e.g., the Consolidated Fund of India, that case anyway stands quite independent of how strong the current stream of state revenue is.

The trends in the US concerning the increase in state revenue due to the addition of a potential tax base have also been confirmed by independent research. For instance, it has been acknowledged that "rapid growth has persisted in every subsequent year as the early-adopting states continued to see growth and as additional states began taxing recreational cannabis"[8]. Armikka R. Bryant, discussing the "immense revenue potential" of the marijuana market, stated that, "During the 2014-2015 fiscal year, the taxes imposed on recreational and medical marijuana sales in Colorado raised more than $43 million in retail sales tax and excise tax revenue".[9] Similarly for Washington, the author observed that "For fiscal year 2016, sales in the state grossed over $970 million, resulting in over $185 million in tax revenue".[10]

---

5. Jeffrey A. Miron, *The Budgetary Implications of Marijuana Prohibition*, MARIJUANA POLICY PROJECT, 2 (June 2005), https://www.mpp.org/assets/pdf/issues/economics/budgetary-implications-marijuana-prohibition.pdf; *The War on Marijuana in Black and White: Billions of Dollars Wasted on Racially Biased Arrests*, AMERICAN CIVIL LIBERTIES UNION, 22 (June 2013), https://www.aclu.org/files/assets/aclu-thewaronmarijuana-rel2.pdf.
6. *Fiscal*, BLACK'S LAW DICTIONARY (11th ed. 2019). (Fiscal means (a) 'Of, relating to, or involving financial matters <fiscal year>' b) 'Of, relating to, or involving public finances or taxation <the city's sound fiscal policy>'). We focus on using 'fiscal' in the latter sense in this paper.
7. NITI AAYOG, SPECIAL FEATURE: WOMEN ENTREPRENEURSHIP PLATFORM, 4 ARTHNITI 1, 7-8 (July 31, 2020), https://niti.gov.in/sites/default/files/2020-08/Arthniti_Newsletterjuly2020.pdf; NATIONAL STATISTICAL OFFICE, PRESS NOTE ON ESTIMATES OF GROSS DOMESTIC PRODUCT FOR THE FIRST QUARTER (APRIL-JUNE) 2020-2021, 1 (Aug. 31, 2020) (on file with the Ministry of Statistics and Programme Implementation), http://164.100.117.97/WriteReadData/userfiles/PRESS_NOTE-Q1_2020-21.pdf; *India GDP Q1 Data: India's economic growth slips 23.9% in Q1 of 2020-21*, INDIAN EXPRESS (Aug. 31, 2020), https://indianexpress.com/article/business/economy/gdp-1st-quarter-growth-rate-data-india-april-june-2020-6577114/.
8. Davis, Hill. & Phillips, *supra* note 4, at 19.
9. Armikka R. Bryant, *Taxing Marijuana: Earmarking Tax Revenue From Legalized Marijuana*, 33 GEORGIA ST. UNIV. L. REV. 677 (2017).
10. *Id.*

In this article, we will attempt to make a fiscal case for legalizing and regulating the trade in cannabis by offering evidence from several jurisdictions in the US that have done so. It will be seen by the end of this analysis that all jurisdictions that have taken this decision have seen a steady, growing, and very promising stream of tax revenue added to their state funds. The analysis will show that those jurisdictions that have legalised such use and sales have consistently experienced an increase in state revenue. In the US alone, till the time of writing of this paper, eleven states and the District of Columbia have made the use of cannabis legal for adults.[11] Out of these, ten states (namely, Alaska, California, Colorado, Illinois, Maine, Massachusetts, Michigan, Nevada, Oregon, and Washington, D.C.) have also allowed for the sale of cannabis, which is being taxed and regulated similarly to alcohol.[12]

The Fiscal Case

The fiscal case for cannabis legalization was noted as far back in 1963 by a renowned British journal where it was noted that in addition to "the undoubted attraction of reducing, for once, the number of crimes that a member of our society can commit, and of allowing the wider spread of something that can give pleasure, a greater revenue would certainly come to the State from taxation than from fines. Additional gains might be the reduction of interracial tension, as well as that between generations; for "pot" spread from South America to Britain via the United States and the West Indies."[13] We may note that in 1963 there was no legal prohibition on the cannabis trade in India.[14]

Even before the legalization of marijuana for adult-use sales had begun across the states, various reports and studies were already pouring in predicting how it would serve well for the states to tap into this potential tax base. In 2014, when legislation was introduced in the state legislature of Vermont, the legislature directed the 'Secretary of Administration to produce a comprehensive report on

---

11. *Our American States* - The NCSL Podcast, *Marijuana Overview*, NAT'L CONF. ON ST. LEGIS. (2019), https://www.ncsl.org/research/civil-and-criminal-justice/marijuana-overview.aspx (last visited Sept. 19, 2020).
12. *Replacing Marijuana Prohibition with Sensible Regulations: An overview of state frameworks for regulating marijuana like alcohol*, MARIJUANA POLICY PROJECT, https://www.mpp.org/issues/legalization/regulationlaws/ (last visited September 19, 2020).
13. Editorial, *Pop "Pot"*, 282 THE LANCET 989 (1963).
14. *Raja Ram Jaiswal* v. *State of Bihar*, AIR 1964 SC 828.

the consequences of legalizing marijuana'[15]. The report[16] was prepared by RAND Corporation, the key findings of which were later published as a journal piece[17]. This piece estimated that the people of Vermont spent $125-225 million per year on marijuana, further stating that 'foregoing revenues from even a 1% excise tax has a greater fiscal impact than does enforcing Vermont's prohibition after decriminalization'.[18] Accordingly, the potential tax revenues for the state from cannabis sales were projected to be around $20-75 million per year.[19]

A study[20] conducted by the Tax Foundation gave an estimate that the federal US and the state governments where cannabis was still criminally prohibited were 'forfeiting $28 billion in annual tax revenue'[21]. Another estimate suggests the spending by cannabis consumers in the US at around $30 billion per year.[22] It is interesting to note that the recognition of the fiscal case for cannabis legalization goes back to at least the mid-20th century.

In an affidavit[23] filed by the renowned Harvard economist Jeffrey A. Miron before the Boston Municipal Court in 2008, based on a report[24] prepared by him, it was stated that the U.S. state and federal governments could have collected 'at least $2.4 billion' as tax revenue in 2004, had marijuana been legal.[25] It was also mentioned that the state and federal governments of the U.S.

---

15. Jonathan P. Caulkins & Beau Kilmer, *Considering marijuana legalization carefully: insights for other jurisdictions from analysis for Vermont*, 111 ADDICTION 2082, 2082 (2016).
16. Jonathan P. Caulkins et al., *Considering Marijuana Legalization: Insights For Vermont And Other Jurisdictions* (2015), https://www.rand.org/content/dam/rand/pubs/research_reports/RR800/RR864/RAND_RR864.pdf.
17. Caulkins & Kilmer, *supra* note 15.
18. Caulkins & Kilmer, *supra* note 15, at 2084.
19. Caulkins & Kilmer, *supra* note 15, at 2086.
20. Gavin Ekins & Joseph Bishop-Henchman, *Marijuana Legalization and Taxes: Federal Revenue Impact*, TAX FOUND. (May 12, 2016), https://files.taxfoundation.org/legacy/docs/TaxFoundation_FF509.pdf.
21. CLAYTON J. MOSHER & SCOTT AKINS, IN THE WEEDS: DEMONIZATION, LEGALIZATION, AND THE EVOLUTION OF U.S. MARIJUANA POLICY 15 (2019).
22. Jonathan P. Caulkins et al., *High Tax States: Options for Gleaning Revenue from Legal Cannabis*, 91 OREGON L. REV. 1047, 1047 (2013).
23. Affidavit of Harvard economist Jeffrey Miron submitted in 2008 in the Massachusetts criminal case of *Commonwealth v. Stroup and Cusick*, No. 0701CR7230, (Boston Mun. Ct, 2008), https://norml.org/wp-content/uploads/pdf_files/brief_bank/Miron_Affidavit.pdf.
24. Jeffrey A. Miron, *The Budgetary Implications of Marijuana Prohibition*, MARIJUANA POLICY PROJECT (June 2005), https://www.mpp.org/assets/pdf/issues/economics/budgetary-implications-marijuana-prohibition.pdf.
25. *Supra* note 23, at 2.

combined spent around $7.7 billion in marijuana prohibition in the year 2004.[26] According to an official estimate, the total expenditure on marijuana consumption in the U.S. for the years 1988-2000 stood at approximately $143.5 billion.[27] A sample calculation carried out by the U.S.'s *Congressional Research Service*, based on a federal government report[28] which pegged the U.S. cannabis market size at $41 billion for the year 2010, estimated the annual potential excise tax collection from cannabis trade to be $9.1 billion and the projected revenue gain to be $6.8 billion.[29] One may note that these potential tax revenue estimates, combined with the other costs incurred by the federal and state governments (including the social enforcement costs of cannabis prohibition laws), together constitute massive budgetary costs borne by the governments.[30] In discussing the budgetary costs of cannabis prohibition laws, Jon Gettman summed up the following as the benefits of a legalized and well-regulated trade regime: a) restoration of 'the capital flow in the illegal marijuana market to legitimate and taxable economic channels'; b) elimination of the 'criminal justice and border security costs' related to illegal cannabis market which would allow the government to 'provide for the reallocation of resources to other pressing drug, immigration, and homeland security issues'; c) possibility of the deflation of teen indulgence in the cannabis trade, also reducing cannabis use among adolescents; d) the elimination of outward flow of capital through domestic

---

26. *Id.* The affidavit further mentioned the endorsement of the report by more than 500 economists, including three Nobel laureates, who had later signed an 'open letter to President Bush' demanding an "open and honest debate about marijuana prohibition", further adding, "We believe such a debate will favor a regime in which marijuana is legal but taxed and regulated like other goods." *Id*, at 2-3. For news about the open letter, *refer to* Ezekiel Edwards & Rebecca McCray, *Hundreds of Economists: Marijuana Prohibition Costs Billions, Legalization Would Earn Billions*, ACLU (Apr. 26, 2012, 4:29 PM), https://www.aclu.org/blog/smart-justice/sentencing-reform/hundreds-economists-marijuana-prohibition-costs-billions.
27. William Rhodes et al., *What America's Users Spend on Illegal Drugs 1988-1998*, OFFICE OF NAT'L DRUG CONT'L POL'Y 22 (Dec. 2000), https://www.ncjrs.gov/ondcppubs/publications/pdf/spending_drugs_1988_1998.pdf.
28. B. Kilmer et al., *What America's Users Spend on Illegal Drugs: 2000-2010*, OFFICE OF NAT'L DRUG CONT'L POL'Y 4 (Feb. 2014), https://obamawhitehouse.archives.gov/sites/default/files/ondcp/policy-and-research/wausid_results_report.pdf.
29. JANE G. GRAVELLE & SEAN LOWRY, *Federal Proposals To Tax Marijuana: An Economic Analysis*, R43785 CONG. RESEARCH SERV., 14-15 (2014), https://fas.org/sgp/crs/misc/R43785.pdf.
30. JON GETTMAN, *Lost Taxes And Other Costs Of Marijuana Laws* 34-37 (2007), http://norml.org.nz/downloads/Gettman_Lost_Taxes.pdf. It is stated that, "Consequently, marijuana arrests cost taxpayers $10.7 billion in 2004. Taken together, the lost tax revenue from the diversion of funds to the marijuana market and the cost of marijuana arrests produce a budgetary cost to local, state and the federal government of $41.8 billion." *Id*, at 36.

production of cannabis; and e) the shifting of all 'fiscal costs related to marijuana use from all taxpayers to marijuana users themselves by way of excise taxes'.[31]

Canada is reported to have generated 186 million Canadian dollars in tax revenue within the first five-and-a-half months post-legalization of cannabis use for recreational purposes in early 2019.[32] One may note that often the discussions around fiscal benefits of legalization of cannabis trade do not include those about the possibility of revenue generation from the use of hemp as an industrial and agricultural commodity[33], or those about its medical uses[34] (medical cannabis may be taxed as well).

Cannabis use decriminalization and its legalization for recreational use have been a policy matter of interest in Europe as well.[35] For instance, in the Netherlands, the sale of cannabis is allowed subject to certain restrictions in establishments called 'coffee shops', and the government 'does not prosecute members of the public for possession or use of small quantities of soft drugs'.[36]

---

31. *Id*, at 37.
32. *Cannabis generates C$186 million in tax revenue in Canada in first months of legalization*, REUTERS (June 20, 2019), https://in.reuters.com/article/us-canada-cannabis/cannabis-generates-c186-million-in-tax-revenue-in-canada-in-first-months-of-legalization-idINKCN1TK2YV.
33. JEAN M. RAWSON, CONG. RESEARCH SERV., RL32725, HEMP AS AN AGRICULTURAL COMMODITY (2005), https://fas.org/sgp/crs/RL32725.pdf.
34. CHARLES DOYLE, CONG. RESEARCH SERV., MARIJUANA FOR MEDICAL PURPOSES: A GLIMPSE OF THE SUPREME COURT'S DECISION IN *UNITED STATES V. OAKLAND CANNABIS BUYERS' COOPERATIVE* AND RELATED LEGAL ISSUES (2005), https://crsreports.congress.gov/product/pdf/RS/RS20998; MARK EDDY, CONG. RESEARCH SERV., MEDICAL MARIJUANA: REVIEW AND ANALYSIS OF FEDERAL AND STATE POLICIES 32 (2010), https://fas.org/sgp/crs/misc/RL33211.pdf; Cannabinoids as Antioxidants and Neuroprotectants, U.S. Patent No. 6,630,507 (filed Feb. 2, 2001) (issued Oct. 7, 2003) (patent rights assigned to the U.S. Department of Health and Human Services);, *Potential Merits of Cannabinoids for Medical Uses, Before the Subcomm. on Criminal Justice, Drug Policy, & Human Res. H. Comm. on Gov't Reform*, 108th Cong. (2004) (Robert J. Meyer, Dir. of Office of Drug Evaluation II), https://www.govinfo.gov/content/pkg/CHRG-108hhrg96746/html/CHRG-108hhrg96746.htm; Letter from Robert D. Evans, A.B.A. Gov't Affairs Office, to Honorable John Conyers, Ranking Member Committee on the Judiciary, H.R. (May 4, 1998). (The American Bar Association 'supports federal legislation to establish a program under which [seriously ill] patients can be treated with marijuana...').
35. *See* generally, European Monitoring Centre for Drugs and Drug Addiction (EMCDDA), *Cannabis legislation in Europe: An overview*, PUBLICATIONS OFFICE OF THE EUROPEAN UNION (June 2018), https://www.emcdda.europa.eu/system/files/publications/4135/TD0217210ENN.pdf (Discussing the cannabis legislations in the EU countries, with a special focus on cannabis for 'recreational use').
36. GOV'T OF THE NETHERLANDS, https://www.government.nl/topics/drugs (last visited Oct. 14, 2020).

The tolerance[37] of these coffee shops during the 1980s and 90s resulted in annual revenue estimates which claimed a turnover of 210-283 million euros.[38] It has been reported that in 2008 alone, the Dutch coffee shops paid 400 million euros as taxes to the government on the income generated from the sales of cannabis amounting to over 2 billion euros.[39] For 2013, the total turnover of the coffee shops at the time was estimated to be somewhere ranging from 875 million to 1.25 billion euros.[40] While the social enforcement costs of laws regarding crimes involving soft drugs are pitched at 160 million euros per year[41], the annual tax revenue from these shops is placed at 400 million euros.[42] Even in Spain, with the springing up of 'legally constituted'[43] Cannabis Social Clubs across the country, there has been a heavy generation of income through the cannabis market. A study cited by the *Transnational Institute* pegged the yearly spending at 1,163 million euros, and mentioned that 'if all cannabis sales were liable to VAT', around 200 million euros could be generated as tax revenue, also creating 'an estimated 40,000 jobs', with revenue generation amounting to 400 million euros 'in social security and income tax distributions'.[44] According to an

---

37. *See* GOV'T OF THE NETHERLANDS, https://www.government.nl/topics/drugs/toleration-policy-regarding-soft-drugs-and-coffee-shops (last visited Oct. 14, 2020). (Mentions the toleration policy regarding soft drugs and coffee shops.)
38. European Monitoring Centre for Drugs and Drug Addiction, *EMCDDA INSIGHTS: Cannabis production and markets in Europe*, OFFICE FOR OFF'L PUB'NS OF THE EUROPEAN COMMUNITIES 73 (2012), https://www.emcdda.europa.eu/attachements.cfm/att_166248_EN_web_INSIGHTS_CANNABIS.pdf.
39. *How To Regulate Cannabis: A Practical Guide*, TRANSFORM DRUG POL'Y FOUND. 90 (Oct. 2016), http://fileserver.idpc.net/library/Cannabook%202nd%20Ed%20Digital.pdf; Phillip Smith, *Europe: Dutch Marijuana Tax Revenues at $600 Million a Year, Crop Is Country's Third Largest Export*, STOPTHEDRUGWAR.ORG (May 09, 2008, 12:00 AM), https://stopthedrugwar.org/chronicle/2008/may/09/europe_dutch_marijuana_tax_reven.
40. Marianne M.J. van Ooyen-Houben, *The Dutch Coffee Shop System, Tensions and Benefits*, 25 MICH. ST. INT'L L. REV. 623, 658-59 (2017), https://digitalcommons.law.msu.edu/cgi/viewcontent.cgi?article=1228&context=ilr.
41. Jean-Paul Grund & Joost Breeksema, *Coffee Shops and Compromise: Separated Illicit Drug Markets in the Netherlands*, GLOBAL DRUG POL'Y PROGRAM 52 (July 2013), https://www.opensocietyfoundations.org/uploads/4516426f-086e-405c-9385-76363993d8f2/coffee-shops-and-compromise-20130713.pdf.
42. Steve Rolles, *Cannabis policy in the Netherlands: moving forwards not backwards*, TRANSFORM DRUG POL'Y FOUND. 1 (Dec. 2014), https://www.unodc.org/documents/ungass2016/Contributions/Civil/Transform-Drug-Policy-Foundation/Cannabis-policy-in-the-Netherlands.pdf.
43. Tom Blickman, *Cannabis policy reform in Europe: Bottom up rather than top down*, Series on Legislative Reform of Drug Policies No. 28, TRANSNATIONAL INSTITUTE 9 (Dec. 2014), https://www.tni.org/files/download/dlr28.pdf.
44. *Id*, at 10.

international development organization *Health Poverty Action*, the introduction of a 'legal cannabis market' in the United Kingdom could result in the generation of 1 to 3.5 billion euros as annual tax revenues.[45]

Notwithstanding the niceties of taxation systems at different levels and their variance across regions, the one thing that emerges pretty clearly from this brief examination below is that the legalized cannabis market has proved to be a steady and reliable source of state revenue, providing the state with potential tax bases waiting to be tapped.

Evidence Supporting the Fiscal Case

California

The legalization of cannabis for the use of adults and the establishment of a regulated cannabis market was approved by California voters through a ballot initiative[46] in November 2016, which ultimately resulted in the promulgation of the Medicinal and Adult-Use Cannabis Regulation and Safety Act[47]. California's revenue records have noted a massive inflow of revenue since the legalization of the cannabis trade. The total revenue thus earned in the form of cultivation tax, excise tax, and sales tax, from the beginning of 2018 till June 2020 amounts to a massive $1.4472 billion.[48] Table 1 provides more details.

Table 1[49]

Year	Revenue	Annual Increase
2018 (Jan-Dec)	$ 397.1 million	—
2019 (Jan-Dec)	$ 635.8 million	$ 238.7 million
2020 (Jan-June)	$ 414.3 million	N.A.

45. Jamie Doward, *Legalizing cannabis 'could earn Treasury £3.5bn'*, THE GUARDIAN (June 2, 2018), https://www.theguardian.com/society/2018/jun/02/legalise-cannabis-treasury-3bn-drugs.
46. Proposition 64: Marijuana Legalization. Initiative Statute., LEGIS. ANALYST'S OFF. (2016), https://lao.ca.gov/ballot/2016/Prop64-110816.pdf.
47. Medical and Adult-Use Cannabis Regulation and Safety Act, West's Ann. Cal. Bus. & Prof. Code § 26000, 2017 (U.S.).
48. Cannabis Tax Revenues, CAL. DEP'T OF TAX & FEE ADMIN. (2020), https://www.cdtfa.ca.gov/dataportal/dataset.htm?url=CannabisTaxRevenues.
49. *Id.*

Washington

Washington, on November 6, 2012, legalized the cannabis trade, and 'replaced marijuana prohibition with a model that legalizes marijuana for adults and taxes and regulates it like alcohol'[50] through Initiative Measure No. 502[51]. The retail shops started functioning on July 8, 2014.[52] The Annual Reports of the Washington State Liquor and Cannabis Board for the fiscal years since 2015 have consistently observed a huge inflow of revenue, as can be gleaned from Table 2.

Table 2[53]

Fiscal Year	Revenue	Annual Increase (rounded off)	Source
FY 2015 (July 1, 2014 to June 30, 2015)	$ 65.71 million	—	Annual Report Fiscal Year 2015
FY 2016	$ 189 million	$ 123.53 million	Annual Report Fiscal Year 2016
FY 2017	$ 319 million	$ 129.87 million	Annual Report Fiscal Year 2017
FY 2018	$ 367.4 million	$ 48.30 million	Annual Report Fiscal Year 2018
FY 2019	$ 395.5 million	$ 28.14 million	Annual Report Fiscal Year 2019

50. *I-502: An Overview of Washington's New Approach to Marijuana*, MARIJUANA POLICY PROJECT, https://www.mpp.org/states/washington/washingtons-i-502/.
51. Initiative Measure No. 502, CODE REVISER'S OFF. (July 8, 2011), https://lcb.wa.gov/publications/Marijuana/I-502/i502.pdf.
52. *Supra* note 50.
53. Annual Report Fiscal Year 2015, WASH. ST. LIQUOR & CANNABIS BOARD 16 (2015), https://lcb.wa.gov/publications/annual_report/2015-annual-report-final-web.pdf; Annual Report Fiscal Year 2016, WASH. ST. LIQUOR & CANNABIS BOARD 17 (2016), https://lcb.wa.gov/sites/default/files/publications/annual_report/2016-annual-report-Final-opt.pdf; Annual Report Fiscal Year 2017, WASH. ST. LIQUOR & CANNABIS BOARD 15-16 (2017), https://lcb.wa.gov/sites/default/files/publications/annual_report/2017-annual-report-final2-web.pdf; Annual Report Fiscal Year 2018, WASH. LIQUOR & CANNABIS BOARD 15-16 (2018), https://lcb.wa.gov/sites/default/files/publications/annual_report/2018-annual-report-web2.pdf; Annual Report Fiscal Year 2019, WASH. LIQUOR & CANNABIS BOARD 14-15 (2019), https://lcb.wa.gov/sites/default/files/publications/annual_report/2019-annual-report-final2.pdf.

Oregon

Oregon voters 'approved an initiative regulating marijuana for adult use in November 2014, and the state's first adult-use stores opened in October 2016'[54]. Ballot Measure 91 (titled the Control, Regulation, and Taxation of Marijuana and Industrial Hemp Act of 2014) after being democratically approved, was made operative from January 1, 2016, by the Oregon Legislative Assembly through House Bill 3400.[55] A research report released in September 2014 by Oregon's Legislative Revenue Office estimated decent net revenue from legalized cannabis trade for the upcoming fiscal years and stated that:

> *Legalization of marijuana will convert the current black market for marijuana to a gray market as tax and regulatory compliance are slow to take hold. The legalized regulated market is likely to achieve higher efficiency and more innovation with time and as circumstances improve. These technological advances are likely to exert downward pressure on the legal retail price in the future and drive a shift from the gray market to the legal recreational market.*[56]

The report highlighted the necessity of acknowledging the slow yet sure grip of the state government over the pre-existing black market for marijuana and the revenues that would come out of its capture over time. As anticipated, the state did indeed accrue increasing revenues over the coming fiscal years. There has been a consistent increase in the total cannabis tax since the opening of its first adult-use stores in 2016. Table 3 provides more details.

Table 3[57]

Fiscal Year	Revenue (rounded off)	Annual Increase (rounded off)
FY 2016	$ 20.65 million	—

54. *Marijuana Tax Revenue in States that Regulate Marijuana for Adult Use*, MARIJUANA POLICY PROJECT, https://www.mpp.org/issues/legalization/marijuana-tax-revenue-states-regulate-marijuana-adult-use/.
55. House Bill 3400, OR. ST. LEGIS. (June 24, 2015), https://olis.leg.state.or.us/liz/2015R1/Downloads/MeasureDocument/HB3400/Enrolled.
56. OR. LEGIS. REVENUE OFF., RESEARCH REPORT #3-14, THE REVENUE IMPACT OF MARIJUANA LEGALIZATION UNDER MEASURE 91, 1 (Sept. 2014), https://www.oregonlegislature.gov/lro/Documents/RR%203-14%20Measure%2091.pdf.
57. OR. DEP'T OF REVENUE RES. SEC., OREGON MARIJUANA TAX STATISTICS: ACCOUNTING INFORMATION, (Aug. 28, 2020), https://www.oregon.gov/dor/programs/gov-research/Documents/Financial-reporting-receipts-public.pdf.

Fiscal Year	Revenue (rounded off)	Annual Increase (rounded off)
FY 2017	$ 70.26 million	$ 49.61 million
FY 2018	$ 82.2 million	$ 11.94 million
FY 2019	$ 102.09 million	$ 19.89 million
FY 2020	$ 133.15 million	$ 31.06 million

Colorado

In November 2012, the voters of the state of Colorado approved Amendment 64[58], 'an initiative to regulate marijuana for adults', and 'on January 1, 2014, the state became the first with legal adult-use sales'.[59] Table 4 provides more details.

Table 4[60]

Year	Revenue (rounded off)	Annual Increase (rounded off)
2014	$ 46.1 million	—
2015	$ 104.76 million	$ 58.66 million
2016	$ 167.16 million	$ 62.40 million
2017	$ 220.69 million	$ 53.53 million
2018	$ 243.47 million	$ 22.78 million
2019	$ 279.16 million	$ 35.69 million

58. Amendment 64, COL. GEN. ASSEMBLY (Aug. 29, 2012), https://www.leg.state.co.us/LCS/Initiative%20Referendum/1112initrefr.nsf/c63bddd6b9678de787257799006bd391/cfa3bae60c8b4949872579c7006fa7ee/$FILE/Amendment%2064%20merged.pdf; Amendment 64 Implementation, ST. OF COL., https://www.colorado.gov/pacific/sites/default/files/13%20Amendment%2064%20LEGIS.pd.
59. *Supra* note 54.
60. *Supra* note 54.

Alaska

Alaska voters approved the voter initiative Measure 2[61] in November 2014[62], which came into effect in February 2015[63], following which possession and use of cannabis were legalized for adults over the age of 21. Since the opening of adult-use cannabis stores beginning October 2016[64], the state government has collected substantial revenue. Table 5 provides details.

Table 5[65]

Fiscal Year	Revenue (rounded off)	Annual Increase (rounded off)
FY 2017	$ 1.75 million	—
FY 2018	$ 11.08 million	$ 9.34 million
FY 2019	$ 19.20 million	$ 8.12 million
FY 2020	$ 24.54 million	$ 5.34 million

Nevada

Cannabis was legalized for adult-use sales and consumption through a successful voter initiative in Nevada on November 8, 2016[66], with the actual sales

61. AS 17.38 (Ballot Measure 2), ALCOHOL & MARIJUANA CON'L OFF., https://www.commerce.alaska.gov/web/portals/9/pub/MCB/StatutesAndRegulations/MJ_Ballot Measure2.pdf.
62. ALASKA DEP'T OF HEALTH & SOC'L SERV., MARIJUANA USE AND PUBLIC HEALTH IN ALASKA – 2020, 1 (Jan. 2020), http://dhss.alaska.gov/dph/Director/Documents/marijuana/MarijuanaUse_PublicHealth_Alaska_2020.pdf; *Supra* note 54.
63. ALASKA DEP'T OF HEALTH & SOC'L SERV., MARIJUANA EDUCATION, http://dhss.alaska.gov/osmap/Pages/marijuana.aspx; AS 17.38 - Statutes (Effective 7/25/18), ALCOHOL & MARIJUANA CON'L OFF., https://www.commerce.alaska.gov/web/Portals/9/pub/MCB/StatutesAndRegulations/AS17.38.pdf.
64. *Supra* note 54.
65. Marijuana Tax Reports, ALASKA DEP'T OF REVENUE, http://tax.alaska.gov/programs/programs/reports/index.aspx?60000.
66. Statewide Ballot Questions 2016: To Appear on the November 8, 2016 General Election Ballot, OFF. OF SEC'Y OF ST., NEVADA 14-33 (2016) Carson City: State of Nevada, https://www.nvsos.gov/sos/home/showdocument?id=4434.

beginning in July 2017[67]. An attractive amount of cannabis tax revenues (from sales for both medical and recreational use) have since been collected. Table 6 provides details.

Table 6[68]

Fiscal Year	Revenue (rounded off)	Annual Increase (rounded off)
FY 2018	$ 69.76 million	—
FY 2019	$ 99.185 million	$ 29.43 million
FY 2020	$ 105.181 million	$ 5.996 million

Massachusetts

The people of Massachusetts voted in favor of adult-use sales through the ballot initiative Question 4 on November 8, 2016[69] (Secretary of the Commonwealth 2016: 12-24), with the sales finally beginning in November 2018[70]. The cannabis tax revenue, as anticipated, has been steadily picking up since then. Table 7 provides details.

Table 7[71]

Year	Revenue (rounded off)	Annual Increase (rounded off)
2018 (Nov-Dec)	$ 2.798 million	—
2019	$ 75.67 million	$ 72.87 million
2020 (Jan-Aug)	$ 64.14 million	—

---

67. *Supra* note 54.
68. Marijuana Statistics and Reports: Marijuana Tax Revenue, Department of Taxation, DEP'T OF TAX'N, ST. OF NEVADA, https://tax.nv.gov/Publications/Marijuana_Statistics_and_Reports/.
69. SEC'Y OF THE COMM., THE COMM. OF MASSACHUSETTS, INFORMATION FOR VOTERS: 2016 BALLOT QUESTIONS 12-24 (2016), https://www.sec.state.ma.us/ele/elepdf/IFV_2016.pdf.
70. *Supra* note 54.
71. *Supra* note 54.

Michigan

Cannabis trade was also recently legalized[72] in Michigan by a ballot proposal[73] in November 2018 by the people of Michigan, with the actual sales starting in December 2019[74]. Table 8 provides details.

Table 8[75]

Year	Revenue (rounded off)	Annual Increase
2019 (Dec)	$ 1.118 million	—
2020 (Jan-July)	$ 34.539 million	—

Illinois

HB1438[76] was signed into law on June 25, 2019[77], thus allowing for legalization and regulation of adult-use sales in Illinois. The government has declared that with the beginning of sales in January 2020, the state "earned $52 million in revenue during the first six months of Illinois' new adult-use industry"[78].

Conclusion

A recent study conducted on the magnitude of substance abuse in India, by the Ministry of Social Justice and Empowerment of the Government of India in

72. Michigan Regulation and Taxation of Marihuana Act: Initiated Law 1 of 2018, MICH. COMP. LAWS. ANN. § 333.27951, https://www.legislature.mi.gov/(S(un0bpjzkhqvupvwim2rvqxyv))/mileg.aspx?page=getObject&objectName=mcl-Initiated-Law-1-of-2018.
73. Michigan Regulation and Taxation of Marihuana Act Official Full-Text for Proposal 18-1, ST. OF MICHIGAN, https://www.michigan.gov/documents/sos/Full_Text_-_CRMLA_635255_7.pdf.
74. *Supra* note 54.
75. *Supra* note 54.
76. Cannabis Regulation & Tax Act: HB1438 Enrolled, ILLINOIS GEN. ASSEMBLY, https://ilga.gov/legislation/101/HB/PDF/10100HB1438lv.pdf.
77. *Supra* note 54.
78. *Gov. Pritzker Announces $52 Million in Adult-Use Cannabis Tax Revenue in First Six Months of Industry*, ILLINOIS NEWS (July 14, 2020), https://www2.illinois.gov/news/release?ReleaseID=21813.

2019 pointed out that "after Alcohol, Cannabis and Opioids are the next commonly used substances in India"[79]. It stated:

> About 2.8% of the population (3.1 crore individuals) reports having used any cannabis product within the previous year. The use of cannabis was further differentiated between the legal form of cannabis (bhang) and other illegal cannabis products (ganja and charas). Use of these cannabis products was observed to be about 2% (approximately 2.2 crore persons) for bhang and about 1.2% (approximately 1.3 crore persons) for illegal cannabis products, *ganja* and *charas*. States with the highest prevalence of cannabis use are Uttar Pradesh, Punjab, Sikkim, Chhattisgarh and Delhi.[80]

Indicating the lower levels of dependence amongst cannabis users (prevalence of cannabis use in India being lower than the global average[81]), the report further stated:

> The proportion of people with problem cannabis use (i.e., those with harmful or dependent pattern of cannabis use) is rather modest. At the national level, about 0.25% (one in eleven cannabis users) suffers from cannabis dependence. However, there is a substantial difference between bhang and ganja/charas in terms of dependent use – while just about one in sixteen users of bhang were dependent on cannabis, this figure was one in seven in case of ganja/charas users.[82]

---

79. MIN'Y OF SOCIAL JUSTICE & EMPOWERMENT, MAGNITUDE OF SUBSTANCE USE IN INDIA, 2019 at 2, (India), http://socialjustice.nic.in/writereaddata/UploadFile/Magnitude_Substance_Use_India_REPORT.pdf.; cited in Neha Singhal & Naveed Ahmad, *A Case For De-Criminalization of Cannabis Use in India*, VIDHI CENTRE FOR LEGAL POL'Y 5 (Aug. 20, 2020), https://vidhilegalpolicy.in/wp-content/uploads/2020/08/Cannabis_Final.pdf.
80. MIN'Y OF SOCIAL JUSTICE & EMPOWERMENT, MAGNITUDE OF SUBSTANCE USE IN INDIA, 2019 at 2, (India), http://socialjustice.nic.in/writereaddata/UploadFile/Magnitude_Substance_Use_India_REPORT.pdf.
81. *Id*, at 4.
82. *Id*, at 3. This may be compared with the dependence pattern of alcohol use. "Nationally, about 14.6% of the population (between 10 and 75 year of age) uses alcohol. In terms of absolute numbers, there are about 16 crore persons who consume alcohol in the country...

    At the national level, as many as 19% of current users of alcohol consume alcohol in a dependent pattern. The prevalence of dependent pattern of alcohol use in the general population (10-75 years) is estimated to be 2.7%, or 2.9 crore individuals. States with high prevalence (more than 10%) of alcohol use disorders are: Tripura, Andhra Pradesh, Punjab, Chhattisgarh and

(Footnote No. 82 contd.)

Notwithstanding the questions that might be raised against the terming of cannabis consumption as 'drug abuse' in light of the low dependence rates, if the current laws against such consumption are to be enforced exhaustively, more than 3 crore individuals would find themselves behind the bars, and the already 'crumbling' criminal justice system 'would cave in entirely'.[83] On the other hand, one may instead prefer examining the potential revenue generation by taxing cannabis use and trade. We may also factor in the current high social enforcement costs that the taxpayers have to ultimately bear as a result of such criminalization.[84] A research study[85] conducted in Mumbai by the *Vidhi Centre for Legal Policy* revealed that in the year 2018, '81,778 persons were arrested under the NDPS Act', out of which 59% were held for possession of 'drugs' and substances for personal use.[86] 10,669 cases before the Magistrate Courts were analysed during the course of the research, with the conclusion that 99.9% of the cases were related to the 'consumption of a narcotic substance', with a further revelation that where 'information on the kind of substance' was available, 87% of those cases were of cannabis consumption.[87] The authors of the study stated that "We find therefore, that Mumbai's NDPS arrests, which are the highest in the country, are primarily arrests of cannabis consumers. This suggests that criminalization of cannabis consumption is pushing a substantial number of people into the criminal justice system."[88] The study also concluded that the criminal laws most adversely affected the poor and marginalized sections

---

(Footnote No. 82 contd.)

Arunachal Pradesh. An additional 2.5% of people in the country (about 2.7 crore individuals), consume alcohol in a harmful manner. In other words, about 5.2% of the population (more than 5.7 crore individuals) are affected by harmful or dependent alcohol use and need help for their alcohol use problems. Nearly one in five alcohol users suffers from alcohol dependence and needs urgent treatment." *Id*, at 2-3.

83. Neha Singhal & Naveed Ahmad, *A Case For De-Criminalization of Cannabis Use in India*, VIDHI CENTRE FOR LEGAL POL'Y 6 (Aug. 20, 2020), https://vidhilegalpolicy.in/wp-content/uploads/2020/08/Cannabis_Final.pdf.
84. *Id.* ("Although there is no current research on the cost of enforcing cannabis prohibition in India, studies conducted abroad find that on an average, incarceration costs are 2-6 times higher than money spent on health and social services.")
85. Neha Singhal & Naveed Ahmad, *Criminalisation Leads to Exploitation: The Mumbai Story No One Knows About*, VIDHI CENTRE FOR LEGAL POL'Y (Sept. 8, 2020), https://vidhilegalpolicy.in/research/criminalisation-leads-to-exploitation-the-mumbai-story-no-one-knows-about/.
86. Singhal & Ahmad, *supra* note 83, at 5.
87. *Id.*
88. *Id*, 5-6.

of the society.[89] Contrary to general perceptions, high figures for arrests of drug use may be taken to be indicative of 'a sure sign of a failed law and a failed policy.[90] The prevalence of cannabis use in India with low dependency rates, the ineffectiveness of criminal sanctions as regards their deterrent effects, ensuing social enforcement costs due to criminalization, and the adverse effects such criminalization has on marginal sections of the society, provides a strong basis for an argument in favour of legalization and regulation of its trade which would help in revenue generation that could be utilized positively in health and social services.

According to a widely reported[91] study conducted by an independent Berlin-based data-driven campaign outlet *ABCD*, along with an Israel-based firm *Seedo*, New Delhi and Mumbai ranked globally amongst the top-ten cannabis consuming cities in the world, with New Delhi placed at third and Mumbai at the sixth position respectively.[92] The total cannabis consumption per year for New Delhi was reported to be 38.26 metric tons, while for Mumbai the figure was placed at 32.38 metric tons.[93] New Delhi was also ranked 10th amongst the least expensive cities for cannabis, with the price estimated to be US $ 4.38 per gram[94], though the correctness of this price needs to be independently confirmed.

---

89. Singhal & Ahmad, *supra* note 85.
90. Neha Singhal & Naveed Ahmad, *Sikkim's Alternative Model to Tackle Drug Abuse: An Analysis of the Sikkim Anti-Drugs Act, 2006*, VIDHI CENTRE FOR LEGAL POL'Y 11 (Sep. 18, 2020), https://vidhilegalpolicy.in/wp-content/uploads/2020/09/SADA-Final_18.09.2020.pdf; Steve Rolles & Niamh Eastwood, *Drug Decriminalisation Policies in Practice: A Global Summary*, INTERNATIONAL DRUG POLICY CONSORTIUM, http://fileserver.idpc.net/library/Drug-decriminalisation-policies-in-practice.pdf.
91. *Delhi, Mumbai ranked among top 10 cities in cannabis consumption globally, capital bags third spot*, FINANCIAL EXPRESS (Sept. 10, 2019), *available at* https://www.financialexpress.com/india-news/delhi-mumbai-ranked-among-top-10-cities-in-cannabis-consumption-globally-capital-bags-third-spot/1701538/; *Delhi 3rd largest cannabis consumer in the world, Mumbai 6th: Study*, INDIA TODAY (Sept. 13, 2019), *available at* https://www.indiatoday.in/education-today/latest-studies/story/delhi-3rd-largest-cannabis-consumer-in-the-world-mumbai-6th-study-1598845-2019-09-13; *Delhi ranks high 3rd on global weed list*, TIMES OF INDIA (Sept. 10, 2019), *available at* https://timesofindia.indiatimes.com/city/delhi/delhi-ranks-high-3rd-on-global-weed-list/articleshow/71057555.cms.
92. *ABCD 2018 Cannabis Price Index*, ABCD, (Apr. 20, 2018), http://weedindex.io.
93. *ABCD 2018 Cannabis Price Index*, ABCD, (Apr. 20, 2018), http://weedindex.io.
94. *ABCD 2018 Cannabis Price Index*, ABCD, (Apr. 20, 2018), http://weedindex.io. Placing reliance on this study, it was reported, "A study estimated that around 725 crore could be raised in Delhi alone if cannabis is taxed. This number was pegged at 641 crore for Mumbai." Singhal & Ahmad, *supra* note 83, at 5.

In light of all this, two things become clear. First, all jurisdictions in the US that have legalized trade in cannabis have experienced the addition of reliable and steady streams of revenue to the public exchequer. Second, given the fact that cannabis use has been historically prevalent in India[95] and was indeed legally regulated and taxed[96], it would be particularly worthwhile to propose a similar exercise (of calculating the potential tax revenue from legalizing the cannabis trade) to be conducted in the context of India.

95. REPORT OF THE INDIAN HEMP DRUGS COMMISSION, 1893-94, GOV'T OF INDIA (1894); *Supra* note 80, at 7.

96. *Supra* note 14.

Appendix B

List of Affected Provisions in the NDPS Act

S. No.	Provision of the NDPS Act	Description of the Provision	Text of the Provision
1.	Section 2(i) read with Section 2(xiv) and Section 2(xxiii)	Definitions	In this Act, unless the context otherwise requires— (i) "addict" means a person who has dependence on any narcotic drug or psychotropic substance;
2.	Section 2(iii)	Definitions	"cannabis (hemp)" means— a. *charas*, that is, the separated resin, in whatever form, whether crude or purified, obtained from the cannabis plant and also includes concentrated preparation and resin known as hashish oil or liquid hashish: b. *ganja*, that is, the flowering or fruiting tops of the cannabis plant (excluding the seeds and leaves when not accompanied by the tops), by whatever name they may be known or designated; and c. any mixture, with or without any neutral material, of any of the above forms of cannabis or any drink prepared therefrom;
3.	Section 2(iv)	Definitions	"cannabis plant" means any plant of the genus cannabis;

S. No.	Provision of the NDPS Act	Description of the Provision	Text of the Provision
4.	Section 2(vii-a) read with Section 2(xiv) and Section 2(xxiii)	Definitions	"commercial quantity", in relation to narcotic drugs and psychotropic substances, means any quantity greater than the quantity specified by the Central Government by notification in the Official Gazette;
5.	Section 2(vii-b) read with Section 2(xiv) and Section 2(xxiii)	Definitions	"controlled delivery" means the technique of allowing illicit or suspect consignments of narcotic drugs, psychotropic substances, controlled substances or substances substituted for them to pass out of, or through or into the territory of India with the knowledge and under the supervision of an officer empowered in this behalf or duly authorised under Section 50-A with a view to identifying the persons involved in the commission of an offence under this Act;
6.	Section 2(vii-d) read with Section 2(xiv) and Section 2(xxiii)	Definitions	"controlled substance" means any substance which the Central Government may, having regard to the available information as to its possible use in the production or manufacture of narcotic drugs or psychotropic substances or to the provisions of any International Convention, by notification in the Official Gazette, declare to be a controlled substance;
7.	Section 2(viii-a) read with Section 2(xiv)	Definitions	"essential narcotic drug" means a narcotic drug notified by the Central Government for medical and scientific use;
8.	Section 2(viii-b) read with Section 2(xiv) and Section 2(xxiii)	Definitions	[Section 2(viii-b)] "illicit traffic", in relation to narcotic drugs and psychotropic substances, means— [ii] cultivating the opium poppy or any cannabis plant; [iii] engaging in the production, manufacture, possession, sale, purchase, transportation, warehousing, concealment, use or consumption, import inter-State, export inter-State, import into India, export from India or transhipment of narcotic drugs or psychotropic substances;

S. No.	Provision of the NDPS Act	Description of the Provision	Text of the Provision
			(iv) dealing in any activities in narcotic drugs or psychotropic substances other than those referred to in sub-clauses (i) to (iii); or (v) handling or letting out any premises for the carrying on of any of the activities referred to sub-clauses (i) to (iv); other than those permitted under this Act, or any rule or order made, or any condition of any licence, term or authorization issued, thereunder, and includes— 1. financing, directly or indirectly, any of the aforementioned activities; 2. abetting or conspiring in the furtherance of or in support of doing any of the aforementioned activities; and 3. harbouring persons engaged in any of the aforementioned activities;
9.	Section 2(ix) read with Section 2(xiv) and Section 2(xxiii)	Definitions	"International Convention" means— a. the Single Convention on Narcotic Drugs, 1961 adopted by the United Nations Conference at New York in March, 1961; b. the Protocol, amending the Convention mentioned in sub-clause (a), adopted by the United Nations Conference at Geneva in March, 1972; c. the Convention on Psychotropic Substances, 1971 adopted by the United Nations Conference at Vienna in February, 1971; and d. any other international convention, or protocol or other instrument amending an international convention, relating to narcotic drugs or psychotropic substances which may be ratified or acceded to by India after the commencement of this Act;

S. No.	Provision of the NDPS Act	Description of the Provision	Text of the Provision
10.	Section 2(x) read with Section 2(xiv) and Section 2(xxiii)	Definitions	"manufacture", in relation to narcotic drugs or psychotropic substances, includes— 1. all processes other than production by which such drugs or substances may be obtained; 2. refining of such drugs or substances; 3. transformation of such drugs or substances; and 4. making of preparation (otherwise than in a pharmacy on prescription) with or containing such drugs or substances;
11.	Section 2(xi) read with Section 2(xiv) and Section 2(xxiii)	Definitions	"manufactured drug" means— (a) all coca derivatives, medicinal cannabis, opium derivatives and poppy straw concentrate; (b) any other narcotic substance or preparation which the Central Government may, having regard to the available information as to its nature or its nature or to a decision, if any, under any International Convention, by notification in the Official Gazette, declare to be a manufactured drug, but does not include any narcotic substance or preparation which the Central Government may, having regard to the available information as to a decision, if any, under any International Convention, by notification in the Official Gazette, declare not to be a manufactured drug;
12.	Section 2(xii)	Definitions	"medicinal cannabis", that is, medicinal hemp, means any extract or tincture of cannabis (hemp);

S. No.	Provision of the NDPS Act	Description of the Provision	Text of the Provision
13.	Section 2(xiv)	Definitions	"narcotic drug" means coca leaf, cannabis (hemp), opium, poppy straw and includes all manufactured drugs;
14.	Section 2(xx) read with Section 2(xiv) and Section 2(xxiii)	Definitions	"preparation", in relation to a narcotic drug or psychotropic substance means any one or more such drugs or substances in dosage form or any solution or mixture, in whatever physical state, containing one or more such drugs or substances;
15.	Section 2(xxii)	Definitions	"production" means the separation of opium, poppy straw, coca leaves or cannabis from the plants from which they are obtained;
16.	Section 2(xxiii)	Definitions	"psychotropic substance" means any substance, natural or synthetic, or any natural material or any salt or preparation of such substance or material included in the list of psychotropic substances specified in the Schedule;
17.	Section 2(xxiii-a) read with Section 2(xiv) and Section 2(xxiii)	Definitions	"small quantity", in relation to narcotic drugs and psychotropic substances, means any quantity lesser than the quantity specified by the Central Government by notification in the Official Gazette;
18.	Section 2(xxv) read with Section 2(xiv) and Section 2(xxiii)	Definitions	"to import into India", with its grammatical variations and cognate expressions, means to bring into India from a place outside India and includes the bringing into any port or airport or place in India of a narcotic drug or a psychotropic substance intended to be taken out of India without being removed from the vessel, aircraft, vehicle or any other conveyance in which it is being carried. *Explanation.*—For the purposes of this clause and clause (xxvi), "India" includes the territorial waters of India;

S. No.	Provision of the NDPS Act	Description of the Provision	Text of the Provision
19.	Section 2(xxviii-a) read with Section 2(xiv) and Section 2(xxiii)	Definitions	"use" in relation to narcotic drugs and psychotropic substances, means any kind of use except personal consumption;
20.	Section 3 read with Section 2(xxiii)	Power to add to or omit from the list of psychotropic substances	The Central Government may, if satisfied that it is necessary or expedient so to do on the basis of - a. the information and evidence which has become available to it with respect to the nature and effects of, and the abuse or the scope for abuse of, any substance (natural or synthetic) or natural material or any salt or preparation of such substance or material; and b. the modifications or provisions (if any) which have been made to, or in, any International Convention with respect to such substance, natural material or salt or preparation of such substance or material, by notification in the Official Gazette, add to, or, as the case may be, omit from, the list of psychotropic substances specified in the Schedule such substance or natural material or salt or preparation of such substance or Material.
21.	Section 4 read with Section 2(xiv) and Section 2(xxiii)	Central Government to take measures for preventing and combating abuse of and illicit traffic in narcotic drugs, etc.	1. Subject to the provisions of this Act, the Central Government shall take all such measures as it deems necessary or expedient for the purpose of preventing and combating abuse of narcotic drugs and psychotropic substances and the illicit traffic therein [and for ensuring their medical and scientific use]. 2. In particular and without prejudice to the generality of the provisions of sub-section (1), the measures which the Central Government may take under that sub-section include measures with respect to all or any of the following matters, namely:—

S. No.	Provision of the NDPS Act	Description of the Provision	Text of the Provision
			a. coordination of actions by various offenders, State Governments and other authorities— (i) under this Act, or (ii) under any law for the time being in force in connection with the enforcement of the provisions of this Act; b. obligations under the International Conventions; c. assistance to the concerned authorities in foreign countries and concerned international organisations with a view of facilitating coordination and universal action for prevention and suppression of illicit traffic in narcotic drugs and psychotropic substances; d. identification, treatment, education, after care, rehabilitation and social re-integration of addicts; [(da) availability of narcotic drugs and psychotropic substances for medical and scientific use;] e. such other matters as the Central Government deems necessary or expedient for the purpose of securing the effective implementation of the provisions of this Act and preventing and combating the abuse of narcotic drugs and psychotropic substances and illicit traffic therein. (3) The Central Government may, if it considers necessary or expedient so to do for the purposes of this Act, by order, published in the Official Gazette, constitute an authority or a hierarchy of authorities by such name or names as may be specified in the order for the purpose of exercising such of the powers and functions of the Central Government under this Act and for taking measures with respect to such of the matters referred to in sub-section (2) as may be mentioned in the order, and subject to the supervision and control of the

S. No.	Provision of the NDPS Act	Description of the Provision	Text of the Provision
			Central Government and the provisions of such order, such authority or authorities may exercise the powers and take the measures so mentioned in the order as if such authority or authorities had been empowered by this Act to exercise those powers and take such measures.
22.	Section 6	The Narcotic Drugs and Psychotropic Substances Consultative Committee	1. The Central Government may constitute, by notification in the Official Gazette, an advisory committee to be called "The Narcotic Drugs and Psychotropic Substances Consultative Committee" (hereafter in this section referred to as the Committee) to advise the Central Government on such matters relating to the administration of this Act as are referred to it by that Government from time to time. 2. The Committee shall consist of a Chairman and such other members, not exceeding twenty, as may be appointed by the Central Government. 3. The Committee shall meet when required to do so by the Central Government and shall have power to regulate its own procedure. 4. The Committee may, if it deems it necessary so to do for the efficient discharge of any of its functions, constitute one or more sub-committees and may appoint to any such sub-committee, whether generally or for the consideration of any particular matter, any person (including a non-official) who is not a member of the Committee. 5. The term of office of, the manner of filling casual vacancies in the offices of and the allowances, if any, payable to, the Chairman and other members of the Committee, and the conditions and restrictions subject to which the Committee may appoint a person who is not a member of the Committee as a member of any of its sub-committees, shall be such as may be prescribed by rules made by the Central Government.

S. No.	Provision of the NDPS Act	Description of the Provision	Text of the Provision
23.	Section 7-A read with Section 2(xiv) and Section 2(xxiii)	National Fund for Control of Drug Abuse	1. The Central Government may, by notification in the Official Gazette, constitute a Fund to be called the National Fund for Control of Drug Abuse (hereafter in this Chapter referred to as the Fund) and there shall be credited thereto— a. an amount which the Central Government may, after due appropriation made by Parliament by law in this behalf, provide; b. the sale proceeds of any property forfeited under Chapter V-A; c. any grant that may be made by any person or institution; d. any income from investment of the amounts credited to the Fund under the aforesaid provisions. [(2) The Fund shall be applied by the Central Government to meet the expenditure incurred in connection with the measures taken for— a. combating illicit traffic in narcotic drugs, psychotropic substances or controlled substances; b. controlling the abuse of narcotic drugs and psychotropic substances; c. identifying, treating, rehabilitating addicts; d. preventing drug abuse; e. educating public against drug abuse; and f. supplying drugs to addicts where such supply is a medical necessity. (3) The Central Government may constitute a Governing Body as it thinks fit to advise that Government and to sanction money out of the said Fund subject to the limit notified by the Central Government in the Official Gazette.]

S. No.	Provision of the NDPS Act	Description of the Provision	Text of the Provision
			(4) The Governing Body shall consist of a Chairman (not below the rank of an Additional Secretary to the Central Government) and such other members not exceeding six as the Central Government may appoint. (5) The Governing Body shall have the power to regulate its own procedure.
24.	Section 8 read with Section 2(xiv) and Section 2(xxiii)	Prohibition of certain operations	No person shall— a. cultivate any coca plant or gather any portion of coca plant; or b. cultivate the opium poppy or any cannabis plant; or c. produce, manufacture, possess, sell, purchase, transport, warehouse, use, consume, import inter-State, export inter-State, import into India, export from India or tranship any narcotic drug or psychotropic substance, except for medical or scientific purposes and in the manner and to the extent provided by the provisions of this Act or the rules or orders made thereunder and in a case where any such provision, imposes any requirement by way of licence, permit or authorisation also in accordance with the terms and conditions of such licence, permit or authorisation: Provided that, and subject to the other provisions of this Act and the rules made thereunder, the prohibition against the cultivation of the cannabis plant for the production of *ganja* or the production, possession, use, consumption, purchase, sale, transport, warehousing, import inter-State and export inter-State of *ganja* for any purpose other than medical and scientific purpose shall take effect only from the date which the Central Government may, by notification in the Official Gazette, specify in this behalf.

S. No.	Provision of the NDPS Act	Description of the Provision	Text of the Provision
			[Provided further that nothing in this section shall apply to the export of poppy straw for decorative purposes.]
25.	Section 8-A	Prohibition of certain activities relating to property derived from offence	No person shall— a. convert or transfer any property knowing that such property is derived from an offence committed under this Act or under any other corresponding law of any other country to from an act of participation in such offence, for the purpose of concealing or disguising the illicit origin of the property or to assist any person in the commission of an offence or to evade the legal consequences; or b. conceal or disguise the true nature, source, location, disposition of any property knowing that such property is derived from an offence committed under this Act or under any other corresponding law of any other country; or c. knowingly acquire, possess or use any property which was derived from an offence committed under this Act or under any other corresponding law of any other country.
26.	Section 9 read with Section 2(xiv) and Section 2(xxiii)	Power of Central Government to permit, control and regulate	1. Subject to the provisions of Section 8, the Central Government may, by rules— a. permit and regulate- (i) the cultivation, or gathering of any portion (such cultivation or gathering being only on account of the Central Government) of coca plant, or the production, possession, sale, purchase, transport, import inter-State, export inter-State, use or consumption of coca leaves;

S. No.	Provision of the NDPS Act	Description of the Provision	Text of the Provision
			(ii) the cultivation (such cultivation being only on account of Central Government) of the opium poppy; (iii) the production and manufacture of opium and production of poppy straw; [(iii-a) the possession, transport, import inter-State, export inter-State, warehousing, sale, purchase, consumption and use of poppy straw produced from plants from which no juice has been extracted through lancing;] (iv) the sale of opium and opium derivatives from the Central Government factories for export from India or sale to State Government or to manufacturing chemists; (v) the manufacture of manufactured drugs (other than prepared opium) but not including manufacture of medicinal opium or any preparation containing any manufactured drug from materials which the maker is lawfully entitled to possess; [(v-a) the manufacture, possession, transport, import inter-State, export inter-State, sale, purchase, consumption and use of essential narcotic drugs: Provided that where, in respect of an essential narcotic drug, the State Government has granted licence or permit under the provisions of Section 10 prior to the commencement of the Narcotic Drugs and Psychotropic Substances (Amendment) Act, 2014, such licence or permit shall continue to be valid till the date of its expiry or for a period of twelve months from such commencement, whichever is earlier.]

S. No.	Provision of the NDPS Act	Description of the Provision	Text of the Provision
			(vi) the manufacture, possession, transport, import inter-State, export inter-State, sale, purchase, consumption, or use of psychotropic substances; (vii) the import into India and export from India and transhipment of narcotic drugs and psychotropic substances; b. prescribe any other matter requisite to render effective the control of the Central Government over any of the matters specified in clause (a). (2) In particular and without prejudice to the generality of the foregoing power, such rules may— a. empower the Central Government to fix from time to time the limits within which licences may be given for the cultivation of the opium poppy; b. require that all opium, the produce of land cultivated with the opium poppy, shall be delivered by the cultivators to the officers authorised in this behalf by the Central Government; c. prescribe the forms and conditions of licences for cultivation of the opium poppy and for production and manufacture of opium; the fees that may be charged therefor; the authorities by which such licences may be granted, withheld, refused or cancelled and the authorities before which appeals against the orders of withholding, refusal or cancellation of licences shall lie; d. prescribe that opium shall be weighed, examined and classified according to its quality and consistence by the officers authorised in this behalf by the Central Government in the presence of the cultivator at the time of delivery by the cultivator;

S. No.	Provision of the NDPS Act	Description of the Provision	Text of the Provision
			e. empower the Central Government to fix from time to time the price to be paid to the cultivator for the opium delivered; f. provide for the weighment, examination and classification, according to the quality and consistence, of the opium received at the factory and the deductions from or additions (if any) to the standard price to be made in accordance with the result of such examination; and the authorities by which the decisions with regard to the weighment, examination, classification, deductions or additions shall be made and the authorities before which appeals against such decisions shall lie; g. require that opium delivered by a cultivator, if found as a result of examination in the Central Government factory to be adulterated, may be confiscated by the officers authorised in this behalf; h. prescribe the forms and conditions of licences for the manufacture of manufactured drugs, the authorities by which such licences may be granted and the fees that may be charged therefor; [(ha) prescribe the forms and conditions of licences or permits for the manufacture, possession, transport, import inter-State, export inter-State, sale, purchase, consumption or use of essential narcotic drugs, the authorities by which such licence or permit may be granted and the fees that may be charged therefor;] i. prescribe the forms and conditions of licences or permits for the manufacture, possession, transport, import inter-State, export inter-State, sale, purchase, consumption or use of psychotropic substances, the authorities by which such licences or permits may be granted and the fees that may be charged therefor;

S. No.	Provision of the NDPS Act	Description of the Provision	Text of the Provision
			j. prescribe the ports and other places at which any kind of narcotic drugs or psychotropic substances may be imported into India or exported from India or trans-hipped; the forms and conditions of certificates, authorisations or permits, as the case may be, for such import, export or transhipment; the authorities by which such certificates, authorisations or permits may be granted and the fees that may be charged therefor.
27.	Section 9-A read with Section 2(xiv) and Section 2(xxiii)	Power to control and regulate controlled substances	1. If the Central Government is of the opinion that, having regard to the use of any controlled substance in the production or manufacture of any narcotic drug or psychotropic substance, it is necessary or expedient so to do in the public interest, it may, by order, provide for regulating or prohibiting the production, manufacture, supply and distribution thereof and trade and commerce therein. 2. Without prejudice to generality of the power conferred by sub-section (1), an order made thereunder may provide for regulating by licences, permits or otherwise, the production, manufacture, possession, transport, import inter-State, export inter-State, sale, purchase, consumption, use storage, distribution, disposal or acquisition of any controlled substance.
28.	Section 10 read with Section 2(xiv) and Section 2(xxiii)	Power of State Government to permit, control and regulate	1. Subject to the provisions of Section 8, the State Government may, by rules— a. permit and regulate— (i) the possession, transport, import inter-State, export inter-State, warehousing, sale, purchase, consumption and use of poppy straw [except poppy straw produced from plants from which no juice has been extracted through lancing]; (ii) the possession, transport, import inter-State, export inter-State, sale, purchase, consumption and use of opium;

S. No.	Provision of the NDPS Act	Description of the Provision	Text of the Provision
			(iii) the cultivation of any cannabis plant, production, manufacture, possession, transport, import inter-State, export inter-State, sale, purchase, consumption or use of cannabis (excluding *charas*); (iv) the manufacture of medicinal opium or any preparation containing any manufactured drug from materials which the maker is lawfully entitled to possess; (v) the possession, transport, purchase, sale, import inter-State, export inter-State, use or consumption of [manufactured drugs (other than prepared opium and essential narcotic drugs)] and of coca leaf and any preparation containing any manufactured drug; (vi) the manufacture and possession of prepared opium from opium lawfully possessed by an addict registered with the State Government on medical advice for his personal consumption: Provided that save in so far as may be expressly provided in the rules made under sub-clauses (iv) and (v), nothing in Section 8 shall apply to the import inter-State, export inter-State, transport, possession, purchase, sale, use or consumption of manufactured drugs which are the property and in the possession of the Government: Provided further that such drugs as are referred to in the preceding proviso shall not be sold or otherwise delivered to any person who, under the rules made by the State Government under the aforesaid sub-clauses, is not entitled to their possession: b. prescribe any other matter requisite to render effective the control of the State Government over any of the matters specified in clause (a).

S. No.	Provision of the NDPS Act	Description of the Provision	Text of the Provision
			(2) In particular and without prejudice to the generality of the foregoing power, such rules may— a. empower the State Government to declare any place to be a warehouse wherein it shall be the duty of the owners to deposit all such poppy straw as is legally imported inter-State and is intended for export inter-State or export from India; to regulate the safe custody of such poppy straw warehoused and the removal of such poppy straw for sale or export inter-State or export from India; to levy fees for such warehousing and to prescribe the manner in which and the period after which the poppy straw warehoused shall be disposed of in default of payment of fees; b. provide that the limits within which licences may be given for the cultivation of any cannabis plant shall be fixed from time to time by or under the orders of the State Government; c. provide that only the cultivators licensed by the prescribed authority or the State Government shall be authorised to engage in cultivation of any cannabis plant; d. require that all cannabis, the produce of land cultivated with cannabis plant, shall be delivered by the cultivators to the officers of the State Government authorised in this behalf; e. empower the State Government to fix from time to time, the price to be paid to the cultivators for the cannabis delivered; f. prescribe the forms and conditions of licences or permits for the purposes specified in sub-clauses (i) to (vi) of clause (a) of sub-section (1) and the authorities by which such licences or permits may be granted and the fees that may be charged therefor.

S. No.	Provision of the NDPS Act	Description of the Provision	Text of the Provision
29.	Section 11 read with Section 2(xiv) and Section 2(xxiii)	Narcotic drugs and psychotropic substances, etc., not liable to distress or attachment	Notwithstanding anything to the contrary contained in any law or contract, no narcotic drug, psychotropic substance, coca plant, the opium poppy or cannabis plant shall be liable to be distrained or attached by any person for the recovery of any money under any order or decree of any court or authority or otherwise.
30.	Section 12 read with Section 2(xiv) and Section 2(xxiii)	Restrictions over external dealings in narcotic drugs and psychotropic substances	No person shall engage in or control any trade whereby a narcotic drug or psychotropic substance is obtained outside India and supplied to any person outside India save with the previous authorisation of the Central Government and subject to such conditions as may be imposed by that Government in this behalf.
31.	Section 14	Special provision relating to cannabis	Notwithstanding anything contained in Section 8, Government may, by general or special order and subject to such conditions as may be specified in such order, allow cultivation of any cannabis plant for industrial purposes only of obtaining fibre or seed or for horticultural purposes.
32.	Section 20	Punishment for contravention in relation to cannabis plant and cannabis	Whoever, in contravention of any provision of this Act or any rule or order made or condition of licence granted thereunder, - a. cultivates any cannabis plant; or b. produces, manufactures, possesses, sells, purchases, transports, imports inter-State, exports inter-State or uses cannabis, shall be punishable,— [(i) where such contravention relates to clause (a) with rigorous imprisonment for a term which may extend to ten years, and shall also be liable to fine which may extend to one lakh rupees; and

S. No.	Provision of the NDPS Act	Description of the Provision	Text of the Provision
			(ii) where such contravention relates to clause (b),— A. and involves small quantity, with rigorous imprisonment for a term which may extend to [one year], or with fine which may extend to ten thousand rupees, or with both; B. and involves quantity lesser than commercial quantity but greater than small quantity, with rigorous imprisonment for a term which may extend to ten years, and with fine which may extend to one lakh rupees; C. and involves commercial quantity, with rigorous imprisonment for a term which shall not be less than ten years but which may extend to twenty years and shall also be liable to fine which shall not be less than one lakh rupees but which may extend to two lakh rupees: Provided that the court may, for reasons to be recorded in the judgment, impose a fine exceeding two lakh rupees.]
33.	Section 21 read with Section 2(xi)	Punishment for contravention in relation to manufactured drugs and preparations	Whoever, in contravention of any provision of this Act or rule or order made or condition of licence granted thereunder, manufactures, possesses, sells, purchases, transports, imports inter-State, exports inter-State or uses any manufactured drug or any preparation containing any manufactured drug shall be punishable,— a. where the contravention involves small quantity, with rigorous imprisonment for a term which may extend to [one year], or with fine which may extend to ten thousand rupees, or with both;

S. No.	Provision of the NDPS Act	Description of the Provision	Text of the Provision
			b. where the contravention involves quantity, lesser than commercial quantity but greater than small quantity, with rigorous imprisonment for a term which may extend to ten years, and with fine which may extend to one lakh rupees; c. where the contravention involves commercial quantity, with rigorous imprisonment for a term which shall not be less than ten years but which may extend to twenty years, and shall also be liable to fine which shall not be less than one lakh rupees but which may extend to two lakh rupees: Provided that the court may, for reasons to be recorded in the judgment, impose a fine exceeding two lakh rupees.
34.	Section 22	Punishment for contravention in relation to psychotropic substances	Whoever, in contravention of any provision of this Act or any rule or order made or condition of licence granted thereunder, manufactures, possesses, sells, purchases, transports, imports inter-State, exports inter-State or uses any psychotropic substance shall be punishable,— a. where the contravention involves small quantity, with rigorous imprisonment for a term which may extend to [one year], or with fine which may extend to ten thousand rupees, or with both; b. where the contravention involves quantity lesser than commercial quantity but greater than small quantity, with rigorous imprisonment for a term which may extend to ten years, and with fine which may extend to one lakh rupees; c. where the contravention involves commercial quantity, with rigorous imprisonment for a term which shall not be less than ten years but which may extend to twenty years, and shall also be liable to fine which shall not be less than one lakh rupees but which may extend to two lakh rupees:

S. No.	Provision of the NDPS Act	Description of the Provision	Text of the Provision
			Provided that the court may, for reasons to be recorded in the judgment, impose a fine exceeding two lakh rupees.
35.	Section 23 read with Section 2(xiv) and Section 2(xxiii)	Punishment for illegal import into India, export from India or transhipment of narcotic drugs and psychotropic substances	Whoever, in contravention of any provision of this Act or any rule or order made or condition of licence or permit granted or certificate or authorisation issued thereunder, imports into India or exports from India or tranships any narcotic drug or psychotropic substance shall be punishable,— a. where the contravention involves small quantity, with rigorous imprisonment for a term which may extend to [one year], or with fine which may extend to ten thousand rupees, or with both; b. where the contravention involves quantity lesser than commercial quantity but greater than small quantity, with rigorous imprisonment for a term which may extend to ten years, and with fine which may extend to one lakh rupees; c. where the contravention involves commercial quantity, with rigorous imprisonment for a term which shall not be less than ten years but which may extend to twenty years, and shall also be liable to fine which shall not be less than one lakh rupees but which may extend to two lakh rupees: Provided that the court may, for reasons to be recorded in the judgment, impose a fine exceeding two lakh rupees.
36.	Section 24 read with Section 2(xiv) and Section 2(xxiii)	Punishment for external dealings in narcotic drugs and psychotropic	Whoever engages in or controls any trade whereby a narcotic drug or a psychotropic substance is obtained outside India and supplied to any person outside India without the previous authorisation of the Central Government or otherwise than in accordance with the conditions (if any) of such authorisation

S. No.	Provision of the NDPS Act	Description of the Provision	Text of the Provision
		substances in contravention of Section 12	granted under Section 12, shall be punishable with rigorous imprisonment for a term which shall not be less than ten years but which may extend to twenty years and shall also be liable to fine which shall not be less than one lakh rupees but may extend to two lakh rupees: Provided that the court may, for reasons to be recorded in the judgment, impose a fine exceeding two lakh rupees.
37.	Section 25	Punishment for allowing premises, etc., to be used for commission of an offence	Whoever, being the owner or occupier or having the control or use of any house, room, enclosure, space, place, animal or conveyance, knowingly permits it to be used for the commission by any other person of an offence punishable under any provision of this Act, shall be punishable with the punishment for that offence.
38.	Section 25-A	Punishment for contravention of orders made under Section 9-A	If any person contravenes an order made under Section 9-A, he shall be punishable with rigorous imprisonment for a term which may extend to ten years and shall also be liable to fine which may extend to one lakh rupees: Provided that the court may, for reasons to be recorded in the judgment, impose a fine exceeding one lakh rupees.
39.	Section 26	Punishment for certain acts by licensee or his servants	If the holder of any licence, permit or authorisation granted under this Act or any rule or order made thereunder or any person in his employ and acting on his behalf— a. omits, without any reasonable cause, to maintain accounts or to submit any return in accordance with the provisions of this Act, or any rule made thereunder;

S. No.	Provision of the NDPS Act	Description of the Provision	Text of the Provision
			b. fails to produce without any reasonable cause such licence, permit or authorisation on demand of any officer authorised by the Central Government or State Government in this behalf; c. keeps any accounts or makes any statement which is false or which he knows or has reason to believe to be incorrect; or d. wilfully and knowingly does any act in breach of any of the conditions of licence, permit or authorisation for which a penalty is not prescribed elsewhere in this Act, he shall be punishable with imprisonment for a term which may extend to three years or with fine or with both.
40.	Section 27 read with Section 2(xiv) and Section 2(xxiii)	Punishment for consumption of any narcotic drug or psychotropic substance	Whoever consumes any narcotic drug or psychotropic substance shall be punishable,— a. where the narcotic drug or psychotropic substance consumed is cocaine, morphine, diacetylmorphine or any other narcotic drug or any psychotropic substance as may be specified in this behalf by the Central Government by notification in the Official Gazette, with rigorous imprisonment for a term which may extend to one year, or with fine which may extend to twenty thousand rupees, or with both; and b. where the narcotic drug or psychotropic substance consumed is other than those specified in or under clause (a), with imprisonment for a term which may extend to six months, or with fine which may extend to ten thousand rupees, or with both.
41.	Section 27-A	Punishment for financing illicit traffic	Whoever indulges in financing, directly or indirectly, any of the activities specified in sub-clauses (i) to (v) of clause (viii-a) of Section 2 or harbours any

S. No.	Provision of the NDPS Act	Description of the Provision	Text of the Provision
		and harbouring offenders	person engaged in any of the aforementioned activities, shall be punishable with rigorous imprisonment for a term which shall not be less than ten years but which may extend to twenty years and shall also be liable to fine which shall not be less than one lakh rupees but which may extend to two lakh rupees: Provided that the court may, for reasons to be recorded in the judgment, impose a fine exceeding two lakh rupees.
42.	Section 27-B	Punishment for contravention of Section 8-A	Whoever contravenes the provision of Section 8-A shall be punishable with rigorous imprisonment for a term which shall not be less than three years but which may extend to ten years and shall also be liable to fine.
43.	Section 28	Punishment for attempts to commit offences	Whoever attempts to commit any offence punishable under this Chapter or to cause such offence to be committed and in such attempt does any act towards the commission of the offence shall be punishable with the punishment provided for the offence.
44.	Section 29	Punishment for abetment and criminal conspiracy	1. Whoever abets, or is a party to a criminal conspiracy to commit, an offence punishable under this Chapter, shall, whether such offence be or be not committed in consequence of such abetment or in pursuance of such criminal conspiracy, and notwith-standing anything contained in Section 116 of the Indian Penal Code (45 of 1860), be punishable with the punishment provided for the offence. 2. A person abets, or is a party to a criminal conspiracy to commit, an offence, within the meaning of this section, who, in India, abets or is a party to the criminal conspiracy to the commission of any act in a place without and beyond India which -

S. No.	Provision of the NDPS Act	Description of the Provision	Text of the Provision
			a. would constitute an offence if committed within India; or b. under the laws of such place, is an offence relating to narcotic drugs or psychotropic substances having all the legal conditions required to constitute it an offence punishable under this Chapter, if committed within India.
45.	Section 30	Preparation	If any person makes preparation to do or omits to do anything which constitutes an offence punishable under any of the provisions of [Sections 19, 24 and 27-A and for offences involving commercial quantity of any narcotic drug or psychotropic substance] and from the circumstances of the case it may be reasonably inferred that he was determined to carry out his intention to commit the offence but had been prevented by circumstances independent of his will, he shall be punishable with rigorous imprisonment for a term which shall not be less than one-half of the minimum term (if any), but which may extend to one-half of the maximum term, of imprisonment with which he would have been punishable in the event of his having committed such offence, and also with fine which shall not be less than one-half of the minimum amount (if any), of fine with which he would have been punishable but, which may extend to one-half of the maximum amount of fine with which he would have ordinarily (that is to say in the absence of special reasons) been punishable, in the event aforesaid: Provided that the court may, for reasons to be recorded in the judgment, impose a higher fine.
46.	Section 31	Enhanced punishment for offences after previous conviction	1. If any person who has been convicted of the commission of, or attempt to commit, or abetment of, or criminal conspiracy to commit, any of the offences punishable under this Act is subsequently convicted of the commission of, or attempt to commit, or abetment of, or criminal conspiracy to commit, an

S. No.	Provision of the NDPS Act	Description of the Provision	Text of the Provision
			offence punishable under this Act with the same amount of punishment shall be punished for the second and every subsequent offence with rigorous imprisonment for a term which may extend to [one and one-half times of the maximum term] of imprisonment, and also be liable to fine which shall extend to [one and one-half times of the maximum amount] of fine. 2. Where the person referred to in sub-section (1) is liable to be punished with a minimum term of imprisonment and to a minimum amount of fine, the minimum punishment for such person shall be [one and one-half times of the minimum term] of imprisonment and [one and one-half times of the minimum amount] of fine: Provided that the court may, for reasons to be recorded in the judgment, impose a fine exceeding the fine for which a person is liable. 3. Where any person is convicted by a competent court of criminal jurisdiction outside India under any corresponding law, such person, in respect of such conviction, shall be dealt with for the purposes of sub-sections (1) and (2) as if he had been convicted by a court in India.
47.	Section 31-A	Death penalty for certain offences after previous conviction	1. Notwithstanding anything contained in Section 31, if any person who has been convicted of the commission of or attempt to commit, or abetment of, or criminal conspiracy to commit, any of the offences punishable under [Section 19, Section 24, Section 27-A and for offences involving commercial quantity of any narcotic drug or psychotropic substance] is subsequently convicted of the commission of, or attempt to commit, or abetment of, or criminal conspiracy to commit, an offence relating to,— a. engaging in the production, manufacture, possession, trans-portation, import into India, export from India or transhipment, of the narcotic

S. No.	Provision of the NDPS Act	Description of the Provision	Text of the Provision
			drugs or psychotropic substances specified under Column (1) of the Table below and involving the quantity which is equal to or more than the quantity indicated against each such drug or substance, as specified in Column (2) of the said Table: (vii) Hashish - 20 kgs (viii) Any mixture with or without any neutral material of any of the above drugs - [lesser of the quantity between the quantities given against the respective narcotic drugs or psychotropic substances mentioned above forming part of the mixture] (x) THC (Tetrahydrocannabinols, the following isomers: 6a (10a), 6a(7), 7, 8, 9, 10, 9 and their stereochemical variants) - 500 grams (xiv) Salts and preparations of the Psychotropic substances mentioned in (ix) to (xiii) - 1,500 grams; b. financing, directly or indirectly, any of the activities specified in clause (a), [shall be punished with punishment which shall not be less than the punishment specified in Section 31 or with death]. (2) Where any person is convicted by a competent court of criminal jurisdiction outside India under any law corresponding to the provisions of [Section 19, Section 24 or Section 27-A and for offences involving commercial quantity of any narcotic drug or psychotropic substance] such person, in respect to such conviction, shall be dealt with for the purposes of sub-section (1) as if he had been convicted by a court of India.
48.	Section 32	Punishment for offence for which no	Whoever contravenes any provision of this Act or any rule or order made, or any condition of any licence, permit or authorisation issued thereunder for which no

S. No.	Provision of the NDPS Act	Description of the Provision	Text of the Provision
		punishment is provided	punishment is separately provided in this Chapter, shall be punishable with imprisonment for a term which may extend to six months, or with fine, or with both.
49.	Section 32-A	No suspension, remission or commutation in any sentence awarded under this Act	Notwithstanding anything contained in the Code of Criminal Procedure, 1973 (2 of 1974) or any other law for the time being in force but subject to the provisions of Section 33, no sentence awarded under this Act (other than Section 27) shall be suspended or remitted or commuted.
50.	Section 32-B	Factors to be taken into account for imposing higher than the minimum punishment	Where a minimum term of imprisonment or amount of fine is prescribed for any offence committed under this Act, the court may, in addition to such factors as it may deem fit, take into account the following factors for imposing a punishment higher than the minimum term of imprisonment or amount of fine, namely:— a. the use or threat of use of violence or arms by the offender; b. the fact that the offender holds a public office and that he has taken advantage of that office in committing the offence; c. the fact that the minors are affected by the offence or the minors are used for the commission of an offence; d. the fact that the offence is committed in an educational institution or social service facility or in the immediate vicinity of such institution or faculty or in other place to which school children and students resort for education, sports and social activities;

S. No.	Provision of the NDPS Act	Description of the Provision	Text of the Provision
			e. the fact that the offender belongs to organised international or any other criminal group which is involved in the commission of the offence; and f. the fact that the offence is involved in other illegal activities facilitated by commission of the offence.
51.	Section 33	Application of Section 360 of the Code of Criminal Procedure, 1973 and of the Probation of Offenders Act, 1958	Nothing contained in Section 360 of the Code of Criminal Procedure, 1973 (2 of 1974) or in the Probation of Offenders Act, 1958 (20 of 1958) shall apply to a person convicted of an offence under this Act unless such person is under eighteen years of age or that the offence for which such person is convicted is punishable under Section 26 or Section 27.
52.	Section 34	Security for abstaining from commission of offence	1. Whenever any person is convicted of an offence punishable under any provision of Chapter IV and the court convicting him is of opinion that it is necessary to require such person to execute a bond for abstaining from the commission of any offence under this Act, the court may, at the time of passing sentence on such person, order him to execute a bond for a sum proportionate to his means, with or without sureties, for abstaining from commission of any offence under Chapter IV during such period not exceeding three years as it thinks fit to fix. 2. The bond shall be in such form as may be prescribed by the Central Government and the provisions of the Code of Criminal Procedure, 1973 (2 of 1974), shall, in so far as they are applicable, apply to all matters connected with such bond as if it were a bond to keep the peace ordered to be executed under Section 106 of that Code. 3. If the conviction is set aside on appeal or otherwise, the bond so executed shall become void.

S. No.	Provision of the NDPS Act	Description of the Provision	Text of the Provision
			4. An order under this section may also be made by an appellate court or by the High Court or Sessions Judge when exercising the powers of revision.
53.	Section 35	Presumption of culpable mental state	1. In any prosecution for an offence under this Act, which requires a culpable mental state of the accused, the court shall presume the existence of such mental state but it shall be a defence for the accused to prove the fact that he had no such mental state with respect to the act charged as an offence in that prosecution. *Explanation.*—In this section "culpable mental state" includes intention, motive, knowledge of a fact and belief in, or reason to believe, a fact. 2. For the purpose of this section, a fact is said to be proved only when the court believes it to exist beyond a reasonable doubt and not merely when its existence is established by a preponderance of probability.
54.	Section 36	Constitution of Special Courts	1. The Government may, for the purpose of providing speedy trial of the offences under this Act, by notification in the Official Gazette, constitute as many special Courts as may be necessary for such areas as may be specified in the notification. 2. A Special Court shall consist of a Single Judge who shall be appointed by the Government with the concurrence of the Chief Justice of the High Court. *Explanation.*—In this sub-section, "High Court" means the High Court of the State in which the Sessions Judge or the Additional Sessions Judge of a Special Court was working immediately before his appointment as such Judge. 3. A person shall not be qualified for appointment as a Judge of a Special Court unless he is, immediately before such appointment, a Sessions Judge or an Additional Sessions Judge.

S. No.	Provision of the NDPS Act	Description of the Provision	Text of the Provision
55.	Section 36-A	Offences triable by Special Courts	1. Notwithstanding anything contained in the Code of Criminal Procedure, 1973— a. all offences under this Act which are punishable with imprisonment for a term of more than three years shall be triable only by the Special Court constituted for the area in which the offence has been committed or where there are more Special Courts than one for such area, by such one of them as may be specified in this behalf by the Government; b. where a person accused of or suspected of the commission of an offence under this Act is forwarded to a Magistrate under sub-section (2) or sub-section (2-A) of Section 167 of the Code of Criminal Procedure, 1973, such Magistrate may authorise the detention of such person in such custody as he thinks fit for a period not exceeding fifteen days in the whole where such Magistrate is a Judicial Magistrate and seven days in the whole where such Magistrate is an Executive Magistrate: Provided that in cases which are triable by the Special Court where such Magistrate considers— (i) when such person is forwarded to him as aforesaid; or (ii) upon or at time before the expiry of the period of detention authorised by him; that the detention of such person is unnecessary, he shall order such person to be forwarded to the Special Court having jurisdiction; (c) the Special Court may exercise, in relation to the person forwarded to it under clause (b), the same power which a Magistrate having juris-diction to try a case may exercise under Section 167 of the Code of Criminal

S. No.	Provision of the NDPS Act	Description of the Provision	Text of the Provision
			Procedure, 1973, in relation to an accused person in such case who has been forwarded to him under that section; (d) a Special Court may, upon perusal of police report of the facts constituting an offence under this Act or upon complaint made by an officer of the Central Government or a State Government authorised in his behalf, take cognizance of that offence without the accused being committed to it for trial. (2) When trying an offence under this Act, a Special Court may also try an offence other an offence under this Act with which the accused may, under the Code of Criminal Procedure, 1973, be charged at the same trial. (3) Nothing contained in this section shall be deemed to affect the special powers of the High Court regarding bail under Section 439 of the Code of Criminal Procedure, 1973, and the High Court may exercise such powers including the power under clause (b) of sub-section (1) of that section as if the reference to "Magistrate" in that section included also a reference to a "Special Court" constituted under Section 36. (4) In respect of persons accused of an offence punishable under Section 19 or Section 24 or Section 27-A or for offences involving commercial quantity the references in sub-section (2) of Section 167 of the Code of Criminal Procedure, 1973 thereof to "ninety days", where they occur, shall be construed as reference to "one hundred and eighty days": Provided that, if it is not possible to complete the investigation within the said period of one hundred and eighty days, the Special Court may extend the said period up to one year on the report of the Public Prosecutor indicating the progress of the investigation and the specific reasons for the detention of the accused beyond the said period of one hundred and eighty days.

S. No.	Provision of the NDPS Act	Description of the Provision	Text of the Provision
			(5) Notwithstanding anything contained in the Code of Criminal Procedure, 1973, the offences punishable under this Act with imprisonment for a term of not more than three years may be tried summarily.
56.	Section 36-B	Appeal and revision	The High Court may exercise, so far as may be applicable, all the powers conferred by Chapters XXIX and XXX of the Code of Criminal Procedure, 1973 (2 of 1974), on a High Court as if a Special Court within the local limits of the jurisdiction of the High Court were a Court of Session trying cases within the local limits of the jurisdiction of the High Court.
57.	Section 36-C	Application of Code to proceedings before a Special Court	Save as otherwise provided in this Act, the provisions of the Code of Criminal Procedure, 1973 (2 of 1974), (including the provisions as to bail and bonds) shall apply to the proceedings before a Special Court and for the purposes of the said provisions, the Special Court shall be deemed to be a Court of Session and the person conducting a prosecution before a Special Court, shall be deemed to be a Public Prosecutor.
58.	Section 36-D	Transitional Provisions	1. Any offence committed under this Act on or after the commencement of the Narcotic Drugs and Psychotropic Substances (Amendment) Act, 1988, which is triable by a Special Court shall, until a Special Court is constituted under Section 36, notwithstanding anything contained in the Code of Criminal Procedure, 1973, be tried by a Court of Session. 2. Where any proceedings in relation to any offence committed under this Act on or after the commencement of the Narcotic Drugs and Psychotropic Substances (Amendment) Act, 1988 are pending before a Court of Session, then, notwithstanding anything contained in sub-section (1), such proceeding shall be heard and disposed of by the Court of Session:

S. No.	Provision of the NDPS Act	Description of the Provision	Text of the Provision
			Provided that nothing contained in this sub-section shall affect the power of the High Court under Section 407 of the Code of Criminal Procedure, 1973 to transfer any case or class of cases taken cognizance by a Court of Session under sub-section (1).
59.	Section 37	Offences to be cognizable and non-bailable	1. Notwithstanding anything contained in the Code of Criminal Procedure, 1973 (2 of 1974), - a. every offence punishable under this Act shall be cognizable; b. no person accused of an offence punishable for [offences under Section 19 or Section 24 or Section 27-A and also for offences involving commercial quantity] shall be released on bail or on his own bond unless— (i) the Public Prosecutor has been given an opportunity to oppose the application for such release, and (ii) where the Public Prosecutor opposes the application, the court is satisfied that there are reasonable grounds for believing that he is not guilty of such offence and that he is not likely to commit any offence while on bail. (2) The limitations on granting of bail specified in clause (b) of sub-section (1) are in addition to the limitations under the Code of Criminal Procedure, 1973 (2 of 1974), or any other law for the time being in force on granting of bail.
60.	Section 38	Offences by companies	1. Where an offence under Chapter IV has been committed by a company, every person, who, at the time the offence was committed was in charge of, and was responsible to, the company for the conduct of the business of the company as well as the company, shall be deemed to be guilty of the offence and shall be liable to be proceeded against and punished accordingly:

S. No.	Provision of the NDPS Act	Description of the Provision	Text of the Provision
			Provided that nothing contained in this sub-section shall render any such person liable to any punishment if he proves that the offence was committed without his knowledge or that he had exercised all due diligence to prevent the commission of such offence. 2. Notwithstanding anything contained in sub-section (1), where any offence under Chapter IV has been committed by a company and it is proved that the offence has been committed with the consent or connivance of, or is attributable to any neglect on the part of any director, manager, secretary or other officer of the company, such director, manager, secretary or other officer shall be deemed to be guilty of that offence and shall be liable to be proceeded against and punished accordingly. *Explanation.*—For the purposes of this section,— a. "company" means any body corporate and includes a firm or other association of individuals; and b. "director", in relation to a firm means a partner in the firm.
61.	Section 39	Power of court to release certain offenders on probation	1. When any addict is found guilty of an offence punishable under Section 27 [or for offences relating to small quantity of narcotic drug or psychotropic substance] and if the court by which he is found guilty is of the opinion, regard being had to the age, character, antecedents or physical or mental condition of the offender, that it is expedient so to do, then, notwithstanding anything contained in this Act or any other law for the time being in force, the court may, instead of sentencing him at once to any imprisonment, with his consent, direct that he be released for undergoing medical treatment for detoxification or de-addiction from a hospital or an institution maintained or recognised by Government and on his entering into a bond in the form prescribed by the

S. No.	Provision of the NDPS Act	Description of the Provision	Text of the Provision
			Central Government, with or without sureties, to appear and furnish before the court within a period not exceeding one year, a report regarding the result of his medical treatment and, in the meantime, to abstain from the commission of any offence under Chapter IV. 2. If it appears to the court, having regard to the report regarding the result of the medical treatment furnished under sub-section (1), that it is expedient so to do, the court may direct the release of the offender after due admonition on his entering into a bond in the form prescribed by the Central Government, with or without sureties, for abstaining from the commission of any offence under Chapter IV during such period not exceeding three years as the court may deem fit to specify or on his failure so to abstain, to appear before the court and receive sentence when called upon during such period.
62.	Section 40	Power of court to publish names, place of business, etc., of certain offenders	1. Where any person is convicted of any of the offences punishable under Section 15 to Section 25 (both inclusive), Section 28, Section 29 or Section 30, it shall be competent for the court convicting the person to cause the name and place of business or residence of such person, nature of the contravention, the fact that the person has been so convicted and such other particulars as the court may consider to be appropriate in the circumstances of the case, to be published at the expense of such person in such newspapers or in such manner as the court may direct. 2. No publication under sub-section (1) shall be made until the period for preferring an appeal against the orders of the court has expired without any appeal having been preferred, or such appeal, having been preferred, has been disposed of.

S. No.	Provision of the NDPS Act	Description of the Provision	Text of the Provision
			(4) The expenses of any publication under sub-section (1) shall be recovered from the convicted person as if it were a fine imposed by the Court.
63.	Section 41	Power to issue warrant and authorisation	1. A Metropolitan Magistrate or a Magistrate of the first class or any Magistrate of the second class specially empowered by the State Government in this behalf, may issue a warrant for the arrest of any person whom he has reason to believe to have committed any offence punishable under this Act, or for the search, whether by day or by night, of any building, conveyance or place in which he has reason to believe any narcotic drug or psychotropic substance or controlled substance in respect of which an offence punishable under this Act has been committed or any document or other article which may furnish evidence of the commission of such offence or any illegally acquired property or any document or other article which may furnish evidence of holding any illegally acquired property which is liable for seizure or freezing or forfeiture under Chapter V-A of this Act is kept or concealed. 2. Any such officer of gazetted rank of the department of central excise, narcotics, customs, revenue intelligence or any other department of the Central Government including the para-military forces or the armed forces to be empowered in this behalf by general or special order by the Central Government, or any such officer of the revenue, drugs control, excise, police or any other department of the State Government as is empowered in this behalf by general or special order of the State Government if he has reason to believe from personal knowledge or information given by any person and taken in writing that any person has committed an offence punishable under this Act or that any narcotic drug or psychotropic substance or controlled substance in respect of which any offence under this Act has been committed or any document or other article which may furnish evidence of the commission of such offence or any illegally acquired property or any document or other article which may furnish

S. No.	Provision of the NDPS Act	Description of the Provision	Text of the Provision
			evidence of holding any illegally acquired property which is liable for seizure or freezing or forfeiture under Chapter V-A of this Act is kept or concealed in any building, conveyance or place, may authorize any officer subordinate to him but superior in rank to a peon, sepoy or a constable to arrest such a person or search a building, conveyance or place whether by day or by night or himself arrest such a person or search a building, conveyance or place. 3. The officer to whom a warrant under sub-section (1) is addressed and the officer who authorised the arrest or search or the officer who is so authorised under sub-section (2) shall have all the powers of an officer acting under Section 42.
64.	Section 42	Power of entry, search, seizure and arrest without warrant or authorisation	1. Any such officer (being an officer superior in rank to a peon, sepoy or constable) of the departments of central excise, narcotics, customs, revenue intelligence or any other department of the Central Government including para-military forces or armed forces as is empowered in this behalf by general or special order by the Central Government, or any such officer (being an officer superior in rank to a peon, sepoy or constable) of the revenue, drugs control, excise, police or any other department of a State Government as is empowered in this behalf by general or special order of the State Government, if he has reason to believe from personal knowledge or information given by any person and taken down in writing that any narcotic drug, or psychotropic substance, or controlled substance in respect of which an offence punishable under this Act has been committed or any document or other article which may furnish evidence of the commission of such offence or any illegally acquired property or any document or other article which may furnish evidence of holding any illegally acquired property which is liable for seizure or freezing or forfeiture

S. No.	Provision of the NDPS Act	Description of the Provision	Text of the Provision
			under Chapter V-A of this Act is kept or concealed in any building, conveyance or enclosed place, may, between sunrise and sunset,— a. enter into and search any such building conveyance or place; b. in case of resistance, break open any door or remove any obstacle to such entry; c. seize such drug or substance and all materials used in the manufacture thereof and any other article and any animal or conveyance which he has reason to believe to be liable to confiscation under this Act and any document or other article which he has reason to believe may furnish evidence of the commission of any offence punishable under this Act or furnish evidence of holding any illegally acquired property which is liable for seizure or freezing or forfeiture under Chapter V-A of this Act; and d. detain and search, and, if he thinks proper, arrest any person whom he has reason to believe to have committed any offence punishable under this Act: Provided that in respect of holder of a licence for manufacture of manufactured drugs or psycho-tropic substances or controlled substances granted under this Act or any rule or order made thereunder, such power shall be exercised by an officer not below the rank of sub-inspector: Provided further that if such officer has reason to believe that a search warrant or authorisation cannot be obtained without affording opportunity for the concealment of evidence or facility for the escape of an offender, he may enter and search such building, conveyance or enclosed place at any time between sunset and sunrise after recording the grounds of his belief.

S. No.	Provision of the NDPS Act	Description of the Provision	Text of the Provision
			(2) Where an officer takes down any information in writing under sub-section (1) or records grounds for his belief under the proviso thereto, he shall within seventy-two hours send a copy thereof to his immediate official superior.
65.	Section 43	Power of seizure and arrest in public place	Any officer of any of the departments mentioned in Section 42 may— a. seize in any public place or in transit, any narcotic drug or psychotropic substance or controlled substance in respect of which he has reason to believe an offence punishable under this Act has been committed, and, along with such drug or substance, any animal or conveyance or article liable to confiscation under this Act, any document or other article which he has reason to believe may furnish evidence of the commission of an offence punishable under this Act or any document or other article which may furnish evidence of holding any illegally acquired property which is liable for seizure or freezing or forfeiture under Chapter V-A of this Act; b. detain and search any person whom he has reason to believe to have committed an offence punishable under this Act, and if such person has any narcotic drug or psychotropic substance or controlled substance in his possession and such possession appears to him to be unlawful, arrest him and any other person in his company. *Explanation.*—For the purposes of this section, the expression "public place" includes any public conveyance, hotel, shop, or other place intended for use by, or accessible to, the public.
66.	Section 44	Power of entry, search, seizure and arrest in offences relating to	The provisions of Sections 41, 42 and 43, shall so far as may be, apply in relation to the offences punishable under Chapter IV and relating to coca plant, the opium poppy or cannabis plant and for this purpose references in those sections

S. No.	Provision of the NDPS Act	Description of the Provision	Text of the Provision
		coca plant, opium poppy and cannabis plant	to narcotic drugs, or psychotropic substance [or controlled substance], shall be construed as including references to coca plant, the opium poppy and cannabis plant.
67.	Section 45	Procedure where seizure of goods liable to confiscation not practicable	Where it is not practicable to seize any goods (including standing crop) which are liable to confiscation under this Act, any officer duly authorised under Section 42 may serve on the owner or person in possession of the goods, an order that he shall not remove, part with or otherwise deal with the goods except with the previous permission of such officer.
68.	Section 46	Duty of land holder to give information of illegal cultivation	Every holder of land shall give immediate information to any officer of the Police or of any of the departments mentioned in Section 42 of all the opium poppy, cannabis plant or coca plant which may be illegally cultivated within his land and every such holder of land who knowingly neglects to give such information, shall be liable to punishment.
69.	Section 47	Duty of certain officers to give information of illegal cultivation	Every officer of the Government and every panch, sarpanch and other village officer of whatever description shall give immediate information to any officer of the Police or of any of the departments mentioned in Section 42 when it may come to his knowledge that any land has been illegally cultivated with the opium poppy, cannabis plant or coca plant, and every such officer of the Government, panch, sarpanch and other village officer who neglects to give such information shall be liable to punishment.
70.	Section 48	Power of attachment of crop illegally cultivated	Any Metropolitan Magistrate, Judicial Magistrate of the first class or any Magistrate specially empowered in this behalf by the State Government [or any officer of a gazetted rank empowered under Section 42] may order attachment of any opium poppy, cannabis plant or coca plant which he has reason to believe to

S. No.	Provision of the NDPS Act	Description of the Provision	Text of the Provision
			have been illegally cultivated and while doing so may pass such order (including an order to destroy the crop) as he thinks fit.
71.	Section 49	Power to stop and search conveyance	Any officer authorised under Section 42, may, if he has reason to suspect that any animal or conveyance is, or is about to be, used for the transport of any narcotic drug or psychotropic substance [or controlled substance], in respect of which he suspects that any provision of this Act has been, or is being, or is about to be, contravened at any time, stop such animal or conveyance, or, in the case of an aircraft, compel it to land and— a. rummage and search the conveyance or part thereof; b. examine and search any goods on the animal or in the conveyance; c. if it becomes necessary to stop the animal or the conveyance, he may use all lawful means for stopping it, and where which means fail, the animal or the conveyance may be fired upon.
72.	Section 50	Conditions under which search of persons shall be conducted	1. When any officer duly authorised under Section 42 is about to search any person under the provisions of Section 41, Section 42 or Section 43, he shall, if such person so requires, take such person without unnecessary delay to the nearest gazetted officer of any of the departments mentioned in Section 42 or to the nearest Magistrate. 2. If such requisition is made, the officer may detain the person until he can bring him before the gazetted officer or the Magistrate referred to in sub-section (1). 3. The gazetted officer or the Magistrate before whom any such person is brought shall, if he sees no reasonable ground for search, forthwith discharge the person but otherwise shall direct that search be made.

S. No.	Provision of the NDPS Act	Description of the Provision	Text of the Provision
			4. No female shall be searched by anyone excepting a female. 5. When an officer duly authorised under Section 42 has reason to believe that it is not possible to take the person to be searched to the nearest Gazetted Officer or Magistrate without the possibility of the person to be searched parting with possession of any narcotic drug or psychotropic substance, or controlled substance or article or document, he may, instead of taking such person to the nearest Gazetted Officer or Magistrate, proceed to search the person as provided under Section 100 of the Code of Criminal Procedure, 1973. 6. After a search is conducted under sub-section (5), the officer shall record the reasons for such belief which necessitated such search and within seventy-two hours send a copy thereof to his immediate official superior.
73.	Section 51	Provisions of the Code of Criminal Procedure, 1973 to apply to warrants, arrests, searches and seizures	The provisions of the Code of Criminal Procedure, 1973 (2 of 1974) shall apply, in so far as they are not inconsistent with the provisions of this Act, to all warrants issued and arrests, searches and seizures made under this Act.
74.	Section 52	Disposal of persons arrested and articles seized	1. Any officer arresting a person under Section 41, Section 42, Section 43 or Section 44 shall, as soon as may be, inform him of the grounds for such arrest. 2. Every person arrested and article seized under warrant issued under sub-section (1) of Section 41 shall be forwarded without unnecessary delay to the Magistrate by whom the warrant was issued. 3. Every person arrested and article seized under sub-section (2) of Section 41, Section 42, Section 43 or Section 44 shall be forwarded without unnecessary delay to—

S. No.	Provision of the NDPS Act	Description of the Provision	Text of the Provision
			a. the officer-in-charge of the nearest police station, or b. the officer empowered under Section 53. (4) The authority or officer to whom any person or article is forwarded under sub-section (2) or sub-section (3) shall, with all convenient despatch, take such measures as may be necessary for the disposal according to law of such person or article.
75.	Section 52-A	Disposal of seized narcotic drugs and psychotropic substances	1. The Central Government may, having regard to the hazardous nature, vulnerability to theft, substitution, constraint of proper storage space or any other relevant consideration, in respect of any narcotic drugs, psychotropic substances, controlled substances or conveyances, by notification in the official Gazette, specify such narcotic drugs, psychotropic substances, con-trolled substances or conveyance or class of narcotic drugs, class of psychotropic substances, class of controlled substances or conveyances, which shall, as soon as may be after their seizure, be disposed of by such officer and in such manner as that Government may, from time to time, determine after following the procedure hereinafter specified. 2. Where any [narcotic drugs, psycho-tropic substances, controlled substances or conveyances] has been seized and forwarded to the officer-in-charge of the nearest police station or to the officer empowered under Section 53, the officer referred to in sub-section (1) shall prepare an inventory of such [narcotic drugs, psychotropic substances, controlled substances or conveyances] containing such details relating to their description, quality, quantity, mode of packing, marks, numbers or such other identifying particulars of the [narcotic drugs, psychotropic substances, con-trolled substances or conveyances] or the packing in which they are packed, country of origin and other particulars as the officer referred to in sub-section (1) may consider relevant to the identity of the [narcotic drugs, psychotropic

S. No.	Provision of the NDPS Act	Description of the Provision	Text of the Provision
			substances, controlled substances or conveyances] in any proceedings under this Act and make an application, to any Magistrate for the purposes of— a. certifying the correctness of the inventory so prepared; or b. taking, in the presence of such Magistrate, photographs of [such drugs, substances or conveyances] and certifying such photographs as true; or c. allowing to draw representative samples of such drugs or substances, in the presence of such Magistrate and certifying the correctness of any list of samples so drawn. (3) Where an application is made under sub-section (2), the Magistrate shall, as soon as may be, allow the application. (4) Notwithstanding anything contained in the Indian Evidence Act, 1872 (1 of 1872) or the Code of Criminal Procedure, 1973 (2 of 1974), every court trying an offence under this Act, shall treat the inventory, the photographs of [narcotic drugs, psychotropic substances, controlled substances or conveyances] and any list of samples drawn under sub-section (2) and certified by the Magistrate, as primary evidence in respect of such offence.
76.	Section 53	Power to invest officers of certain departments with powers of an officer-in-charge of a police station	1. The Central Government, after consultation with the State Government, may, by notification published in the Official Gazette, invest any officer of the department of central excise, narcotics, customs, revenue intelligence [or any other department of the Central Government including paramilitary forces or armed forces] or any class of such officers with the powers of an officer-in-charge of a police station for the investigation of the offences under this Act. 2. The State Government may, by notification published in the Official Gazette, invest any officer of the department of drugs control, revenue or excise [or any

S. No.	Provision of the NDPS Act	Description of the Provision	Text of the Provision
			other department] or any class of such officers with the powers of an officer-in-charge of a police station for the investigation of offences under this Act.
77.	Section 53-A	Relevancy of statements under certain circumstances	1. A statement made and signed by a person before any officer empowered under Section 53 for the investigation of offences, during the course of any inquiry or proceedings by such officer, shall be relevant for the purpose of proving, in any prosecution for an offence under this Act, the truth of the facts which it contains, - a. when the person who made the statement is dead or cannot be found, or is incapable of giving evidence, or is kept out of the way by the adverse party, or whose presence cannot be obtained without an amount of delay or expense which, under the circumstances of the case, the court considers unreasonable; or b. when the person who made the statement is examined as a witness in the case before the court and the court is of the opinion that, having regard to the circumstances of the case, the statement should be admitted in evidence in the interest of justice. (2) The provisions of sub-section (1) shall, so far as may be, apply in relation to any proceedings under this Act or the rules or orders made thereunder, other than a proceeding before a court, as they apply in relation to a proceeding before a court.
78.	Section 54	Presumption from possession of illicit articles	In trials under this Act, it may be presumed, unless and until the contrary is proved, that the accused has committed an offence under this Act in respect of— a. any narcotic drug or psychotropic substance or controlled substance; b. any opium poppy, cannabis plant or coca plant growing on any land which he has cultivated;

S. No.	Provision of the NDPS Act	Description of the Provision	Text of the Provision
			c. any apparatus specially designed or any group of utensils specially adopted for the manufacture of any narcotic drug or psychotropic substance or controlled substance; or d. any materials which have undergone any process towards the manufacture of a narcotic drug or psychotropic substance or con-trolled substance, or any residue left of the materials from which any narcotic drug or psychotropic substance or controlled substance has been manufactured, for the possession of which he fails to account satisfactorily.
79.	Section 55	Police to take charge of articles seized and delivered	An officer-in-charge of a police station shall take charge of and keep in safe custody, pending the orders of the Magistrate, all articles seized under this Act within the local area of that police station and which may be delivered to him, and shall allow any officer who may accompany such articles to the police station or who may be deputed for the purpose, to affix his seal to such articles or to take samples of and from them and all samples so taken shall also be sealed with a seal of the officer-in-charge of the police station.
80.	Section 56	Obligations of officers to assist each other	All officers of the several departments mentioned in Section 42 shall, upon notice given or request made, be legally bound to assist each other in carrying out the provisions of this Act.
81.	Section 57	Report of arrest and seizure	Whenever any person makes any arrest or seizure under this Act, he shall, within forty-eight hours next after such arrest or seizure, make a full report of all the particulars of such arrest or seizure to his immediate official superior.

S. No.	Provision of the NDPS Act	Description of the Provision	Text of the Provision
82.	Section 57-A	Report of seizure of property of the person arrested by the notified officer	Whenever any officer notified under Section 53 makes an arrest or seizure under this Act, and the provisions of Chapter V-A apply to any person involved in the case of such arrest or seizure, the officer shall make a report of the illegally acquired properties of such person to the jurisdictional competent authority within ninety days of the arrest or seizure.
83.	Section 58	Punishment for vexatious entry, search, seizure or arrest	1. Any person empowered under Section 42 or Section 43 or Section 44 who— a. without reasonable ground of suspicion enters or searches, or causes to be entered or searched, any building, conveyance or place; b. vexatiously and unnecessarily seizes the property of any person on the pretence of seizing or searching for any narcotic drug or psychotropic substance or other article liable to be confiscated under this Act, or of seizing any document or other article liable to be seized under Section 42, Section 43 or Section 44; or c. vexatiously and unnecessarily detains, searches or arrests any person, shall be punishable with imprisonment for a term which may extend to six months or with fine which may extend to one thousand rupees, or with both. (2) Any person wilfully and maliciously giving false information and so causing an arrest or a search being made under this Act shall be punishable with imprisonment for a term which may extend to two years or with fine or with both.
84.	Section 59	Failure of officer in duty or his connivance at the contravention of	1. Any officer, on whom any duty has been imposed by or under this Act and who ceases or refuses to perform or withdraws himself from the duties of his office shall, unless he has obtained the express written permission of his official

S. No.	Provision of the NDPS Act	Description of the Provision	Text of the Provision
		the provisions of this Act	superior or has other lawful excuse for so doing, be punishable with imprisonment for a term which may extend to one year or with fine or with both. 2. Any officer on whom any duty has been imposed by or under this Act or any person who has been given the custody of - a. any addict; or b. any other person who has been charged with an offence under this Act, and who wilfully aids in, or connives at, the contravention of any provision of this Act or any rule or order made thereunder, shall be punishable with rigorous imprisonment for a term which shall not be less than ten years but which may extend to twenty years, and shall also be liable to fine which shall not be less than one lakh rupees but which extend to two lakh rupees. *Explanation.*—For the purposes of this sub-section, the expression "officer" includes any person employed in a hospital or institution maintained or recognised by the Government or a local authority under Section 64-A for providing de-addiction treatment. (3) No court shall take cognizance of any offence under sub-section (1) or sub-section (2) except on a complaint in writing made with the previous sanction of the Central Government, or as the case may be, the State Government.
85.	Section 60	Liability of illicit drugs, substances, plants, articles and conveyances to confiscation	1. Whenever any offence punishable under this Act has been committed, the narcotic drug, psychotropic substance, controlled substance, opium poppy, coca plant, cannabis plant, materials, apparatus and utensils in respect of which or by means of which such offence has been committed, shall also be liable to confiscation.

S. No.	Provision of the NDPS Act	Description of the Provision	Text of the Provision
			2. Any narcotic drug or psychotropic substance [or controlled substances] lawfully produced, imported interstate, exported interstate, imported into India, transported, manufactured, possessed, used, purchased or sold along with, or in addition to, any narcotic drug or psychotropic substance [or controlled substances] which is liable to confiscation under sub-section (1) and the receptacles, packages and coverings in which any narcotic drug or psychotropic substance [or controlled substances], materials, apparatus or utensils liable to confiscation under sub-section (1) is found, and the other contents, if any, of such receptacles or packages shall likewise be liable to confiscation. 3. Any animal or conveyance used in carrying any narcotic drug or psychotropic substance [or controlled substances], or any article liable to confiscation under sub-section (1) or sub-section (2) shall also be liable to confiscation, unless the owner of the animal or conveyance proves that it was so used without the knowledge or connivance of the owner himself, his agent, if any, and the person-in-charge of the animal or the conveyance and that each of them had taken all reasonable precautions against such use.
86.	Section 61	Confiscation of goods used for concealing illicit drugs or substances	Any goods used for concealing any narcotic drug, [psychotropic substance or controlled substance] which is liable to confiscation under this Act shall also be liable to confiscation. *Explanation.*—In this section "goods" does not include conveyance as a means of transport.
87.	Section 62	Confiscation of sale proceeds of illicit drugs or substances	Where any narcotic drug, [psychotropic substance or controlled substance] is sold by a person having knowledge or reason to believe that the drug or substance is liable to confiscation under this Act, the sale proceeds thereof shall also be liable to confiscation.

S. No.	Provision of the NDPS Act	Description of the Provision	Text of the Provision
88.	Section 63	Procedure in making confiscations	1. In the trial of offences under this Act, whether the accused is convicted or acquitted or discharged, the court shall decide whether any article or thing seized under this Act is liable to confiscation under Section 60 or Section 61 or Section 62 and, if it decides that the article is so liable, it may order confiscation accordingly. 2. Where any article or thing seized under this Act appears to be liable to confiscation under Section 60 or Section 61 or Section 62, but the person who committed the offence in connection therewith is not known or cannot be found, the court may inquire into and decide such liability, and may order confiscation accordingly: Provided that no order of confiscation of an article or thing shall be made until the expiry of one month from the date of seizure, or without hearing any person who may claim any right thereto and the evidence, if any, which he produces in respect of his claim: Provided further that if any such article or thing, other than a narcotic drug, psychotropic substance [controlled substance] the opium poppy, coca plant or cannabis plant is liable to speedy and natural decay, or if the court is of opinion that its sale would be for the benefit of its owner, it may at any time direct it to be sold; and the provisions of this sub-section shall, as nearly as may be practicable, apply to the net proceeds of the sale.
89.	Section 64	Power to tender immunity from prosecution	1. The Central Government or the State Government may, if it is of opinion (the reasons for such opinion being recorded in writing) that with a view to obtaining the evidence of any person appearing to have been directly or indirectly concerned in or privy to the contravention of any of the provisions of this Act or of any rule or order made thereunder it is necessary or expedient so to

S. No.	Provision of the NDPS Act	Description of the Provision	Text of the Provision
			do, tender to such person immunity from prosecution for any offence under this Act or under the Indian Penal Code (45 of 1860) or under any other Central Act or State Act, as the case may be, for the time being in force, on condition of his making a full and true disclosure of the whole circumstances relating to such contravention. 2. A tender of immunity made to, and accepted by, the person concerned, shall, to the extent to which the immunity extends, render him immune from prosecution for any offence in respect of which the tender was made. 3. If it appears to the Central Government or, as the case may be, the State Government, that any person to whom immunity has been tendered under this section has not complied with the conditions on which the tender was made or is wilfully concealing anything or is giving false evidence, the Central Government or, as the case may be, the State Government, may record a finding to that effect and thereupon the immunity shall be deemed to have been withdrawn and such person may be tried for the offence in respect of which the tender of immunity was made or for any other offence of which he appears to have been guilty in connection with the same matter.
90.	Section 64-A	Immunity from prosecution to addicts volunteering for treatment	Any addict, who is charged with an offence punishable under Section 27 or with offences involving small quantity of narcotic drugs or psychotropic substances, who voluntarily seeks to undergo medical treatment for de-addiction from a hospital or an institution maintained or recognised by the Government or a local authority and undergoes such treatment shall not be liable to prosecution under Section 27 or under any other section for offences involving small quantity of narcotic drugs or psychotropic substances:

S. No.	Provision of the NDPS Act	Description of the Provision	Text of the Provision
			Provided that the said immunity from prosecution may be withdrawn if the addict does not undergo the complete treatment for de-addiction.
91.	Section 66	Presumption as to documents in certain cases	Where any document— (i) is produced or furnished by any person or has been seized from the custody or control of any person, in either case, under this Act or under any other law; or (ii) has been received from any place outside India (duly authenticated by such authority or person and in such manner as may be prescribed by the Central Government) in the course of investigation of any offence under this Act alleged to have been committed by a person; and such document is tendered in any prosecution under this Act in evidence against him, or against him and any other person who is tried jointly with him, the court shall— a. presume, unless the contrary is proved, that the signature and every other part of such document which purports to be in the handwriting of any particular person or which the court may reasonably assume to have been signed by, or to be in the handwriting of, any particular person, is in that person's handwriting; and in the case of a document executed or attested, that it was executed or attested by the person by whom it purports to have been so executed or attested; b. admit the document in evidence, notwithstanding that it is not duly stamped, if such document is otherwise admissible in evidence; c. in a case falling under clause (i), also presume, unless the contrary is proved, the truth of the contents of such document.

S. No.	Provision of the NDPS Act	Description of the Provision	Text of the Provision
92.	Section 67	Power to call for information, etc.	Any officer referred to in Section 42 who is authorised in this behalf by the Central Government or a State Government may, during the course of any enquiry in connection with the contravention of any provision of this Act— a. call for information from any person for the purpose of satisfying himself whether there has been any contravention of the provisions of this Act or any rule or order made thereunder; b. require any person to produce or deliver any document or thing useful or relevant to the enquiry; c. examine any person acquainted with the facts and circumstances of the case.
93.	Section 68	Information as to commission of offences	No officer acting in exercise of powers vested in him under any provision of this Act or any rule or order made thereunder shall be compelled to say whence he got any information as to the commission of any offence.
94.	Section 70	Central Government and State Governments to have regard to international conventions while making rules	Whenever under this Act Central Government or the State Government has been empowered to make rules, the Central Government or the State Government, as the case may be, subject to other provisions of this Act, may while making the rules have regard to the provisions of the Single Convention on Narcotic Drugs, 1961, the Protocol of 1972 amending the said Convention and of the Convention on Psychotropic Substances, 1971 to which India is a party and to the provisions of any other international convention relating to narcotic drugs or psychotropic sub-stances to which India may become a party.
95.	Section 71	Power of Government to establish centres for	1. The Government may establish, recognize or approve as many centres as it thinks fit for identification, treatment, management, education, after-care, rehabilitation,

S. No.	Provision of the NDPS Act	Description of the Provision	Text of the Provision
		identification, treatment, etc., of addicts and for supply of narcotic drugs and psychotropic substances	social re-integration of addicts and for supply, subject to such conditions and in such manner as may be prescribed, by the concerned Government of any narcotic drugs and psychotropic substances to the addicts registered with the Government and to others where such apply is a medical necessity. 2. The Government may make rules consistent with this Act providing for the establishment, appointment, maintenance, management and superintendence of, and for supply of narcotic drugs and psychotropic substances from, the centres referred to in sub-section (1) and for the appointment, training, powers, duties and persons employed in such centres.
96.	Section 76	Power of Central Government to make rules	1. Subject to the other provisions of this Act, the Central Government may, by notification in the Official Gazette, make rules for carrying out the purposes of this Act. 2. Without prejudice to the generality of the foregoing power, such rules may provide for all or any of the following matters, namely:— a. the method by which percentages in the case of liquid preparations shall be calculated for the purposes of clause (v), (vi), (xiv) and (xv) of Section 2; b. the form of bond to keep the peace to be executed under Section 34; c. the form of bond to be executed for release of an addict-convict for medical treatment under sub-section (1) of Section 39 and the bond to be executed by such convict before his release after due admonition under sub-section (2) of that section; [(ca) the manner in which "controlled delivery" under Section 50-A is to be undertaken;] d. the authority or the person by whom and the manner in which a document received from any place outside India shall be authenticated under clause (ii) of Section 66;

S. No.	Provision of the NDPS Act	Description of the Provision	Text of the Provision
			[(da) the manner in which and the conditions subject to which properties shall be managed by the Administrator under sub-section (2) of Section 68-G; (dc) the fees which shall be paid for the inspection of the records and registers of the Appellate Tribunal or for obtaining the certified copy of any part thereof under sub-section (6) of Section 68-O; (dd) the powers of a civil court that may be exercised by the competent authority and the Appellate Tribunal under clause (f) of Section 68-R; (de) the disposal of all articles or things confiscated under this Act; (df) the drawing of samples and testing and analysis of such samples; (dg) the rewards to be paid to the officers, informers and other persons;] e. the conditions and the manner in which narcotic drugs and psychotropic substances may be supplied for medical necessity to the addicts registered with the Central Government and to others under sub-section (1) of Section 71; f. the establishment, appointment, maintenance, management and superintendence of centres established by the Central Government under sub-section (1) of Section 71 and appointment, training, powers and duties of persons employed in such centres; g. the term of office of, the manner of filling casual vacancies of, and the allowances payable to, the Chairman and members of the Narcotic Drugs and Psychotropic Substances Consultative Committee and the conditions and restrictions subject to which a non-member may be appointed to a sub-committee under sub-section (5) of Section 6; h. any other matter which is to be, or may be, prescribed.
97.	Section 78	Power of State Government to make	1. Subject to the other provisions of this Act, the State Government may, by notification in the Official Gazette, make rules for carrying out the purposes of this Act.

S. No.	Provision of the NDPS Act	Description of the Provision	Text of the Provision
		rules	2. Without prejudice to the generality of the foregoing power, such rules may provide for all or any of the following matters, namely:— a. the conditions and the manner in which narcotics drugs and psychotropic substances shall be supplied for medical necessity to the addicts registered with the State Government and others under sub-section (1) of Section 71; b. the establishment, appointment, maintenance, management, superintendence of centres established under sub-section (1) of Section 71 and appointment, training, powers and duties of persons employed in such centres; c. any other matter which is to be, or may be, prescribed. (3) Every rule made by a State Government under this Act shall be laid, as soon as may be after it is made, before the Legislature of that State.
98.	Section 81	Saving of State and special laws	Nothing in this Act or in the rules made thereunder shall affect the validity of any Provincial Act or an Act of any State Legislature for the time being in force, or of any rule made thereunder which imposes any restriction or provides for a punishment not imposed by or provided for under this Act or imposes a restriction or provides for a punishment greater in degree than a corresponding restriction imposed by or a corresponding punishment provided for by or under this Act for the cultivation of cannabis plant or consumption of, or traffic in, any narcotic drug or psychotropic substance within India.